Third Time Lucky

Living the Nightmare

JW LAWSON

THIRD TIME LUCKY

First Edition

DEDICATION

I dedicate this book to the victims and survivors of abuse.
There are a lot of you.

CONTENTS

ACKNOWLEDGMENTS

I would like to express my gratitude to the many people who helped me on this journey: to all those who provided support, talked things through with me, offered comments and assisted with the proofreading and design. The list is endless, but special thanks go to my wonderful husband Andrew who funded the entire project, Georgia and Caz Butler, and Catherine Haywood.

There is, however, one person who deserves an extra-special thank you: my friend, Dawn Lawson, who has never stopped encouraging, supporting and sympathising with me over the past few years. Your belief in Third Time Lucky, and me, ensured that I remained driven and focused until the book was complete. Without you, this book would still be a dream.

Thanks to you, it's now a reality.

PART ONE

"The pursuit of truth and beauty is a sphere of activity in which
we are permitted to remain children all our lives."

Albert Einstein

1. THE BEGINNING

It was 25th November 2014. Hard to believe that another year had almost passed.

There was so much to do.

Christmas was coming, and fast. There was stacks to do, in fact, and only a few weeks to get organised.

Beth began to panic.

She untangled herself from her bedding and caught a glimpse of her reflection in the full-length mirror on her wardrobe. Yep, she looked rough. Her hair was a mess. It was bedraggled, and her roots needed doing – again. Yet she knew that, after her chores, she would transform herself into something quite stunning. It was amazing how good you could look after just a few hours of pampering and a great deal of meticulously applied make-up. She smiled as she went to the bathroom, picturing how she would look in a few hours' time.

"Pretty good for a forty-three-year-old," she muttered to herself.

Dave stirred. "You okay in there?"

"Sure," Beth replied, looking forward to her busy day ahead.

She straightened the towels, polished the chrome on the sink tap and jumped into the shower, reminding herself to stand very still to avoid splashing the tiles.

* * *

1994: Elise

Elise awoke to find herself in a strange bedroom. The filthy roller-blind hung from a broken rail, allowing the grey November daylight to filter through the nicotine-stained window panes. Torn wallpaper clung desperately to the damp walls, and a light bulb above the bed flickered, and then died.

Next to her was a stranger. Unshaven, at least sixty years old and naked. He snored loudly and stank of booze and fags. His hideously fat gut moved up and down in rhythm with his heavy breathing. Elise slid out of bed and tried to recollect how she got there. She didn't need much prompting to remember.

Her underwear was discarded on the floor, along with an empty packet of ribbed condoms. A half-drunk bottle of vodka and a packet of Marlboro cigarettes were on a dingy cabinet, along with a twenty-pound note. She immediately jolted back into reality and remembered exactly where she was.

Fighting back tears, she gathered her clothes and ran into the hallway, clutching the money she had worked so hard to get.

* * *

2004: Lizzie

Her back hurt. She had asked the staff a hundred times for another sodding mattress, but they always refused, saying that hers was perfectly adequate. It really pissed her off and, now that her sleep meds were wearing off, she was in a foul mood.

The stupid bitch in the bed next to her didn't help either. *She* never had problems sleeping. She spent most of her life bloody unconscious – crazy fat cow.

The nurses and their annoying, whining voices and the shrill of the phones all bloody night also irritated Lizzie beyond the point of anger. She loathed everybody. She hated this hell-hole, but knew that she would have to be extremely well behaved over the coming months. Her release would mean a new beginning for her; a fresh start. She took a quick shower, combed her hair and put on her tracksuit.

It was almost 7 a.m. – breakfast time – and Lizzie hoped that her recent behaviour would allow her the privilege of enjoying a bowl of cereal instead of soggy toast. The weak, piss-flavoured coffee would be revolting but she would drink it anyway because, today, Lizzie was going to be a good girl.

"Mummy's little angel," she mumbled quietly as she shuffled into the breakfast queue.

2. I DON'T LIKE MONDAYS

2014: Beth

Beth applied the protective serum and straightened her hair. She started to like her reflection in the mirror. Although her roots were showing, the blonde highlights against the autumn-brown lowlights now looked amazing. Her huge brown eyes and baby-pink lips somehow portrayed an innocent, childlike image. She liked that. Her trim, size eight figure carried every outfit well and her breasts were firm and pert despite her age – she loved her breasts even more than her hair. She pouted in front of the mirror and studied herself admiringly.

Beth relished the fact that some people still asked her for ID despite her age and that, when dressed for her shopping trips, heads would always turn to admire her beauty. She was a stunner – no doubt about it. Later on today, if she had time, she would go shopping in Hemel Hempstead.

She loved the shops – clothes shops in particular. She simply adored clothes, especially figure-hugging outfits that accentuated her breasts and tiny waist. She relished the attention she got from passers-by, but she had so much to do before she could go.

Must rush.
House is filthy.
Ironing to do.
Panic.

Dave, freshly showered and wearing his work overalls, tiptoed into the bedroom. "There's a cup of tea downstairs for you, love. I'm off now." He pecked her on the cheek and gently shut the door behind him.

She heard his car engine roar into life, and Beth dreaded the thought of the mess he had made. The shower would be filthy, and as for the teabags … God only knew where he had put them. She so hoped that he had tidied up after himself but, when she entered the kitchen, she knew that her plans for the day were wrecked. There would be no shopping trip for her. She had to clean.

She had so much to do, and so little time.

* * *

1994: *Elise*

The so-called communal bathroom stank. Urine formed tiny puddles on the broken tiles close to the filthy toilet, and the shower didn't work. Elise was having a bad day already.

After rescuing an encrusted clump of soap that was stuck to the bathroom sink, she washed her face, trying desperately to remove the thick mascara she had worn the night before. It smudged, making her look even more exhausted than she actually felt. She scrubbed harder and harder, trying to eradicate every shred of evidence that she was a prostitute. Finally, she had removed most of the mascara and red lipstick and, behind the mask of Rimmel, lay a tired, but very pretty face: innocent, with delicate features, etched with a little sadness. But attractive anyhow.

She managed to foam the soap in the tepid tap water and meticulously cleaned her slight body from neck to toe, so that no trace of him remained. He had disappeared, along with the night before. Then she caught sight of her bruises. Deep purple marks welted across her arms and there were teeth marks on her left breast. She hadn't erased everything after all.

Elise trembled. She needed something to get through today. Her fix. Yes, that would make things better. It always did. But how the hell could she afford it? Twenty quid was nothing compared to what she needed. She began to shake. Withdrawal symptoms were kicking in. Her body shuddered violently. Her vision became blurred and she felt nauseous. More work needed to be done.

Elise re-entered the bedroom she had just escaped from, removed her clothes and edged towards the snorting creature under the threadbare sheets.

She caressed his legs, directing her hands towards his crotch, gently scratching him with her bitten nails. That didn't seem to bother him, and he turned towards her with a leer on his unshaven, bloated face.

* * *

2004: Lizzie

Lizzie had forgotten that it was Monday. She hated Mondays with a vengeance and remembered that song from ages ago where a girl who, just like her, hated them too. She shot everybody dead.

Good idea, Lizzie thought as she placed four cornflakes on a spoon and swallowed.

Every day, after breakfast, Lizzie was forced to have one-on-one care until the community group, which was held at 8.30 a.m. She would be watched constantly to ensure that the cereal she had eaten for breakfast stayed in her stomach and she didn't throw up. She had bulimia and she wanted to puke, but nobody trusted her to keep her food down any more, which is why she had this stupid one-on-one every sodding day.

The forty-five minutes of being constantly watched got on Lizzie's tits, big-time. The nurse watching her was a nice enough woman; black, with a huge stomach and knockers that rested on her waist. She had an infectious laugh that made Lizzie smile, and her hair was almost shaven, which Lizzie figured was easier to manage than wild afro curls. Her name was Gloria.

Lizzie knew Gloria was only doing her job and she also knew that she was one of the better nurses here. So, today, she would actually behave herself and keep her breakfast down.

The skinny, balding guy chairing the community group, however, left a lot to be desired. Full of his own self-righteousness, Mr Hillier bellowed the rules of St Thomas's Hospital to the 'inmates' (that's the term Lizzie used, as she felt like a prisoner there). He barked his orders across the room, distressing some of the inmates with his latest threat; if anybody so much as touched another patient, they would be punished.

Lizzie shuddered when she thought of Jason – her one and only friend in this place, and the only person who was ever kind enough to hold her hand. How she despised Mr Hillier and his ridiculous rules and regulations.

Someone started to sob, and moaned that the rules were unfair. A young lad with a nervous twitch sniggered while he deliberately stroked another patient's arm and laughed when he was swiftly removed from the room by a nurse. Lizzie, however, chose to ignore the defiant inmate and set her daily goal – to be a good girl. To be *Mummy's little angel.*

Then she could go home.

* * * * *

3. SUFFERING

2014: Beth

The teabags were there, right on the worktop, and had left a filthy dark stain that would be impossible to remove. Beth bit her gold necklace in indecision then reached for the cleaning cupboard desperately – if she didn't get to the stains quickly, then they would spread. They would end up destroying the units, the floor and then the entire kitchen. This was an emergency.

She frantically sprayed Mr Muscle over all the kitchen surfaces. The doorbell rang. She wasn't expecting anybody. Who could it be? She faced a dilemma. Would she risk losing her kitchen or would she face a tragedy if she didn't answer the door? What if it was the police, who had to relay a message that one of her kids had been killed? What if Dave had been in a car accident? Jesus, this really was going to be a bad day.

Beth decided that the latter was the most important. After all, she did want a new kitchen, as this one had been fitted a couple of years ago and she fancied one of those pyrolytic ovens and induction hobs. Dave could take out another loan to pay for it and, due to him having contacts in the industry, it would be heavily discounted. She couldn't wait to tell him.

Beth tentatively opened the door, only to be greeted by the postman. "Morning. Could you sign for this, please?"

Beth scowled at him. How dare he disturb her from her cleaning duties, only to ask for a filthy letter to be signed for with an even filthier pen? She grabbed a clean tissue from her pocket, wiped the pen and signed for the letter which, no doubt, had numerous harmful germs on it. Then she locked the door, discarded the letter and ran to the cloakroom to wash her hands – three times. The first wash got rid of the dangerous stuff that would definitely harm her. The second time made sure that any 'leftover' germs were destroyed and the third time was, well, *third time lucky*. Beth believed in 'third time lucky' and knew that if she didn't say it, she – or, even worse, her family – would come to harm. No way was she going to chance that.

After another hour of scrubbing the surfaces, cleaning the oven and hob, washing the floor and polishing the appliances, all traces of the teabags had gone. Beth felt relieved, but then remembered that Dave had used the shower. And so her cleaning regime started once more – this time the bathroom and, of course, the sink in the cloakroom too, as she had washed her hands there after receiving the letter which she dared not open. The towels all had to be washed too, but she decided that she had touched enough germs for one day. Dave could put them in the washing machine when he got home that evening, and paper towels would have to do until then.

It was eleven o'clock before Beth could finally relax. The bed was immaculate; the duvet cover was positioned at perfect right-angles to correspond with the square bedstead. She discarded her latex gloves, wiped her hands with antibacterial lotion, dried them on a paper towel and sat down.

She fancied a coffee – a strong one with three sugars, and a cigarette. Heck, she hadn't even had time to smoke this morning but, as she inhaled, her head buzzed and she felt so much better. All she had to do now was pluck up the courage to open that letter, then she could finally go out.

* * *

1994: Elise

Elise used to love sex – or, as her friends would correct her – making love. Her ex-boyfriend had been a nice guy. He worked hard for a living, owned a three-bedroomed detached house and drove a new Range Rover.

His ex-wife had screwed him financially but, through sheer determination and hard work, he had rebuilt his life and only had a few emotional scars from the years of anxiety she had caused him. He also had a three-year-old son whom he saw every other weekend and, apparently, idolised. Other than these minor complications, he was pretty perfect.

Elise had come along by chance. They had met at a friend of a friend's New Year's Eve party (which Elise had gate-crashed) and had hit it off straight away. Elise liked him from the moment she set eyes on him. Although he was far older than her and had greying, thinning hair, his blue eyes were gentle and kind. They glistened in admiration of this very unconventional and wacky young woman in front of him who was, despite her spiky hair and outrageous clothes, absolutely stunning. He imagined that she was already spoken for or had a string of attractive boyfriends.

Elise was, however, single. She had finished with her long-term boyfriend some months before and, as the bells of Big Ben chimed, Elise and David embraced, then tenderly brushed lips. The memories of the former year melted away: a new year had just begun. Elise held on tightly to this kind man. For the first time in years, she actually felt safe.

* * *

His torso was heavy on her slight frame. As he thrust his erect penis into her, he bit Elise's shoulder over and over. Each thrust felt more painful than the last, and the stench of his stale breath drifted across to Elise's blindfolded face. She was helpless, and had no idea what he was going to do to her next. Her wrists were bound with rope to the battered bedstead, her ankles spread and tied, and he pumped harder and harder into her frail body.

Grunting aloud and cursing Elise for not satisfying him, he withdrew and slung the used condom in her face.

"Suck me, bitch," he yelled, forcing his engorged penis into her trembling mouth. Elise could smell him – he smelled stale from the previous night's sex, and sweaty – but she sucked hard and rapidly, desperately hoping to bring him to climax. She was good at oral and, since it didn't hurt, she preferred it to sex. She imagined that she was with David – the kind and gentle man whom she had idolised. She pictured his muscular body, the fine hairs running down his chest to his navel. She visualised him lying on their crisp, white bed linen, eyes closed, mouth slightly open, breathing heavily with the ecstasy she was giving him.

The fat, hideous man jerked, then groaned loudly. As the warm, salty semen burst into her mouth, he released himself, grunted and untied her ankles. Elise gagged at the foul taste in her mouth but fought to keep it down. She couldn't vomit now – not when she was so close to getting paid. All he had to do was free her wrists, then she would be on her way.

She could feel the weight of his body lying on the sheet next to her. Elise wanted to go, but sensed her ordeal wasn't quite over.

"What's your name, bitch?" the hideous monster asked.

"Jackie," she replied, in almost a whisper.

He muttered some obscenities and started to masturbate, without success. Forcing his flaccid penis into Elise's hand, he demanded she make him hard, then straddle him.

"Make me come again, bitch, then I'll pay you."

It took another two hours before Elise finally earned her much-needed forty pounds. All she had to do now was find her friend, then she really would feel free. At least for a little while.

* * *

2004: Lizzie

The community group session seemed to drag on for hours, although Lizzie had only been sitting there for forty minutes.

Most of the inmates were there following suicide attempts, some due to drug addiction, some with eating-disorders and the others, in Lizzie's opinion, were simply seeking attention – just like the fat girl she shared her room with. Whatever the reason for their admission, she chose to ignore them all – other than Jason who, despite having a very low mental age, she liked. He was twenty-five years old and had been admitted due to his violent tendencies but Lizzie had never witnessed anything other than gentleness. He had a kind face and always smiled at Lizzie – unlike the others, who cried most of the time.

Lizzie was there following a suicide attempt. She had spent a week in hospital, later becoming an inmate. She also suffered from bulimia which, compared to the suicide attempt and overdose, wasn't really a big deal.

It was almost time for their tea-break – or, at least, Lizzie felt that it should be. She fancied a cup of tea, or even that disgusting piss-weak coffee. The fact that it was only quarter past nine and she had a meeting with a shrink coming up irritated her somewhat. Christ, time dragged here. She was bored shitless already and she wasn't even halfway through the morning.

Dr Davies was, however, a decent bloke. Actually, he was a fantastic psychiatrist and, despite her protests, Lizzie enjoyed talking to him. He genuinely appeared to be interested in her and always listened intently to everything Lizzie had to say. She never felt foolish or stupid when she shared her secrets with him. He didn't laugh at her either – unlike her mother, who had belittled her all her life.

Lizzie sat down on the floor and bent her legs, almost adopting the lotus position. For some reason, she felt relaxed sitting like this and recalled reading a book on yoga as a young girl. It eased the stress for her then and, subconsciously, helped her now.

Dr Davies covered his usual questions then paid particular attention to Lizzie's bulimia. After she had given him perfect responses, Dr Davies decided to take Lizzie off lithium, due to the chronic side-effects she was suffering from, particularly the vomiting. Lizzie dare not admit that she was inducing that 'symptom' by sticking her fingers down her throat, and instead smiled at Dr Davies. She hated the stuff – it made her thirsty and she constantly needed to pee. So, coming off it sounded quite appealing, although she knew that she would have to work harder than ever to hide her puking problem.

"We're going to try a different medicine for you, Lizzie, which may suit you better," the doctor explained. "It's called Zyprexa, and we'll monitor your progress over the next few weeks. Hopefully, you'll gain a little weight too and start to feel less depressed. We'll also prescribe you Sonata, which is stronger than the medication you're currently taking. I know that you're suffering from insomnia, Lizzie, so I hope this will help too."

Lizzie suddenly felt very depressed. She knew that Dr Davies was only doing what he felt was best for her, and she understood that changing her meds might help her improve and start to feel a little healthier. Lizzie realised that she was skinny, but she liked the way she looked. Her mum was an alcoholic and morbidly obese. The years of drinking a couple of bottles of gin a day and pigging out on junk food had taken their toll, and there was no way that Lizzie would ever allow herself to get fat. She loathed her mother and her monstrous appearance, and she feared that this new medication would change her appearance, make her look like her mother, a thought she dreaded.

"Please, Dr Davies," Lizzie begged, "Can you leave the daily medication out? I'm doing really well and I'm scared of the side-effects. We can try a week without them and see how I am. Remember, I didn't need those drugs before I came here, and I can prove I don't need them now."

Tears welled in Lizzie's brown eyes. A single droplet hung on her long eyelashes then dripped onto her cheek. She wiped it away and looked pleadingly at Dr Davies. "Please," she cried, "please help me."

The kind-hearted doctor went to stroke Lizzie's arm, then remembered that he was not permitted any physical contact.

"I am," he whispered as he closed the door and left Lizzie alone.

* * * * *

4. BETH'S JOURNEY

2014

The letter could wait. After the morning she had endured, Beth simply could not face any more stress. Both her children were away at the moment. Kirsty, her younger child, aged nineteen, was staying with her bohemian boyfriend in Paris and Robert, fourteen months older, was in his final year of his degree at Birmingham University. Both kids, however, were due home for Christmas so Beth needed to get a move on. And she had loads of presents to buy; all on Dave's credit card.

Beth didn't have to work – or, at least, that's what she wanted to believe. She had always found it emotionally hard to be a parent and had never had a proper job. Simply coping with everyday life had been a battle. However, now that both the children were grown up, excuses about being busy looking after them or running the home were wearing rather thin with Dave.

Beth recalled the extremely heated discussion they had had only a week or so ago, when, once again, Dave had been horrified at his credit card bill. It was over a thousand pounds – and all on clothes. Clothes that Beth would not wear, but would donate to a charity shop with the labels still on them. Clothes that made her look like a cheap little trollop – but he dare not tell her so. Clothes that she didn't need and he couldn't afford to pay for. But Dave knew where these kind of discussions could lead, and wanted a quiet life. And so, after suggesting she get a part-time job in a supermarket, and receiving a deluge of excuses, then abuse, he dropped the subject. For now, at least.

Beth took one final look in her driver's mirror and tended to her already perfectly groomed hair. She started the engine, opened the driver's window and lit her second cigarette of the day as she started the forty-minute drive to Hemel Hempstead. Sometimes it could take thirty-five minutes, other times longer, but generally she allowed forty minutes. This meant she never felt under pressure because she was running late, and often allowed Beth to take a detour en route. It was quite a pretty ride to Hemel once she had driven through Dunstable, which had declined over the years. When she was little, it had been a bustling market town but now, other than banks, charity shops and estate agents, most of the shops had closed down and were boarded up. She rarely stopped there these days.

She passed the rolling hills of Whipsnade Zoo. Beth smiled. She recollected her annual trips here with Nanny and Granddad, eating curled-up sandwiches and drinking warm squash while snuggling up with them on a tatty red picnic blanket. She remembered feeding the penguins and asking their keeper whether they enjoyed the warmer weather in England. Sometimes, Beth wished for snow so that they could slip and slide and play in their natural environment. She loved snow too, but wasn't allowed to play out in it with her friends, due to her asthma. (If she got a chest infection, she would cough a lot in the night, and her mummy needed her sleep.)

The highlight of the zoo was, however, always the same. Nanny, Granddad and Beth would jump aboard the open-topped bus that toured the zoo. She would then be allowed an ice cream – but only one. Beth couldn't get enough of the sweet, sickly stuff and would scoff the lot within a few minutes, but Nanny was under orders from Beth's mummy not to spoil her too much. Nanny always took notice of her daughter and never broke the rules. Nor did Beth. She daren't.

Once her hands had been wiped and her face cleaned, Beth would run as fast as her skinny legs would take her to the splash zone. The afternoon sea lion show would start and she always insisted that they were there half an hour before the show started so that she didn't miss any of the fun. She would cross her spindly legs on the concrete seating and wait with bated breath for the sea lions to start their amazing tricks and acrobatics. Beth would imagine swimming with them, riding on their backs and feeding them fish afterwards as a treat. She sometimes wished that she could be a sea lion too. They didn't get told off for being naughty, and they could play as much as they wanted to.

Beth accelerated towards Dagnall; she grabbed another cigarette from her packet, lit up and shot back into reality. Those were some of the happiest memories of her life and she treasured each and every one of them, but now she had to drive fast and concentrate on the road, not on childhood memories. She could relive them again later.

As she headed towards the Old Town, Beth looked briefly across the Old High Street towards St Mary's Church and the enormous Gadebridge Park. She would find time, someday, to go back there. It also held some good memories for her. But she didn't have enough time today; she was running late. She had been driving for forty-five minutes, daydreaming about the past, and now she had messed up. The whole trip would be wrecked if she didn't get a move on.

Beth dashed towards one of the open car parks in the town centre. It was packed and she drove round and round, cursing at every driver in her way. She was in a hurry, for Christ's sake, and none of these stupid housewives or retirees seemed to care. She eventually opted for the large multi-storey car park close to Debenhams, which she loathed. Although clean and brightly lit, it frightened Beth. She imagined being followed, watched from dark, unlit corners, then murdered, left rotting for days before being found by a cleaner. These places freaked her out.

After pulling on her woollen gloves, Beth purchased a parking ticket and entered the lift. Pressing the button for the mall, her heartbeat calmed and she took a deep breath in relief. The brightly lit mall welcomed her with sparkling lights, and tasteful Christmas decorations adorned the high roofline and windows. She had made it and now, for a short while, Beth could relax.

* * * * *

5. FOR ELISE

1994

Elise was freezing. The blast of cold air outside the building sent her reeling and she rubbed her arms in an attempt to warm up and get rid of her goose bumps. It didn't work. The cheap imitation-silk vest clung to her chest as she tried to run in the ridiculously high-heeled boots she had bought the day before from the local market. And as for her short leather skirt – well, that offered no warmth either. It was hopeless. She had to rush or she would freeze to death. She also needed her fix.

It was a long way to Hockwell Ring – at least a mile and a half, or three thousand steps, give or take a few. It was often frightening, but the walk was one that Elise was extremely familiar with. She knew which short-cuts to take, which houses to dodge and, most importantly, *who* to avoid. There had been a lot of trouble here with shootings and murders recently, and she, for one, wasn't going to be part of that. She had enough to contend with. She bowed her head and continued on her journey.

Elise knew which flat he would be in today. He'd told her last night before she went to work.

"Meet me there at eleven," he'd yelled when she'd entered the car. It was now half past but she wasn't too worried. He'd be totally spaced anyway, and in that state of mind, time never mattered.

She tottered towards the high-rise flats. Elise felt a surge of relief burst through her. The familiar butterflies rushed through her tummy and suddenly she didn't feel the cold any more. The violent tremors stopped too. She was in safe territory now and Leroy would be there to offer her what she needed.

It was a long way up to his flat and the battered lift, like the shower this morning, was broken. Elise decided that her boots were going to be hopeless on the stairs, so removed them before starting the long climb to Leroy's haven. She could smell disinfectant from the freshly cleaned floors as she caught her breath after climbing up the fifth flight of concrete steps. A small child opened the door to his mother's flat, revealing a stressed woman holding a screaming baby and bellowing for him to come back indoors. An Asian man glared at Elise before locking his door and checking it three times before descending the stairs.

It wasn't the nicest place to live, but for some reason Elise wished she lived there. It felt like home, in a peculiar way, and she felt she belonged there. She increased her pace and finally reached flat 117A. She rang the doorbell.

Leroy was thin and lanky and his face could have told a thousand stories. Elise was fascinated by his scars and often wondered how he got them. She imagined him in a forest, fighting off bears and ending up torn to shreds, but alive. He would then be rescued by wolves that would bring him up as their own, before Leroy would escape and enter the real world as a hero.

The reality was far less dramatic. Leroy hadn't been attacked by wild creatures – his attacker was behind bars for stabbing him twice in the leg and slashing his face with a kitchen knife. Leroy had been in the wrong place at the wrong time and had ended up being a victim, along with others, of a gang fight. He was the 'wrong' shade of black and came from a rival gang's housing estate, which had been enough to justify the attack. Not that Leroy agreed.

"You bloody coming in, then?" Leroy enquired as Elise stood shivering at his open door. "It's freezing."

Elise entered the warm living room and inhaled the wonderful smell of weed. The remnants of the smokes were in an ashtray, and she wondered whether he had any left.

"You got a smoke?" Elise asked, winking at Leroy. Leroy opened his Marlboro packet and chucked one across the room.

"Not a cigarette, tosser," she yelled playfully. "Marijuana. I need to feel mellow before the big hit."

Leroy stood up. His six feet five inch frame towered above Elise as she huddled under a soft throw on the worn sofa. He leaned towards her, brushed her fringe away from her cheeks and smiled. He liked her hair away from her face; it made her look so young and innocent. He had secretly fancied her for weeks and regularly fantasised about her being his girlfriend. Then, the stark reality of who she was – what she was – would hit him and the romanticism would disappear in a flash.

"You got the cash you owe me?" Leroy asked, raising his eyebrows and opening his eyes in a wide and slightly intimidating manner. "Hundred quid and it's yours."

Elise looked sheepishly at him and rummaged through her cheap handbag. Grabbing her purse, she presented him with three crumpled notes. "I got sixty quid, Leroy. That's all I have. Please?"

Leroy moved away from Elise and stood in front of the ceiling-high window, his back to her. He stared out at the skyline, which was adorned with council houses and burned-out cars. Turning back to Elise, he stared at her pityingly. He knew how desperate she was, how much she needed the stuff, but he could not weaken. Money was short – he owed people big-time, and knew that, if he didn't cough up, he'd have another scar to add to his collection.

"Told ya last night, no more favours. You gotta pay full whack now, Lise, cos this stuff ain't cheap and I had to change me contact. If you ain't got the dosh, you ain't getting your heroin."

Elise shuddered at the thought of not getting her hit. Slowly removing the throw from her now-warm body, she grabbed Leroy's hand in desperation. She gripped his fingers tightly, forcing her broken nails into the folds of his skin, and started to scream, then sob.

"Leroy – please. You know I can't survive without it. You know I need it to work. I'll die without it – look at me. *Look at me!* I'm begging you – just this once. I'll pay you the rest soon, I promise. Cross my heart and hope to die. I absolutely, totally promise that I'll pay you tomorrow. Just one fix, Leroy. Please, just one more, then I'll stop pestering you. Please, Leroy, I'm begging…"

Leroy released Elise's limp hand and put his arms around her tiny body. She was shaking violently and tears were streaming down her cheeks towards her lips. She was an addict, he knew that now. Leroy was hoping to get clean soon, as he had a new job to aim for, but what else did Lise have? He knew the answer as he lifted her up, tucked her under the throw and retrieved a sterile plastic packet from the cabinet next to the television.

* * * * *

6. LIZZIE'S BAD MISTAKE

2004

Lizzie felt sick. A feeling of nausea was building rapidly and she began to heave, forcing bile into her dry mouth. She could not puke. She *must not* puke, or they would put her back on that stuff again and she couldn't face that. Lizzie retched at the vile taste then swallowed the bile just as the door opened.

The man who ran the daily community group stood in the doorway and beckoned to Lizzie. Mr Hillier was authoritarian and going bald; he only ever spoke to the 'inmates' during the group sessions, barking orders at them rather than having a conversation.

All that Lizzie wanted to hear right now was a friendly voice. A warm smile would have done, or just a kind gesture. She knew that he would not answer her wishes. In his eyes, she, and all the other *prisoners*, were drug-riddled lunatics who were fit for nothing. Or at least that's how Lizzie thought he felt. She slouched towards him, scowling as he pointed towards the canteen.

Lizzie waited in the queue, and planned her vengeance. *God, I wish I could get revenge on that balding prick,* she thought. She despised him. Revenge would shut him up once and for all and give her a laugh. But that could wait, as it was tea-break now and she liked the digestive biscuits that came with her coffee.

She waited patiently for her turn. Lizzie and the other inmates were relieved from the tedium of queuing by a fifteen-stone girl called Leanne. She screamed, a high-pitched, grinding shrill note that echoed through the canteen, before running desperately for the window, frantically flapping her arms. Within a few seconds, a specialist team was called to sedate and restrain her. They took her away immediately. Normality resumed, and the residents continued with their tea and biscuits as though nothing had happened.

Lizzie liked events like this. They amused her, although she knew that she couldn't share her feelings with anybody else, not even Jason, as he was a real gossip. She particularly enjoyed Leanne's little episodes, especially when she found out that Leanne regularly heard alien voices and saw things that weren't there. She planned to write a book about her stay at the hospital someday, or even tell her kids about it. But that could wait.

She didn't eat her biscuit after all. Instead of wasting the digestive, she hid it in her knickers to give it to Jason instead. He loved sugary foods, and whenever his mum visited him, she would bring him a bag of goodies like Mars Bars and Snickers. She would also read to him – sometimes extracts from the daily newspaper to keep him up to date with world events or, on other occasions, articles from a trashy gossip magazine. Either way, Lizzie thought that it was a nice thing to do and wished that her mum was like that.

It was 'free' time now. Every inmate had half an hour or so to relax and chill. Some chose to watch TV in the impersonal TV room, which had a green patterned carpet and uncomfortable plastic chairs placed around the walls.

Today, most of the inmates opted to watch trash TV, but Lizzie chose escapism, in the form of her treasured book. Jason would sometimes join her and ask her to read to him, which she enjoyed as much as he did. Lizzie felt quite honoured to be asked and so, today, as Jason sat beside her, discreetly holding her hand and sucking the biscuit Lizzie had saved for him, she started to read him her latest story – a scary one.

Gloria, the kind black nurse, had given Lizzie the book and, although she was fully aware that she was breaking St Thomas's rules, she had felt a great deal of satisfaction knowing that she was extending a little kindness to one of her patients. Lizzie knew that she had to be careful whenever she read the book and made sure that the pages were always open and the cover was never displayed. She didn't want Gloria to get into any trouble.

She started to read the James Patterson novel aloud. Jason shuddered and gripped her hand tightly. Although he was a patient here and had fantasised about killing the bastard who mugged his mum, the psychotic nature of the kidnapper in this book disturbed him. He wasn't keen on *Along Came a Spider* and asked Lizzie to stop reading it to him. She shrugged and silently continued to read. Lizzie secretly had a crush on Alex Cross, the detective in the novel. He sounded like a nice man – brilliantly clever but also a very loving and caring father; something Lizzie wished desperately she still had.

Her dreams about Alex Cross came to an abrupt halt when Mr Hillier spotted Lizzie and Jason holding hands. He briskly approached the pair, separating them and scolding them for breaking the 'no touching' rule. Their punishment was no free time for a week. Their leisure time would be replaced by therapy sessions where they would discuss why rules and regulations should be obeyed.

Lizzie felt an enormous surge of rage build up within her and, before she knew what she was doing, she had hit Mr Hillier in the nose with a perfect left hook.

"You low-life bastard!" she bawled while being dragged from the room and sedated by a couple of faceless workers. However, she couldn't help but smirk when she saw the blood gushing down his feeble face, and felt a huge sense of satisfaction when she witnessed him sniffling like a baby towards the gents' toilets, holding a blood-drenched tissue to his nose.

Then the consequences of her actions hit her. She had been a bad girl and Mummy's little angel would have to be punished.

* * * * *

7. BETH'S FEAR

2014

It was a magical time of the year, and the shops in the Marlowes were more appealing than ever. Beth skipped joyfully as festive songs were played. She hummed to one of her favourites, 'Silent Night', and took a moment to reflect on past Christmases. She remembered the enormous real Christmas tree in her huge living room, decorated with fairy lights and angels, Dad smoking his pipe, wearing his pyjamas and tartan slippers, Granddad and Nanny sipping sherry, the dog curled up by the open fire … and Mummy. Her thoughts ended there and she made her way to her favourite boutique, Serendipity.

There was something very special indeed about this shop. Whether it was the appealing frontage, with soft lighting and tasteful dress designs, or the decadent interior, Beth wasn't sure, but she immediately felt at home as soon she walked through the large Georgian door. Every single outfit here moulded perfectly to Beth's curves and fitted like a glove. The skirts weren't too long, the dresses weren't too short, and the jeans hugged her backside like Dave wished he could! She could buy the stock of the entire shop and waste nothing on charity donations.

A Christmassy little black number jumped out at Beth. It looked like silk and had tiny diamante stones around the neckline, which plunged to a low V. She knew this stunning dress was an absolute must for her, especially at this time of the year.

Keeping her gloves on, she sorted through the sizes. There were tens, twelves and fourteens but no eights. No sodding eights. She frantically rummaged through the dresses on the next rack, just in case a size eight had been put there, but no joy. She was devastated. Beth believed that this dress had been designed just for her – she had to have one, now! It was critical, otherwise something terrible would happen. She regained her composure and looked for a shop assistant.

A young, dumpy girl wearing jeans that were far too tight for her was helping another customer. The short, indecisive woman irritated Beth as she tried to decide which dress to buy for her friend's wedding. Black seemed inappropriate, although it slimmed her down, but should she be brave and go for the red one instead? The shop assistant listened intently and recommended that she try both on. Beth was becoming impatient and a familiar, nagging anger was starting to build inside her. She swore silently to herself, wishing that the stupid fucking customer would piss off and buy something from somewhere else. She was far too fat for Serendipity stuff and should go to a supermarket instead where they did frumpy clothes for old people like her. Serendipity had been created for Beth, and she wanted her little black dress desperately.

The shop assistant caught Beth's eye and smiled warmly.

"Hello, can I help you with anything?"

Beth calmed down and tried to act rationally. She had worked hard to control her emotions so far, and could carry it off for a few more minutes. Pointing to the little black dress, she asked whether the shop had any size eights. "You have every other size except mine. I have to attend an important function tonight, and I *need* this dress."

The shop assistant looked a little surprised at Beth's tone of desperation, but promised to take a look in the stock room for her.

"We tend to keep new stock in the shop," she added, "but I'll have a look just in case. Hold on a minute."

Beth turned away, impatiently flicking through the accessories and jewellery. She spotted some 'bling' earrings, a thick bracelet and necklace, and knew they would match the dress perfectly. Just a new handbag, shoes and stockings, and then she'd be done.

Mrs Indecisive exited the changing room with both dresses and looked for the shop assistant, who was nowhere to be found. Tutting loudly, she hung the far-too-small outfits on the clothes rail and left the store. *Good*, Beth thought, sniggering at the image of the woman with rolls of fat protruding from the slinky dress.

She moved towards the changing room and peeked at the sizes of the discarded items of clothing. Fourteens, both of them. *Huh, they'd swamp me. I could go camping in them,* Beth thought. Then, out of the corner of her eye, she spotted *the* little black dress. It was hanging there, almost *begging* Beth to pick it up. But the size was what mattered most. It had to be right. It had to be an eight, as this dress was meant just for her. Her heart racing, she pulled the label from the back of the dress. It was a size eight. Beth squealed with delight and felt a huge sense of relief surge through her body. It would, of course, have to be dry cleaned, as somebody else had worn it, but that didn't matter now – she had exactly what she needed.

Gathering her accessories and selecting a small black clutch bag, Beth dashed to the counter excitedly. She felt like she had felt the Christmas when she was six. Her nanny and granddad had bought her a walking, talking doll. It was the popular tall one, with life-like hair and pretty brown eyes just like hers, and every single girl at her school had asked Santa for one. Most didn't have their wishes granted, but Beth had, and she had cherished that doll. Funny; she couldn't recall what had happened to it.

Beth was bought back to reality when the checkout girl asked for payment. This was always a tricky time, as Beth's gloves were woollen and thick and she sometimes pressed the wrong numbers on the keypad. Beth retrieved her credit card from her pocket, where she kept it to save fumbling in her purse, placed it in the card machine and keyed in the code. The transaction failed. She made a second attempt and the transaction failed again. Beth felt her blood pressure rising. She flushed and felt sick with the stress of it all. "Third time lucky," she said to herself and keyed in the number one last time. The credit card machine rejected payment for the third time, and her card was frozen.

"Do you have another card, Madam?"

Beth felt her heart thudding. The card was in her purse, which held trillions of germs from the air. But she had no choice.

"Hold on," she whispered before removing her glove.

Beth took three deep breaths for luck and unzipped her handbag. Her purse was nestled between an umbrella and a packet of cigarettes. She closed her eyes, grabbed the purse, opened it, took the card, placed it in the card holder, opened her eyes and entered the code. The reader flashed that the payment had been accepted. Beth snatched her card, threw it in her bag and grabbed her purchases.

Beth vomited in the public toilet; she knew that she would have to work extra hard at cleaning up now. She was smothered in polluting, dangerous filth which would transfer into her car, then her home, and kill her, and everybody she loved. The soap in the dispenser had run out. She had cleaned herself twenty times and so, with bleeding hands and a red-raw face, she counted her steps back to the multi-storey car park. Only eight hundred and twenty-one steps to go, then she would be safe.

Eight hundred and twenty.

Eight hundred and nineteen.

Third time lucky.

* * * * *

8. ELISE'S TERROR

1994

Elise kissed Leroy on the lips. It wasn't sexy or seductive but, as he gave her the syringe, she felt not just an enormous sense of relief, but *love*. Whether the latter was purely due to the fact that he had given in to her pleas, or she genuinely cared for the guy, was irrelevant: she was, at long last, going to feel *better*.

Pulling the blanket away from her arms, she found a vein. This one was still in good condition compared to the others, which were completely shot. Elise forced her hand around her arm to create some pressure and the blue vein bulged through her skin, awaiting relief.

Elise pressed the heroin through the syringe. Leroy looked away. This was a sight he had seen a thousand times before, but his stomach still turned as he pictured his little friend destroying her life. Selling drugs to strangers was one thing, but this was different – he cared for Elise.

The silence was broken by hysterical laughter and a thud as Elise fell off the sofa and kicked her legs in the air. She felt euphoric. Heck, life was good. Her giggles echoed through the small living room as she recollected everything fantastic she had ever experienced. Her friends, Leroy, the ecstasy his stuff gave her – they all made her feel so wonderful, and she felt warm and snug and safe.

Leroy turned towards Elise, who was flushed and looked healthy. Her breathing was slowing down and she was mellow, humming a song and smiling. Her aching muscles had disappeared, and the pain from her bites and bruises from her client the night before had dissipated. Wow, she felt good – *and* incredibly horny. Beaming a daft smile at Leroy, she trotted towards his bedroom, jumped onto his bed and passed out.

Leroy knew this feeling well, and he yearned for it too. But tomorrow he was visiting a drug rehab clinic to discuss finally kicking the habit and stopping selling drugs, once and for all. He needed to be clean for his new job, and so he made do with another joint. The effects of marijuana were pleasing but very short-lived. He always needed three or four joints now just to start feeling remotely high, but joints were cheaper than the hard stuff and far less addictive.

Beat the heroin addiction first, then give up the joints, he thought while inhaling the weed, closing his eyes in pleasure.

His peace was temporary as Leroy was interrupted by deafening thumps on his front door.

"Hudson, we know you're in there, so be a good man and open the fucking door."

Leroy felt like shitting himself. He knew that voice and knew from its tone that Craig was seriously pissed off. Leroy could ignore it and pretend to be out, but he knew better. His door, then shortly after, his head, would be kicked in. Not something he relished.

Leroy found it hard to collect his thoughts or formulate any kind of plan. The hammering on the door was getting louder, but he felt incredibly chilled and mellow. He knew he was in deep shit but, Christ, why the hell wasn't his brain taking this threat seriously? He would quit weed tomorrow as well.

Leroy managed to half compose himself and staggered towards the door.

"Okay, man, okay. Craig, hold on," he whispered, edging towards the front door, a half-witted grin on his face. Despite his ridiculous smile, his stomach was churning with nerves and his heart rate trebled when the door was almost pushed off its hinges the moment Leroy unlocked it.

Craig forced his way into the living room. Behind him was his henchman Duke. "Where's my fucking cash, man?" Craig demanded, grabbing Leroy around the neck. Leroy sensed the danger he was in and realised that Craig was in no mood for joviality. He was intimidating at the best of times, with a hideous gangsta tattoo that spread from his shaved head down to his neck. He'd even had his prisoner number tattooed across his forehead, just to remind people how hard he was, and that he'd done time for his crimes. Twice.

Leroy knew that he had to tread bloody carefully with this thug.

Duke, who didn't have any tattoos but chose to decorate his enormous muscular body with piercings instead, removed his shoe, grabbed something from it, and then pointed a Swiss army knife at Leroy's throat.

Leroy felt that his heart was going to explode, it was pounding so hard. He tried not to show his terror. He was petrified. He also feared for Lise who, despite being in cloud cuckoo land in his bedroom, was also in grave danger. Leroy hoped she would stay in his room.

"Hey man, take that knife away, it's kinda intimidating," he begged. Craig nodded at Duke, who edged the knife closer to Leroy's neck. Barely able to speak, Leroy tried to work out how he could worm his way out of this situation. Jesus, he had two hundred quid plus the extra sixty from Lise. He owed Craig five hundred pounds. Although no great mathematician, he knew that he was two hundred and forty quid short.

"I got just over half, Craig – I can give ya that now and the rest tomorrow. Me punter ain't shown up wiv it today, man, like he should've, but he ain't gonna let me down. I swear on me ma's life – I will have your dosh within twenty-four hours."

The knife pushed harder into Leroy's neck. It drew blood – just a small cut, but enough to scare Leroy senseless. Craig pulled the knife away then lunged it towards Leroy's jugular before stopping just millimetres away from the bulging artery.

"Excuses, excuses, excuses, Leroy. I hear this last week, I hear it yesterday and now, I hear it today. I am tired, man – no, I'm bloody exhausted of hearing that shit coming out of that rancid mouth of yours. You want trouble? You fucking got it. You're a dead man, did ya hear me? A dead man, unless you cough up now."

Leroy did hear him. He had to think quickly. He broke away from Craig's grip in the hope that he wouldn't stab him to death. Craig waited as Leroy opened a drawer close to the TV.

The money was in an envelope – or, at least, some of it was. Leroy passed it to Craig, then added the sixty quid that Lise had given him. Craig and Duke paced towards him, counted the notes and moved even closer to Leroy. "And the rest?"

"Told ya – tomorrow. This time tomorrow I'll have it. If I ain't, then kill me. I'm serious, man; just give me twenty-four more hours. Ain't a lot in the big picture of things, is it?"

Craig saw red. Who the fuck did this prick think he was, asking him to wait? *Nobody* ordered Craig around, not even his bloody mother. Craig felt a familiar rage build in his gut, one that had caused him to stab his younger brother in the chest; a rage that had resulted in the prisoner number on his forehead. He shoved Duke out of the way with his elbow then, pushing Leroy towards the window, smashed his enormous fist into Leroy's ribcage. Once, twice, three times – each time harder than the last, each time more furious. He wanted this motherfucker dead.

Leroy fell to the floor, fighting for breath. He was in agony. Writhing in pain, he tried to curl into a ball but failed miserably. He could barely move.

Craig was far from satisfied, though. Grabbing Leroy's dreadlocks, he dragged his head back and pulled his body up in one vicious yank. Leroy's limp body hung like a rag doll as Craig clenched his hands around his neck and pummelled his head against the full-length window. It cracked. One more blow and the window would shatter, killing Leroy. Craig had often wondered what it would be like to watch someone bleed to death. He smiled and geared himself up for the final blow.

Craig clenched his fist, threw his arm back, and then stopped abruptly. A sob distracted him from his moment of glory. He was flummoxed. His clenched fist relaxed. Elise approached him, holding a tiny package in her hand. Falling to her knees and trembling in terror, she stared up at Craig, begging with her terrified eyes for some kind of mercy.

"Please," she whispered, "take this."

In her tiny hand was a pink silk pouch, sealed at the top with crimson ribbon. She lifted it up to Craig and begged him again to take it.

"It's all I have," she sobbed, tears streaming down her distraught face. "It's a gold watch, with diamonds and everything. It has be worth at least a grand – just take a look … please, just one look."

She had gained Craig's attention. He had enjoyed watching her pathetic begging, but was very interested in Elise's statement. *Could that piece of crap really be worth a grand?* He knew his stuff, though, so if she was bullshitting, she too would be going through that bloody window.

Snatching the package from Elise, he pulled the watch out and inspected it closely. Lise studied his face in the hope that his menacing expression would change. He gave nothing away.

The first thing Craig looked for on any item of jewellery was the hallmark. It was there all right. All eighteen fucking carats of it. *One point for the girl — she weren't lying about that.* Next, he studied the face of the watch. The hands were intact and the second hand was still working. He compared the time against his Gucci — spot-on. The jewels were there too — thirteen of them. Twelve for the hours and one in the centre. *There are diamonds as well. No shit, this is a decent piece of jewelry — worth a fair bit. At least a fuckin' grand.*

Leroy stayed silent and didn't dare move from his spot by the window. His chest was killing him, and he desperately needed to lie down. But he remained motionless, frozen by fear. Elise was on her knees, shaking violently. Both stared at Craig. They could hardly breathe for fear of what might happen next.

Turning towards Leroy, Craig spat on his face.

"You got twenty-four hours," he yelled, placing the watch carefully in his pocket and walking towards the front door. "I'll take this as a bonus for the shit you caused me today. You have twenty-four hours, prick."

"Tomorrow."

Within seconds, the door had slammed shut behind them and peace was restored. The booted foot slamming through the wood at the bottom of the door was a gentle reminder of what was to come.

Twenty-three hours and fifty-eight minutes to go.

* * * * *

9. LIZZIE'S NIGHTMARE

2004

Lizzie felt like crap. She ached from head to toe and had stomach cramps, as if her period was due. Forcing her eyes open, she wondered what time it was. She tried to focus on the large wall clock but the hands and numbers blurred, forming a black shadow around its face.

She knew that it wasn't bedtime, as it was still light outside. It was pouring with rain and she could hear the wind. A storm seemed to be brewing.

Dragging herself out from under the covers, she brushed her fringe away from her eyes and studied the stark room. Although warm and functional, it wasn't the most welcoming of places. The bedding was white and slightly rough on her skin, the floor tiles always felt cold on her feet and the walls were bare, other than the clock that she couldn't see properly and a bizarre picture painted by the crazy girl in the next bed.

Health and safety notices were strategically placed on the doors, by the sink and above the bath taps, and there was a soap dispenser screwed to the white bathroom tiles. It was always empty. Lizzie missed real soap, and wished that she could have some of the lovely Pears soap that Granny used to have when she was a little girl.

She still felt drugged. That Ativan stuff had certainly done the trick – she must have passed out after only a few minutes. Lizzie tried to recollect who had given her the sedative, but her mind clouded over like the sky outside. She could recall the faceless bodies dragging her to her room, placing her in bed, mumbling a few words then disappearing into thin air. She still felt drowsy.

Lizzie slumped back onto her single pillow after trying to fluff it up, without success. It was so incredibly uncomfortable, and her neck ached constantly. She knew, however, that there was no point in asking for a second one. Like so many of the requests she had made since being admitted, this one would be ignored.

Lizzie snuggled under her covers. She shivered and gently rubbed her skinny arms in an attempt to warm herself up. It worked, and the goose bumps dissipated. She curled her knees towards her chest and closed her eyes. She badly needed to rest...

* * *

The wind was howling and Lizzie could hear a door slamming in the distance. It was probably a shed door, left open or blown open in somebody's garden out there in the real world. She dreamed of the garden it was in: with long grass verges, deep flower beds with rose bushes, and mature trees. There was a greenhouse at the very bottom and a path with crazy paving leading to it. A child's rickety swing was nearby. It was a dull yellow and the chains squeaked as the wind blew the swing back and forth. Nearby was a tatty half-built shed. Its green door had flaking paint and was swaying on its hinges in the gusts of wind hitting it. Like the swing chain, which squeaked too. They both needed some oil.

The house to which the garden belonged was huge. It was at least three storeys high, with large bay windows enveloped within pointed arches. The roof was steep-pitched, with grey slates, and two asymmetrical chimneys thrust up into the sky, one at each end of the roof.

Lizzie looked at the gable window. It was small and unobtrusive, hidden discreetly from view. Only people in the back garden would be able to see it. A discoloured net curtain was flapping frantically, escaping through a crack in the window, then shooting back into the room. She wondered why the owners hadn't had it repaired. It seemed peculiar that such a beautiful home should be spoiled by that one silly flaw.

The sound of barking distracted Lizzie. A golden-coated, long-haired retriever bounded towards her, its tail wagging and its tongue hanging out. He bounced towards Lizzie, and then spotted a half-chewed tennis ball in the rose bed. Stopping dead, he gazed at Lizzie, then back at the ball. She knew what he wanted (or didn't want!) so she clambered into the mud and retrieved the ball for him. Jumping in the air, slobbering excitedly, the dog beseeched Lizzie with his eyes to chuck the ball. She wisely considered the glass panes in the greenhouse and held the ball tightly. Running into the shed, she rummaged through some discarded junk in a wooden box and pulled out a tatty lead. Alfie sprinted towards her, sat down by her shoes and waited patiently for the lead to be attached to his collar.

The gate from the back garden appeared gigantic to Lizzie. Looking up, she wondered how she could unlatch the bolt at the top. The lower one was simple, but the top bolt was virtually impossible to reach. She ran back to the shed and noticed some old stepladders that Daddy used to reach the branches of the trees when they needed pruning in the autumn. They would do. Dragging the wooden legs across the soaked lawn took all her strength. Lizzie then assembled the stepladder and climbed as far as the middle rung. The bolt was stiff but she managed to finally yank it open and escape, leaving the gate wide open and flapping in the wind.

The walk to the park was magnificent. Although it was cold and raining, Lizzie felt very cosy in her grey duffle coat. Her shoes, although caked in mud, were comfortable. Mummy always bought her Start-rites which, although clunky and old-fashioned, did the job and looked after Lizzie's feet. The girls at school laughed at her as they paraded around in their fashionable footwear but, right now, Lizzie didn't care what they thought. She was having fun!

Alfie was always as good as gold whenever Lizzie walked him. He was five years old and seemed to sense that Lizzie was young too. He never pulled or yanked her when she walked him, and slowed his pace so that her little legs could keep up with him.

The Avenue looked stunning as she passed through. The rows of individually designed mansions seemed to smile at her as she walked by. With their brightly lit windows and soft warm lighting, she imagined happy families sitting together, singing songs or playing games. Lizzie pictured the bright orange flames flickering in the open fire, with children, all snug and warm in their dressing gowns and slippers, cuddled up on a fluffy rug nearby. There would be fresh bread baking in the oven and their mummy would wear an apron and their daddy would read to them. She skipped cheerfully past these wonderful homes with their wonderful families.

Alfie's pace increased. The park was nearby. Langstone Park was one of Lizzie's favourite places in the world. It had everything from man-made hills which you could slide down on your bottom when the grass was wet enough, to the most amazing playground, which was where Lizzie was heading.

The playground was a huge enclosed area surrounded by a red picket fence and two gates. At the far end of the play area, towards the sandpit, was one of those huge hills she adored. Lizzie felt the butterflies build in her tummy – she loved this place so much.

She opened the squeaky gate, holding Alfie's lead tightly. Lizzie remembered the countless times she had played on the bright red swing. She'd work her little legs as hard as they would go then, when she was as high as the clouds, she would jump off and pretend to fly like an eagle. Lizzie stroked Alfie and ran towards the hopscotch, grabbing a pebble on the way. Throwing the stone, she jumped, aiming for the numbers, and got as far as number four before Alfie picked the stone up in his mouth and dropped it at her feet. Lizzie knew he wanted to play, but she had one more important thing to do before Alfie had his fun!

One of the hills on the edge of the playground had a huge slide at the top of it. Lizzie clambered up the wooden steps, sat at the top of the steel slide and squealed with excitement as she slid down. Alfie waited patiently at the bottom, wagging his tail as Lizzie went flying off the end into a muddy puddle.

Other than Lizzie and Alfie, the playground was empty. Most kids preferred to be indoors in this weather, but Lizzie was different. She inhaled the fresh, clean air deep into her lungs, left the playground, released Alfie from his lead and chucked the tennis ball as far as she could. Alfie, within a few seconds, skidded, grabbed the ball in his slobbering mouth, ran to Lizzie and dropped it at her feet. The game continued for another hour, with Alfie running to and fro with the ball, becoming more and more bedraggled with every muddy trip. It was raining hard now and Lizzie was starting to feel damp though her coat. Alfie was drenched but didn't seem to care.

Looking at her little red wristwatch, Lizzie panicked. It was almost four o'clock and she should be at home, doing her homework. Grabbing Alfie by the collar, placing the lead back on to it, she ran as fast as her legs would take her, along the winding paths, past the trees and back towards The Avenue. She had a stitch, which always happened when she ran, and slowed her pace. Fallen leaves from the oak trees lining The Avenue squashed beneath her feet and she kicked them playfully in the air. Alfie tried to catch them in his mouth but failed miserably, chopping at the air with his jaws instead. Lizzie laughed at him. Alfie seemed to laugh back at her. He was her very best friend. Her only friend, really.

When she approached the path leading to her back garden, Lizzie stopped dead in her tracks. The gate was closed. She pushed it but it wouldn't budge. Her heart pounded. She would have to use the front door. She dragged her legs, scraping her shoes on the ground as she walked around the side of the house. She edged towards the front driveway. Lizzie slowed to almost a standstill. The elegant front porch was illuminated by a large wrought-iron lantern and she noticed the umbrellas placed neatly in a disused urn. She realised that she should have used one while walking Alfie, as she was soaking wet. A large crow distracted her when it landed on one of the enormous chimneys. The smoke billowing from the chimney pots dissuaded him from staying longer and, with a loud squawk, he flapped his wings and disappeared. Lizzie dawdled, wishing she could fly away too.

Unlatching the wrought-iron gates leading to the driveway, Lizzie looked for Daddy's Jaguar. It wasn't there. She held her breath in anticipation of Mummy's mood. Sometimes Mummy didn't seem to care that Lizzie was dirty. She would sway around the living room, a glass in her hand, and dance to music by that strange person, Bob Dylan. Sometimes, though, she *did* care.

Lizzie stood on tiptoe and rang the doorbell. Loud chimes echoed through the hallway. The door from the lounge opened, and an enormous shadow appeared and switched the hall light on after closing the lounge door behind her. This was a bad sign.

Mummy unlatched the front door and opened it. She stared at Lizzie hatefully.

Lizzie stood on the doormat, motionless, her head bowed. Alfie bounded into the hall, lead still attached to his collar, and shook himself, scattering mud all over the parquet flooring. Lizzie dared not look at the mess he was making but instead lifted her eyes to see if Mummy had a drink in her hand and smelled of that funny smell. She didn't.

A gargantuan hand grabbed Lizzie's pigtails and yanked her into the hall. With a forceful slap across the back of her head, she threw Lizzie on to the hard wooden tiles, wrenching her shoes off and pulling at her woollen tights. They wouldn't budge, due to them being sopping wet and sticking to her legs, but Mummy would not give up trying to remove them. Lizzie's skinny legs felt as if they were being pulled out of their sockets as Mummy finally scraped the tights off her. Lizzie was cold, but remained silent.

Lifting her face forcefully, her mummy tugged Lizzie's head back by her pigtails and met her eyes.

"You have been an extremely naughty girl, Elizabeth.

What do naughty girls deserve?"

Lizzie said nothing.

The little brown plastic pegs holding her soaking duffle coat together were torn off one by one.

"You will be cold at school now," Mummy leered at Lizzie. Then, without undoing the back zip, she forced the grey pinafore over Lizzie's head. The zip scratched the back of Lizzie's neck as the dress got stuck. Lizzie didn't flinch. Yanking her polo-neck from her back, Mummy shook it violently. She glared at the child standing in front of her. Lizzie bowed her head, shivering from cold.

"Look at you, trembling like a jelly and whimpering like a pathetic baby," Mummy roared.

Lizzie remained as still as she possibly could in her vest and pants. She was very cold. Alfie, sensibly, stayed hidden, but Lizzie could hear him whimpering. She wanted to hug him, but dare not move.

The shoe hit the back of Lizzie's head. Lizzie jolted with pain and tears welled up in her eyes.

Don't cry, Lizzie, she thought, although she wanted to bawl her eyes out with pain. Mummy seized the other shoe and headed towards Lizzie with it. Pointing at the mud and leaves caked on the sole, she lowered her huge frame towards Lizzie. She scraped the mud from the bottom of the shoe with her hand, rubbed it all over Lizzie's face, slapping her hard first, and then forced the sticky sludge into her hair.

"Open your mouth," she demanded.

Lizzie clenched her teeth as tightly as she could.

"Open your mouth!" her mother bellowed again.

Lizzie hoped that the neighbours could hear and would rescue her soon. She clenched her teeth more tightly than ever.

Mummy became furious. Ramming her fingers between Lizzie's lips, she dug her nails into her gums – once, twice, three times. Lizzie could feel the blood seep through her milk teeth and gasped. She opened her mouth, fighting for breath.

Shoving a clump of mud into Lizzie's mouth, she ordered her to chew at least twenty times, and then swallow. Lizzie gagged at the earthy clumps but had to swallow so she could breathe again. Her mother released Lizzie's nose just in time. She was having an asthma attack. She needed Ventolin.

Lizzie knew that her mummy was furious. She had cursed Lizzie's father numerous times, blaming him for this flaw, and shoved the blue inhaler at Lizzie, almost hitting her in the eye. She yelled obscenities at the child, then fell silent.

Lizzie overheard sobbing coming from the living room. Her mother opened the door. Lizzie saw Andrew standing in his play pen, tears streaming down his face. Her mother lifted him up, wiped the tears from his cheeks and smiled at her baby. She kissed his forehead gently, cuddled him and sat down with him, holding him close to her chest. Rocking him tenderly in her arms, she noticed Lizzie shivering in the hall. Gently placing Andrew back in his play pen, she returned to her daughter.

"Take your medicine *now,* then I'll clean you up," she demanded. Lizzie shuffled into the downstairs cloakroom, closed the door behind her, and sat on the toilet seat, taking deep breaths as she took her inhaler. She could hear her mummy singing a lullaby to Andrew. He cooed back at her. Lizzie relaxed a little and her chest felt a little clearer. She could almost feel her airways opening wider to let the much-needed air into her lungs.

The door flew open. Mummy was back.

She screamed at Lizzie, calling her a filthy monster as she stripped off her remaining clothes. She filled the wash basin with cold water. Caking a hard flannel with the caustic soap she had retrieved from the cleaning bucket, she scrubbed Lizzie brutally, making her skin burn. The soap stung, making Lizzie's eyes stream.

"Cry baby bunting," Mummy sneered, scrubbing her back and bottom with the flannel. Lizzie flinched. It hurt.

Mummy forced the flannel across Lizzie's neck, digging her nails behind her hairline as she did so. "Time to wash out that foul mouth of yours now – open wide."

This time Lizzie obeyed. Her gums were sore, but she welcomed the thought of removing the muddy taste from her mouth. Opening her mouth wide, Mummy foamed up the soap and placed a fistful on Lizzie's tongue. Lizzie's tummy heaved at the disgusting taste and burning sensation. She tried to reach the sink to spit it out. She felt sick. Mummy blocked her path.

"No, Elizabeth," she demanded again. "Swallow."

Lizzie swallowed. It burned her throat and she wanted to cry out in pain. Mummy smiled, enjoying the sight in front of her.

"Now hold your breath, child," she demanded, forcing Lizzie's face towards the sink. Lizzie closed her eyes and tried to control her breathing as her mother turned on the cold tap and ran the freezing water through Lizzie's hair. The mud had solidified into hard clumps and, as the woman scrubbed and pulled, Lizzie wondered whether she would have any hair left afterwards. Then she yanked Lizzie's head up. She got some scissors. Then a comb. Pushing Lizzie against the tiled wall, Mummy laughed. She snarled at her cowering daughter.

"Your choice, Elizabeth," she screamed before studying Lizzie, who was dripping water all over her nicely polished tiles.

Through stifled tears, Lizzie begged for the comb. Dragging it through her sopping locks was agonising. Mummy watched silently, her arms crossed. Lizzie continued to comb through the knots, then stopped. Mummy was giving her *that* look.

The comb remained stuck in Lizzie's tangled hair, but that didn't matter anymore. She edged towards her mummy and took her hand. Her eyes met her mummy's, and a single tear rolled down her cheek.

"I'm sorry, Mummy," Lizzie whispered, releasing her clammy fingers. "I really am."

Mummy sneered.

"And Elizabeth – what do you say now?" she demanded, glaring at the child.

"I'm so sorry," the little girl sobbed. "I promise never to be naughty again. I promise to be Mummy's little angel."

The woman wiped her hand on her cardigan and sniggered. Her cold features gradually warmed at the sense of power she was feeling.

"Good girl," she whispered into Lizzie's ear, pushing her out of the room and into the hallway. "Now, off you go to your room and get your nightie on before Daddy gets home."

Lizzie trudged up the first flight of stairs. She could hear the wind bellowing outside and the torrential rain hitting the windows.

A trickling down her legs distracted her. Horrified, Lizzie sobbed. Huge, salty tears welled in her brown eyes, and rolled down her cheeks into her mouth. She was burning up. Beads of sweat formed on her forehead and on the back of her neck. Lifting her arm, she tried to wipe her brow. A large hand stopped her. Lizzie screamed. She could bear no more. It was too much for her. She could take no more punishment.

"No!" she wailed. "Leave me alone! Please don't hurt me, I'm begging you – please leave me be. I promise to be a good girl, Mummy, I promise."

* * *

Gloria held Lizzie's hand a little longer before wiping her brow again with a damp cloth. Her concerned face filled with emotion as she studied the poor young woman. Lizzie looked so fragile and vulnerable, and terribly sad. Gloria wanted to hold her and make everything better. She wanted to tuck her into bed every night and protect her from the big bad world, but she knew this was impossible.

Lizzie stirred and sat up abruptly, blinking at her surroundings. Unlatching her hand from Lizzie's, Gloria poured her a glass of cold water and placed it on the bedside table, next to the book she had rescued after this afternoon's incident.

"That nightmare again, sweetheart?" Gloria enquired tenderly.

"Yes, that nightmare again," Lizzie replied softly, turning away from Gloria to hide the tears that were streaming down her face.

* * * * *

10. VOICES

2014: Beth

Beth couldn't face the dry cleaners. Before this afternoon's incident, she had planned to pop into a dry cleaner in the Old Town, have a coffee in one of the small cafés she knew, then, if she had the time, take a stroll through the park. But those plans had all been destroyed.

As she secured her seatbelt, her eyes smarted – she must have left some soap in them when she was cleaning up. She dared herself to look in the interior mirror, then dismissed the thought. Beth knew how dreadful she must look, without the reminder of a monstrous reflection in front of her. Mumbling to herself, she reversed the car, drove down the winding ramps and exited the multi-storey car park into the real world once again.

It was raining – nothing too heavy but enough to prompt the automatic windscreen wipers of her Vauxhall into action. They systematically wiped the remnants of water from her screen, almost hypnotising Beth before she reached the junction. Her eyes were now streaming – that darn liquid soap had, no doubt, caused permanent damage to her eyes, judging by how much they were running. Switching on her hazard lights, she stopped her car and looked in the mirror.

Her eyes were, as she had imagined, almost red-raw from the frantic cleaning they had been subjected to. Her long eyelashes had clumped together with the soap remnants, sticking across her swollen eyelids, and her face was puffy. She had also cut her lip, which was swelling up like a balloon. God, she looked a mess. A car tooted its horn and the driver, a young woman, cursed at Beth.

"Stupid cow," she hollered as she passed, shooting a single finger in the air then turning left at the junction Beth was blocking. Beth was too consumed by her reflection to notice the children in the rear of the car laughing at the crazy woman talking to herself.

Beth rummaged through the glove box and retrieved a pair of large sunglasses. She hadn't worn them for years as they were *so* out of fashion, but being large-framed, with jet-black lenses, they were her saviour. After applying a coat of lip gloss, she indicated right and started her journey home.

Her head was thudding. Not one of those niggling headaches she regularly suffered from; this was, she believed, a migraine. Beth could feel the blood pumping through her veins and blood vessels, waiting to burst behind her eyes and temples. She needed a painkiller, and fast.

Fumbling though her handbag, she tried to drive with one hand, and found a packet of pills. Not reading the label, she figured that, whatever they were, they would ease this pain and help her to concentrate. A nagging voice in her head stopped her. *No, Beth, stop! Don't take them, don't.*

Beth listened intently to the warning, tossed the packet onto the passenger seat and opted for a cigarette instead. It helped a little and the migraine slowly subsided.

When she reached home, Beth tried to recall how she had got there. She'd forgotten the route she had taken, the roads she had driven down and felt that, somehow, her brain had been working on autopilot. She turned her engine off, unlatched the seatbelt, and, still with gloved hands, grabbed her handbag. Beth took a deep breath and tried to compose herself for what lay ahead. She had a mountain of work to do. With hindsight, she admitted to herself that going shopping had been a terrible mistake. She knew there would be a price to pay for her stupidity. She looked at herself one last time before she got out of the car. Her hideous face was her penance.

Beth unlocked the front door; she caught sight of the unopened letter. It was still there on the oak cabinet, despite her wishing it had gone. A friend of hers had a vivid imagination and swore blind she could make things disappear if she thought hard enough about it. Beth had tried this morning, but she had failed. She surmised that, as well as being crazy, her so-called friend was a liar too.

"Good riddance to bad rubbish," Beth muttered to herself, removing her boots and leaving them outside on the doormat. Dave could clean them later.

Wandering through the hallway, she opened the door to her immaculate kitchen. It sparkled with cleanliness, the stainless-steel appliances polished and uniformly positioned on the worktop. She desperately needed a cup of coffee but decided against it. The kettle looked so lovely right now and if she accidentally dripped some water on it while filling it up, it would be wrecked. She turned to the fridge, grabbed a carton of orange juice, cleaned the straw with her antibacterial wipes, and sipped it quietly. She felt much better now – until she remembered the bag with the dress.

The horror of the shopping experience threw Beth's mind into chaos. The bag – *that bag* – was still in her car, polluting every single inch of it. *She* had been in the car. Shaking from head to toe and sobbing in desperate panic, she stripped off her clothes and gloves, burst upstairs into the en-suite and ran into the shower.

The hot water eased some of Beth's anxiety almost immediately. Just the thought of the germs had made her feel sick but, once she had applied the shampoo, then conditioner to her hair, she felt much happier knowing that one part of her body had been freed from the bacteria.

Although her face was still terribly sore, Beth gently applied some cleanser. It stung a little but, again, so long as her face was clean, it was well worth a little pain. She cleansed the remainder of her body, and her heart rate returned to normal. She felt able to face the endless chores ahead.

She had to finish the ironing. Although that was essential, it always made the whole house dusty, so she would polish the house first, then vacuum and attempt to cook a meal for Dave. She would then apply her makeup and straighten her hair the way Dave liked it. She wouldn't, however, wear her little black dress. That was being saved for Christmas Day – and needed dry-cleaning anyway.

Beth removed herself very carefully from the shower and trod gently on her favourite bath mat. It was brand new and so fluffy that every time she got out of the shower, her wet feet would be embedded into the thick pile, leaving an indentation. Dave thought it was terribly cute when he compared his size elevens to Beth's threes. She hated that element about her new mat, and tossed it into the wash basket to launder later.

Pulling on her latex gloves, Beth dressed in a simple cream polo-necked jumper and skinny jeans. She towel-dried her hair, brushed it and decided that she would allow it to dry naturally. Beth knew that blow-drying hair could damage it, and avoided it unless absolutely necessary. She would apply her makeup later.

She wandered down the stairs. The telephone rang. Beth hadn't expected any telephone calls, especially today. She hadn't planned this and she had so much work to do. "It could be a bad call," she said to herself, recalling the terrifying thoughts she had experienced earlier with the postman about the police and her kids. Grabbing a wipe, she cleaned the handset and answered.

"Hello."

The line was silent.

Beth's hand began to shudder and her stomach churned with anxiety. Perhaps she was being watched and, rather than follow her in the multi-storey car park and then kill her, they were making sure she was at home.

Her *killer* coughed quietly and spoke very softly to Beth.

"Please excuse me, madam, I have a cold! Mrs Lewis; am I through to the householder – is that Mrs Lewis?"

Beth panicked. They knew her boyfriend's surname now. Her palms were beginning to sweat, and in a trembling voice she answered, "No, she doesn't live here; she's gone."

The caller asked whether the new homeowner would be interested in changing their energy supplier. They could guarantee a financial saving of at least £150 a year if she agreed now. But this offer was only available today and Beth had to make a decision now.

She could feel her heart thumping in terror. It felt as though, any minute now, it would burst through her ribcage. She was petrified and knew that the caller wanted her details so they could cut off her electricity before breaking in and murdering her. Beth's knees gave way and she collapsed onto the floor. The handset fell from her hand.

Beth couldn't recall how long she had been lying on the hard wooden floor when she finally came round. Her headache was back and she dragged her body up, crawling on all fours into the living room. After closing the curtains, she collapsed onto the

44

sofa and closed her eyes. She needed to relax. For once, she agreed that the chores could wait until tomorrow – if she survived, that was.

* * *

Dave had had a seriously tough day at work. Although the chancellor was assuring everybody that Britain was on the road to recovery, he knew differently. His company, a bespoke furniture manufacturer, had suffered its worst financial year since its formation over fifty years ago. His father had founded the business and, shortly after he had retired, Dave had transitioned into the role of managing director. The title meant nothing to him, though – he loved getting involved with the carpentry and always preferred being hands-on than sitting in a stuffy office in front of a computer. Today had been an office day, and Dave's computer had thrown out some frightening statistics. If he didn't win some new business within the next few weeks, he would have to make the two of his carpenters redundant or Regency Furniture would become history.

He grabbed his coat, set the security alarm and headed for his car. A loud and very familiar voice welcomed him.

"Dave, over here! We're off for a pint – you coming?"

The soon to be redundant workers beckoned Dave from their van, but he very politely declined.

"Work to do at home, lads," he replied. "Next time, maybe."

Closing the doors of the van, the workers laughed. One of them placed his thumb on his head.

"That woman indoors ain't 'alf got ya by the short and curlies!" he jested, beeping the horn and waving as he headed towards the White Horse for a well-earned pint of beer and packet of peanuts.

Dave managed a smile. They were smashing chaps, both of them. The elder of the two, Mike, had worked for his company for forty years. He was one of the first apprentices his dad had taken on and, edging towards retirement with very little in his pension fund, he always volunteered for every minute of overtime he could get. Charlie was in his mid-thirties, had a stay-at-home partner, like Dave, and ten-year-old twins. He too was struggling for money; having kids and running a home was very expensive. Dave certainly knew that.

The drive home seemed to take an age. Traffic was solid. It was raining heavily. The constant braking and stop-starting ground on Dave's nerves. He just wanted to go home, see his girlfriend, eat his meal and put his feet up while watching TV. He might even treat himself to a glass of the Côtes du Rhône he had been saving.

When he approached the cul-de-sac leading to his home, Dave swore as he remembered he had cancelled his credit card only the day before. Beth had gone shopping today and he had forgotten to tell her. He desperately hoped she hadn't tried to use it, but feared the worst.

He neared his house; Dave slowed down nervously. His earlier excitement about spending a relaxing evening had diminished into a feeling of concern. He knew that if Beth had tried to use the cancelled card, she would be in a terrible state now. Her OCD would be awful, along with the paranoia she often suffered from. When she was stressed, the two got so much worse and Dave sometimes found it so hard to deal with.

He remembered the good days they had shared, however, and smiled. His blue eyes sparkled and he recalled happier times, when Beth was well. During the healthy days, as he called them, his relationship was, in his opinion, perfect. The house, although clean, wasn't sterile. Beth would be more casual about her appearance, and she would start baking again. When she could concentrate fully, Beth was an amazing cook. Nothing fazed her and her skills in the kitchen were simply breath-taking. Dave figured that this was something to do with her creative flair. She was also an incredible artist.

Sadly, over the past month or so, Beth's mental wellbeing had been declining again. She appeared to have submerged into what Dave imagined to be a dark shadow of her healthy self and, as well as becoming obsessive, she had stopped eating regular meals, just picking at snacks and pushing her dinner away. Any form of affection was also banned. If he so much as tried to touch her, Beth would tense up and back away from him.

She was, he feared, very poorly again, despite the medication, but, as always, he would support and protect Beth. Somebody had to.

The hallway was in darkness. He wiped his shoes on the mat, and edged towards the kitchen light. The room was empty and pitch black. There was no sign of cooking. He felt the kettle; it was cold.

He wandered towards the dark living room and opened the door. The TV that he had yearned for on his way home was on standby and the curtains had been drawn, along with the blind – which, under most circumstances was purely for decoration. His eyes caught a silhouette against the back wall, behind the sofa.

Dave knew the routine well.

Tiptoeing towards the image on the wall, he whispered softly towards the shadow.

"Beth, it's me, Dave, your boyfriend."

He paused. There was no reaction.

"I work for Regency Furniture and we have two children, remember. Kirsty is in Paris and Robert's in Birmingham. They're coming here soon to see their mum – you. Please don't be frightened, Beth. Nobody is going to hurt you. I'm here to protect you. Just come out from where you're hiding and it will all be okay.

Dave remained motionless, waiting for a sign.

The shadow moved. The room was filled with a tense silence. Dave edged backwards towards the light switch. He didn't want to startle Beth, so slowly turned the switch so that the lighting would be soft and wouldn't glare into her eyes, which she hated. The shadow shifted again. A large object appeared to be protruding from the arm of the silhouette. It was shaking.

Dave tried to stay calm. He was feeling nervous too, and his muscles were tense with stress. His throat felt dry. His vocal cords tightened and, as he tried to speak, his voice faltered. *Damn, I have to keep my voice sounding like mine! Beth will go mad otherwise.* He softened his voice to a whisper. He was exhausted, and just wanted to put his feet up and relax, but the next few minutes were critical. He must not frighten Beth. Although he couldn't show it, Dave was also becoming impatient. He just wanted this episode over.

Beth was hiding from her *killer* and was doing a good job of it. She knew that he would try to pretend to be Dave – he was clever, granted, but to Beth it was absolutely obvious. His wobbling voice, just a moment ago, was the big giveaway – the evidence she had needed.

The *killer* had probably followed Dave too and learned his mannerisms in an attempt to trick her. But Beth had worked everything out. She was very proud of herself and her friends would be too.

You want to kill me, huh? Like hell, she thought, crawling towards the edge of the sofa. Beth suddenly felt extremely powerful and strong. She convinced herself that she could overpower this monster and that, with careful tactics, just as he thought he was safe, she could get him. She shimmied quietly again and crouched just low enough to peek over the top of the sofa. She saw the *killer's* silhouette. He was looking at his mobile phone and was probably texting his accomplice, who would pick him up after the murder. She had to make her move now, or it would be too late. She silently stood and ran towards the *killer*, aiming a hockey stick at his neck. Dave instinctively sensed the rapid movement and raised his arm, just in time, to obstruct Beth's weapon. He firmly held her other hand as she kicked him in the testicles time and time again.

"You pathetic bastard!" she screamed hysterically, spitting in Dave's face. "My friends told me all about you. They warned me about you! Go on, then, kill me if it will make you happy!"

Beth's face looked alien to Dave. Her normally soft brown eyes appeared black, and her features were contorted. Still firmly holding her, he tossed the hockey stick into the hall, loosened his grip on her wrist and looked her in the eyes. She bowed her head, mumbling nonsensical words to herself. Dave felt relieved that the worst was over. In a few minutes, peace would be restored.

"Beth, it *is* me," he whispered gently to the trembling woman in front of him. "I'm Dave, and I can prove it. Do I have a scar?"

Beth angled her head and moved her eyes towards her *killer*. Boy, he was good.

Staring coldly at the *murderer*, Beth smirked.

"Scar? Nah, no scar," she responded angrily, knowing that Dave had a huge scar across his lower tummy. She had accidentally caught him with a knife once, but there was no way she would let on about that.

Dave had expected this reaction and secured Beth's wrists with one strong hand. He then lifted up his shirt. A seven-inch-long deep purple scar jumped out at her. Beth's eyes focused on the healing wound and gradually her head cleared. She studied the purple scar and counted how many stitches Dave had. She counted thirty-five small indentations on his skin.

"Thirty-five stitches," Dave said lowering his shirt and gently restraining Beth.

Although still disorientated, Beth wished she could remember more about the scar, but it was impossible to access all the information she needed. Her head felt foggy and was starting to thud again. She was thirsty too. But one thing was for sure, though – she wished that she hadn't hurt *her* Dave. He hadn't deserved *that*.

Her Dave.

It *was* him!

Beth immediately felt a huge weight lift off her shoulders when she realised that the *killer* had gone and Dave had, once again, rescued her. Her muscles relaxed and, with that, so did Dave. Moving his arms around her waist, he embraced Beth and kissed her tenderly on the forehead. It was almost over now.

Beth's eyes welled up with emotion; her *protector* held her close to him. She inhaled his familiar smell deep into her lungs. Her breathing synchronised with his and she closed her eyes, feeling peaceful. Opening her eyes to meet Dave's, she froze.

From the corner of her eye, she noticed the hockey stick that she must have retrieved from Robert's wardrobe. She'd kept it out of sentiment and could never find the courage to throw it away, although, quite frankly, Robert didn't care. His hockey days were long over.

Beth tried to recollect how the stick had got into the hall, but it was beyond her muddled mind. Her scared eyes met Dave's. He cuddled Beth and looked at her reassuringly, although he feared her response to his question.

"They're back again, Beth, aren't they?" Dave whispered while holding Beth closely to him. Beth didn't reply. She pulled her body away and sat on the floor, looking defiantly at him, her legs curled beneath her. She was hiding something; Dave knew that look well.

The penny dropped and Dave's stomach heaved with the thought of it. *Her pills. Where the hell were they?*

Dave recalled the last time he had witnessed Beth taking her medication. Every morning, before making her cup of tea, he'd leave a glass of water on the bedroom cabinet with the tablet and watch her drink the water. Beth would often pretend to swallow the pill, but he had worked that one out years ago. And so, he would check her tongue and inside her mouth to ensure that she had swallowed the medication. But, over the past few weeks, he had let the routine slip. The financial pressures of work and home had taken their toll on him and he had overlooked this one simple, but essential, duty.

"Your tablets, Beth – where are your pills?"

Beth crumpled into a ball and started to rock backwards and forwards. This motion relaxed her in times of great pressure, and she needed to switch off from this ghastly situation. She believed that secretly Dave was probably trying to kill her with the poison in the medication. She also knew that, sometimes, the drugs made her feel better – just like the shopping trips.

Beth jolted suddenly. Her body stiffened and her muscles twitched. Running desperately into Dave's arms, she screamed hysterically, pointing towards the front door.

"The bag, the shopping bag, Dave – it's in my car. It has to be destroyed or it could harm us all!"

She was shaking and wanted to throw up. Pulling at Dave's shirt, Beth continued to point towards the front door.

"The car, Dave – take it away, take it away."

Dave ran through the hallway, grabbed the car keys from a kitchen cupboard and opened the passenger door.

The pack of clozapine almost jumped out as Dave scrabbled across the floor of the car, searching for the carrier bag. He lifted the packet and studied it closely. The seal had not been broken. Beth, as he had feared, had not been taking her medicine.

Placing the packet in his pocket, he opened the boot and retrieved the bag from Serendipity. Locking the car, he entered the hall almost boiling with fury. He must calm down before speaking to Beth. He headed for the drinks cabinet in the dining room and poured himself a neat whisky. Slugging back a large mouthful, Dave plodded to the living room, switched on the TV and relished the warmth the alcohol was creating, and the numbness. His mind, for a moment, felt rested.

Beth was in her bedroom. She attached the letter she had received this morning to some tweezers and gripped them firmly with her right hand. Her hand shook as she read the address on the left-hand corner. It was in red print, which she hated. She despised the sending address even more. She held her breath and found the courage to open the letter. Beads of sweat were forming on her forehead. She wiped them away with her left hand and held her breath as she pulled out the letter. It was dated 20th November. A Friday.

Her next appointment with Jonathan Davies, consultant psychiatrist, was typed in a clear font. It was scheduled for 10 a.m. at the usual place on 6th December – another Friday. The letter also mentioned that if she failed to attend this appointment, she would be charged. Beth placed the neatly folded letter back in the envelope.

Opening the bottom drawer, she pulled it off its runners. Gently positioning it on the cream bedroom carpet, she was relieved to see a tatty rectangular brown box. It had a painting on the front, with lots of love hearts and kisses. Beth's eyes lit up as she recollected painting the image. She then shot back to reality.

Using her tweezers, she opened the box and removed a fine sheet of pink tissue paper. She positioned the envelope so that it would fall precisely on the neatly stacked pile of other correspondence she had received. Beth replaced the tissue paper and closed the box. Returning the drawer to its original position, she checked her reflection in the mirror, beamed at herself and headed for the landing stairs, speaking softly.

"Like the others, this letter can wait."

Her friends were a few steps in front of her and turned around to wave at Beth. They agreed with her very wise decision and watched cheerfully as she happily slipped down the stairs towards her beloved Dave.

Holding hands and skipping off into the distance, the girls nodded their heads in agreement. They would deal with Dr Jonathan Davies soon. But first, they had to remove the true enemy.

Dave.

Beth's killer simply had to die before she did.

"Third time lucky, girls," they giggled to each other.

Third time lucky, Beth thought as she passed the brown carrier bag, entered the living room and spotted Dave sleeping, and a spilled bottle of whisky on her lovely cream carpet.

* * * * *

11. OVERDOSE

1994: Elise

The small living room of Flat 117a was full of an eerie silence. Elise remained deadly still, slumped on the floor. The rush from her fix had worn off long ago, and, despite still feeling numb, she knew that she and Leroy were in deep trouble. She forced her stiff limbs together, stretched her spine, and headed towards the crumpled mess lying on the floor.

The cut on Leroy's neck had stopped bleeding, thank heavens, but Elise could see he was in agony. He was groaning and curled up, clutching his chest. Beads of sweat had formed on his forehead and were trickling into his half-open mouth. Elise bent down and stroked his hand. Her concerned eyes met his.

Leroy's heavy eyes tried to focus on the woman approaching him. He vaguely recollected the events of a few hours before: Craig, Duke and the money. *Christ, the money.* He only had a few hours before he had to pay up.

He closed his eyes in an attempt to dismiss the memories but the excruciating throbbing within his chest prevented this. With each breath he took, a searing pain shot through his ribcage. It felt, Leroy imagined, like a hot poker piercing his lungs with every breath he took. But he would be okay. Leroy always survived.

Elise headed for the telephone. She knew that he needed help. She pressed the number nine. As she pushed the button again, a firm hand stopped her.

"No, Lise, I'll be fine. No ambulance, no police – we'll sort this out ourselves." She heard the anxiety in Leroy's voice and cut off the telephone call.

Leroy struggled, but somehow managed to unfold his crippled body and stand up. He shuffled over to the kitchenette at the far end of the living room, grabbed a chipped mug and poured himself a glass of water. Jesus, he needed some painkillers, and urgently. Opening the tatty brown cabinet, he snatched a packet of paracetamol, removed four, and gulped them down. Elise watched, slumped on the sofa. She was still dazed by the earlier events. She was also thirsty.

Joining Leroy in the kitchen, Elise filled the old mug and downed the fresh, cold water within a few seconds. Leroy held Lise's hands, recollecting how she had saved him from a possible horrific death. Pecking her gently on the cheek, he limped towards the comfortable sofa and tentatively sat down, placing the throw behind his back for support. He flinched with pain but tried to hide it.

Elise wasn't stupid. She recognised the fact that Leroy was suffering – she had been in similar situations on endless occasions. Her worried eyes focused on the telephone once again, and then met his. He shuffled closer to her on the sofa.

"Lise, I don't need an ambulance," he stuttered, still smarting from the soreness in his chest. He hoped that the paracetamol would soon kick in – if it didn't, he sure as hell would need some help. He closed his eyes and breathed slowly. *How the hell am I going to get out of this mess?*

The stark realisation of the danger he was in played through Leroy's mind as the painkillers started to absorb into his bloodstream. He recollected Lise, her little pink bag and *that* watch, and knew that she had saved his life. He also knew that Lise had been penniless – almost destitute, which is why she sold her body. None of it made any sense to him.

Elise curled up on the sofa, resting her head very gently on Leroy's legs. She smiled at him warmly while he stroked her forehead.

"Lise, I need to thank you," Leroy whispered. "You saved my life, I sure as hell know that, and I owe you big time. Lise, the watch; the watch you gave to Craig – where the hell did you get it?" He couldn't help it, but the tone of his voice was questioning. Elise felt this was more of an accusation. Lifting her head away from Leroy, she edged away from him and shifted towards the other end of the sofa.

She recalled her precious gift, one of her most treasured possessions, and fought back the tears as she faced Leroy. "I can't say," she responded, bowing her head and curling her feet beneath her. Elise thought about the beautiful watch, which was now in the possession of a thug and probably being traded in a dodgy deal. It had broken her heart giving it up, and the thought of it being in somebody else's possession almost destroyed her.

She remembered every part of the watch and how it had felt on her wrist. She had been told to never forget about the precious diamonds. There were thirteen of them. *One for each year you've been on planet Earth*, Nan had said, struggling for breath but still managing to laugh as she said it.

Elise recollected the pride she had felt when her nan had given her the watch. She also remembered leaving the stark hospital ward crying her eyes out and running home afterwards. It was one of the happiest, yet saddest, days of her life. A weird contrast, Elise thought, as she tried to fathom how to explain the story to her friend.

Elise had told Leroy nothing important about her life. All he knew was that she was a hooker and a druggie. He had met her on the streets a few months ago and had taken pity on the sopping wet, scantily dressed girl with an old carrier bag in her hand and just a few pence in her plastic purse. After some persuasion, he had bought her a coffee in a nearby McDonald's and they had been 'sort of' friends ever since. But she had never felt any desire to tell him much about her former life. It hadn't seemed important. Not until now.

Elise only once, had confided to Leroy when she was as high as a kite and her inhibitions were down. He'd enquired how she'd ended up on the streets, although his motives at that point had been far from honourable. Somehow, though, despite the spaced woman giggling in front of him, he had done the decent thing and let her answer his question before covering her up in one of his large sweatshirts. The condoms sitting in his back pocket remained unused.

Elise remembered the moment she had told Leroy that she was an orphan. She had fabricated a story about how her parents had died (they had been involved in a horrific car crash and were killed on impact). She had no other family and was moved to a children's home, which, as soon as she was sixteen, she ran away from. That's how she had ended up on the streets. Leroy had believed her and had never felt the need to question her further.

Somehow, she had to find the courage to explain how she had got the watch. She respected Leroy and she owed him the truth. But sometimes the truth hurt. She suddenly felt freezing cold. The fan heaters had packed up months ago and, despite them not chucking out much heat, they had at least taken the chill off the room. Elise yearned for some warmth. She shivered and Leroy tucked her under the throw. He winced with pain as he moved, but knew that she was suffering more at the moment than he was.

Elise smiled tenderly at her friend as she warmed up. She bowed her head and tried to find the courage to explain how she had got the watch. Leroy deserved an honest explanation after the kindness he had extended to her over the past few months.

Despite his obvious flaws, Elise respected Leroy. He was, she knew, deep down, a good man with a very kind heart. Brought up by a caring and spiritual family, he'd been taught never to steal. He had never lied, and he sometimes accompanied his sister and nieces to church. On one occasion, much against her wishes, he'd dragged Elise there with him. Despite her protests, she'd actually enjoyed the singing and closeness of the church. *One big family, united together,* she recalled the minister stating as a prelude to a prayer. She had liked being part of a family, even if it belonged to God.

Shuffling closer towards Leroy, Elise stuttered as she started to speak. "The truth is, I didn't steal that watch, Leroy, I promise you. It was a gift to me – a gift from my nan just before she died."

Leroy listened intently to Lise's story. He thought that she had no family, and squinted as Elise continued her tale.

"I lied to you about having no family. I did have some; I just chose to block them out of my mind, if that makes sense to you. Sometimes, when memories are painful, if you think hard enough, they can go away; mine were painful, Leroy – dreadfully painful."

Leroy's warm eyes met Elise's as she softly spoke to him. She was very emotional while she explained the problems she had encountered at home and the hell she had given her parents.

"I was rebellious from the moment I came into the world – or at least that's what my mum would tell me. We always clashed; we seemed to wind each other up all the time and, well, one thing would lead to another and we'd end up scrapping." Elise struggled to continue. Her eyes flicked across the living room, looking for an easy way to explain everything. Other than the ticking of an old wooden mantle clock and the kitchen tap dripping, the room was eerily silent. Leroy's breathing had eased into a steady rhythm and the pain in his chest was gradually subsiding. Elise gazed at the window, stood up and covered Leroy with the throw. Edging towards the TV, she opened a drawer and removed a small packet of pot and some papers. Leroy watched as Lise precisely positioned the weed along the middle of the paper, licked the edge and rolled it into a perfect joint. Taking a deep breath after lighting it, she finally relaxed a little. Leroy couldn't resist smiling at his little friend as a familiar, daft grin spread across her face. Elise walked towards Leroy, offering him a drag before taking back the joint and continuing her story.

"My dad was weak." She remembered endless occasions on which she and her mother had ended up with fistfuls of each other's hair in their hands after a brawl. She studied her wrist, which had a permanent reminder of their fights, and covered her eyes in an attempt to eliminate the memories. Elise thought back to her father and how, whenever she heard his car, she would initially feel relief, then always extreme disappointment. She told Leroy about all the times he had arrived home from a work trip, only to be welcomed by her mother, who lied about how Elise had been naughty. Her father had never asked Elise for her version of the story. Not once.

"In fact, he was terrified of my mum and I remember her slapping him across the face whenever he intervened to stop one of our arguments. I knew, deep down, he wanted to help me – but, well, he was never strong enough to confront her and, more importantly, protect me."

Elise continued, becoming more confident as she explained her life before prostitution. The joint was doing a good job. "I was hard work, Leroy, and I mean hard *bloody* work. Everything my mum asked me to do, I defied, or at least I tried to. She enrolled me into a ballet school once, and instead of going there, I played with my best friend, got filthy and wrecked my leotard. Another time, I got chucked out of the private school my mother had sent me to, for being defiant and rebellious; my behaviour, the head mistress had said, was disruptive to the other students. I then had to go to a state school, which wasn't much better."

Elise felt that an enormous weight was being lifted off her shoulders as she told her life history to the sleepy guy on the end of the sofa. The painkillers were, at last, working. Even though his eyes were closed, Leroy was listening intently. "Carry on," he whispered, moving closer to Lise.

Elise stubbed out the remainder of her joint, inhaled deeply and sat down on the carpet close to Leroy. She curled her body into a ball and held her head in her hands, replaying the events of her nan's death, the watch, and running home from hospital, desperately fighting back tears.

Elise had hidden the watch in a little pink bag which she had been given at a wedding. It had contained sugar-coated almonds which she had loathed, as they reminded her of perfume, but the bag was so pretty she had kept it. The pink bag was hidden in a secret box that she placed underneath her mattress. As her mother rarely entered the room, Elise knew that her gift would never be discovered and that this, along with some other secret possessions, would always be safe there.

Memories of later events flooded Elise's mind. She continued her story with precise detail. Her mind swam. She recollected each moment as though it was happening to her all over again. It felt so real – and right now, it was real once again....

The discomfort in her tummy was getting worse. Elise had felt a dull ache all day, but now the pain was radiating across her back, as well as her stomach. She attributed this to hunger and possibly grief at losing her nan but, somehow, this ache was different to the hunger pains she had encountered before. Elise's heart also felt empty, but she fought back the tears. The stabbing pains in her abdomen dug deeper and deeper.

Clutching her tummy, she went up the long flight of stairs to the bathroom. When she pulled down her pants. Elise was horrified. She was bleeding heavily and her underwear was covered in blood, which was running down her legs and bottom. She was dying for sure. This was her penance for hiding her nan's watch.

Elise filled the bathroom sink with warm water, smothered the flannel with soap and scrubbed herself clean. Hiding her soiled knickers in her hand, she ran upstairs to her room, only to find her mother standing on the landing. She grabbed Elise's blood-covered hands and stared coldly at her daughter's terrified face. Snatching the underwear, she walked into the bathroom and threw a pack of sanitary towels at her daughter.

"You'll need these," she yelled, descending the stairs and heading for her own bedroom. Tutting loudly, she slammed the door shut, leaving her confused daughter shaking helplessly on the landing floor. Elise soon discovered that she wouldn't die. Not this time, anyway.

The ticking of the clock bought her back to reality. Leroy was dozing, but stirred. Elise uncurled her body and slumped next to him on the sofa. She continued quietly to stare into space, her voice close to a whisper.

"It was puberty that was the toughest. Blame it on the hormones or the fact that I was a little cow, I don't know, but my moods became horrendous and I spent most of my life shut away in my room. I never spoke to them or ate with them. I started to nick my mum's booze, smoke weed and sleep around. I did everything I could to hide the pain I was in – and it worked... sometimes."

Bowing her head in shame, Elise then thought of her nan, who was so very different to her mother. She had a tiny frame and dazzling grey eyes, and she always spoke softly to her granddaughter, and often held her hand or hugged her. Elise had loved the scent her nan had used; it was a delicate aroma of lavender and roses, which always seemed to fill the house – except when Nan was baking, which was one of her favourite pastimes. Elise had loved helping Nan, licking the sweet mixture from the mixing bowl and the spatula covered in butter cream.

She warmly described her to Leroy: she baked Elise fairy cakes and taught her to paint. When she was very little, she had also been allowed to sleep at her nan's, but that soon came to an abrupt end. Those happy days, along with so much else, had been forbidden.

Despite pleading desperately with her daughter, Elise's nan wasn't allowed to see her granddaughter any more. But, as usual, Elise had rebelled, playing hooky from school and sneaking to the safe confines of her nan's house for the day. Her nan had never let on. It had been their little secret.

Elise's mind clouded over as she remembered the day she ran away from home. "My mother was drunk and was, as always, causing aggro. I was going to a party and had spent frigging hours getting ready; you know what it's like with girls," she laughed, winking at Leroy as she recalled flicking through a fashion magazine, studying the latest supermodels and hoping to look like Cindy Crawford once she had finished. Her tight leggings, thick makeup and highlighted hair hadn't exactly replicated the supermodel look of the nineties, but she remembered how pleased she had been with the end result. "Well, I'd finished doing my hair and makeup when the bitch heard me walking down the stairs. I blame the bloody stiletto heels on my shoes but, hey ho, shit happens! The cow stopped me in my tracks; I'd nicked a bottle of her booze and I reckon that's what set her off."

Elise hesitated before she continued her story. "She hurt me that time, Leroy; not just a slap, but she *really* hurt me. I remember using makeup to hide the bruises. But, the worst thing was..."

Elise couldn't continue. The pain was etched across her face. She recollected her mother dragging her into the kitchen by her long hair, and immediately switched off – those memories were far too painful to explain.

Leroy was still listening. He snuggled closely to Elise, although his ribs were still frigging killing him. "Carry on, Lise," he whispered reassuringly. Elise's heart felt as though it was in her mouth as the horrendous memories replayed though her mind. Cowering like a child, she snuggled up to Leroy, her eyes welling up with tears.

"I can't, Leroy," she sobbed, shutting down her memories in an instant. Elise rolled another joint, sharing it with Leroy, who needed to chill as much as she did. Taking a deep breath, she tried to continue. It was impossible – Leroy would never understand.

They were starving. Elise's tummy rumbled with hunger and Leroy, hearing the noise, struggled out of his warm cocoon and headed for the kitchen. Elise watched him as he attempted to cook. After almost cremating a pack of bacon and eating the pile of sandwiches, he switched on the TV. Leroy asked Elise the question one more time.

"So – the watch, Lise. Did you really tell me the truth?"

Elise felt hurt but could understand Leroy's reasons for questioning her. She had lied to him before but, this time, her story was for real.

"It *was* my nan's, Leroy. She gave me the watch just before she died and I promised her that, first, I would never, ever let my mum find out and, second, I would treasure it for ever. I broke that promise tonight."

Elise lowered her head. Her eyes welled up yet again. The pain she felt inside was too much. She couldn't talk any more. She was also tired but she had to work. She turned towards Leroy as he finished the sandwiches. He was a terrible colour and although Elise wanted to say that he looked as white as a sheet, she didn't think he'd see the funny side. She was also aware that Craig would be back in the morning demanding his money. She would have to work trebly hard to get that type of cash. It would be a 'no limits' night if she was to raise the money she needed. She shuddered at the thought of what was to come, and yawned with exhaustion.

Leroy mirrored Elise and beckoned for her to join him on the bed for a cuddle. She had been so brave sharing all that shit with him and, hell, to sacrifice her one and only possession just to save his skin was something else. Man, she was one hell of a woman. Leroy collapsed on the bed and Elise joined him soon after, snuggling up close to him and resting her eyes.

Elise couldn't sleep. The rekindled emotions of their earlier conversation churned around in her mind, preventing her from switching off. The memories of her parents, her nan, the party, the boyfriends and the fights with her mother went round in her mind like a roundabout at a funfair. Her whole life had been like a rollercoaster ride. Elise hoped that somehow, maybe soon, the ride would stop and she would be able to jump off and make something of her life.

In the distance, she could hear the whirring of helicopter blades. The noise increased as the machine hovered over the nearby streets, and police sirens blared in unison as they weaved their way through the estate below. Despite being so high up, reflections of the blue flashing lights filtered through the window in the bedroom, flicking across the walls and hitting the Bob Marley poster that took pride of place over the bedstead.

Elise undressed then tucked herself under the duvet, trying not to disturb Leroy, who at last was sleeping. She studied his face and ran her finger down his scar, kissing it gently afterwards. His features were relaxed and he looked so peaceful. He had a big day tomorrow after settling his debt with Craig. Quitting drugs would be as tough as facing that thug, and Elise admired him so much for trying to turn his life around.

She plumped up her pillows and considered her future. If Leroy could beat his addiction, she could too. She needed to face reality, fight her own demons and make a new life for herself. Perhaps, after tonight's shift, she would join Leroy at the clinic and try to quit heroin too. Then, like normal girls of her age, she could get a regular job with regular hours and lead a regular life – as she had not so long ago.

Making a pledge to give up the drugs very soon, she crept into the living room for a shot of heroin, then collapsed into a deep sleep next to her friend.

* * *

The pain in Leroy's ribs had returned with a vengeance. Despite taking a concoction of painkillers while Elise slept, along with a couple of spliffs, the seething agony in his chest was becoming more intense with every breath he took. Struggling out of his bed, Leroy fell on all fours and rolled on the bedroom carpet in agony. He needed some relief desperately, and he needed it fast. He struggled to his feet and staggered to the chest of drawers in his front room. He had enough heroin. He knew that he was planning to quit tomorrow, but at this moment his thoughts were focused on eradicating the agony within his chest. He retrieved the small packet of powder, poured it onto a teaspoon, flicked the lighter and filled the syringe. Frantically pumping the vein on his left arm, he inserted the needle and took a deep breath.

"One last time, Leroy," he muttered. "One last shot."

Elise awoke at the shrill of sirens seventeen floors below Leroy's flat. The police, thanks to the gangs, were regulars in this area, and, thinking about the police helicopter in the night, she figured that some small-time criminals had entered into rival territory, scrapped and – hopefully – been arrested. Perhaps one of them had her watch.

Opening her eyes, she turned to the empty half of the bed. The indentation in the mattress reminded Elise of her own bed when she was a child. The springs on Leroy's were broken too.

Elise got up, plodded into the front room – and then froze. Leroy was slumped on the floor, eyes wide open, and appeared to be foaming at the mouth. The stench of vomit stopped Elise in her tracks before she composed herself and ran towards him. Throwing herself onto the carpet, Elise checked his airway; he didn't appear to be breathing. She tried to remember the first aid course she had learned at Brownies, and applied pressure to his chest with her hands. She pumped with all the strength she could muster then placed her mouth over Leroy's, struggling not to retch at the stench, but managing somehow.

"Come on, Leroy, wake up," she screamed, pumping his chest and forcing her own air into his lungs. He did not respond.

The ambulance only took a few minutes to arrive. After ascending the endless flights of stairs, two out-of-breath paramedics hammered at the door then burst into the living room. Elise led them to Leroy, lying motionless on the floor. They'd seen this type of situation numerous times, but each time, it was distressing.

The female paramedic checked for a heartbeat; there was none. As her colleague started CPR, the female calmly asked Elise what he had taken. "Heroin, I think, along with other stuff," Elise replied, her eyes as wide as saucers as she watched their attempts to resuscitate him. The paramedic forced some liquid into Leroy's nostrils. It had no effect.

The scene in front of her reminded Elise of the movie *Pulp Fiction*, when they gave the overdosed girl a shot of something into her heart. But this wasn't a movie, this was for real, and the whole situation was much scarier than some far-fetched film.

To Elise, it felt as though time was standing still. After a while, the paramedics abandoned their attempts at resuscitation. Leroy appeared to have died of an overdose, although his chest injuries could also have been a contributory factor. An autopsy would, no doubt, reveal the cause of death but, for now, they could do no more. Collecting their equipment and facing Elise, the female paramedic looked at her sympathetically, then at her watch.

"Time of death?" she asked her colleague.

"15.25," he responded, watching as his friend as she documented everything including the date: 24th October 1994.

The room was filled with darkness. The alien voices echoed through the walls, bounced from the window and slammed through her heart like an arrow. Their words were nonsensical, sluggish and deep, like a record playing at half its normal speed. Their actions were in slow motion as they lifted Elise's arms away from Leroy – *'the body'*, they had called him.

Leroy was just sleeping, and would wake up when he felt better. The dark man in the bodysuit shouldn't be moving Leroy like that, because he had a sore chest. He really should know better.

The woman in the bodysuit shouldn't be using her radio – it might disturb him. He needed his sleep. Tomorrow was his big day. The day he was going to quit drugs. The bodysuits just didn't seem to understand.

The TV was still on, which could really distress Leroy. He hated this cartoon.

"Turn the TV off. Leroy doesn't like cartoons. Do it *now* – do you hear? Do it now – please."

The bodysuits didn't seem to hear her. The distorted images continued to bound across the television screen. They appeared to jump out and mock Elise, darting behind the furniture and clambering across the ceiling.

The lady in the suit put down her radio. More people in bodysuits came into the room, running around and interfering with everything. Elise couldn't understand what all the fuss was about. Her mind clouded with the cacophony of sound, and her stomach heaved at the smell in the room. She tried to focus on the cartoon characters that were hiding in every corner of the flat, laughing at her. The bodysuits were chasing her – trying to kill her, no doubt.

Then, nothing.

Darkness enveloped her.

Black clouds shrouded the depths of her mind.

Everything went silent.

Then black.

* * * * *

12. CONSEQUENCES

2004: Lizzie

The stony silence in Lizzie's room was broken by the clattering of cups and spoons on the refreshment trolley. Gloria gathered the crockery and poured Lizzie a cup of tea, making sure that it was strong and sweet.

She stirred the tea methodically, staring out of the window at the world outside. The rain had, at last stopped and the wind had dropped, but none of this had any relevance to the dilemma she faced right now in this stark, impersonal room with the desperate young woman sobbing silently.

It would have been so simple to walk away from this situation. Gloria had a good enough excuse; she needed to complete her rounds within the next hour. But observing Lizzie relive her nightmare again and again distracted Gloria from resuming her normal duties, and she edged towards the bed and stroked her hair very gently.

"Let's clean you up, young lady, after you've had a nice cup of tea."

The tears had finally subsided and Lizzie wiped her face on the sleeve of her nightdress in the hope that the evidence of her nightmare would disappear. She closed her eyes as she felt Gloria's soft touch, and wished that she could run away from this place and find somebody just like Gloria to look after her. She needed a little tenderness from time to time, but the harsh reality was that there was no fairy-tale ending to her story. This little angel had nowhere left to run.

As Gloria started to remove the bed linen, Lizzie turned to face her. Her nightdress was sopping, and she felt cold and uncomfortable, but Gloria just smiled kindly and continued to strip the bed. Lizzie lifted her nightdress so as not to soak the chair and sipped her tea. Her mind had cleared a little and she felt more like her old self.

Angry.

For as long as she could remember, she had combated her feelings by getting angry. As a child, she had realised that crying was not the answer. Her mother had continually reminded her that 'cry babies' were not welcome in her home. And so Lizzie had learned to cope in a different way, away from an audience – away from everybody – in the depths of her own mind. Every time she swore in her head, she felt a little better. It was a coping mechanism that she had maintained for years, and it worked. Most of the time.

Lizzie placed the empty cup on the trolley and Gloria finished making her bed with fresh linen. She placed the soiled bedding in a large plastic bag, and smiled at her, suggesting that she clean herself up then join the rest of the residents in the communal lounge. Gloria entered the bathroom and started to run a bath for her. She fished in her pocket and retrieved a small bottle of bubble bath, pouring it under the warm tap, and beckoned for Lizzie to strip off and clean up. Closing the door behind her, she resumed her afternoon duties.

The aroma of the bubble bath filled the room with the scent of flowers. Once the foam had reached the centre of the bathtub, Lizzie turned off the taps and slipped off her nightdress. Standing at the edge of the bath, she whisked the water around with her hand and stood motionless in front of the water. She had not had a bath for at least ten years, and the terror of drowning enveloped her body, causing her to shudder from head to toe. Taking a deep breath, she lifted one leg and placed it in the warm water. It felt soothing against her skin. Closing her eyes, Lizzie found the courage to place her other leg in the bath and sit down carefully. Her heart was racing and she checked the door to ensure it was still closed. She listened intently for any sign of an intruder although she knew that nobody would be able to enter her room. The coast was clear and for now, she was safe.

She immersed her aching body in the warmth. She could feel the tension from her aching muscles and the anger inside her head dissipate. Her body relaxed and, with it, her mind. Lizzie shut her eyes again and tried to remember the last time she had felt like this. It had been a long time since she had felt comfortable with her own body, and it felt nice. The medication they had given her earlier today must have worn off, but something deep inside her had changed. She felt positive and secure, knowing that she had a friend in Gloria and she trusted her; something that Lizzie had not been able to do for many years.

She set herself a personal goal as she foamed the soap on the sponge and cleaned herself. She had to eliminate the nightmares from her mind, along with the hatred and anger that consumed her. She would, from now on, combat her emotional issues, attend regular therapy sessions with that nice Dr Davies, and recover. She would gradually wean herself off the medicines they insisted on giving her, she would eat properly, and then she would leave this place and lead a normal life, which would include Gloria – her friend.

Her thoughts were interrupted by a tap on her door and the friendly voice she had just been thinking about.

"Lizzie, are you okay in there?" Gloria enquired. "I've got you a nice warm towel."

The bathroom door opened and Gloria placed the towel nearby, respecting Lizzie's privacy. She fluffed up the bed pillow and waited for a reaction from Lizzie. There wasn't one.

Nervously, she edged towards the bathroom door.

"Lizzie, are you alright?"

Lizzie stood dripping on the cold tiles and stared at the towel she had been offered. Tiptoeing towards it, she kicked it to ensure that it genuinely was what Gloria had stated and as it sat, crumpled on the floor, she realised that Gloria had, once again, shown her another act of kindness. She rubbed her body dry, applied deodorant and brushed her hair before entering her room.

Gloria was relieved to see Lizzie and hugged her closely, kissing her forehead before dressing.

"Thank you," Lizzie whispered softly, "You have no idea how much this means to me."

Gloria sat on the bed and smiled back at the young woman. Despite breaking all the rules of St Thomas's Hospital, she felt ecstatic; she believed that she could indeed help the young woman fight the demons inside her mind and to finally lead a normal life in the outside world. Lizzie did too, and when they exited her bedroom, both women were smiling.

The gibberish chatter of the inmates of St Thomas's Hospital came to an immediate halt as soon as Lizzie and Gloria entered the communal room. The large TV boomed the daily news in the background: Emlyn Hughes, a once-famous footballer, had just died. Lizzie stood close to her friend and immediately felt uneasy in the cold atmosphere surrounding her. A skinny patient, still in his pyjamas, grabbed the remote control and turned it off, glaring at Lizzie as he did so. Lizzie snuggled closer to Gloria, her heart pounding with anxiety.

The room filled with tension. Each patient stopped and stared at her, their frightened expressions grinding deep into her soul. Lizzie glanced across the room at the blank faces gazing at her and moved even closer to Gloria for comfort. Gloria, however, felt as tense as Lizzie did, and guided her towards the reading corner so that she could enjoy a little privacy without feeling like a circus freak – a term Lizzie had often used in this place. Lizzie sat down and snatched the top book from the pile. It was a fairy-tale, but that didn't matter, as she wouldn't be reading today anyhow. She just needed to convince the others that she was not a threat to them.

She turned the pages. A young lad with a limp moved away from his chair, muttering that she was *the naughty one*. He nervously shuffled towards the opposite end of the room, as did the crazy girl, Leanne, who imagined that aliens were everywhere. Leanne gripped the lad's arms frantically, pulling him towards the window, which would be a safe exit point should the bad girl attack her.

The silence continued for what felt like hours, although in reality it was just a few minutes. As Lizzie leafed through the pages, she felt a familiar feeling lurch through her body. She fought the voices in her head and continued to ignore the background noise. The others quietened, reassured by her actions, and were able to resume their afternoon's entertainment, watching Peppa Pig.

Wankers, Lizzie thought as she flicked through the pathetic fairy-tale which involved ridiculous princesses and princes all living a perfect life in a perfect sodding castle. The anger was consuming her, and the voices were becoming louder in her mind. Slamming the book hard onto the surface of the bookcase, she jumped up suddenly, flapped her arms and yelled "Boo!" at the inmates to frighten them. It worked.

Mayhem struck the room. Everyone shouted for assistance. Lizzie laughed hysterically at the idiots around her. She had forgotten how entertaining it was to wind up the inmates, and, suddenly, all thoughts of remaining calm had disappeared. *Calm is good*, Lizzie thought. *But hell, it's fun scaring the shit out of these pricks.*

Gloria ran across the room, trying to calm the patients with softly spoken words. They were restless and nervous, and some had left the area to report the incident. Lizzie felt a rush of adrenalin burst through her body, knowing that she controlled this entire situation. She could sit down quietly and be a good girl, which is what she had intended to do before they had all stared at her as though she was a leper, or she could cause havoc by petrifying them. She had made her decision.

The bald, swollen-nosed idiot entered the room, with a group of snivelling snitches behind him. He boldly strode towards Lizzie, then stopped immediately. Meeting her eyes, he looked coldly at her.

"Well, Lizzie, what type of situation do we have here?" he questioned loudly. The inmates hid behind one another.

Lizzie bowed her head. She wanted to beat the crap out of Mr Hillier, but knew that she had already pushed the boundaries too far today. Meeting his cold eyes, she apologised.

"I'm sorry Mr Hillier, truly I am. They all scared me, staring at me like that. I wanted to be a quiet, good girl, I promise you, but they wouldn't stop looking at me and, well, I lost it – just for a minute, and I really promise never to do it again. I promise to be an angel."

Mr Hillier moved towards the books and lifted up the copy that Lizzie had been reading. His expressionless face met hers.

"You like reading, don't you, Lizzie?"

Lizzie was confused, but not stupid. She knew the mind games this idiot played, and she wasn't as thick as he thought she was. Meeting his eyes, she screwed up her nose and turned her head away from him.

"I hate reading. My mother would force me to read when I was a little girl. I had to learn the lines from each chapter and recite them to her. Every time I failed, my punishment was more reading and so, no, Mr Hillier, I do not like it. In fact, if I never had to read again, I would be the happiest person in this hospital."

Lizzie crossed her fingers behind her back, hoping desperately that her lie would work.

"Well, Lizzie," he responded, "For once you will approve of my decision." He turned and exited the communal room, beckoning Gloria to join him.

"See that she has no more books, Gloria," he demanded as the patients sniggered behind him, pointing in Lizzie's direction. Gloria slowly walked towards Lizzie, dreading her reaction.

Lizzie was back in her room and gazing out of the window. The clouds from before had dispersed and the mottled sky reminded her of an image produced randomly from an artist's palette. Gloria had gently explained that for now, Lizzie had better obey the rules, and she had suggested that, perhaps, after her additional sessions with Dr Davies, she could learn how to paint in her free time. Little did Gloria know that Lizzie could draw, and paint, but, along with so many other things, she had stopped that some time ago.

Lizzie was distracted by her stomach rumbling. She hadn't eaten since yesterday and realised suddenly how hungry she was. She looked at the clock on the wall – it was 4.15 p.m. Tea would be at 5 p.m., then, perhaps, if Mr Hillier had gone home, she could sit quietly away from her bedroom and away from the idiots who had been mocking her.

It seemed to take forever, but finally it was tea time. Lizzie combed her hair, put on her slippers and joined the queue in the canteen, forcing herself to smile at the inmates.

Tonight's dinner was mince with mash, peas and swede, which Lizzie really didn't care for. She wished that she had been around for lunch, which had been chicken nuggets and chips, but she had been asleep then. Reluctantly, she plopped the meal on her plate and sat down by herself at a table in the far corner of the room. She made an ornate design out of the peas and mash, creating a happy face, before forcing the food down her throat. Her stomach initially heaved but as she continued to eat, the heaving stopped and, surprisingly, she started to feel more human. She scraped the plate clean, and felt a deep sense of satisfaction and pride. She remembered the lectures she had been given where she was reprimanded for not eating, which meant she might have to stay longer in the hospital. Lizzie would always cry after these sessions. But for once, she looked forward to her weigh-in the next day. She desperately yearned for praise and felt that she had earned it today, despite the earlier events.

A familiar person edged towards Lizzie's table, ignoring the roaming eyes following his every move. Jason smiled before putting his plate on the table. He plonked himself down on the wooden chair, scraping the legs noisily across the floor as he pushed himself in. Lizzie was pleased to see a friendly face and smiled warmly at him. He cleared his plate in record speed, then whispered quietly to her so as not to raise suspicion from the others. Moving his head close to Lizzie's ear, he covered his mouth with his hand.

"Lizzie, I've been trying to find you all day." It was obvious he hadn't heard about her little episode. "Anyway," he continued, "You'll never believe it."

Excitedly, he pulled his chair closer to the table and explained that his meeting with Dr Davies had gone very well and that, if he continued to maintain the improvements he had shown, he would be allowed to go home.

"If all goes as planned," Jason added, "I can go home on Saturday."

Lizzie watched his joyful expression as he counted the number of days on his fingers.

"That's five days, Lizzie," he exclaimed. "Five bedtimes, five dinners and then home time."

Lizzie's mind was in turmoil. Part of her wanted to beg him to stay as he was her only friend here but, when she studied his face, she also felt elated for him. He deserved a bit of luck and, at last, he could be given another chance.

After their main course, they joined the queue of inmates. Lizzie and Jason watched, amused, as the patients' turmoil spread throughout the queue.

"They're facing a real dilemma today," Lizzie giggled. "Choices aren't a good thing, and there are two desserts on offer! Will they choose the rice pudding, that looks like frogspawn with disgusting strawberry jam blobbed in the middle, or chocolate pudding? Decisions, decisions," she added sarcastically as she made her choice: the chocolate sponge with chocolate sauce.

Lizzie settled down to enjoy her dessert. She watched the queuing patients, who appeared to be having a full-blown conference. Eventually they had all selected their desserts and shuffled back to their seats. Lizzie and Jason hurriedly piled the sponge and custard into their bowls and gulped the food down. Jason then beamed at Lizzie while rummaging through his trouser pockets. Holding his fist firmly shut, he beckoned for her to sneak outside the canteen. Almost skipping with joy, he guided her towards the TV room, which was deserted, and offered her a seat. Lizzie, confused by his sudden elation, obediently sat next to him.

"Close your eyes, Lizzie," he ordered. He took her hand and allowed something to drop into it. Lizzie screwed her eyes together, trying to imagine what on earth Jason was giving her. Jason released his hand and asked Lizzie to promise to keep a secret.

"It's my gift to you," he whispered tenderly. "Take it now, go back to your room and, when you get a private moment, you can look at it properly. My mum came up with the idea because you – well, you've been so kind to me, what with the reading and that…"

Jason became flustered and Lizzie, fully aware of the no touching policy, scanned the room for spies. The clattering emanating from the canteen continued and, very quickly, she brushed her lips against Jason's mouth and ran out of the room, down the corridor and towards her bedroom. Jason, blushing, re-entered the canteen, hoping for some of the lovely rice pudding, which would turn pink when mixed with jam.

Lizzie dashed into her room, then stopped dead in her tracks. Although it was only half past six, the stupid fat cow who shared the room with her was sitting on her bed, attempting to embroider some ridiculous tapestry thing. Lizzie glared at her then, realising that she hadn't even threaded the bloody great needle, sniggered. The fat girl glared at Lizzie, although she didn't really know why.

Lizzie guessed that this girl was one of the snitches who had reported her to Mr Hillier. Of course, there was no way she would let on that she knew this, as Little Miss Snitch would run to him again, but Lizzie aimed to get her own back. She wasn't quite sure how yet, but she'd work something out within the next few days.

Hiding the secret gift in her tracksuit pocket, she smiled falsely at the girl. "What're you doing?" she enquired, knowing full well what the silly cow was attempting.

"Tapestry," she replied, holding the mishmash of stitches up proudly towards Lizzie. Lizzie studied the mess in the girl's hand and counted to ten before she responded. A familiar nagging voice wanted to mock the girl, but Lizzie realised that she had to be a model inmate if, like Jason, she was ever going to escape.

Lizzie moved a chair closer towards the girl's bed. The green crosses on the tapestry were randomly stitched and, just below them, pale yellow crosses merged with one another, forming something reminiscent of a pile of puke. The girl stared proudly at her, itching for a compliment, and her eyes begged for some feedback. Lizzie studied the image again and imagined her artist's palette, the random colours on the canvas, merging to form beautiful images of the countryside.

Turning towards the girl, she smiled. "Your tree is beautiful," she whispered kindly. Guiding the girl's hand towards the rear of the material, Lizzie pointed out that if she liked the green thread, she could make some hills in the background. Then, if she really wanted to, the orange could be the sun.

"But first," Lizzie added, "Let me help you with this." The fat girl, for once beamed a genuine smile at Lizzie. She had always been useless at everything. Bullied at school for being overweight and stupid, Sara had tried desperately to find a skill. Having one talent would have made all the difference to her but, until now, she hadn't realised that her talent lay in stitching. Her elation showed on her face and her blue eyes shone brightly as Lizzie effortlessly threaded the needle, knotted the end and returned the needle to Sara.

Lizzie for once, felt good. She still planned to pay Sara back for snitching on her but, as she watched her carefully stitch the squares, biting her lip in concentration, she felt a sense of pride. Perhaps, after all, this girl, like Lizzie, simply needed somebody to praise her. As she slid her chair back where it belonged, Lizzie turned towards the girl, giving her a thumbs-up.

"I love your tapestry, Sara; you should be very proud of yourself."

Sara's heart skipped a beat as she meticulously sewed. She now wished that she hadn't told Mr Hillier about the bad girl. The bad girl actually was just like her, really. Nobody understood Sara either.

Lizzie settled onto her bed and toyed with the idea of removing the little item from her pocket. Although Sara was concentrating hard with her blunt needle, she may notice, and Lizzie knew she was not to be trusted. She lowered her head to her pillow and gazed at the spotlights above her, imagining that they were stars or distant planets millions of miles away.

A tap at the door startled both women. A nurse entered the room with small plastic containers, water and tablets. Without acknowledging the women, she passed them their medication, watched as they swallowed and exited the room, closing the door behind her. Lizzie, as soon as the coast was clear, spat the pills into her hand and flushed them down the toilet.

The wall clock ticked quietly. It felt later than it actually was, but Lizzie was tired. She put on some clean pyjamas, hid Jason's gift in her top, tucked herself under her fresh bed linen, remembered the kindness that Gloria had shown her and snuggled under the covers.

Sleep came easily this time and Lizzie's dreams would be, she hoped, nice. The events of the day disappeared, and she relished the thought of her meeting the next day with Dr Davies who, she hoped, would be pleased with her progress.

The fat girl in the next bed slept well too. For once, Lizzie wasn't bothered by her loud snoring. Her dreams of hills, trees and the sun shining on her back consumed her mind, along with thoughts of kindness and love. Life was going to be so much better soon, and everybody would be so very proud of her.

"Mummy's little angel," she muttered in her sleep, cuddling her pillow and smiling.

"Mummy's little angel," repeated the monster standing in her daughter's bedroom, with a sneer on her face, "will be punished."

* * * * *

PART TWO

JONATHAN

'Men are not prisoners of fate, but only prisoners of their own minds.'

Franklin D. Roosevelt

13. JONATHAN

Despite appearances, Jonathan had not been born with a silver spoon in his mouth. The first of five children, Jon had been brought up in the less salubrious part of Tunbridge Wells in a terraced council house in a very average street.

His parents were hard-working, honest folk who believed that children should be seen and not heard, and should always respect their elders. They had a strong work ethic, along with a belief that you gained nothing without effort and hard work.

As the first son, Jonathan had been privileged enough to enjoy the sole attention of his mum and dad until he was two years old. His mum had doted on her very pretty child, with his wavy dark hair that flopped into his eyes, long curly eyelashes and infectious smile. She would show him off proudly to her friends when he was a placid baby and, later, the well-behaved toddler. Jonathan was the perfect son – although at times his father secretly wished that his little boy was more boisterous and masculine.

When Jamie, the second son, arrived in 1971, then his sister Lucy ten months later, life changed dramatically. Money became scarcer and Jonathan saw less and less of his parents. His mum seemed to spend most of her life cleaning and cooking, and Dad had to find a second job just to make ends meet. Jonathan, however, remained content in his little world, which was pretty simple really. He had a nice, clean home, a bed to sleep in, food in his belly and a family he loved very much. Nothing could have changed his contentment with life. He was easily pleased.

His family grew to seven over the next few years, and the once spacious three-bedroomed home became a cramped environment, with four boys sharing one bedroom and Lucy having a room to herself. While his brothers and sister spent most of their time playing in the large back garden, Jon relished the peace and quiet of his bedroom. With his head in a book and his tape recorder playing in the background, life couldn't have been any more perfect.

Jonathan's siblings were so different from him. When Jon was seven, he realised during his birthday party just how unique he was. His brothers were all extremely boisterous, fighting for attention from their parents and squabbling over who got the largest piece of birthday cake. Jonathan didn't care less about the size of his portion or, indeed, about the ultimate prize in the game of pass the parcel – none of that was important to him. He just felt blessed to be lucky enough to have a party and that his mum, despite her lack of time and money, had created a masterpiece of a cake, in the form of a giant football, smothered with butter cream and icing sugar.

As the years passed, the differences between Jonathan and his siblings became even more pronounced. He would watch his brothers in the garden with Dad, eagerly assisting him with his carpentry as he built a giant tree house. They would fight for his attention while enthusiastically learning the difference between a right angle and a perpendicular. This work, to Jonathan, held absolutely no appeal, although he knew that if he really wanted to, he could teach himself woodwork, metalwork or anything he so chose. Jonathan, however, opted for learning instead, and he sat quietly on his bottom bunk, his head deep inside a book.

From the moment he had learned his first few words, Jonathan had been fascinated by literature. The wonder of the simple *Peter and Jane* books from his earliest school days had absorbed his mind completely. The phonics, the letters, the shape of words and finally the sentences that made sense of everything never ceased to amaze him. From the age of seven, Jonathan would sit flicking through his pocket-sized dictionary. His personal challenge was to learn one new word every day.

At the age of seventeen, Jonathan had learned a total of 5,000 new words, all of which he understood fully and could apply to everyday life. He spoke eloquently and was polite and well-mannered. His friends at school, however, never ribbed him about his intellect or posh voice; in fact, rather than take the mickey out of him, everybody wanted to be Jonathan's friend, including some of the teachers. However, regardless of his apparent perfection, his parents worried frantically about their son.

Despite the simplicity of Jon's private world of learning, his mother was secretly anxious about her son. She was used to the antics and misbehaviour of her other four children, and had constant reports from school about their wild behaviour. In contrast, Jonathan had never been in trouble. He had been a quiet child who would rather listen to his siblings than participate in conversation. Funnily enough, however, they would always run to Jonathan for advice whenever they were in trouble or were feeling insecure. He had a natural ability to listen and, when appropriate, advise – which, despite their different personalities, they heeded and valued.

When his brothers hit the early stages of puberty, their main priority was attracting members of the opposite sex. Jonathan would cover his ears as his brothers fantasised over the hottest girls in the school and tried to masturbate quietly under their covers. They would sneak in their dad's bedroom and pinch *The Joy of Sex* from under his mattress, giggling at the images.

Jonathan, however, preferred to study, and had recently become fascinated by three things: pie charts, the origin of words, and the human body, particularly the brain and how it worked. His brothers, he understood, were entering a critical stage of their lives; he'd recently read a medical encyclopaedia and had memorised the words that gave a clear and concise explanation of puberty. In boys, a hormone released by the pituitary gland signalled the testicles to produce a hormone called testosterone, which spurred the development of the secondary sex characteristics, such as the growth of facial hair and a deeper voice. Fluctuating levels of hormones could also bring on adolescent mood swings. These ups and downs were tough for both child and parent to deal with, but were an inevitable part of puberty. Jon's parents certainly knew that well enough.

Jonathan, however, although in the final stages of adolescence, had learned to apply his emotions and concerns in one simple and logical way. He believed that everything in his life could be represented by a pie chart, later to become known as Jon's 'pie'.

His obsession with 'pie' started at school, when, during a maths lesson, each student was told to create a chart for homework. Most kids analysed the expenses of running a home or a car – Jon analysed the importance of every aspect of his life. He neatly drew around a plate, creating sections and marking them with percentages representing how important each section was. He shaded the important part of his chart in red, then the less important sections – the 'what ifs' – in grey. The grey areas were irrelevant to him and, although visible on his chart, didn't really become part of his pie – the red section – unless they became real issues or concerns and he felt he had to act upon them.

As puberty took over his siblings' lives, Jon managed his with relative ease. There were some important matters that he wanted to change, and these represented about a third of his life – or, as he imagined, a third of his pie. One example was that he needed to improve his grades in maths and science. It *was* important, and he *could* change things by studying harder. That change to his life would mean that he could achieve a higher grade in his exams, so he could go on to study A-Levels at school, thus allowing him to enter university and someday get a decent and highly paid job. Hence, the importance of this part of his pie. It dictated his future and was worth worrying about.

Then came the remaining grey area, which included his brothers, sister, parents and many silly things in his life that weren't worth fussing about. He'd listened to his mother worrying about how she would cope if his dad passed away when the children were young: "What will I do about money?" "How will I cope?" "What will I tell the children?"

Jon knew that his mum worried about lots of things – most of which were unlikely to happen and had never happened. It caused her unnecessary anxiety and concern, and he subsequently pledged to worry about nothing until it actually became something – a real issue, or part of his pie. In that instance, the insignificant, grey piece of pie would move to one of the important sections and Jon would then worry about it and make any changes that were necessary to improve the situation.

And so Jonathan continued to enjoy a relatively carefree life while his siblings, who did not subscribe to his pie theory, had more chaotic lives, worrying about this and that.

Jonathan was seventeen and studying for A-Levels when his parents approached him and asked for a private chat. Gathering his books into a tidy pile without even questioning why, he left his studies behind and sat quietly in the dining room. His parents stared anxiously at him. His father was the first to speak.

"Jonathan," he muttered, trying to clear his throat and looking anxiously at his wife. "We're a little worried."

Jonathan raised his head and opened his eyes wide as both parents nervously shuffled in their seats.

"It's just that um, well, your brothers are never in. They go to discos, they fool around with girls… But you're always here, and, well, we were wondering whether something was worrying you."

Jonathan thought of his pie. Nope, he was fully prepared for his forthcoming exams. Nothing was worrying him. He smiled at his parents reassuringly.

"No, Mum, Dad, I'm fine thanks. Looking forward to next year then graduating in whatever I decide to do; life's cool."

His father stuttered and started to pick at his fingernails. Mum, sensing his embarrassment, chipped in.

"Jonathan, I'm going to be straight with you. Do you like boys?"

Jonathan's stomach fluttered with the adrenalin rush he felt and the ludicrous situation he was in. He knew precisely what his parents were meaning to ask: was he a homosexual? He wanted to laugh in their faces and deny everything. He knew, however, from their expressions that they were genuinely concerned – and he sort of understood their anxiety. His private world of study had never involved girls but nor had it included boys, other than his siblings and peers, who constantly approached him for advice.

Reassuringly, he smiled gently at his parents. "Listen, Mum, Dad, I love to learn but I also love to help people by listening. This involves both boys and girls, and no, I have no preference. I am not homosexual but, then, I haven't yet been involved with a girl, although I must admit that some do turn my head."

He thought of the hot head girl who had a huge rack and superb arse, then in an instant discarded the thought of giving her one. The last thing he needed now was an erection.

His nervous parents sipped their tea, unconvinced that their son was straight, but as Jonathan excused himself, they shrugged in confusion.

"No pie," Jonathan responded, as he shot upstairs and back to his room.

They had no idea what he was talking about.

* * * * *

14. BETH'S FRIENDS

2014

The beeping and vibration of his mobile phone awoke Dave with a start. As he tried to regain his bearings, Beth shot out of the living room and back into the kitchen. He heard a drawer slam, then the back door. She obviously needed another cigarette.

His eyes focused on the tiny screen in front of him, and he reached for the messages. Three missed calls and four text messages. He looked at the number. It was familiar. He had dialled it earlier and the messages were all from the same sender: Jonathan Davies.

Dave checked that Beth was okay before he replied to his text. She was sitting in the cold, gazing up at the sky while taking deep drags from her cigarette. The hot tub in the garden had been uncovered, and the heat from the water rose to form a light mist above it. Stubbing out her cigarette, she turned towards Dave and smiled.

"I need to relax," she whispered, picking up the butt from the decking and wrapping it in a tissue before placing it in the bin. She ran upstairs, removed her gloves, washed her hands and a few moments later reappeared in her tiny bikini with a towel neatly positioned under her arm. Dave sighed with relief, knowing that he had at least thirty minutes of peace to make his call.

He shut the back door behind him, and shivered. It wasn't just the cold autumn air that hit him, but the fact that he was having to take matters further behind Beth's back. She needed help desperately but he knew that, without his intervention, she would never visit Jonathan or resume taking her medicine. He dialled the number and waited. The answerphone kicked in almost immediately.

'Hello, you have reached the office of Jonathan Davies, I am sorry that I am unable to take your call right now, but it is important to me. Please leave a message and I will contact you as soon as I can. However, if this is an emergency, please contact me on my mobile.'

Dave left his name and number and waited anxiously for his call. After hanging around in the kitchen for ten minutes, he contemplated calling the emergency number, but resisted. Beth, although in a bad way, wasn't in a critical state. The poor doctor was obviously tied up in a meeting or with another client. The call could wait.

* * *

The meeting with the board of directors had dragged on far longer than Jonathan had anticipated. Despite the phenomenal number of clients they had on their books, costs were escalating and due to a third of their customers being referred by the NHS (at Jonathan's insistence), finances were becoming very tight. Jon studied their designer suits and watches, and figured that, as always, he would be the one who would have to change.

His colleagues insisted that Jonathan review the situation urgently and seek more private patients, as they had. After all, they could charge practically what they wanted – as desperate, wealthy people would pay a fortune to speak to an expert. Jonathan cringed at the thought. Although he wanted to help everybody, rich or poor, often the less fortunate needed his help more. The social problems surrounding them and their unhealthy environments often triggered addictions, depression and numerous other conditions and, although wealthier clients also suffered, his poorer clients were often ignored until they hit the point of desperation.

He waved at his colleagues as he excused himself from the boardroom. He was conscious that he had missed numerous calls, due to his phone's constant vibration during the meeting.

Pouring himself a cup of cold coffee from the percolator, Jonathan flicked through his missed calls and messages. Jennifer, bless her, had called a couple of times, reminding Jon to pick up the kids from the childminder as she had a parents evening. The others were all from the same caller, Dave Lewis, who he had tried to contact earlier today.

He dialled the number; a breathless voice greeted him. Dave, while sitting in the garden watching Beth, had left the phone on the kitchen worktop and had had to run in from the garden so as not to miss the call. He regained his composure and his breathing slowed. He explained the situation with Beth and how concerned he was. "I'm so sorry to bother you, Dr Davies," he added, "but I just don't know who to turn to."

Strictly speaking, Jonathan should not have been speaking to his client's partner. He was fully aware of client confidentiality and the Data Protection Act, but he listened intently as Dave explained the situation he was in and the desperation he felt.

The fact that Dave usually attended Beth's meetings with Jonathan made this conversation an exception to the rule. Jonathan knew his patient well and understood why her partner was so distressed.

Opening the filing cabinet, he retrieved the letters he had sent to Beth and explained that she had failed to attend the previous two appointments and, for obvious reasons, she needed to maintain contact with him. That was why Jonathan had tried to speak to Dave. Although his colleagues wouldn't understand, Jonathan cared genuinely about his patients' wellbeing, in particular Beth's.

Dave remained silent. He hadn't seen the letters: Beth was obviously in denial and had thrown them away. And she had ignored the calls too.

Flicking to the calendar page on his mobile, he checked his itinerary for the next day. Jonathan had a full schedule, but agreed to slot Beth in for an hour, during his lunch break, if Dave could make it. Dave immediately agreed.

"Thank you, Dr Davies. I don't know what I'd do without you."

Placing the mobile on the side cabinet he headed for the garden to discuss the news with Beth.

She stood on the kitchen floor, naked. Her discarded bikini was nowhere to be seen, and the water from the hot tub dripped onto the tiles. Beth stared at the puddles beneath her feet, shivered, then glared hatefully at Dave.

Her friends had been right all of the time about him, her so-called boyfriend. Deep down, Beth had known that Dave, just like everybody else, was out to destroy her, but sometimes he had pretended to care about her, even love her – and, stupidly, her defences had dropped. She had been a silly fool and, as she stood in the kitchen, nothing seemed to matter anymore.

Her friends were still enjoying themselves in the garden. They had annoyed her earlier today with their constant giggling and nagging, and she had hoped that, by going into the hot tub, they would calm down and allow her to relax. Some hope. Instead of allowing Beth to chill, they had forced her to spy on Dave.

"He's up to something!" they bellowed at her. "Go and see, Beth, go and see now."

Beth hadn't wanted to. The warmth of the water and the aroma of the bubbles eased the tension she had felt all day and, for the first time, she was actually enjoying herself. She loved the fact that, despite the weather being so bitterly cold, she could be warm outside while being able to study the endless sky above her. Even the horrors of Dave trying to attack her in the living room, and then spilling his drink on her beautiful carpet, had dissipated. Logic had kicked in temporarily. After she had returned the kitchen knife to the drawer, Beth had realised how daft she was acting. Dave wasn't trying to hurt her, she told her friends. And he didn't mean to spill the drink. They just laughed in her face and mocked her for being so naïve and stupid.

She glared at the despicable traitor in front of her while he tried to pretend that he cared about her by wrapping a towel around her shoulders and rubbing her dry. She was rigid with rage, and wished that he would die in a hideous accident so that she and her friends could just get on with their lives. And as for him thinking that a nice hot cup of coffee would fix everything? Well, he had another bloody shock coming his way.

Dave was worried. He studied the trembling woman in front of him. Her eyes were once again vacant and her lips pursed angrily. Her thin arms dangled and he noticed some tiny scars on them, which were new. He cringed, realising that, on top of everything else, Beth could be self-harming. Jesus, she was in a bad way, his poor, tortured little angel.

The kettle was ruined. He never took care when filling it up with water. She had told him time and time again to turn the tap *one* notch only, then to carefully fill the kettle with just enough water. But no, *oh no*, he set the tap to maximum and the sodding water missed the dammed kettle and spewed all over the stainless steel. The crap in the water stained everything – she had told him that too. And stains attracted germs. And germs killed people, just like Beth. He really was beyond help.

She did not want to drink the coffee, despite being thirsty; she knew what he was up to. Oh yes, her friends knew too.

Coffee, my arse, she thought, slamming the cup on the worktop and shattering it into pieces, punching it time and time again. Dave tried to stop her by pushing her towards the hallway.

"Beth, no, stop, Beth, please – it will be alright."

She didn't care what he was saying and crushed her hands together, smiling insanely at Dave. The broken shards of china dug deep into her palms and she stood, amused, watching the blood run down her hands, onto her feet, then the floor. This was fun, or at least her friends thought it was as they sniggered behind her.

Dave was beyond exhausted. He calmed Beth, cleaned her wounds and bandaged her hands. She wasn't resisting any more, which helped a little, but each movement he made was meticulously studied by her, and her friends.

He tried to tempt Beth to eat a little or even drink something, but his efforts were in vain. She pursed her lips then screamed incomprehensible words at him. She knew what he wanted – to drug her with that poison – and so, tomorrow, she would eat and drink once he was gone. Until then, she would rather starve to death or die of thirst.

After an exhausting battle to help Beth put her pyjamas on, Dave tucked her into bed hoping that she would rest, or sleep. She turned away from him and sobbed quietly into her pillow. Lifting her streaky face and turning towards Dave, she cried real tears.

"Why did you call that man, Dave?" she asked sadly. "I trusted you. I really did."

Dave tried to cuddle Beth but she pushed him away with her damaged hands. He felt dreadful – riddled with guilt, as he knew that he was partly responsible for the sorry state his girlfriend was in. His head throbbed with tension and his eyes welled up in pity.

"Because I love you, Beth" was all he could say before he turned towards the bathroom to undress and shower.

Beth wished she could believe him as she closed her eyes in exhaustion. She knew that only two people really loved her – not her kids, not Dave, nor her parents – and they were snuggled up close to her, protecting her from the evil monster standing in the bathroom door.

"Night night, Beth," they whispered tenderly.

"Night night," she replied, kissing two vacant areas close to her pillow. "Don't let the bed bugs bite."

* * *

Despite his aching muscles and throbbing headache, there was no point in trying to sleep. It was only seven o'clock in the evening and, under different circumstances, Dave would have crashed on the bed and slept until the middle of the following day.

Beth had finally settled down. Her tossing and turning had subsided and she now lay peacefully, curled under the covers, cuddling a pillow. It was a funny little habit and, despite all tonight's shocking events, Dave still thought she looked cute. He quietly closed the bedroom door and went downstairs to make himself something to eat.

After eating a few pieces of cheese on toast, he cleaned the kitchen and collapsed onto the sofa. His mind was numb and he reflected not just on the situation with Beth, but on work and his kids. For the first time in months, he started to feel sorry for himself. He was strong, but right now, right this minute, he needed somebody to comfort *him*. It had always been him comforting Beth and, yes, he understood why, but over the years, nobody had ever asked how *he* was or how *he* felt. Sometimes life was so bloody unfair and cruel. He started to weep.

His mobile phone distracted him. He intended to ignore the call, but noticed that it was Kirsty. Coughing in an attempt to hide the fact he had been sobbing, he answered the call.

"Hey Dad, how are you?" Kirsty asked in her usual chirpy manner. "Been trying to catch Mum, but her mobile is always on answerphone. Is everything okay?"

He could have told his daughter the truth, but what was the point in involving her and causing yet another person anxiety? She couldn't help. Only Jonathan Davies could, it seemed.

"Hi, Kirsty! Boy, am I pleased to hear from you. I'm good, ta. Mum's been a bit under the weather with a cold, but she'll be fine in a couple of days. She's curled up in bed now, sleeping. How are you? How's gay Paree?"

Kirsty didn't answer her dad's questions. Although she was only nineteen, she was not an idiot. Her dad, it appeared, had a very short memory; she had lived with her mum and seen what she could be like. Thankfully, her older brother and her dad had got her though childhood and youth pretty unblemished, but she could remember some of the darker times.

"Dad, tell me the truth now – is Mum okay – really? Please don't lie to me."

Dave almost weakened. There he was, just a few minutes ago feeling consumed with self-pity as he had nobody to talk to and now, when he had been given the chance to let off steam, he wouldn't tell the truth.

"Oh Kirsty, please don't worry, sweetheart. It's work. Things are tough, and over the next few days I've got to lay Mike and Charlie off. I feel so bloody bad, Kirst. Mike's been with us all his working life, you know, and what the hell will Charlie do? He's got two kids and a mortgage."

Kirsty backed down from confronting her dad and totally understood his stress – well, kind of. She was lucky enough to have a well-off boyfriend whose parents had bought him an apartment in Paris in order to culturally educate him. She wasn't sure whether getting high on dope and pissing it up in a bar every night was indeed *cultural* – but, heck, it was fun and it meant that, so long as he got his monthly allowance, he could support her too.

She looked at the time on her phone and realised she was running late. "Well, okay, Dad," she replied. "Give Mum a hug from her best girl and, hey, one for you too. See you soon, Pops. Byeeeeee."

With that, the call was over.

Dave studied his mobile for a moment. The call had lasted just over two minutes, but even that simple chat with his precious daughter had made an amazing difference to how he felt. He blew his nose and sent a text to the boys at work, asking them to open up for him, as he wouldn't be in until the afternoon. Then, feeling completely shattered, he took a sleeping pill, brushed his teeth and fell into a much-needed deep sleep.

* * *

The lovely aroma of freshly baked bread awoke Dave. He thought for a brief moment that he was dreaming but, as the homely smell wafted through the bedroom and into his nostrils, he knew he was not imagining things. The bright red digits on the bedroom clock shone brightly. It was 6.30 a.m. and pitch black outside. Beth's side of the bed was empty.

He tried to fathom what was going on, and was startled by the image standing at his bedroom door. Beth was dressed in her favourite skinny jeans and well-tailored crew-necked top. Her makeup was soft and warm and she had plaited her hair the way Dave had always liked it. She beamed at him, and lowered the tray onto his bedside cabinet.

"I've made you breakfast, darling," she exclaimed. "Fresh bread, bacon, eggs and your favourite – hash browns. Oh, and some freshly squeezed orange juice; the coffee's just brewing, back in a mo."

With that, Beth skipped down the stairs, humming cheerfully, to tend to the coffee.

A few minutes later, she dashed back into the bedroom. She plopped down on the end of the bed and gazed tenderly at Dave. "Eat your breakfast, love, before it gets cold."

Dave wasn't hungry, but obediently took the tray and picked at the food. Beth watched him as he added bacon to the thickly sliced bread, dipped his sandwich into the soft egg yolk and ate his meal.

"Dave," she whispered, moving closer to his side of the bed. "I need to apologise."

Lowering her head, she stared at her bandaged hands.

"I haven't been well," she added. "And you're right – I do need to take my medicine. Without it, I – well, I just can't control myself. Those voices, the ones that I've told you about, they always come back. I end up doing what *they* tell me to do and, although I know it's wrong, at the time it just feels right. I *know* that you love me. God, who the hell would put up with this behaviour unless it *was* love? And so, from today, I promise, cross my heart and hope to die, to take my pills and to be a good girl."

Dave didn't react. He sipped his orange juice and studied the clock. 6.45 a.m.

This was nothing new to him. In fact, every single time Beth had an appointment with Dr Davies, she would act as though she was normal, show him her medicine packet with the empty tabs, and offer to seduce him. The problem was, she could never remember this pattern. But Dave could.

He finished his breakfast, and thanked her for the delicious meal, kissing her lightly before making his excuses to visit the bathroom.

Beth scowled as he ran the tap. Her friends were as furious as she was, and figured that the only way of making him forget the appointment with the evil doctor was to distract him. Beth had already thought of that and, when he returned, freshly showered and naked, she was lying on the bed in a black lace teddy, smiling seductively in his direction.

Beth ran her bandaged hand across her breasts and beckoned her man to join her. "Come here, baby," she whispered, blowing Dave a kiss. "It's been so long; I need you."

Under different circumstances, Dave would have jumped at the opportunity to make love with Beth. She had a stunning figure and knew, every time, which buttons to press; she was an amazing lover. However, as he watched her trying to lure him into her arms, his penis said it all. It was flaccid. He couldn't exploit her and, more importantly, he would not exploit her. She was sick. Pulling on his boxer shorts, he turned away.

"I'm sorry Beth," he said, as he left the room. "Too much stress at the moment, what with work and – well, you know, everything else, I'm just not in the mood."

She saw no point in trying any more. The bastard didn't appreciate anything she did for him. She didn't choose to bloody get up at four in the morning to bake him a pissing loaf – her stupid friends had made her do that. And as for the sex, bollocks to that too. She didn't fancy the ageing prick. Christ, look at him – grey hair, flabby gut and old. She was far too good for him; didn't he bloody realise that?

Ripping the teddy off her body, she slammed the bathroom door and took her second shower of the day.

"Get his filthy germs off me," she hollered, hoping that the pathetic, ageing bastard downstairs could hear her. Dave could, but chose to ignore it. He'd heard far worse than that in the past.

Beth wouldn't get dressed, and spent the remainder of the morning sulking in her bedroom with her friends. Although she was a little more subdued than he'd expected, Dave still wasn't convinced she had taken her medicine. She'd deliberately left the packet on the worktop in the kitchen, which showed one empty tab, but she could easily have flushed it down the loo. She'd done that before too.

It was midday. Dave had spoken to the boys at work, who were enjoying being the boss for the day and were finishing off an oak cabinet for a local customer. Everything was under control, except for Beth.

Refusing to dress, she lay on the carpet, gripping on to the bed with her sore hands, which could not be covered with her latex gloves. Her dead weight didn't stop Dave. He lifted her up, pulled some knickers and a tracksuit on her, and carried her to the car. She spat at him while he clipped her seatbelt into the fastener, then lit a cigarette, blowing the smoke defiantly into his face. Turning the stereo up full blast, she wound the electric windows up and down for the whole journey, in the hope that he would crash the car and kill them both. It didn't work.

It only took ten minutes to reach the small car park at Dr Davies's practice. Dave reversed into a vacant parking spot, opened the door for Beth and lifted her out of the seat. She pulled his hair spitefully and kicked, aiming for his testicles, but her efforts were in vain. Seeing Dave struggling to open the main entrance door, Jonathan jumped out of his seat to assist him, and welcomed him and Beth with a warm smile.

"Hello, Beth, Dave," he chirped, his warm eyes meeting theirs. "Do come through."

Jonathan was not shocked, or even surprised, to see Beth in this condition. He had been her psychiatrist for many years now and had seen her in a much worse state. *I can help her*, he thought before sitting down opposite them. "Coffee or tea?" he enquired.

"Coffee, please," said Dave, making himself comfortable. "No sugar and white."

Beth refused to meet Jonathan's eyes and turned her head away in a deliberate attempt to avoid him. *God, this is boring.* She picked at the flaking green leather on the chair, pulling it hard then making little piles of the remnants on her bandage. *Looks like bogies,* her friends said as they grinned in Beth's direction, disregarding the trillions of germs that were sitting on her bandages. Beth smiled back at the girls, who were now giving Jonathan the evil eye.

"So, Beth," Jon asked his distracted client, "how are things?"

Beth ignored him and continued fiddling with the chair.

"I see that you've grown your nails," he added, noticing her pink nail varnish. "If you remember, the last time you were here, you were nibbling them and stated that you wanted to stop biting them. Well done, Beth, they look lovely."

Beth kept her head bowed but looked up to see his face. He wouldn't notice that tiny movement, she thought. She noticed that he was wearing glasses. *Four eyes,* her friends silently sniggered as Beth looked down to study her neatly painted nails. She had done well and was actually quite proud of herself; she had chewed her nails all her life – until recently. It was the germ factor that had prompted her to stop, but she wasn't going to tell Dr Davies that.

Jon moved his chair away from his desk, leaned back and placed his hands behind his back before approaching Beth again.

"Beth," he said in a firmer voice. "It's been six months since we last had a chat and, from what Dave has told me, you've been a little under the weather recently." Jonathan never called a client *ill* or *poorly,* as the stigma of mental illness often stereotyped patients into these categories.

He continued. "I know that the medicines you *were* taking" (he emphasised the word *were* so that Beth knew that he knew) "had some side- effects, Beth. How are the nightmares now that you've stopped taking them? Have they got any worse?"

The girls were ordering Beth to keep her trap shut. If she started yacking to that doctor and blurted out that they were back, he would force her to take that poisonous medicine – which would kill them.

"Remember, Beth," they yelled, "Third time lucky."

Beth heard their warning and followed their movements carefully. They were now behind the doctor and pretending to slit his throat with their hands. "I *know*," she angrily replied to them. She ignored Jonathan again, who was busy observing her.

Dave cleared his throat and answered the question on Beth's behalf. She glared at him viciously and with complete contempt when he explained that she had ceased taking the pills for a number of weeks and had admitted that the voices were back. Her OCD had spiralled out of control too, and Dave was concerned that Beth was self-harming. He pulled up Beth's sleeve and showed Dr Davies the thin scars on her forearm.

Pouring himself and Dave a coffee, Jonathan moved to the edge of his desk and looked down at Beth.

"They look sore, Beth. How did you hurt yourself?"

She didn't know what injury he was referring to. Her hands? Her arms?

"I dropped a cup."

'No, Beth," they screamed, running towards her. "Stop!"

"The cup smashed and I was upset."

"Why were you upset, Beth?"

"Dave was trying to poison me."

"Why do you say that?"

"I just know it."

"How do you know, Beth?"

"*They* told me."

The voices in her head boomed and squealed and screamed, demanding that she shut the fuck up now. Beth studied Jonathan drinking his coffee, then Dave. She was thirsty. She ignored the girls.

Sensing this, Jonathan grabbed a cup from a tray, poured Beth a coffee, added a little milk and three sugars. "I hope you still take sugar," he said, smiling as he passed Beth the cup. She tentatively sipped at the coffee and relaxed a little, knowing that at least *he* wasn't going to poison her.

"Biscuit?"

Beth chose a custard cream from the tatty tin Dr Davies removed from his old wooden filing cabinet. Jonathan helped himself to a couple of digestives.

"Don't tell Jennifer or the girls," he laughed, explaining that he was supposed to be on a diet. He tapped his tummy. Beth smiled.

"So," he added, "you were telling me about your sore hands, Beth, and saying that *they* told you Dave was trying to poison you. Are *they* the friends you've mentioned before to me? The friends that come and go when you do and don't take your medicine?"

Beth continued to nibble at her biscuit, separating the halves so that she could lick the cream. Her friends were glaring in her direction, one of them frantically biting her nails.

"Don't say anything!" they demanded.

She stuck the cream onto her little finger and licked the sweet goo. Beth gazed vacantly at Jonathan. "I don't know what you're talking about."

'Well done, Beth," they rejoiced. "Good girl."

"Your friends," Jon added.

"I don't have any friends," Beth responded.

"Yes, you do," they giggled. "Us!"

Jonathan reconsidered his questioning techniques and dropped the subject for a moment. "So, what have you been doing with yourself recently, Beth?"

"Nothing."

"Well," he added, "the last time we met, you were going to start painting again. Didn't that happen?"

"No."

"Why not? You have a brilliant talent, don't you, Beth? Remember the paintings you showed me last time you were here? How did you feel when you showed them to me?"

She didn't remember anything as she had been so drugged up last time. The roof could have fallen on her head and she wouldn't have noticed.

"I don't remember," she responded honestly.

Jonathan thought back. Heck, this was a tough one, and she really was playing up today. However, he had seen far worse from Beth, and admired her for how she had managed her illness in the past. He continued, using a different and very deliberate tactic.

"And how about your shopping trips? You loved Milton Keynes, I recall?"

Beth looked directly into Jonathan's eyes. As well as losing his sight, his memory was failing too.

"It's not Milton Keynes. I go to Hemel."

"Oh yes," he replied, his eyes twinkling behind his metal-rimmed spectacles. "I remember now – the Martlowes."

"Marlowes," she responded. "M - A - R - L - O - W - E – S."

"And do you still go to that park – Gay Bridge?"

Beth laughed. God, he really was losing it.

"Gadebridge," she replied, smirking at the forgetful twit in front of her. "And no, I haven't been for ages. I will though, when, you know, when I'm a bit better."

The girls were sulking in the corner of the room.

"So you want to get better, Beth?"

"Yes. Christmas is just around the corner and everyone's coming this year."

"Everyone?"

Jonathan looked in Dave's direction. He was staring down at his knees. God, he needed some new trousers – these ones were falling to bits.

Jon couldn't allow his nervousness to show, and took a large gulp of his now-cold coffee and a deep breath to calm him down.

"Dave?" he asked, distracting him from his thoughts. Dave looked up at the doctor, then towards Beth, who was nodding anxiously at the doctor.

Beth bit the chain of her necklace and stuttered her reply. "Yes, *everybody*'s coming, and so I need to start taking my medicine again, don't I?"

"Do you, Beth?"

"Yes. I want this to be a special day. I've got so much to do, and so little time."

Beth started to panic. Her eyes glazed as she thought of the chores and endless presents she had to buy and gift-wrap, and the cards and the decorations. The Christmas pudding and the cake joined her panic list – they must be made soon, or they would taste awful, and everyone would laugh at her because she couldn't even manage a simple roast and dessert.

"Why do you say that, Beth?"

"What?"

"There's so little time?"

She looked at Jonathan and felt that familiar anger build inside her. How dare he?

"As if you would have a clue, Dr Davies! You ponce around this office in your pathetic suit and tie, without a worry in the world. You go home and the little wife has cooked your dinner and washed the dishes and cleaned the mess you left in *her* house.

Your kids are fed and watered and ready for bed and you just swan in and bingo – all done."

"Bravo, Beth," her friends cheered, clapping their hands in delight.

Jon said nothing. He moved back to his chair, sipped the remnants of his coffee and returned to his questioning.

"What do you plan to cook, Beth? Are you a great chef as well as a good painter?"

"Dinner and dessert," she replied after finishing the last of the biscuit.

"Sounds good. Don't forget the penny in the pudding and – most importantly – don't forget to take your medicine, or you may burn the turkey or forget about the penny and swallow it!" He grinned and pretended to choke.

Beth looked towards her friends, who were sticking their fingers down their throats and asking Beth to find them a bucket. Beth ignored their antics then met Dave's eyes. He was smiling and so was she.

"I won't," she said, fighting the voices in her head.

Jonathan was conscious of the time, and aware that his next client would be waiting for him. He was also ravenous.

"I'll write you another prescription," he said, scribbling in surprisingly neat handwriting. "These won't give you nightmares, Beth, or the dry mouth you've had with clozapine. I trust you enough to know that you *will* take them. After all, as you said, you have a lot to do in order to make your Christmas perfect. Take care, and I'll see you on the sixth of December. And, remember, keep up the good work with the nails. I hope to see a painting next time. In fact, why don't you hand-paint your special Christmas cards, Beth? I am sure that people will treasure them."

"Hand-paint your cards, Beth," they mocked as she and her killer boyfriend left the office.

"Goodbye, Dr Davies," Dave said, smiling and waving in his direction, feeling a huge sense of relief.

"Bye, Dr Davies," Beth muttered while Dave gently held her hand. "And thank you."

"Creep!'" they yelled at Beth as she sat in the car seat holding her prescription.

Beth didn't hear them. She was too busy deciding which picture to paint on her Christmas cards, and whether the cake should have reindeers or snowmen on the icing.

* * * * *

15. JENNIFER

1986

The coming year was probably the most important year of Jonathan's life so far. Two key events were to influence him in dramatic ways, and became very important segments of his pie; segments that could be changed if he so chose. But each portion, for now, would shape his future perfectly and offer him the security he had always hoped for.

He was seventeen and a half, in the last term of his A-Level studies, when the first memorable event occurred. She was in his year but was a few months older than Jon, and she was desired by every red-blooded male in the school.

The kids would eagerly watch her as she demonstrated her natural prowess in the gym. Her elegant, slim body would arch and somersault, balance on the beam and move delicately across the matted area through the sports hall. She effortlessly and very elegantly performed gymnastics, completely oblivious of the audience she had attracted. Boys would hang around, watching slyly from the glass doors outside, as she performed her magic.

Jenny was not only athletic but brilliantly academic as well. Jon had known her only through his studies. They both excelled at English and science, but she was studying physics rather than Jon's subject, biology.

Until that memorable April evening, the only conversation they had ever enjoyed had been during a brief encounter outside the staff room when he had bumped into her, dropped his books and blushed as bright as a beacon while stuttering an apology to her. Jenny, sensing the anxiety he was suffering, bent down and helped him gather his books. Their eyes met and for a brief moment an embarrassed silence surrounded them. Her smile soon eased the awkwardness and had melted Jonathan's heart.

From that moment on, other than his revision, Jennifer Paige had become one of the most important pieces of his pie.

He kept her a secret from everybody, especially his family, who he knew would throw a torrent of questions at him. How old was she? Was she fit? Had he, you know, got intimate with her? No, as far he was concerned, Jennifer would remain a private, hidden pleasure in his life, just like the chocolate bars he would sometimes sneak into bed.

It was spring and the A-Level students were studying hard, sitting mock exams and past A-Level papers. Jon was reasonably pleased with his estimated grades so far – he needed at least three A-Levels at a decent grade in order to attend one of the better universities, although he had absolutely no idea what he wanted to do, career-wise. His teachers predicted at least two grade As and, at a minimum, a B in maths and sociology. However, despite his consistently solid performance Jonathan strived for perfection – one of his few flaws. He was rarely happy with his achievements and always felt that he could have attained more, had he worked just that little bit harder. He wanted four straight As and knew that he would have to work all the hours God sent to achieve his goal.

Jenny did not appear to have any flaws whatsoever. With predicted As in the four subjects she was studying, she had already received offers from various colleges at Cambridge and Oxford Universities to study English, should she attain the expected results. This star pupil had everything. Or so it appeared.

They had been working hard one April afternoon and, without realising it, Jenny had missed the school coach home. As she fumbled through her bag looking for a coin for the telephone box, Jonathan came to the rescue. Even though it was six miles to Wadhurst, he offered to escort her home safely. He knew a few shortcuts across the parks, and reassured her that he could be trusted. Jennifer jumped at the opportunity to spend some time with Jon. Since their rather awkward encounter by the staff room, she had thought of him often. She didn't know why – there were far better looking guys in her year, but something she could not put her finger on had triggered new emotions in her that day.

The walk went far too quickly. Two hours and ten minutes after leaving the school, and having deliberately dawdled most of way home, Jenny stopped at her long driveway. It was empty, and no lights were on. Her parents had their own legal practice and were obviously working late tonight. She turned the key in the lock, and thanked Jonathan for getting her home safely. He politely nodded and waved as he turned away to take the long walk back to Tunbridge Wells. While jogging out of the driveway, he heard her call his name.

"Jon, hey Jonathan, don't go yet. Come in for a drink and a snack."

Without hesitation, Jonathan performed the fastest sprint of his life, almost skidding into the large hallway where the girl of his fantasies stood smiling.

It was like a dream. Despite his ability to form articulate sentences, Jon could barely breathe, yet alone speak. The drink had not materialised, nor had the snack but, instead he had had the most remarkable, spectacularly beautiful sensation he had ever experienced in his seventeen and a half years. Although it had lasted only a couple of minutes, his smile spread from ear to ear. Not only was Jenny superbly fit and agile, amazingly intelligent *and* beautiful, she was seriously hot as well. Hotter than any volcano, or even the sun, she had made a man out of a lad in a few spectacular minutes.

Jon couldn't remember his walk home, nor the ticking off he received from his father for being late. All he could remember was the soft touch of her lips, her silky flesh and the most incredible sensation as he climaxed in the throes of passion with the most beautiful girl in the whole of Royal Tunbridge Wells.

From that moment on Jennifer Paige and Jonathan Davies were an item. They would spend every free moment together, revising. Every lunchtime, they would huddle on an old bench at the back of the school, trying to sneak the odd kiss here.

Jonathan's peers could not understand what the hottest girl in the school saw in him, although they surmised that the only thing he had over them must have been tucked inside his underwear. Jennifer, however, was falling hook, line and sinker for Jon – although she kept cool, as she knew that in a few months they would go their separate ways.

Following a number of interviews at various universities, Jennifer had made her choice. She would read English and wanted to become a teacher. Like Jon, she was passionate about language, in particular modernist poetry and the cultural contexts of literature. She hoped for a place at either St Catherine's or St Anne's College and figured that, being in Oxford, she would be close to major roads and motorways and, hopefully, wouldn't have to travel too far to meet Jon at weekends.

Up to now, Jon hadn't thought past university. Being so laid back did have its disadvantages and, following constant nagging from his parents, his teachers *and* Jennifer, he actually put some serious thought into his vocation in life. He liked people and for some reason that he could not comprehend, they liked him too. He was also a great listener; he knew that, especially now he had a girlfriend: God, could she talk. He adored English; he could do the same degree as Jennifer, maybe? Jonathan considered that option carefully, remembering the peace and quiet he yearned for. As much as he cared for Jen, he still needed his own space from time to time.

He'd made one decision then: he would not apply to Oxford. He was bright, loved listening and was completely fascinated by the human body. *Good Lord*, he thought, shocking himself. *I could be a doctor!* Sure, it would take years (although he hadn't got a clue quite how many years it would take) and it would cost him a small fortune. But it was what he wanted to do.

"Jen," he exclaimed during their usual lunchtime snogging session on the bench, "I'm going to be a doctor."

"More like a psychiatrist," she giggled, brushing her hand over his floppy fringe and pecking him on the cheek.

And so, on that bright-skied, sunny afternoon in April, Jonathan made the biggest decision of his life with his incredibly perceptive girlfriend.

She did better than he did in A-Levels, and attained the four A grades she had wanted. Jonathan didn't do so badly: three As and a B, and a place at one of the top medical schools in the United Kingdom for the next six years of his life.

Oxford!

* * * * *

16. HELP ME

1994: Elise

She could hear a beeping sound but she had no idea where it was coming from. It was pitch black and her mind was a whirlpool, with incoherent thoughts rushing through her head.

She didn't know whether she was dead or alive.

"Where am I? Help me – please."

She forced her eyes to remain closed, too terrified to open them and discover that she was in hell.

She felt a piercing pain from something sharp, then felt a jolt of electricity pulsate through her body.

"Think of something nice, Elise."

Everything went dark and for a short while, Elise was reliving her former life. Her very own fairy-tale with her idyllic life and beautiful prince…

It was a perfect day. The air felt so clean and pure. Elise wandered towards her lovely house, smiling at the friendly faces and waving at the children as they ran home from school. She skipped with joy through the winding paths then across a large park with tennis courts, anticipating the excited reaction she would get from David. He was, without any doubt, the best thing that had ever happened to her apart from – well, apart from today, when she had heard the most incredible news *ever*.

Elise had never really believed that anybody could ever replace her nan – that was, until David came along and swept her off her feet. She recalled daydreaming – as a child in the darkness of her cold bedroom – of a fairy-tale prince who would rescue her and take her away from the wicked witch that kept her prisoner. And, although *she* had actually escaped that night from her evil captor, her prince had been there and had taken her into his arms, rescuing her from that terrible woman and her terrible life.

She rubbed her stomach, finding it hard to believe that, instead of the stomach bug she thought she'd contracted, inside her was a tiny little being, a baby. A little miracle for her and David, made from complete and utter love.

They had only been together for a few months, but that didn't matter. Her heart skipped a beat every time she saw him, and his kind gentle voice sent shivers down her spine. She loved the way he would kiss the nape of her neck, stroke her face, and tenderly kiss her eyelids before she went to sleep. He'd even bought her a big teddy with a huge love heart on its chest that would protect her every bedtime when he wasn't there.

David sometimes had to work long hours and stay away from home. He had a very important job, she knew that much, and occasionally, when he had tight deadlines, he would work through the night to get the job done on time and meet his customers' expectations. That didn't stop him from calling Elise every few hours just to remind her that he was thinking of her and was missing her like crazy.

"Oh, and by the way," he would say before finishing the call, "did I tell you how much I love you?"

He got her every time, and every single time he said that lovely little phrase, her heart melted.

She had never felt so special. David had given her something that she had never believed in her wildest dreams would come true and now, it seemed, the fairy-tale had just got even better.

She ran into the hallway and burst through into the front room. David was sitting on the sofa, bouncing his son on his knee and singing a daft song to him. Tommy was giggling hysterically with his dad as, every now and then, David would slip him through his knees, pretending to drop him, then catch him before he hit the carpet. It was a simple game that they both enjoyed, and Elise's face lit up as they played so innocently, demonstrating their love for each other.

Placing Tommy on the sofa, David popped on the TV, fed a video into the VCR and hugged Elise. "So how's my baby?" he asked, wrapping his arms around her waist and pecking her on the lips. Smiling like a Cheshire cat, Elise moved David's hand to her tummy and gently placed her hands over his.

"Your baby is exactly six weeks and two days old, and he or she is doing absolutely fine," she replied, almost bursting with elation.

David was silent. His eyes met Elise's and a single tear sat in the corner of his left eye, then trickled down his cheek. He held her gaze for a moment longer and studied her. Then, gathering her into his arms, he held her closely, kissing her frantically on her neck, her lips and then her tummy.

Elise smiled warmly at Tommy, who seemed to be oblivious to his father's actions. Although she hadn't known the child for long, Elise had grown very fond of him and wondered how he would adapt to his new life with a half-brother or sister. He didn't appear to suffer from jealousy: when he first met Elise, he had simply smiled at her and asked whether she was going to be his second mummy! She secretly hoped that she would be kinder than Tommy's birth mum who, since having an affair and leaving David for her lover, had become obsessed with money and screwing David financially – despite him being the innocent parent in the break-up. Tommy remained engrossed in *Toy Story* – until, that was, his dad and Elise popped his jacket on him and took him out for a treat. To Tommy, it was the best meal ever. He had always loved Pizza Hut – and, wow, to get a pudding too, with a real ice-cream machine and as many sweets as he wanted? It had to be one of the best nights of his life! He also quite liked this lady, despite her silly haircut. When they told him he would soon have a baby brother or sister, Tommy liked that idea too. It would be cool to have somebody to play with at Daddy's and he couldn't wait to tell his mum when he went home later.

Elise, although only in the very early stages of her pregnancy, had a little bump already. Because she was so skinny, she showed early, and every day she would look in the mirror at her new shape and smile. She had also stopped smoking, which, funnily enough, had been quite easy. Every time she had craved a smoke, she would strip off her clothes and look at her tiny bump, picturing her baby, who now had tiny arms and legs and a face, and a daft nickname – Blob. That took away any urge for nicotine, and soon she never even thought of cigarettes.

With the money she had saved from stopping smoking, she would buy provisions and clothes for Blob. The staff at Mothercare knew Elise by name now. She would catch the bus into town, do David's banking then wander round her favourite store studying prams, pushchairs, blankets and clothing. She had enough romper suits in pink and blue to clothe a dozen babies, and had never considered buying a neutral colour such as white. But none of that bothered her or David. She washed each item by hand, folded them neatly and placed them in the hand-made baby drawers in the spare bedroom.

It was a Tuesday morning when David received his first call of the day from Elise. She'd usually call during what she perceived to be his tea break (at 10 a.m. – although he never took breaks, but didn't have the heart to tell her so), but today she rang at 9 a.m. He ran to the phone, immediately worried that something had happened to his princess, or little Blob.

She was breathless as she excitedly told David her news. "It's like a butterfly, David, you would never believe it. Blob flutters all the time," she exclaimed. He wished he could go home right now and hug his little angel. David was consumed not only by adoration for this remarkable woman, but admiration too. After all she had gone through, with her years of torment and pain, she was so easily pleased and so incredibly perfect. He decided then and there that he wanted to spend the rest of his life with her.

It was the third trimester of her pregnancy and Elise proudly wore her dungarees, which emphasised the size of her huge bump. She had decided to challenge herself to decorate Blob's nursery after studying numerous baby books and wanting something different from the teddy bear and lamb wallpaper available in DIY stores. It was by chance that she came upon her idea; Tommy was watching *Bambi* when Thumper jumped across the screen.

"That's it!" she yelled excitedly, staring at the screen in front of her, "Bunnies – Blob will love bunny rabbits, and Thumper will be looking down on Blob's cot when he or she is sleeping."

David smiled lovingly at Elise who spent hours designing the room to scale on graph paper, drawing squares on the bedroom wall then painstakingly painting every rabbit body, ear and tail, plus hills and trees, to perfection.

After three weeks, the nursery was almost complete. Standing back approvingly, Elise summoned David to join her upstairs and, with a fine brush in her hand, invited him into the room. "Close your eyes," she said, before dipping a brush into her paint pot.

With the pink paint, she drew the word *Mummy* just below Thumper's feet, then, taking the blue paint pot, she painted *and Daddy* next to it. Then in bright red she wrote *love,* with a heart, and finally, in blue, *you.*

Standing next to David, she told him to uncover his eyes. He scanned the amazing portraits along each wall, then saw Elise's final contribution. It was so simple, yet beautiful, and, once again, he wept with joy as he stroked her bump and looked at Blob's beautiful room. Her brown eyes were filled with pride.

But David had a surprise for her too! Guiding Elise down the stairs and outside, then opening the rear door of his work van, he asked Elise to close *her* eyes. She laughed at her boyfriend copying her.

"You can open them now, Elise," David said excitedly.

Standing in the cold evening air, she shivered in anticipation of her surprise, before opening her eyes wide. The cot was white, with hand-crafted spindles. On the back of the cot, Thumper, carved from the same oak and painted to match hers on the bedroom wall, was smiling broadly and looking down at where Blob would sleep. The opposite end of the cot had a perfectly formed Bambi with huge eyes, a little button nose and a cute little tail.

With eyes like saucers, she stroked each spindle with her delicate fingers and felt the contours of the top railings. The tears streamed down her cheeks as she admired this work of art, knowing that David had been working overtime – not for his customers, as he'd said, but for her and their Blob.

"David," she whispered, smothering his face with kisses, "Thank you. Thank you. I have never, ever received anything so beautiful in all my life. I love you, David, and I always will."

Meeting her tear-filled eyes, David fell to his knees, kissed her bump and held Elise's hands. "Elise, my darling – will you marry me?"

She had never expected anybody to want to spend the rest of their life with her. She had been brought up to believe that she was completely unworthy of any form of love or affection, and that she would be lucky to find a friend mad enough to put up with her, let alone a husband. Yet, as her baby kicked inside her tummy and the stars shone brightly down on her, she was being asked by the most wonderful man in the world to be his wife.

"I love you so much, Elise," he whispered again after she had immediately accepted his proposal. They excitedly agreed to plan the wedding after the birth of Blob then have a nice holiday somewhere in Cornwall or Devon in a little cottage with Blob and Tommy. They'd have a real honeymoon when the kids were older, but neither of them cared. Just to be a happy family was enough – and in Elise's case it was a dream come true…

* * *

The pain was excruciating. Her stomach heaved and her back felt as though red-hot pokers were being forced through her spinal cord, snapping her vertebrae one by one. Her breathing was laboured and beads of sweat poured down her face. Her heart was pounding so hard that it felt as though, any moment, it would explode into a thousand pieces. She felt sick – not just nauseated, but violently ill, just like she used to when she was little and Mummy had fed her some bad food by accident. She felt the bile rising, bursting into her throat, and she threw up all over the bed.

The agony. Jesus, this is something else.

She shook – but not from cold. This was something new that she had never experienced before. Her whole body was going into spasm, her arms thrashing, her mind swimming with hysterical thoughts, her brain craving relief.

"For God's sake, help me," she screamed. "Help me out of this nightmare."

* * *

The noise from the machine gets louder and the bleeps accelerate. Alarms ring and a lady's voice speaks nearby. The girl slips in and out of consciousness.

"She's in cardiac arrest," the nurse yells.

"She's in shock."

Electricity pumps through her heart.

Her body jumps spasmodically.

Bleeping again, this time slowly.

A continuous monotone noise.

Straight, symmetrical lines on the monitor.

An angel is looking down at the dead girl, who has tubes coming out of her.

White light.

Nan and Leroy watching, begging her to return to her body.

The angel jumps back into the dead girl.

More tubes being forced into her veins.

Counting.

"One."

"Two."

"Three."

"Stand clear!"

Her body jolts.

The lines on the screen are moving again.

Relief.

"She's back with us."

"Jesus, no, we're losing her again."

Parallel lines on the monitor.

A continuous tone.

"Adrenalin!" they yell.

An injection, then paddles on her heart.

"One."

"Two."

"Three."

"Stand clear!"

Bleeping again.

Lines moving on the monitor.

Faceless people watching intently.

"No change – she's stable."

A man's voice: "Thank Christ."

"Blood pressure?"

"140/60."

"Sats?"

"Low. She needs more oxygen."

"Temperature's high, doctor – 39.6."

"Hydrate her, and fast."

"How's the baby?"

"She's still pregnant – no blood loss."

"Just keep her with us."

"Yes, doctor."

Doors closing.

Bleep. Bleep. Bleep.

A man's voice: "Hello, can you hear me?"

No reply.

The man checks her pulse.

"She's still in shock."

"Nurse, report any changes to me immediately."

"Yes, Dr Davies."

The nurse updates the girl's chart.

She checks the monitor.

A man's voice, speaking again. "This can often be the case with a drug overdose. The withdrawal stage is the hardest."

"Keep a close eye on this one, please. It's not just one life here, remember."

"Yes, Dr Davies."

A door closes.

Bleep, bleep, bleep.

The girl moves.

"Leroy!" she screams. "Is that you? Leroy, for God's sake, please help me. I need your help!"

She pulls frantically at the IV lines.

Disorientated. "Please, Leroy – I'm begging you. Just one last hit. One last shot. I'm frightened. Where am I?"

Her body thrashes.

She is burning up.

A nurse restrains the hysterical woman.

Her eyes open.

Confusion.

"Where's Leroy? Help me – please."

A nurse holds the girl's hand.

Bleep. Bleep. Bleep.

"You're in hospital," she says. "You are very poorly but you'll be fine after a while. You've overdosed on heroin. It was a close call. You will get better, so long as you stay calm and allow us to look after you."

"Nan? Where's Nan? Where's Leroy? I need them both."

"Your nan? What's your name, sweetheart? We need to contact your next of kin. Can we call your nan?"

Memories of the paramedics in Leroy's flat.

Stark realisation that Nan and Leroy are dead.

She remembers her dream.

"Dave? Blob? Where are you?"

Her heart rate increases.

A man enters the room.

"Hello," he whispers. "My name is Dr Davies. What's yours?"

"Elise."

The girl shudders with terror.

She pulls at the line in her hand. "It hurts – take it out."

A man's voice.

"Well, hello, Elise."

A doctor checks the IV line. "You've been through a dreadful experience. Try to stay calm. We'll work out how you can overcome your addiction and get well again. After all, you've got your little one to consider as well, Elise."

The girl's eyes open wide.

Confusion.

The doctor points to the tiny bump under the white bed sheet.

"Thankfully, your baby appears to be okay."

"Baby? What baby?"

"Your child, Elise. You're approximately three months pregnant."

"No. I can't be. This can't be happening to me. No more. Let it end. Just let me die, please."

Her blood pressure increases.

Temperature – 40.1.

Darkness.

* * *

Jonathan knew from the horrified expression on the woman's face that she had no idea she was expecting a child. Elise was slipping in and out of consciousness, and he asked the nurses to keep him updated on her progress.

He lowered his head, removed his gloves and thanked the resuscitation team. Jon ran to the men's toilet and soaked his face under a cold tap. *Jesus*, he thought, replaying the events of the horrific afternoon he had just been involved with. *If this if what training to be a psychiatrist involves, I don't think I can do it.*

His second year's placement in a hospital was nearing an end. He picked up the telephone, and rehearsed his words to Jennifer. "I can't do this anymore," he said silently as the telephone rang and rang. "This is too much pie."

"Hello?" said an out-of-breath voice. Jen had just run up two flights of stairs to grab the telephone.

"Jen," he whispered, "thank God you're home."

"Jon, what's up? Are you okay, sweetheart?"

"I need to talk. I need to see you now."

With that, she replaced the receiver, jumped into her battered Mini and drove at top speed to Jon's bedsit close to the Luton and Dunstable Hospital. She knew that this was serious as, in the past seven years Jonathan had never asked to talk. Sure, he chatted to her all the time, but he had always coped well with stress, never offloading his worries onto anybody else. But today he sounded desperate and alarmingly upset.

The journey took just over two hours and, as she hammered on the door of his dingy bedsit, Jon dashed to open it and threw his arms around Jen.

"Oh, thank God you're here," he sobbed, wiping his nose with a drenched tissue.

"Whatever is the matter, Jon?" she asked, tenderly wiping his eyes with a fresh Kleenex from her jacket pocket. Sniffing loudly, his red, sore eyes met Jennifer's.

"This girl today. Jesus, Jen, I've never seen anything so dreadful."

He threw his aching body into an armchair and poured himself a glass of vodka. "Want some?" he enquired before gulping down a large mouthful. Jennifer declined and sat on the arm of his chair, listening intently while he spoke through his tears.

"As if an overdose wasn't bad enough," he continued, bowing his head. "It was her little emaciated body. God only knows how she's survived; she is so painfully thin."

He stroked Jennifer's brow and looked at her pretty face and healthy body; a stark contrast to the shocking image that kept replaying through his mind.

"Oh Jen," he said softly. "You've never seen anything like it – bites, bruises, and Jesus Christ, the…"

He stopped talking and held Jen closely, tears welling again before he continued with the gruelling account of his afternoon.

"Oh God, her scars," he whispered, feeling his stomach heave. "Deep, hideous scars from the base of her spine down her buttocks, on the back of her neck and," he paused, taking a deep breath, "she also has burn marks, like cigarette burns, all over the inside of her legs and pubis. I have never seen anything so horrific in my life."

Jennifer thought of her wonderful, carefree and protected life. She wiped Jon's eyes again and poured him another drink.

"She's suffered so much. It looks as though half of the bones in her body have been broken and left to heal on their own," he added, slugging down another mouthful of his drink. "And the scars I mentioned," he looked directly into Jennifer's eyes as he said it, "They were deliberate, Jen. I have no doubt about that." His eyes glazed over as he continued.

"But," he croaked, "they were hidden from view. Whoever did this to this poor woman did not want them to be seen. They made sure they only burned her where the burns wouldn't be noticed. The monster who did this to her should be shot."

Jen was shocked at Jon's reaction. Up to now, he had always remained calm, no matter how much pressure he was under. He'd even remained composed during their recent wedding, despite Jen falling apart from nerves at the altar.

"She's the worst abuse victim I have ever seen," he whispered, taking a slug of vodka straight from the bottle. Jen held her husband's hand as he snuggled close to her.

"And Jen," he sobbed, meeting her eyes, "I don't know what to do. How the hell can I ask her to give up her only relief – drugs – when, if I had suffered a quarter that this poor woman has endured, I would be exactly the same as her? I'd rather be dead."

Jennifer, like Jonathan, had no appropriate answer. No magic wand could wave away these problems. There simply were no words available to describe how they both felt.

"Poor kid" was all she could say, trying to imagine the agony the girl had suffered. It was impossible.

"Yes," Jon replied, "Poor woman, and poor little baby growing inside her."

"She's pregnant too?" Jen asked, horrified at the thought of an innocent baby already being addicted to drugs.

"Yes," replied Jon. "Christ knows how – there's nothing of her, but she's pregnant. I just hope to God that it was consensual and," he added, looking vacantly out of the window, "that the baby hasn't been affected by the drugs."

Jen shuddered, joined Jon and also took a large mouthful of the vodka.

"What now?" she asked.

"I can't do it, Jen. This training wasn't supposed to become *pie* and, for six bloody years, it was everything I had dreamed of. I've seen some awful stuff, as you know, but this? Jen, how on earth can I help somebody like this poor woman? I'm not God, and I can't perform miracles, which she sure as hell needs. I just can't go on doing this."

Jennifer completely understood. She had never seen Jonathan this upset and distressed. Even after losing his father to lung cancer, he had compartmentalised his loss into his pie, grieved privately and filed it away.

His eyes were empty as he slumped into the chair.

"I've always wanted to travel the world, Jen. Will you come with me?"

Smiling tenderly at her husband, Jennifer agreed and held her husband close to her chest. "Anything for you, Jon," she replied. "Absolutely anything. If we decide to settle somewhere permanent, I can teach," she added.

Jonathan smiled warmly at her. He so loved his wife.

"Thanks, Jen."

His pager beeped with a message from ICU.

"She's sitting up now and taking fluids. She also said that she wants to talk to you tomorrow, if that's okay. She says she trusts you."

"Thank you, Alison," Jonathan replied, placing the pager back on to his belt and feeling an enormous sense of relief.

"Looks like our trip is on hold, Jen," he said, pecking his wife on her forehead. Jennifer didn't question him. "Stay tonight with me, please," he added. "I just need some company and a cuddle or ten."

Jennifer stroked his floppy hair away from his eyes and called the head mistress of her school at home. The answerphone immediately came on.

"Hello, Mrs Johnstone. Jennifer Davies here. I am so sorry, but I have a family emergency and won't be in for a couple of days. See you next week."

Jonathan looked at his wife, shocked at her brazen attitude. Jen grinned cheekily at her floppy-haired husband.

"Time for cuddles," she whispered, leading him to the bedroom. He smiled a genuine smile for the first time in eight hours and, as he fell into his wife's arms, made a silent pledge to help Elise.

She trusts you, the nurse had said.

Jon was pretty sure that trust was something that didn't come easily to Elise and he vowed he would not let her down.

And, as Elise stared blankly at the hospital walls, she wondered where that doctor was – and when her nan and Leroy would be visiting her next.

* * * * *

17. UNWELCOME VISITOR

2004: Lizzie

He hadn't chosen to call her, but after five attempts at phoning Lizzie's first emergency contact and getting no response, he had been forced to call Mrs Pritchard. She was listed as one of Lizzie's next of kin and so, he had reluctantly had to report the earlier incidents of the day to this woman.

From his limited knowledge of Lizzie's family, he understood one thing for sure: that Mrs Pritchard appeared to be a contributory factor towards Lizzie's poor mental health and, from the conversation he'd just had with the woman, he could quite understand Lizzie's wish to never speak to her again.

Norman Hillier was pretty resilient. He'd qualified as a psychiatric nurse over twenty years ago and had progressed to a senior position with St Thomas's Hospital, which he generally enjoyed.

After many years of practice, little affected Norman any more. He'd built a protective mechanism that allowed him to switch off as soon as he left the confines of the hospital so he could resume his everyday life at home with his cats and ageing mother. But, as he replaced the receiver, he was actually shaking. Shocked by her reaction, he updated his notebook and opened the window in his office, breathing in the cool winter air.

He'd had no choice, he reassured himself again, closing the window and writing his report. Not only were the rules in place for the patients of St Thomas's Hospital, there were endless rules and regulations for the staff there too. The bureaucracy within the hospital irritated Norman dreadfully but, as he had learned over years of experience, it was pointless trying to avoid the red tape that, he felt, very often inhibited the staff and caused more problems than it actually solved.

He reread his report on the assault this morning, and felt a twinge of guilt. He'd woken up feeling rotten. The chemotherapy and radiotherapy were reducing the tumour in his stomach, and he'd been told that his overall prognosis was good. He would have to have more surgery, however, if the remaining growth didn't shrink any more – but, as with most things, he would worry about that if it happened.

It was the sickness that had drained him. Chemo was never much fun but its after-effects had flattened Norman – and the fact that, this morning, as he was showering, another clump of hair had fallen into the shower tray and blocked the plughole.

He'd gone into work feeling completely fed up and absolutely ghastly. Being quiet and reserved, he didn't really have many people to talk to on a personal level, although he knew that some of the staff seemed to be genuinely concerned about his illness, including Gloria of course. But he was a private man and tried to maintain a professional stance at work, despite falling apart at home on the odd occasion.

Reflecting on the earlier events, though, Norman acknowledged that he should have called in sick. He was tetchy and irritable and, when he saw Lizzie holding Jason's hand, he'd just snapped. She'd been defiant before to Norman, having taken an instant dislike to him following his community group sessions, but this morning she hadn't really done *that* much wrong. Pangs of guilt washed over him when he recalled the innocence of her tender touch with her friend Jason, and the horror on her face at being reprimanded for such an innocent action. But rules were rules, Norman reassured himself – and, lord, if he had allowed Lizzie to hold hands with Jason, the other patients would think that it was okay to do the same. Heaven knows what that could have led to. It was harsh – *he* had been harsh, yes, but, he had to enforce the regulations. Regrettably, Lizzie had been made an example of.

The telephone interrupted his train of thought, then stopped ringing. He thought nothing of it – this happened on a regular basis.

Finalising his report, he turned to the next document, which had to include a blow-by-blow account of the incident. Reading the warnings before he started, including the threat of legal action if it were proven that the accounts of the victim were untrue,

Norman leafed through these and the appropriate disclaimers and checked his answers again. It was as accurate as possible, and he genuinely wished that he could just chuck the paper into the bin and dismiss the event as a misunderstanding. But, as with so much else in this place, he couldn't, and, like the dreadful telephone call he had made earlier, he had no choice. He signed and dated the report and popped it into a brown folder with the rest of the paperwork.

Norman was startled again by the loud shrill of the telephone which, this time, he answered.

"Norman Hillier," he stated, wondering what on earth was going on in the wards. He was surprised to hear the calm voice of Mrs Pritchard.

"Oh, Mr Hillier, thank you for taking my call. I wanted to apologise for the conversation we had earlier – I was shocked, and didn't react well. I would like to see you today and discuss the various options available for Elizabeth; it is of great concern to Mr Pritchard and myself."

Norman really was not in the mood to meet this woman. He was shattered and his nose was smarting from the thump Lizzie had given it. He made his excuses, explaining that visiting time was normally before tea and that tomorrow would be fine.

"Anyhow, Mrs Pritchard," he added, "Lizzie is asleep now and we will not allow her to be disturbed."

The change in her voice had unsettled Norman, and her threats of legal action against the hospital for not managing her daughter's wellbeing made him back down. He knew that Mrs Pritchard was talking absolute nonsense, but he just wanted this whole incident out of the way, including the meeting with Lizzie's parents.

"Okay," he finally replied, frustrated by his weakness, "I'll be here until eight."

"Thank you so much, Mr Hillier," the eerily warm voice on the line replied. "I am extremely grateful for all that you are doing for my little angel. We will be there as soon as possible."

Norman didn't have the energy to even try to analyse the woman. He'd had enough stress for one day. He swept his fingers through his hair; another clump fell into his hand.

This is pointless, he thought, staring at the grey hair before dropping it into the bin. He would shave his head tomorrow and buy a baseball cap. He shuddered at the thought of the patients' reaction in the community sessions but he didn't care. They needed a little humour in their lives.

Mrs Pritchard and her husband certainly didn't hang about. Soon the headlights of the Jaguar swept over the entrance of St Thomas's Hospital and, before he'd even had a chance to do up the top button of his shirt, the entrance system activated the lights on a panel in his office, and the CCTV showed the silhouette of two very differently shaped individuals.

Norman keyed in the code on the number pad and invited Mr and Mrs Pritchard into his office.

"Good evening, Mr Hillier," the small man in an immaculate, but oversized, suit said, in a quiet, shy voice. The woman, who towered above her husband, removed her coat and handed it to Mr Pritchard, who obediently took it and hung it up on the rear of Norman's door. Standing behind a chair, she glared at him until he pulled it out for her and she almost collapsed into the fabric cushion.

Norman, bemused by the strange pair, smiled and offered them a drink.

"We're not here to discuss refreshments," she said while adjusting her enormous dress (which resembled a wigwam, Norman thought). Mr Pritchard quite fancied a cup of tea, and looked longingly at the kettle.

"Yes please," he replied, nervously avoiding eye contact with his wife. "Tea, no sugar and lots of milk."

She tutted and pursed her lips before addressing Norman. "I need to know one thing, Mr Hillier, and one thing only. What form of punishment are you going to deliver to our daughter as a result of today's disgraceful behaviour?"

Norman was totally unprepared for her directness. Clearing his throat, he responded to both parents, meeting their eyes as he spoke.

"It is not about the punishment, Mr and Mrs Prichard. It's more about how we help Lizzie to manage, firstly her anger issues and secondly..." He paused as he reconsidered his word choice. "...Her ability to comply with some of the regulations we have to impose here."

Her mother's eyes almost bore through Norman as he responded. He shuffled in his seat, edging as far back as possible, and continued. Mr Pritchard nervously sipped his tea, almost disappearing into his huge jacket.

"Lizzie, as you are fully aware, has a number of emotional and physiological issues to contend with. On a positive note, she is responding well in her one-on-one sessions with Dr Davies and, in addition to the encouraging outcome of these meetings, she is fighting her bulimia. I am delighted to report that for two consecutive days, she has eaten three meals a day and kept all of them down."

"Oh, really?" the woman said condescendingly. "Don't you realise, Mr Hillier, what a sly, devious little madam she really is? She fooled me for long enough, didn't she, Richard?"

She glared at her husband.

"Yes, dear," Mr Pritchard responded, nodding his head obediently again, still avoiding eye contact with his wife.

"And, anyway, Mr Hillier," she added, slamming her fist on the table, "we are not here to discuss this so-called progress. We are here to discuss what you propose to do about my daughter's outrageous attitude."

Norman had never felt so uncomfortable – his chemotherapy sessions were more pleasant than this.

Standing up straight in an attempt to feel more authoritative, he looked directly into Mrs Pritchard's eyes. "St Thomas's Hospital will manage the appropriate punishments – as you choose to call them. I have removed Lizzie's privileges temporarily and have replaced these with additional support from Dr Davies. And, as she tends to fantasise a great deal, I have suggested that she ceases reading and considers something more creative. This, I believe, will assist your daughter in her recovery."

"So," she bellowed, lifting her enormous body from the chair and pushing her face close to Mr Hillier, "You are telling me that, really, you are doing absolutely *nothing*. Look at your face, Mr Hillier – Elizabeth did that to you and you are simply brushing the whole matter under the carpet. You are letting her get away with her despicable temper fit. I am appalled!" She sneered at Norman. "I'm also scared for you, Mr Hillier. You have absolutely no idea what she is capable of, do you? No idea at all."

"No, Brenda, that's enough," demanded Mr Pritchard, who stood up and was trying to guide his wife back to her chair. Shoving him away with an elbow, she bellowed again. "Shut up, you stupid little man, just sit down and be quiet." Richard dutifully resumed his position in the chair, and Mrs Pritchard turned her attention once again to Norman.

"She tried to kill me, you know." Her silver-grey eyes were tiny slits as she studied her huge hands and fiddled with her wedding ring. Her shoulders slumped and for a brief moment she was silent. Norman noticed a distinct yellow stain on her index finger. She was a heavy smoker, he surmised, as well as a drinker. A waft of her overpowering perfume, along with mint breath freshener, had not eliminated the smell of alcohol on her breath. *Gin,* Norman thought. *She drinks, she smokes – what else is she trying to hide?*

"Did you hear me?" she screamed at Norman. "Don't you want to know the details? How she tried to murder her mother, after everything I've done for her?"

Norman was tired now. He just wanted to conclude the meeting and go home.

"I already know," he replied. "She explained everything to Dr Davies."

The woman's mouth opened wide with shock. This was not what she had expected. *The little cow,* she thought. *How dare she?* Returning to her seat, she widened her eyes and tried to look upset. Her efforts failed.

"It was awful," she sniffed, looking at Richard for sympathy. "Wasn't it, Richard darling?"

"Yes, just dreadful, my dear; shocking," he obediently replied.

Norman was amazed at how pathetic and weak he was. *Stand up to her, Richard!* he wanted to yell at him, but Norman was far too professional and, he admitted, was pretty scared of Mrs Pritchard as well.

It was as though Mr Pritchard had read Norman's mind: he summoned the strength to ask him a question.

"May we see Elizabeth before we leave? I miss my daughter, and would love to see her, just for a moment. I would be most grateful, Mr Hillier."

Norman gave the request fair consideration and responded immediately.

"I'm sorry, Mr and Mrs Pritchard, but no. Lizzie needs her rest and she has had a very distressing day so it's not a good idea to see her now."

Richard stood up again to face Norman. "Oh please," he whispered. "I have no motive, or agenda. I just want to see my daughter, just for a minute ... please?"

It was so difficult for Norman. On the one hand, he felt empathy for Mr Pritchard, who reminded him of a small, lost child. On the other hand, the aggression of the woman towering over both men in the room disturbed him dramatically. He knew, however, that she could not harm her daughter here or inflict any pain on her and so, after reconsidering his decision, he agreed to allow them to see their daughter for a brief moment.

"You must be quiet," he ordered as he led them through a labyrinth of corridors, past some patients in their dressing gowns, then approached Lizzie's room. Quietly turning the door knob, he opened the door and walked softly and deliberately in front of them.

Mrs Pritchard stared in disbelief at the image before her eyes and snatched the sleeve of Norman's shirt. "Why is Elizabeth sharing a room?" she enquired, staring coldly at the fat girl snoring, then in Norman's direction.

The girl stirred, then turned over.

"That's not why we are here," he replied quietly, trying hard not to disturb his patients.

Richard moved slowly forward and took a moment to watch his daughter as she slept peacefully. He studied her delicate features and long eyelashes, and noticed that her hair looked much thicker than before. It was longer, too, almost reaching her shoulders. He could see that although she was still very slim, she had appeared to have gained a little weight.

He wanted to stroke Lizzie's face but resisted, thanked Mr Hillier and left the room, looking back one last time at the peaceful expression on her face. Lizzie was also talking in her sleep, something she had done ever since she was tiny.

Norman gently touched Mrs Pritchard's arm in an attempt to guide her out of the sleeping girls' bedroom. "Just one moment longer," she begged, and bent to whisper something in Lizzie's ear before she exited the room. Closing the door firmly behind her, she pushed Norman out of her way and caught up with her husband.

"Take me home, Richard," she demanded. Norman sighed, grabbed his jacket and walked home to see his cats and his mother.

* * *

Lizzie stirred in her sleep. She thought she'd heard the door close. Blinking rapidly, she rubbed her eyes and stared frantically around the room for an intruder. Then the smell hit her like a sledgehammer. Panic swept through her body.

Her heart thumping hard, Lizzie jumped out of bed and fell to her knees, checking beneath her bed, then Sara's. Nothing. The smell wafted towards the chest of drawers and, after examining behind the unit, the windowsill and again under her bed, she had satisfied herself that nobody was there. The bathroom was deserted. It appeared that the room was safe and, apart from the two female occupants, empty.

It must have been in her imagination, she figured. She snuggled under her covers, and regretted throwing her medicine down the toilet this evening. She clearly still needed it.

The interruption had disturbed her lovely dreams and now, despite hugging her pillow and tossing and turning, Lizzie simply could not get comfortable. It was still early evening. She realised, after plumping her thin pillow for the umpteenth time, that she was not going to get back to sleep.

She looked across the room at Sara, who was still snoring loudly. She had propped her work of art proudly on the windowsill for everybody to see. Lizzie grinned as she tried to work out what exactly Sara had tried to create on the poorly stitched piece of fabric. She gave up and hopped out of bed, turning towards her chest of drawers, remembering her earlier encounter with Jason.

Lizzie ignored the smell still wafting around the room. Checking Sara again, she tentatively opened the drawer where she had hidden the top with Jason's gift. The drawer creaked slightly, but Sara still remained asleep. She picked up the top, and hid in the bathroom, sitting on the tiles with her back to the door. Although she knew why they wouldn't allow locks on doors, it was at times like this that she wished there was a bolt she could use. Privacy, it seemed, along with so many other simple things, was a luxury inmates were not permitted.

The item chinked and Lizzie tried to imagine what it was. She knew that all she had to do was pull it out of her pocket and open her eyes but trying to guess, running her hands over the item, made the event far more memorable. She thought back to the rare happy occasions of her childhood when she'd received a beautifully gift-wrapped parcel and, rather than rip the paper off, she would spend ages prodding the package, shaking it and trying to guess what was inside. Now, realising that any moment Sara could wake or a nurse could enter the room, she yanked the object from her sweatshirt pocket.

It was a very simple piece of jewellery. The chain, although not Lizzie's taste, looked like silver and was so delicate and fine she figured it would snap quite easily. The detail of the locket, however, grabbed her attention. It looked like a ball or something circular. Lizzie stood up and switched on the light over the bathroom mirror so she could see the object more clearly. Holding it up carefully, she examined the necklace, only to realise that what she had thought was a ball was in fact a little fairy. Upon closer examination, Lizzie noticed some tiny italic letters. As her eyes adjusted to the still poor light, she read the words. They read, *Thank you Lizzie. 2004.*

* * *

To most people, being wide awake at 3 a.m. would feel like a major injustice but to Norman Hillier, this was usual. He'd been an insomniac for nineteen years and, until then, like most of the human race, had slept blissfully for at least seven hours a night.

It was working shifts during his nursing training that had thrown his body clock out of synchronisation and, at the time, Norman cursed his body when it would refuse to sleep, despite feeling physically exhausted. But after a few months of complete disarray, constantly drinking black coffees and despising the night shifts, Norman resigned himself to the fact that this was how life would be and simply got on with it, as he did most things.

However, now Norman relished the fact that, when most folk were sleeping, he was wide awake, and actually enjoyed those bonus hours he acquired through his lack of sleep. His favourite time of the year was spring and summer as, when he woke, so would the birds, and he would enjoy their beautiful song as others slept through it.

So this morning really wasn't much different to any day of Norman's life. He would enjoy the peace and solitude of his private world for at least another three hours, tend to his mother, then walk to work.

But something unsettled him. Norman tried to distract himself by shaving the remaining tufts of hair from his head. He tossed aside the electric razor, rubbed in the foam and shaved, very carefully, until he was completely hair-free. Rubbing his now shiny head with a towel, he studied his unfamiliar reflection in the mirror. He had never really liked his appearance; his face was too thin and his small hazel eyes were too close together. So, really, losing his hair wouldn't make much of a difference to the odd-looking chap staring back at him.

Norman continued his early morning chores, planning the evening meal and checking his diary for mother. She would be happy today. Norman had arranged for a friend to collect her and take her to a day centre where she would have some company, drink cups of tea, chatter about how different things were *back then* and generally skip back three generations. His mother enjoyed reminiscing about her younger days, and would constantly remind Norman not to waste food and to be economical with the heating and gas as, any day now, there could be another war and rations would once again become everyday life. He didn't take any notice of her frugal ways and turned on the central heating to take the chill out of the room.

He still had a few hours of peace left. Norman decided to finish off his notes from the previous day. This was not unusual as, in the early hours of morning, there were no interruptions whatsoever. He balanced his notepad on his knee, grabbed a pen and started to document the meeting between himself and Mr and Mrs Pritchard. It was an extremely articulate account of the meeting, and Norman meticulously wrote precise details in neat handwriting, avoiding emotions or his personal interpretations of the couple's body language. That was, until he reached the section during which Mrs Pritchard had accused Lizzie. Her words replayed in his mind time and time again. *She tried to kill me, you know.*

Of course, he hadn't reacted to her. That's precisely what Mrs Pritchard had wanted when she had declared that her daughter was a potential killer – as well, he recollected, as being *sly and devious*. But the nagging doubts he had felt earlier were back, and he now understood why he had felt so unsettled. *Her* body language had been off. During the meeting, Mrs Pritchard had been a dictating, aggressive and controlling woman – *until* she had played her trump card and had failed to get a reaction from Norman.

He thought of two possible reasons for her submissive manner after her allegation: she had not provoked the shock reaction from Norman she had anticipated or, heaven forbid, she was telling the truth. Norman shuddered as he wrote the final account of his meeting, knowing that this document, along with the others, would have to be presented to the hospital's management team – and, equally important, to Jonathan Davies. But he knew that he had done the right thing, as the vision of Mrs Pritchard staring down at her hands and nervously fiddling with her wedding ring replayed in his mind again and again.

* * * * *

18. PROGRESS

Jonathan and Jen had agreed, after receiving their A-Level results during the summer of 1987, that they would only see each other during weekends while studying at Oxford. It had been a very simple and logical decision – both needed to concentrate on their studies in order to achieve their ultimate goal, a first-class degree. In order to accomplish that, they would resist the temptation to spend their days in bed and would actually do some work instead.

And so they spent the summer before starting their degree courses relaxing in the sunshine, making love and – much to Jon's annoyance – working. Although the last thing he wanted was to be apart from Jen, Jonathan had decided to get a job during the summer break. He had no choice; he needed the money if he was ever going to enjoy a social life at university.

Despite receiving a grant for his studies and his parents providing Jonathan with the first month's rental for his accommodation (which *was*, they had reinforced, ten years' worth of Christmas and birthday gifts), he was penniless. He was only too aware that, as well as feeding himself, having to pay £40 rent a week and paying for his own clothes, the books alone for his medical degree would cost hundreds, possibly even thousands, of pounds.

Although he had never done a day's gardening in his life and didn't have a clue what the difference was between a flower and a weed, Jonathan had decided that, rather than sit cooped up in an office all day, he would like to work outdoors. He subsequently managed to convince some of his old school friends that he, as well as being a great listener, was in fact the equivalent of Percy Thrower. And so, having given himself a crash course in the art of gardening and design, Jon tossed aside his old encyclopaedia, borrowed his dad's tools and gloves and started a very temporary career as a landscape gardener.

It was on his first day as a gardener that he realised his ridiculous mistake. Jonathan had cycled through the busy streets of Royal Tunbridge Wells to a leafy, affluent-looking avenue. Every home was individual, with winding drives, cars he could only ever dream of owning, and huge, ornately landscaped gardens. His first contract was through one of his peers at school whose father was a stockbroker. Jon in his naivety, when asked whether he could tend to gardens, had jumped at the opportunity. After agreeing an extortionate fee, he looked forward to earning the equivalent of his first month's rent in the space of just a few days.

The minute he knocked on the door and observed the body language of the scantily clad woman in front of him, Jonathan immediately sensed that gardening would not be his sole responsibility. He had always been very perceptive.

The lawn mowing was something else. Jon had been used to watching his dad struggle with a heavy old manual mower but, as he soon realised, his dad's machine belonged in a museum and the new electric hover contraptions were the only way forward. After almost electrocuting himself, Jonathan learned not only the basics of electrical safety, but how to fix severed wires in record speed, and with an audience. Mrs Milligan simply would not leave Jon alone and followed him constantly, which not only distracted him from his gardening but bothered him deeply.

The thought of the next two days of being followed by some flirtatious, sex-starved housewife horrified him – although later, when he told his pals at university, they constantly reminded him what a great opportunity he had missed. He soon learned why, when they forced him to watch *The Graduate*, but that day, escaping from this house was his priority and he worked extra-long hours to finish the work ahead of schedule.

After tending to the ornate flower beds and managing to remember the difference between chrysanthemums and dandelions, Jon managed to dodge the endless offers of drinks and snacks from Mrs Milligan, trim the conifers and tend to the tomatoes in the greenhouse before finally collapsing in a heap on the neatly striped lawn.

She didn't hang around. In fact, Jon believed she should have been an athlete instead of a housewife, as she sprinted across the lawn to him. Puffing and panting before sitting cross-legged next to Jon, she tried to seduce him with words, but failed miserably.

"He doesn't understand me," she said – of her work-obsessed husband – to Jon, pouting and looking down at her slender legs, then studying Jon's crutch invitingly. Jon at this point seriously reconsidered his career choice, fearing that he would attract nymphomaniacs instead of genuine cases, but disregarded it in moments.

"Caroline says that you're going to Oxford to study medicine," she added, moving closer to Jon and pulling her skirt up even higher.

"Yes," he replied, nervously and deliberately avoiding eye contact with her. She clearly needed something to fill her time – other than young men. After explaining that he wanted to become a psychiatrist, however, the woman clammed up, made her excuses and ran back to the safety of her home.

Jon was never asked to return, but was given a £50 bonus if he promised not to mention their little conversation. He never did – until the effects of too much vodka after a disastrous rugby match resulted in him telling three pals. He reminded himself to stick to beer in future.

His next job was at the local Wimpy restaurant. Jon worked two shifts a day, taking a few hours' break in the afternoon to meet Jen, then working as chief burger flipper from 4 p.m. until closing time. The money, with the overtime, soon mounted up and, before he knew it, Jonathan had saved a grand total of £1342 – and ten pence. This would be enough to buy the books he needed and pay for his accommodation, which he had now arranged. It was located within the grounds of Merton College.

Jenny had not been forced to find a job as her parents were not only funding her degree but had also paid for her accommodation in the halls of residence of St Anne's. It was a stark contrast to Jonathan's financial situation, but he felt no jealousy, just elation that they had both got through the gruelling selection process and were fulfilling their dreams.

Oxford had been everything that Jonathan and Jennifer had expected. Although he had never shown any great enthusiasm for architecture, Jonathan had to admit that the historical buildings in

Oxford were quite remarkable. The combination of the ancient architecture mixed with more modern designs seemed to work here, and he spent many an afternoon in the university parks, which were often filled with poets and musicians performing. Jen was also in her element, as the library within Merton College dated from the thirteenth century and had a priceless collection of early books. Fascinated not only by literature but history too, she was in seventh heaven and, despite the pomp, Jonathan was happy too.

The years of lectures and assignments flew by for Jennifer, and her hard work paid off. She attained a first-class degree and then did a one-year PGCE course at Oxford. During this, she had classroom experience in a local comprehensive school, which she loved. Finally, she secured a job at a local school and although the salary was quite poor, it felt like a fortune after the years of financial hardship at Oxford.

After paying the bills for her small flat, she gave the rest to Jon, who still had three years left at Oxford, two years of foundation training (as a junior doctor), then another three years of learning and applying the skills of psychiatry. Jonathan would sacrifice eleven years of his life in order to achieve his dream – and Jen, the first five years of her marriage. Life was sometimes lonely for her but, as always, she thought of her husband, knowing that they would enjoy a bright and prosperous future.

* * *

2014: Beth

Although proud of the certificates and accolades on his office wall, Jon rarely looked at them; they simply provided reassurance to his clients that he wasn't some back-street shrink.

It was the large family portrait positioned directly above his desk that Jonathan felt most proud of, and he smiled at it as he entered his cosy office. Jennifer, as always, looked stunning and his daughters, Rebecca and Chloe, looked, thankfully, nothing like their father, except for their smiles. Setting aside his memories of that wonderful day in London, he slipped into work mode, opened his diary and retrieved the files of the clients he would be seeing today. Studying the name of his first client, he thought back to the day he had met her and how, all these years on, he was still a constant in her life and she a constant in his. She really was an amazingly determined woman.

Beth tapped on his door, and Jonathan welcomed her with his usual warm smile, making her a coffee with three sugars.

Beth closed the door behind her and sat on the comfy green chair in front of Jonathan's desk. Jon, fiddling with his laptop, which he had never got the hang of, looked towards the door.

"No Dave, Beth?"

Beth smiled at him. "No Dave," she replied. "Although he's waiting in the car for me – just, well, just in case. He's also using the time to do some quotes for some big contract he wants to win," she added chirpily. Her huge eyes met Jon's as he passed her the coffee and sat back in his chair.

Well, she certainly looked healthier than the last time he had seen her. Her hair was the most noticeable change; she'd had it styled into a neat, shoulder-length bob and, from his experience with Jen, he knew that she'd also had some highlights. Her well-groomed hair glistened as the winter sunshine filtered through the large bay window in his office.

"So," Jonathan said, "how have things been since—" He looked at his notes. "Gosh, it's been almost two weeks since our last meeting."

Beth studied her hands and newly polished nails. She had mastered the art of French polishing, and proudly held them up to show Jonathan.

"I learned how to do this," she smiled, placing her hands back on her lap.

"Well done, Beth, they look great. Did it take long to master? It looks fiddly."

She thought back to when she had first come up with the idea and cringed, recollecting the spilled pink varnish on her carpet following her clumsiness. The fact that she had hysterically thrown the remaining white nail polish across the bedroom after the first disaster, then had emptied the contents of her other varnish over the bed linen, made her shudder with embarrassment. Dave, of course, had had to buy not only a new carpet but an entire bed linen collection, something he could ill afford, he had told her.

"No, not too bad," she lied, sipping her coffee and avoiding eye contact with the doctor.

Jonathan studied her reaction and knew immediately that she had not told the truth. A classic symptom of lying is when someone scratches their nose and Beth, wide-eyed, had scratched hers twice.

Returning to his questions, he faced his client. His features were warm but he was serious.

"And your medicine, Beth. How's that going?"

"Fine," she lied, "just fine."

"No side effects?"

"Just one."

"Like?"

"Sickness."

Beth's stomach heaved again. The earliest days had been the worst, and had almost stopped her from taking the dreaded pills. She had felt dizzy and then been sick. The germs had disturbed her. However, almost two weeks on, she had learned to accurately time her dash to the loo, which was imperative and always occurred precisely 53 seconds after the head-spinning had stopped. For the past few days, however, she hadn't thrown up. She guessed that her body was finally getting used to the new medication.

She told Jonathan, who leafed through his notes again.

"I can change them again, Beth, if the side effects are too much."

"No," she replied. "I think I'm getting used to them now and, as the sickness is easing, I'll carry on with them for a while and see how it goes."

"Good, Beth, but any more vomiting, you call me immediately and I'll change them right away."

"Yes, Dr Davies."

Beth was peckish and looked towards the wooden filing cabinet.

"Biscuit?" he smiled, grabbing the tatty tin and placing it in front of Beth. Opening the lid, he pointed to the custard creams and grinned that cheeky grin of his. "I got those in just for you."

Beth looked at him in confusion. She hated custard creams. If they were the last biscuit on the planet, she wouldn't touch them with a barge pole.

Jon was surprised when she took a plain digestive.

"No custard creams today then, Beth?" he laughed.

"It wasn't me who liked them," she replied, picking at the corner of her digestive. "*They* liked them."

"They?"

"Yes, them." She winced. "My friends."

She thought of the girls and their mischievous ways. They would always pull the biscuit halves apart and lick the cream. It hadn't been Beth.

"I miss them," she said sadly. Beth placed her biscuit neatly on the desk which, no doubt, had trillions of germs on it.

"You miss them, Beth? Why is that?"

She spoke softly, lowering her voice almost to a whisper. "They were my only friends and they protected me from – from everything bad, really. I'm scared most of the time now and, without them hanging around, I'm also incredibly lonely." Beth thought of the hours at home when, to fill the emptiness, she would clean and scrub every nook and cranny, just to give her something to do.

Jon moved his chair away from his desk and closer to Beth. She continued. "It's like, well, giving up smoking or drugs or something like that."

Jon couldn't really comprehend this, as he had never smoked or touched drugs. He had, however, seen the effects of withdrawal endless times before, so could understand how hard it was to quit.

"You wouldn't understand," she added, removing her boots and lifting her legs underneath her bottom. This was a good sign. Jon smiled.

"Carry on."

"I know that, every day, I have a set routine, Dr Davies. It involves a shower, cleaning the shower afterwards, having a coffee then my first cigarette of the day. It's the first one that sets me up for the rest of the day and I feel" – she struggled to find the right words – "I feel just, nice, sort of ready for whatever I have to do next. The crazy part is that I don't smoke it all; just one puff is enough.

"Now, if you took that cigarette away from me, I wouldn't feel ready. My brain would be craving the nicotine constantly and

I would be angry and cross. I wouldn't be able to think straight and the rest of my day would be wrecked."

Beth took a sip of her now-cold coffee, which tasted revolting. She gulped the cold liquid, cleared her throat and continued. "But if I knew that another cigarette was sitting there in a packet and could be smoked any time I wanted, well, I would be fine. I probably wouldn't need to smoke it, but would feel reassured knowing that it was there – just in case."

She looked up and laughed. This explanation sounded so ridiculous!

"I haven't really explained myself very well," she added. "But… well, the cigarette; imagine that the cigarette is, *was* my friends."

She squinted, trying to describe her feelings more eloquently. She wished that she could speak better English, like Jonathan, but she had missed so much schooling she struggled with English, along with almost every other subject.

"*They* were always there, Jonathan. Every waking moment of the day. When I was feeling strong, I would ignore them. I could hear them for sure, but I would walk straight past them with my nose in the air." She recollected the countless times they had called her a *stuck-up bitch* and had tried to distract her by causing trouble.

"But it was the bad times, the awful OCD days, when I really needed them."

Beth uncoiled and pulled her boots back on. She opened her handbag and snatched the cigarette packet and lighter from the top.

"I'm sorry, Beth, you can't smoke in here."

Although never a smoker, Jon did not necessarily agree with this new Law. He knew – heck, did he – of the medical consequences of smoking, but his clients often needed relief during their meetings and Jonathan felt that this was their crutch at times of anxiety.

Beth reluctantly removed the unlit cigarette from her mouth and scowled at Jonathan.

"You can go outside if you like – I've got plenty of time. Here, take this."

Jon passed Beth his coat, noticing that she was only wearing a thin jumper.

Throwing it back at him, Beth glared at the not so nice doctor and slammed the door behind her.

Jonathan was, however, pleased with the progress he had seen. She still had a long way to go, but the fact that she had felt strong enough to even speak of her friends was an enormous milestone. He leafed through his files and realised it had been eighteen months since she had mentioned them. The fact that she had even compared them to her addiction to nicotine was admirable.

The door reopened and Beth returned to her seat. She was shivering.

"I'm sorry about that," she said, embarrassed. "I always find it hard to talk about – to explain – my delusional behaviour."

She studied his face for his reaction and, as Jonathan's pupils enlarged, she felt relieved. He had acknowledged what she had just said, and she was proud that she had used the complicated word in the right context.

"Well done Beth – again," was all Jonathan could say. He was a little shocked that Beth had taken the time to research her condition. He figured she must have looked on Google or some other website.

"I have been doing a lot of reading," she added, "about my condition. And, although it is so hard, Jonathan, I'm slowly making progress. I know that I'll never get better, though, not until I—"

She stopped talking.

Jonathan stood up and moved the chair on the other side of his desk next to Beth's. Pulling it closer, he faced her then sat down.

"Beth – now listen. There is no miracle cure for many illnesses, but with the right medication and, in some cases, the right support infrastructure, people can lead a normal life."

"Like me?" she questioned.

"Like you, Beth."

She liked this doctor. Her friends had warned her about him and planned to murder him. Smiling, she told him that.

"They wanted me to kill you, you know."

"Your friends?" Jonathan felt a little uneasy.

"Yes. They told me that you were trying to murder them, *and* me, and that you should be… killed. Then Dave as well." She shuddered at the thought. "He was as bad, they told me, and so, every night, before they went to sleep, they would plan how we would all get rid of you."

"How?" he asked feeling rather nervous.

Beth felt uncomfortable, recollecting when she had stabbed Dave in the stomach – and the other times. Jesus – the other times she had sought revenge…

"It doesn't matter," she replied, shifting her body as far from Jonathan as possible. He moved his chair back, giving Beth the space she needed.

"Clearly, Beth, it did matter – at the time."

"At the time, it seemed to be real. I even considered finding your home and doing something bad."

"Bad?"

"Yes, bad."

"Like what?" Jon's heart was pounding. He thought of Jennifer and his daughters.

"Like cutting your brake pipe or putting a potato in your exhaust. Something like that." She bowed her head in shame.

Jon remained silent.

"But," Beth added, "I never did and I'm pretty sure that when it came to it, I would have chickened out. I nearly always would. Even if I had tried, it would have gone wrong. I'm a failure at everything I do. And always will be." Beth closed her eyes, reminding herself of how hopeless she was.

You hopelessly pathetic little bitch. You can't even get that right, can you? Can you? Is there anything you can do without failing? No, of course not. You can't do anything right. Oh bless, she's crying again – aah, look everybody, look. Smile for the camera, little baby. Aah, diddums. Useless – that's what you are – useless.

Her eyes opened wide. She remembered where she was. A single tear made its way down her cheek and she brushed it away with her hand.

"Tissue?"

"No, I'm fine," she replied, fighting back the tears. "I mustn't cry."

Why not?"

"No reason."

'Daddy's gone a hunting'

Beth looked tired and strained. Jon moved back to his desk and checked the time. She still had another fifteen minutes, but she'd had enough and really should get some rest.

"I don't want to go quite yet." Beth looked at Jonathan, watching the clock. She had read his mind, it seemed.

"I'm not finished."

"Okay, Beth, as long as you feel comfortable with this. It can't be easy."

"It's not, but I need to do this, Dr Davies."

"You do, Beth – yes."

"I need to ask you something."

"Go ahead."

"It's about Christmas."

He looked at Beth, anxiously recalling their last meeting.

"Yes, Beth – are you still planning to have everybody over?"

"That's the problem," she replied, looking at her nail and resisting the temptation to nibble the end. "I'm not sure I'm ready." Beth turned away to stare out of the window. The sun was still shining and the clear sky was baby blue. The frost had disappeared, and the stark trees stood, waiting for the warmth of spring to wake them from their long winter sleep. Beth loved the spring.

"I need to do it." She stood up and walked towards Jonathan, her whole body slumped. "I *have* to do it."

"Why, Beth?" Jon was genuinely concerned about the pressure she was putting herself under. It seemed too soon. Far too soon.

She thought of the girls and why they had been such an important part of her life for so many years. She could have done with them now.

Friends? You don't have any friends, you silly little child. Nobody likes you. I don't like you. So why would you want to have a birthday party? So you could sit alone, sniffling over your birthday cake that nobody wants to share with you? Oh, I get it. I understand – your imaginary friends will be there. Your stupid pretend friends. Even they'll abandon you once they see how pathetic you are. Why celebrate the birth of a lunatic? Crazy, crazy little brat. I wish you had never been born.

'To get a little doggie skin.'

Beth dismissed her painful memories and focused on reality. "A long time ago, during one of our earlier meetings, you told me something."

"What was that, Beth?"

She edged closer to him, wanting to touch his hand for comfort. She resisted. Moving back into her seat, she answered his question.

"You told me that, in order to complete my recovery, I would have to confront my demons." Beth thought of her demon.

'To smother little baby in.'

Jonathan could not remember saying this, but allowed Beth to continue.

"*She* is that demon, Jonathan."

'Stupid, sniffling brat.'

"And until I face her, until I confront her, I will never ever get better; I need to do this and I need to meet her again. It will have to be in a protected environment, and it won't be just her. Kirsty and Robert will be with me, and Dave, along with my dad and some of my other family too. I won't create a scene. I just feel that with the protection of my family I can finally end this torture." She paused and continued, proud of her inner strength. "I deserve to have some peace in my life, as does my family."

Beth thought back to her children. They liked their nan but she knew that they would understand – after Christmas Day everything would make sense.

Jonathan was concerned for her, as well as impressed at the strength and determination she was demonstrating. He had finally recalled a meeting many years before where he had eloquently explained to Beth that sometimes, if you faced the cause of your distress and confronted it, it would help with the recovery process. He had explained that a previous client who had been involved in a serious car accident trembled every time she saw a lorry. She was petrified of every car journey, cowering in the back and screaming at her husband to swerve as soon as a heavy goods vehicle was in her view. She had overcome her terror as soon as she had been persuaded to drive her car in the middle lane of the motorway at the busiest time of the day. From that moment, she no longer feared driving or car accidents. She was indeed cured.

Jonathan could not, however, recollect ever telling Beth to face her demons. He dismissed that part of the conversation and faced Beth again, who was gazing out of the window.

"Beth," he said, feeling genuine empathy for his client. "I quite understand why you want to do this. But so soon? Christmas is only a few weeks away, and I feel that you will be putting undue pressure upon yourself."

She thought of the chores she would have to do within the next few weeks. The whole house would need to be spruced up, but a great deal of the food preparation could be done well before the actual day. She would go shopping this coming week, buy the gifts and wrap them. The tree was in the loft, along with the decorations. Dave could do that. She already had her little black dress. It needed to be dry cleaned, but that wouldn't take long. Yes, there was a lot to do, she admitted. But so little time was left.

"Third time lucky," she whispered at the confused doctor. "So little time, and so much to do."

The remainder of the day flew by for Jonathan. He shut down his dreaded laptop computer, having accidentally deleted most of the notes he had typed during his lunch break, then reflected on his earlier meetings, particularly the one with Beth. He crossed his fingers in the hope that she would, somehow, manage to find the strength to face her mother. Beth was an incredibly courageous woman, but this would be the toughest battle she had ever fought. He closed his door and focused on happier things, like the Chinese takeaway he had promised Jen and the girls, uncrossing his fingers as he did so.

After he waved goodbye to his colleagues, Jon started his car. That was, of course, after he had checked his exhaust pipe. The first thing he did, driving out of the car park, was test his brakes.

* * * * *

19. WITHDRAWAL

1994: Elise

Elise had not felt this dreadful for a long, long time. Her headache was unbearable, pulsating through her temples, and her whole body ached, especially her neck, which was incredibly stiff.

Elise was moved out of intensive care after a day. Following toxicity tests, the doctors established that the heroin she and Leroy had taken contained bleach as well as a concoction of other hideous cleaning chemicals. That's what had killed him, she'd been told after finally realising that he would not be visiting her. His funeral would be held in a few days' time, and she had not been invited by his family.

She was lucky to be alive. She recalled doctors telling her so. Elise didn't feel lucky. If this was life, she wanted it to end.

The news of her pregnancy had horrified her and she had decided to terminate the unborn child as soon as she was released. That decision had been easy to make; even this disaster no longer bothered her. She would make her suicide as painless as possible and she would become a statistic on a list. Nobody would care about *her* funeral.

The nurses were kind enough, offering Elise food and drink every few hours in an attempt to build her up. But, again, after consideration, she decided that sustenance would prolong her worthless life so she would starve or dehydrate to death. They would then be able to use her bed for somebody who was actually worth saving.

She buried her head under the blankets, then heard a familiar voice. She could not recall exactly where she had heard it before, but her curiosity got the better of her and she peeked over her covers to discover who this man was. She tried to focus on the tall chap, who was wearing a white coat and had a name tag on the pocket that she couldn't read. He had dark wavy hair. As he chatted with the nurses, he turned to Elise and smiled at her. Bolting under the covers again, she continued to plan her death and hoped that he would forget her like everybody else had.

Fat chance of that.

Jonathan stood at the end of her bed and checked Elise's charts. Her temperature was a healthy 37.1 and her blood pressure was within the normal range again. Apart from the usual symptoms of shock and withdrawal, she was doing well – physically, at least. Her emotional recovery and rehab were going to be tougher. He had no choice. Unless she started taking methadone soon, she could die. Sudden withdrawal could be deadly for a heavy user, which he suspected Elise was, and so, drawing the curtains around her bed, Jonathan said hello and asked for permission to examine her.

"I won't ask how you're feeling, Elise, as I already know." Jon thought back to the previous cases he had seen, all of which, at the initial point of withdrawal, felt absolutely shocking.

"Tell me, do you feel all of these symptoms or just some?" He cleared his throat. "Restlessness, anxiety, cold sweat with goose bumps (that's why it's called 'cold turkey', he added), excessive salivation, tearing and a runny nose, yawning, sneezing, increased genital sensitivity, muscle spasms – kicking movements ('kicking the habit') and finally, insomnia?"

Elise stared back at the doctor. She nodded, although she wasn't too sure what he had meant by the salivation bit. "You've forgotten one of the classic withdrawal symptoms," she replied, meeting his warm eyes. "Depression and suicidal thoughts." She yanked the covers back over herself after he'd finished checking her out. "That's about it," she concluded sarcastically, turning away from the doctor. "I want to die and I don't care less about the baby; can you help me or will I be forced to do it myself when I am discharged?" Her face was far more serious now as she spoke softly to Jonathan. "I want all of this to end, doctor. I really can't take any more. Can you understand that?"

Jonathan did not respond to Elise's question. He knew the answer already and tried to set his emotions aside. He understood alright, having contemplated quitting his career after the traumatic afternoon and having seen Elise's dreadful scars. Instead, he poured her a glass of water and sat quietly by her side.

"Elise, if you want to stop using heroin, then don't panic. There's still hope. It's still possible for everything to turn out well and for you to give birth to a healthy baby, but the best time to do something about it is now."

"I don't want this baby," she replied coldly. "As for coming off drugs, I can't. It's impossible, doctor, absolutely impossible. They're my only form of escape, and I can't give them up. I have nothing else – nothing and nobody."

He moved closer to Elise and studied her as she spoke. It was clear that, although she was speaking about suicide, she could be helped, if she wanted it. Her face was so incredibly sad and her eyes empty.

"Listen, Elise, there is a future without heroin. Methadone is a synthetic opiate prescribed by doctors as a replacement for heroin. At least you know what's in it. You never know what's been added to heroin to give it more volume and more profit for the dealers. Lots of things can be added to street heroin, such as coffee, quinine, talcum powder, sleeping pills, lactose, brick dust, and sometimes even glass particles, which can be deadly." He hesitated. "The heroin you took contained traces of bleach. Methadone won't hurt your baby either, Elise. And as for having nobody, you do. You have a baby inside you that will love and need its mummy."

Elise cupped her hands over her stomach. She would never have guessed she was pregnant. Her periods had been erratic for years and, apart from that one occasion, precisely thirteen weeks ago, she had always used contraception.

"So, if I took this stuff, if I agreed to the programme, will the baby be okay?" She moved her hands away from her stomach.

"I know that it's easier said than done, but try not to worry too much, Elise. You're doing this for your baby – and for your sake as well. The only downside to methadone treatment is the side effects of NAS on the baby and the difficulties of coming off the methadone after the baby is born." Elise looked confused. Now he really did sound like a flipping teacher. "What's NAS?"

"NAS stands for neonatal abstinence syndrome. It means a new-born baby's withdrawal from drugs he or she was exposed to while in your womb. Several drugs can cause NAS, including alcohol, heroin and methadone, and there will be support for you both once he or she is born."

Elise felt less confused but still concerned. How could she bring a child into her world? It was falling apart and there was no future for her, let alone a baby.

Jonathan continued. "If you decide to have *your* baby, Elise, he or she will display signs of distress, such as high-pitched crying, poor feeding, vomiting, diarrhoea, irritability, sleep problems and tremors." Elise stared at him in disbelief. *Poor kid*, she thought – *an addict before it's even born.*

"But," he added, "the withdrawal will only last for a few days, and you can both begin to be weaned off the methadone safely or switched from the Methadone to Suboxone, in order to come off of the Methadone. The doctors will help you both, and so will I. But it's your decision."

Elise was tired and her brain ached from all the information the doctor had thrown at her. Taking a sip of water, she lifted her blanket and studied her tummy. The stark contrast between her first pregnancy and her feelings of elation and how she now felt was almost too much to cope with. She fought back the tears and made her decision.

"When can I start Methadone, Dr Davies?"

"Now!" he replied, wanting to jump in the air and rejoice to the world. But, as he continued with his rounds, he didn't feel so elated. Not only had Jonathan convinced her to try to quit Heroin, but he had almost forced her to bring a child into a world, who would have very little chance of a future – or, indeed, happiness – with its birth mother.

Once again, he reconsidered his future. Was playing God really a part of it?

* * *

Elise managed to nap for a few hours, learning to ignore the noises of the busy ward surrounding her. It was a 'women only' ward. She wasn't sure what kind of ward it was – some of the other women, like her, seemed to be struggling not only with physical ailments but with their emotions too. Along with the constant humming and buzzing of monitors, there was also howling, screaming and crying.

The clattering of the trolley disturbed Elise. The patients were given a warm drink and some sandwiches. She then realised that she could not maintain her hunger strike. Elise had only eaten a bacon sandwich in the past forty-eight hours and, now that she was feeding her little one, she accepted that she should start eating for two. She eagerly awaited her turn and scoffed the sandwiches in a few minutes. They tasted bland, but her stomach welcomed the sustenance and rumbled as it started to digest.

A lady in the bed adjacent to Elise smiled warmly at her, studying her drips and noticing the speed at which she had downed her lunch.

"You in here for long?" she asked, putting her teeth back in her mouth and trying to chew her ham sandwich. Elise grinned as the teeth slipped out and the woman, embarrassed, gave up and wrapped them in a handkerchief. The woman smiled at Elise and offered her remaining sandwich. "Looks as though you need this more than I do," she said, squeezing her rolls of fat and then studying Elise's frail body. Elise rolled out of bed and, pulling the frame with her fluids attached, walked to the bed and thanked the woman.

"Don't tell anybody," she sniggered, rooting through her handbag while Elise ate the sandwich. "This is for later." She passed a Mars Bar to Elise. "Now that you're eating for two, you need to build yourself up, young lady."

Elise looked shocked and the woman, understanding her reaction, lightly touched her arm. "I overheard your discussion with that nice doctor," she whispered. "You're doing the right thing, my love. I was in the same situation as you once, and look at me now." Elise wondered whether she wanted to look like the woman, and offered a simple shrug in response.

"Oh," she laughed, "that's not what I meant. I've had a minor op on my knee. You'll see my daughter this afternoon when it's visiting time – the child that I believed I didn't want." With that, she picked up her book and continued reading.

"Thank you," Elise replied, taking her Mars Bar and returning to the bed.

"It's nothing," the woman responded sympathetically.

Elise felt a little reassured that she was, at least for now, in a medical ward. She'd heard horror stories about psychiatric units and, although she suspected they were exaggerated, hadn't fancied the thought of being restrained on a bed being given electric shocks. While she finished the chocolate, the tall doctor with floppy hair approached her, having completed his morning rounds and found a few spare moments to see her. He looked tired, she observed. In fact, the bags under his eyes were huge.

"Hello Elise, how are you feeling now that you've eaten something?" he said, noticing the empty packet on her tray.

"A little better, thanks," she replied, screwing the chocolate wrapper into a ball and plopping it next to her water.

"Good to see that you've eaten," he added, relieved. "I know you've had a stressful few days, Elise, but as well as your rehab programme, do you feel able to talk further about your – your personal circumstances?"

Elise glared at the doctor. He looked awkwardly at her charts, clearly embarrassed by his ill-worded question. Elise managed a half smile and looked into the doctor's eyes. He flushed, and now she felt sorry for him.

"What personal circumstances?" she replied then, pointing to her stomach, asked whether he wanted to know how she'd got pregnant.

Sensing she was joking, he relaxed and sat close to her bed. "I have a private room just along the corridor, where we can talk about your situation, if you so wish." The lady in the next bed was disappointed that she wouldn't overhear the next instalment and resumed reading her Jilly Cooper book.

Elise felt ready to talk – just a little. She was concerned about where she would live once she was better, and needed to speak to the doctor about that too.

Grabbing the sides of her cotton NHS gown, she followed Dr Davies into the consultation room, which was as cold and as uninviting as the ward she had just left. Jon noticed Elise shivering, and turned on an old fan heater.

"NHS cutbacks," he added, tapping the cold radiator. Elise tried to maintain her dignity, holding the back of the gown together, and hoping the doctor would not see her bottom. Looking in the opposite direction, he paged a colleague with a request to bring a dressing gown. Elise rubbed her hands on her arms to warm them. Stuttering slightly, Jonathan offered Elise a seat and a glass of water. Settling into a rather hard wooden chair, Jonathan regained his composure and asked the question that he had been dreading for the last couple of hours.

"Elise," he mumbled, recollecting the bruises and bites on her body, "I need to ask something that may be a little painful for you."

Meeting his eyes, Elise asked him to continue. She wanted to talk.

"Your baby – the pregnancy. Was it consensual? I couldn't help but notice your injuries, Elise – the bruises and scars. Has somebody been abusing you?"

Elise's mind churned. *Your baby, your bruises, scars, abuse* – all of them simple words but each one brought back horrific memories – other than the conception of her baby, that was. Elise decided to tackle the easy question first, and moved closer to the heater as she spoke.

"I wasn't raped, if that's what you're thinking." She thought of David and the love they had once felt for each other. She continued. "The baby's dad, David, is also the father of my other child and so…."

Elise recalled the nursery, the birth of her baby and the following blissful months, and wondered what he was doing now. When she had left, he was crawling. She wondered whether he would remember her. She hadn't even had the time to take a photograph of him before she'd been thrown out. Her sad eyes filled with tears.

"And so," she continued, struggling to fight the urge to sob, "it was consensual."

The doctor felt a surge of relief run through him, but this didn't last for long. "Was the father a user too? Did he take drugs?"

"No!" she snapped. "David has never touched a cigarette, let alone drugs, and no, he did not abuse me. He loved me. He was my knight in shining armour." Her voice trailed off and Jonathan could barely hear her as she whispered quietly, staring vacantly. Her pain turned into anger as she recollected, then tried to eliminate her once blissful life.

Regaining her composure, Elise continued. "I left *him*, Dr Davies – but it wasn't through choice. The bruises and bites that you seem so bloody concerned about, they're just part of my job. I was a hooker – get it? A cheap, heroin-addicted prostitute who was so frigging high that I didn't notice the bites. David didn't touch me, do you hear? If it hadn't been for *her* I wouldn't have been in this goddamned situation. She destroyed everything, and now she's taken away the only happiness I ever had." She paused. "He and Blob – sorry, Bob – were my life," she sobbed, her anger turning into sadness. She wiped the tears from her cheeks. "We were going to get married, you know, then *she* wrecked it all."

"Who is *she*, Elise?" Jonathan asked, feeling wretched for putting her through this torment.

"My mother," she replied coldly, before taking another mouthful of water and staring at the indentations on her thighs. Her eyes flicked to the door as a nurse passed Jonathan a dressing gown.

"Pop this on," he said, wanting to comfort her but knowing that he could not touch any of his patients, let alone cuddle them. Elise gratefully slipped on the gown and snuggled into it.

"Thank you," she replied as the nurse left the room. The nurse didn't hear.

None of this made any sense to Jonathan. This David chap sounded decent, and the fact that he was going to marry this woman meant he must have cared about her. Unless, of course, Elise was lying. He asked how she had come to be walking the streets. Her response came easily.

"Desperation, doctor. Have you ever been scared and hungry, with nowhere to go and no money in your pocket? Have you ever been alone and had nobody to call, nobody to run to? My life is – *was* – David and my son. When I had lost them, I gave up the will to live, until some guy offered me heroin in return for sex." She shuddered at the memory of that first time. "I don't expect you to understand, Dr Davies – how can you? But I had no choice. For the past three months, I have been an addict – escaping from my crap life, I suppose. It was the one thing that made me happy. And now I don't even have that, do I?"

Although the methadone was doing its job, Elise missed the euphoria that heroin had provided. She also ached from head to toe and realised that the drug must have helped that too.

"Your baby needs you to stay off the stuff, Elise, doesn't it?"

Lowering her head, she agreed. "It's just so hard, doctor, so incredibly hard. And I have nobody to help me through – I'm completely alone."

Suddenly his pager vibrated. Jonathan read his message and made an excuse to leave the room. "I won't be a moment, Elise," he yelled, running towards the Accident and Emergency department.

After twenty-five minutes, Elise gave up and returned to the ward, under the anxious gaze of the woman in the next bed, who was itching to find out the next instalment of her soap opera. Hunching her shoulders when Elise refused to meet her eyes, she continued to chat to her daughter, wondering what the girl and the doctor had been discussing for so long.

It had been a false alarm. Jon had been on call for the past six hours, and had been paged to A&E three times so far. All calls, shockingly, were suicide attempts *or not,* so it had appeared. He was considering specialising in this field of psychiatry, and, therefore, was always called to the scene. The latest patient, a fifteen-year-old girl, had taken too many paracetamol and her worried mother, aware of her daughter's recent mood swings, had wrongly surmised that she had taken the whole packet to kill herself. The girl, it had seemed had simply failed to read the warnings on the packaging and had swallowed a few too many pills. After having her stomach pumped and a charcoal solution administered, she would be okay and could go home the next day. Jon updated the patient's notes and returned to Ward 33, knowing that his other patient would have given up waiting for him and returned to her bed. He was right.

Puffing slightly, he apologised to Elise, who was bored and jittery. She knew it was psychological, though; she had no craving as such; she just felt anxious.

"Sorry about that," Jon said after his heart rate had resumed its normal rate. Elise looked up at him, amused. She had imagined he would be fitter, being relatively young. She had always loathed exercise and felt a bit of a hypocrite thinking that. "So, have you got time to carry on or shall we call it a day?" she asked, looking distantly at the doctor. She wanted to continue with her account of her life. Jon, nearing the end of his shift, was conscious that Jen was waiting for him and more than likely preparing a hot pot – his favourite. He contemplated skipping the meeting then looked at the young woman in front of him, who was begging him with her eyes for some more of his time. "I need to make a call, then we can resume our chat," he replied, dashing out of the ward.

A few minutes later, he returned, looking a little sheepish. Elise intuitively knew that he had been speaking to a female just from his flushed face. "Woman trouble?" she enquired, smiling. Jon didn't respond but a pang of guilt flooded through him.

But Jon, you promised, and I've gone to so much trouble. Try to make it quick, darling – we've only got a few days together before I have to leave. Please, Jon.

He had chosen his career over his wife, once again, but he knew his decision was the right one as Elise walked towards the door of his consultation room and waited patiently for him to join her.

"Where was I?" she asked, turning on the fan heater, which had switched off automatically. Jon recapped their conversation, reminding Elise that, despite her fear of being alone, she would be supported. "We can talk more about that when you're due to be released, but, Elise, why can't you just call David?"

Elise shuddered at the thought and hesitated before responding. "He believed *her*, doctor. She convinced him that I had lied to him ever since we met. He said he can never trust me again, and he doesn't want me to see Bob again either. *She* twisted his mind, saying that stuff. I should have known, really; I was so bloody stupid believing her and convincing myself and David that she had changed. How can evil ever disappear?" she asked, chewing her nails.

"What do you mean, Elise? Can you tell me or is it too painful?" He watched her study the bleeding quick of her thumbnail. "Do you want to hold off for another time?" Jon was conscious that his meal was waiting for him, a glass of red next to it. He yearned to be with his wife.

"No, it's okay, doctor," Elise replied, wiping the blood from her finger onto the white dressing gown. "Where do I start?"

"Where you feel most comfortable, Elise."

"Okay."

Elise started at the very beginning of her life, and told Jonathan the same story she had so recently explained to Leroy. She even told him about the watch in the little pink bag, which were all she had run away with that dreadful night. The watch had remained in her pocket of her jeans for as long as she could remember, somehow it had become her crutch in times of need. She wished she had taken one of Bob's dummies too.

Jon listened intently as she started to well up. Elise was struggling to tell Jonathan about the time she had run away from home – when her mother had discovered Elise with alcohol, and had punished her.

Elise ran her hands through her hair as she recalled that night. "I paid such a price, Jonathan, for stealing that bottle of vodka. But I don't think that was her real reason. Whenever she looked at me, all dressed up and looking pretty, she looked like she hated me. The bottle was just an excuse to punish me."

Elise paused. She had only ever told David this story and the pain still felt as bad as it had then. "She ran up the stairs and pulled me down by my hair. I can remember thinking I'd spent hours getting it to look perfect – it was so long that I could sit on it." Jon smiled. "Anyway, I fell, but that didn't faze her. Nothing did. She just yanked me up by my hair and dragged me into the kitchen, closing the door after her. She always did that so nobody could hear – strange, really, as my brother was fast asleep and, other than us, the house was empty." Taking a deep breath, Elise continued. "I honestly thought she was going to kill me, doctor. The scissors were sharp and were those long-bladed ones – the type you use to cut carpet. They were *really* big." Elise ran her fingers again through her hair. "She didn't kill me – though afterwards I wished she had. Instead, she forced my face down on to the hard worktop and cut clump after clump of my hair randomly from my skull. Sometimes I could feel the blades piercing my skin; other times, she paused, waving them close to my face. When she had finished, she just laughed and threw my lovely hair over me, mocking me and telling me how stupid I looked. I wanted to cry but dared not. Then she punched me in the eye. She forced me to look into a mirror on the kitchen wall. I looked hideous and she knew – she knew that my looks were all I had. Once again, she was victorious."

Jonathan was shocked at Elise's account of events. In his life, he had never been smacked by either parent, and felt hard done by when they took away his privileges, such as chocolate bars, when he was cheeky to them. It was as though Elise had read his thoughts.

"Hard to believe, huh?" she asked. "Well, there's more." She bowed her head, looking almost ashamed. "She passed out soon after, doctor. I could tell as the LP in the living room had stopped, and the house was silent. When she was drunk and awake, it was always noisy as she would bump into things, but it was quiet – deathly quiet. I don't know what got into me, but I wanted revenge after what she had done to me. I looked a wreck and – well, I decided there and then to kill her." Elise paused and studied her sore finger. "I took a load of aspirin from the yellow packet from the bathroom cabinet, and then dissolved them into her full glass of booze. I then added half a dozen paracetamol just to be sure. She'd always slug back the drink the minute she woke up so I knew that sooner or later, it would be over – for her and for me."

Her huge eyes met Jonathan's. "Then I waited. I watched her from the crack of the living room door and, about an hour later she woke up. I can remember how excited I felt, knowing that she would soon be dead. Evil, I know, but I wanted her out of the way – I *really* wanted her to die. She did stir and I thought she'd seen me, but she hadn't (or so I thought). As she sat up, I remember egging her on in my mind to drink that stuff."

Elise's eyes glazed over as she spoke to the speechless doctor.

"She did, doctor, and I watched and I laughed deep in my belly as she gulped every single drop."

Jonathan continued to listen, trying not to react to Elise's confession. He was shocked – in fact, he hardly believed her tale. She certainly didn't look like a murderer, although he knew from his studies that extreme pressure could push even the most placid individual over the edge.

Elise bowed her head as she concluded her story. "It didn't work, doctor. Within a few minutes of her drinking that stuff, she threw up, the whole flipping lot. I'd forgotten about that – she was often sick after a bingeing session. I'd also forgotten how completely hopeless I was. I never could and, I guess, I never will, get anything right."

"What happened then?" Jonathan asked, trying not to show his shock after Elise's confession.

"I got my rucksack, spiked what was left of my hair with gel, piled on the black eyeliner, threw some clothes in a rucksack and sneaked out of the back door as she had her head down the toilet. Then I went to a party – to get drunk and forget everything that had happened. And that's where I met him."

"Who?"

"My knight in shining armour – my David," she replied sadly. "My beautiful David."

An hour had passed, and Jon knew that his hot pot would be either stone cold or cremated. Pangs of guilt flooded through him as he checked his watch.

"Do you have to go?" Elise asked. "I just need to finish, then you can go home." *Home*, she thought, remembering her former home and the warmth and security it had offered her.

"No, Elise, I'm fine. I've got as long as you need," he lied. Elise felt relief flood through her body – she liked this doctor and, more than that, felt she could trust him.

"I could do with a coffee, though," he added. "Would you like one too?"

"Yes please," Elise replied. "White and very sweet." Jon popped outside to the vending machine and selected the drinks after paying for them. Calling Jen again, he explained that he would be a bit longer, and this time she understood.

"Jonathan, it's okay. I knew when you entered the medical profession how difficult it could be and how, sometimes, our plans would be disrupted. Don't worry – is there anything you need?"

Jon felt overwhelmed by the love he felt for his wife. "Jen, can you do me a favour?"

"Sure, Jon – anything for you," she replied.

"Pop into a charity shop, will you, and get some clothes for my client? She's thin and quite short. See if they have some slippers – small ones. And in the bathroom, there's some shower gel I don't use. Look that out as well."

Jennifer understood and questioned him no further. He was referring to the girl he had treated last night, she knew that, and

Jon was trying to help her. She feared, however, that his efforts would be in vain – being a doctor was one thing but playing God was totally different. She worried that, without his even realising it, this woman was becoming a piece of Jon's pie and, worse, a chunk he could not control.

Setting aside her worries, Jen grabbed her coat and pulled her boots on before hopping into her battered Mini, hoping to reach the charity shop before it closed. She guessed the size and hoped for the best – probably a size ten, with size four feet. Then, after recalling their conversation the previous night, she changed her mind and selected a smaller size. *Emaciated,* Jon had said; *you have never seen anything like it.* This was now becoming Jennifer's pie too and she really didn't feel comfortable with it.

Jon re-entered the warm room and passed Elise her coffee. He felt a sense of relief wash over him. Now that Jen was okay, he felt more comfortable speaking to Elise without the stress of time restrictions. Recapping her account of how she met David, she continued.

"So, from that moment on, it felt as though all of my dreams had come true. Of course, once he'd seen me naked, I had to explain my scars to David but he just cuddled me and comforted me, never questioning anything I said. He even bought me a huge teddy to protect me when he wasn't there," she added sadly. How she missed him.

"Elise – the scars. Are you saying that your mother did that to you too?"

"Yes," she replied coldly, remembering the agony she had endured for so many years. "The cigarette burns were the worst, by miles," she added, opening her thighs slightly and pointing to the now faded scars. "I got used to the others, though."

Once again Jonathan sat in disbelief. Elise's account was so matter-of-fact, almost cold. She had clearly become used to being tortured. Covering her legs with the dressing gown, she looked away from the doctor, and fell silent.

Jonathan completely understood. Recalling parts of their earlier conversation, he broached the subject of Elise's mother again. "You said that she destroyed everything, Elise; after all you say she did to you, are you saying that you allowed her back into your life?" None of this made any sense to him.

Elise was an astute woman. "I know how it looks, doctor. She did cause all of those injuries and, yes, like a fool, like the complete failure I am, I allowed her back into my life – and even worse, into David's and little Bob's." She gulped down the weak coffee.

"How?" he enquired.

"Foolishly," she responded, chewing another fingernail. "Bob was only about three months old. It was a nice warm day and he was suffering a bit from colic, so I decided that we'd walk to the park. Then it started raining so instead of walking him in the pram, I popped him into the car and drove. I didn't really know where we would end up, he was crying and the motion of the car seemed to ease the pain. After about half an hour, he'd nodded off and we ended up close to Harpenden. Do you know it?"

Jonathan nodded. "Carry on if you want to."

"So, with Bob sound asleep, I popped him into the pram and went for a wander around the town. It's ever so quaint, you know, with lots of little boutiques and cafes. As he was still sleeping, I popped into a coffee shop and bought myself a cappuccino. Then he woke up." She smiled, remembering the little squeaks he used to make when he was hungry. "This time, though, it wasn't colic; he needed feeding. I knew his different cries, if that makes sense." Jonathan had no idea what she was talking about. "And so I fed him in the corner of the café, and he calmed down straight away. He loved his food."

"So, what happened then?"

She hesitated. "Then *she* happened, Dr Davies. I knew before I had even looked up that it was her. The voice, her perfume – something told me immediately that she was in that room with me and my baby. Bob sensed that I was upset too, and he started to cry again. I was petrified but had nowhere to run.

"Then she joined us and asked if I wanted a coffee. It was pretty obvious that I already had one, and I was feeding Bob, so I couldn't run away from her. Trust me, if I could have, I would have, doctor. I ignored her, wishing that Bob would finish his feed and let me escape. But he was happy and content and she knew it. She had found me again and she sure as hell wasn't going to let me escape from her evil grip."

"How did that make you feel, Elise, being so helpless?"

She snapped at him. "How do you bloody think I felt?" she yelled. "Oh, I was elated and welcomed her back into my life with open arms." The stress was beginning to show and Elise needed a fix.

Jon kicked himself for being so patronising. "I'm sorry."

"Me too." Elise regained her composure. "She told me she was sorry – sorry for everything; the abuse, the yelling, the hair. It was the drink, she said, and she was a recovering alcoholic, attending weekly sessions with a shrink and going to Alcoholics Anonymous." Jon shuddered; he hated the word *shrink*.

"She then took a little peek at Bob and I can honestly say that I saw a tear in her eye. She didn't let on, but I saw her wipe her face when she turned away. Then she asked me how old he was, and his name. I didn't want to tell her – I was so frightened. I knew that she'd sneer if I told her his nickname, so I told her the truth, so that she wouldn't laugh at me."

Elise wiped her own tears as she spoke. "She looked different, doctor. She had taken the time to dress nicely and her hair was shiny and in a bun. So, after she begged for forgiveness, I eventually backed down. I said she could see us once in a while if she promised to stay off the drink, and it would *always* have to be in a public place – and she agreed. For the first few weeks I kept it a secret from David, then I told him." Elise bowed her head in shame.

"How did he react, knowing your history with your mother?" Jon felt like kicking himself this time, believing that, yet again, he was being patronising. Thankfully, Elise didn't notice his red face.

"He went mad, doctor, and forbade me ever to see her again. I'd got her telephone number and he rang her, threatening to report her to the police and telling her to stay away from me and his baby. He was furious; I had never seen him so angry, until…"

"Until what?"

"Until, until that…"

Elise's head was pounding as she tried to continue with her account of events. She wished she hadn't been so stupid. She missed David and little Bob desperately. She yearned to hold her baby and missed his lovely baby smell, which made her heart skip a beat every time she cuddled him. As the fan heater kicked into life, Elise was bought back to reality.

"She convinced him that she was better, too; that's the scary bit, Dr Davies. David isn't stupid like me; he's always been astute and perceptive, but she did it alright and before we knew it, the weekly trips to a coffee shop became regular visits to the house – *our* house – to see us all and spend time with her grandson. Without me knowing it, she was formulating her devious next move. Why does she hate me, Jonathan? You don't mind me calling you that, do you?"

"Of course not, Elise. Whatever you're comfortable with."

Jon reached into the pocket of his coat and pulled out a Bounty. He was starving and had abandoned all hope of eating within the next few hours. Unwrapping it, he offered Elise one of the bars. She was surprised at his kindness and nibbled at the chocolate before starting the coconut section.

"Thanks again, doctor, you're so kind." She took a deep breath and continued, staring directly into Jonathan's blue eyes.

"I had become a bit worried a few days before. David was looking at me a bit differently, and I couldn't put my finger on why. He was still as affectionate, but there was something in his eyes – something cold – and it worried me. I'd ask him what was wrong and he'd snap back, blaming work or the fact that he hadn't had a good night's sleep in months. But I knew it wasn't that; he'd been fine with Bob and had never complained about work in the past. What bothered me most, though, was that he'd spent time alone with my mother and, ever since, he'd been acting strange around me.

"And then he postponed our wedding. I was totally distraught. It was our future life together and I couldn't understand why everything was changing. He'd bought me loads of bridal magazines and had promised me the fairy-tale wedding I had always dreamed of. *My little princess,* he had said a few weeks before, *would have her fairy-tale wedding – and soon.* There was no limit on how much I could spend, but to be honest, so long as I had the dress and the two men in my life, I would have been happy marrying him in the garden!" Elise finished her chocolate bar and continued.

"He'd been secretly watching me, Dr Davies, although he didn't realise that I had noticed. I'd learned to creep around my mother and sense when she was near, when I was a little girl. And so, whenever I was alone with Bob, he'd be there, very quietly observing me. Then, out of the blue, he called the wedding off too. It was all too much. I snapped, and begged him to tell me what was wrong and why he was being so unkind to me.

"I have never been as devastated as I was that evening. For the first time in our relationship, he shouted at me. He said I was a lying, scheming little cow who just wanted him for his money and that for a while I'd fooled him. And the scars, even the ones here" (she pointed to her bottom) "he said they were all self-inflicted too. I was an attention-seeking, lying, devious bitch who had wormed my way into his life and had deliberately got pregnant so that I could trap him into marriage."

Elise curled her body under the dressing gown and yet again had to wipe her tears away. "But the worst was still to come, doctor. She hadn't played her ace card yet."

"What do you mean by that?"

"She'd been over to our house just the day before and had bathed Bob and put him into his cot. He was sobbing and it wasn't his hungry or colic cry, but when David and I ran upstairs, she was stroking his face and singing a lullaby to him. We went downstairs, believing it had just been colic – which, as you know, he suffered from.

"That wasn't the case, though. I should have known better. I should have followed my instincts." Her heart raced and she fidgeted in an attempt to get comfortable on the hard chair.

"*She* had deliberately hurt my little Bob. The injury was hidden from view, just like mine were, and it wasn't until David changed his nappy that he noticed the mark. My darling baby had been injured, and it was all my fault, Dr Davies – all my fault." Elise recalled David's reaction as he burst into the living room, a look of hatred on his face.

Your mother warned me about your violence, Elise! But I didn't believe her; I loved you so much and I had believed you – but now, oh God, now I know she was telling the truth. Why would she lie? She had nothing to gain, did she? But you, oh, you had everything to gain, didn't you? I've been such a gullible idiot. And to think I was going to marry you. Jesus, what a fool I've been! How could you, Elise – how could you hurt my baby?

"I couldn't believe what he was saying, doctor. She had twisted everything so beautifully; she was always so convincing, what with her posh voice and everything. I tried to tell him that, but he refused to listen to me and carried on shouting in my face."

For once, Jonathan didn't ask any questions. Elise continued to speak.

"He said, Oh, your mother was so right about you, Elise. You tried to murder her once, so she knew what you were capable of, didn't she? But now you've injured our little boy, it's over. Get out, you cheap little bitch, get out and never, ever come back. Do you hear? I will get sole custody of my son. Just pack your bags and go. Get out of our lives, Elise – leave us in peace. I didn't leave, though. I begged him to tell me what she had said. He mentioned the drink and how my mother had told him that I'd tried to poison her after she had made a mess of cutting my hair: she lied, doctor. It wasn't an accident. It was deliberate. And so, with nothing but the clothes on my back and the watch in my pocket, I left. And once again, I was alone and scared. But do you want to know what the worst thing is, Dr Davies?"

Jon nodded. How he loathed her mother.

"The worst thing is that after everything I suffered – the abuse, the violence, the starvation and the emotional torture – nothing could even start to compare to my broken heart. It's still broken," she said. Tears cascaded down her face.

It was impossible for Jon to hide his emotions and for a brief moment, he too felt Elise's sorrow; his eyes also filled with tears. He was not cut out for this and the pie – *his* pie – was now overflowing with 'what ifs'. Once again he seriously questioned his future.

Unable to console Elise, he passed her a tissue. After her tears had passed, he took her back to the ward. Her nosy neighbour was fast asleep.

"Elise," he whispered tenderly. "You will get him back. Justice can and will be done, you know. You will have that fairy-tale wedding."

She didn't believe him. She huddled under her bed covers, and stroked her tiny bump before closing her eyes. "It's just me and you now, little Bump, just me and you." She imagined the tiny baby inside her womb. And, as she drifted into sleep, instead of dreaming about fairy-tale castles and princes, she dreamed of revenge. Someday, somehow, she would repay her mother for all the evil things she had done. Not to her – she didn't care about herself. However, she did care about her darling David and her precious little boy.

But first she had to get better.

* * *

Jonathan was physically and mentally exhausted, and welcomed the sight of the tatty green door of his bedsit. Turning the key, he burst into the front room, to find Jen snuggled up on the sofa, fast asleep, a book in her hand. She stirred and smiled at her husband, sleepily rubbing her eyes.

"What's the time?" she asked, sitting up and trying to focus on the shattered-looking man standing in front of her.

"It doesn't matter, sweetheart. Come on, let's get you tucked up into bed. I'll join you in a minute."

Wobbling as she made her way to the bedroom, Jennifer passed her husband a carrier bag. "There are some clothes in there, and I hope they fit, but Jon, more important than that, I've been doing some research this afternoon."

Jon stood in front of his wife who, despite her bedraggled hair and sleepy eyes, looked beautiful and innocent. He stroked her face; she smiled warmly at her husband.

"There's a charity in a village close to here and they help people just like your patient. It's a rehabilitation place where the residents have their own privacy but earn their keep by working in either a café or in their second-hand furniture shop. I could call them, Jon, and, if you agree, and you can convince Elise, they might even agree to meet you both with a view to possibly accepting her on their programme. What do you think?"

Jon could not think any more. He was drained. But as her words sank in, he held his wife closely and kissed her lips longingly.

"Have I ever told you how much I love you, Jennifer Davies?"

"Yes, you have, Dr Jonathan Davies. And as I have said endless times to you, my sweet dopey husband, I love you too."

Jonathan snuggled close to Jen listening to her heartbeat and gentle breathing as she fell asleep. Once again, through her compassion and kindness, she had convinced him that his career choice was the right one. He hoped that the charity project could help Elise, or even take her in, but, something was nagging at him. He left his sleeping wife and drank a neat vodka after collapsing on the sofa in the living room.

He thought back over his meeting with Elise. Jon couldn't help but question why, for the first time in his life, he felt bitter. This was more than pie – this was a new emotion, and it frightened him. Downing another mouthful of vodka, Jon hoped his feelings towards Elise's mother would disappear; he already despised the woman as much as Elise did.

And that's what worried him the most.

* * * * *

20. TRUST

2004: Lizzie

After bathing and dressing his mother, Norman fed the cats and heated the milk for his mother's Weetabix.

He prepared the stew for their evening meal, peeling the potatoes and chopping the carrots and onions, reminding Mother to check the pot now and again to make sure it didn't go dry and to stir it once in a while. She had been too preoccupied organising her photographs for the old folk to see on her visit to the day centre today to take any notice of him and so, after kissing her on her powdered cheek, Norman popped on his bobble hat and started the short walk to St Thomas's Hospital.

Although not one to feel self-conscious, Norman was aware that his head attire was unusual, and he toyed again with the idea of buying a baseball cap during his lunch break, but decided against it. He needed some humour in his day, and looked forward to the giggles and sniggering of his patients after his dreaded meeting at 8.30 a.m. with his superiors and Dr Jonathan Davies.

* * *

If Jonathan had known how hard it would be for Jen to get pregnant, he would have saved a fortune on contraception. After yet another morning of peeing on a stick and crossing their fingers, they were despondent when they read the negative result. Neither he nor Jen could understand why. They were both healthy, and Jen was extremely fit. "Maybe I'm overdoing it at the gym," she said, after throwing the test in the bin. "I could be putting my body under too much strain doing gymnastics – perhaps I should try something more relaxed. Maybe yoga?"

"Yoga sounds good," Jonathan replied, wanting to scream with anger at the injustice of their situation. He'd seen many patients over the years who only had to sneeze and they would fall pregnant. He'd counselled women who had terminated their babies, for various reasons. Yet that is all he and Jen had wanted for the past two years. They had been precisely timing each lovemaking session, eating the right foods, and reading endless articles about conceiving, yet their wish had not been granted.

Breakfast had been a silent and uncomfortable affair, both stirring the cornflakes around in the bowl, allowing them to go soggy then chucking them down the sink. Jon knew from Jen's fleeting looks at him that she suspected it could be Jon's fault, although he felt it was hers. The statistics of their families said it all. Jen was an only child and Jon had four siblings! However, tossing aside blame for a moment, they shared a strained smile and resigned themselves to the fact that they would have to try even harder at making babies this month.

"Anything for you, Jen," Jon replied playfully after she suggested abandoning the ovulation chart and just *going for it* most evenings. With a cheeky grin, he waved goodbye to Jen and set off on his drive to St Thomas's Hospital. He didn't turn around to smile, though, as he reached his car: he didn't want Jen to see his face, which showed his upset.

The traffic was unusually light for a Tuesday morning, and he arrived at the hospital forty minutes early, something that was absolutely unheard of for him: as well as being famous for his lousy coffee-making abilities, he had a reputation for being late for practically everything.

Norman Hillier, still in his coat and a strange hand-knitted bobble hat, nodded at Jonathan and checked his watch. He asked Jonathan to join him in his office at half past eight for a meeting with management. Jonathan had no idea why Norman was asking him, but agreed.

Abandoning his thoughts of Jen, Jon ran towards his office. "Give me five, Norman. I'll just grab a coffee and join you. Is it really important? I could use the time to sort out my schedule for this morning." Jon hoped that it could wait, as he wanted to buy Jen some flowers to cheer her up.

"Yes, Jonathan, I'm afraid it's important," Norman replied, removing his hat to reveal a shaved head.

From the expression on Norman's face, Jon could tell that something was eating away at the chap. It could be that the cancer had spread, he thought. Grabbing his coffee, Jon took the short walk along the corridor and knocked on Norman's office door.

"Come in, Jonathan," Norman answered quietly, looking at his reflection in a small wall mirror. After replacing his bobble hat, he sat down and offered Jonathan a seat; he retrieved some files and checked some of his notes.

"Jon, I'll get straight to the point," he said, meeting the doctor's confused eyes. "As you are well aware, as part of the protocol within this hospital, whenever an offence or – as in yesterday's case – an assault occurs, specific guidelines must be adhered to." Norman subconsciously rubbed his nose, which was still tender from the thump, and resumed checking his notes before continuing.

"As you know, Lizzie can be rather hot-tempered and we have, in the past, disregarded some of her actions due to her, well, her troubled history."

Jonathan nodded in agreement. Lizzie certainly could speak her mind, as he well knew.

"However," Norman added, "due to the injury I sustained yesterday, we have no choice but to document the events and review Lizzie's mental health programme. I hope you'll agree to additional sessions with her, Jonathan?"

Once more, Jon nodded, wondering why he had been summoned to Norman's office to discuss what was pretty obvious.

Norman stood up and strode towards the large window in his office. It was a bright day, and he watched the car park below as it started to fill with cars and people. He turned towards Jonathan, looking rather sheepish. "I held a meeting yesterday with Lizzie's parents, Mr and Mrs Pritchard, following the assault on me." Norman tried to continue but saw from Jon's body language that he would be interrupted. He was absolutely correct.

Jonathan leapt out of his chair and joined Norman. His eyes were enraged and made Norman feel extremely uncomfortable. He had never seen this side of Jonathan, and he felt intimidated by the normally placid doctor, who was staring coldly at him.

"Did I hear that correctly, Norman? You had a meeting with Lizzie's parents here, without my knowledge and permission?"

Jonathan studied the cars, wishing one of them contained Mrs Pritchard, and he could let rip at her for all she had done to Lizzie. Without allowing Norman to respond, he paced around the office. "You do realise that Mrs Pritchard is the reason that Lizzie is so ill, don't you, Norman? She subjected Lizzie to years of abuse and torment, and almost killed her on several occasions. Why is Lizzie back here again, Norman? Didn't you consider any of that before picking up the telephone? She is the last person you should have called! Didn't you think about reading her notes and calling her boyfriend first? For heaven's sake, what were you thinking of? Her mother, of all people."

Norman lowered his head in shame, wishing that he'd persisted with the first emergency contact. Removing his hat, which was making his head itch, he edged towards his chair and looked sadly at Jon.

"You'll understand my reasons for being forced to discuss the events with Mrs Pritchard once you've had an opportunity to review these documents, Jonathan." He passed Jon the large file containing all the paperwork and opened it for him. Jon chose to disregard Norman's hints that he read them now – he would read them when he had calmed down.

"But that's not why I've called you in, Jon," Norman continued, finishing his tea and retrieving a handwritten note from his jacket pocket. Rereading his account of events, he placed his head in his hands.

"Lizzie's mother made a statement – or an allegation – that disturbed me, Jonathan." His voice sounded strained, and Jon felt a pang of guilt as he studied the bald head of the very sick man in front of him. He shouldn't have snapped – heavens, if Norm could fight cancer with such dignity, Jon sure as hell should be able to cope with his personal problems. It was ridiculous. They were overreacting. A baby would arrive at some point.

"Norman, I'm sorry for snapping."

"Me too," Norman replied, lifting his face from his hands and giving Jon a tired smile. "I'll continue, if I may?"

"Yes, go ahead."

"She – Mrs Pritchard – made an allegation about Lizzie. Initially I dismissed it. As you are no doubt aware from Lizzie's case notes, her mother is dictating and controlling and extremely manipulative. But on this occasion, I regret to say that I believed her." He lowered his head again, remembering how Lizzie's mother had nervously fiddled with her wedding ring.

"Believed what, Norm?"

Norman stared at the notes on his desk then cleared his throat.

"She made an allegation that her daughter had tried to murder her. Despite his apparent weakness, Mr Pritchard agreed with her. I chose to ignore her comment, telling her that you already knew, but the more I thought about her statement, and after observing her body language, the more I actually believed her."

Jon remained silent.

"You do understand, Jonathan, that if such an allegation were proven to be true, Lizzie would have to be removed from St Thomas's to a more…" he hesitated, "a more secure unit?"

Jon fidgeted in his seat, his eyes fixed on the office window. A large black cloud was blowing towards the hospital, blocking out the sunshine.

"We won't have a choice, Jonathan. If Lizzie did indeed attempt to kill her mother, she would be considered a serious threat, not just to the other patients but to the staff here. I will therefore be forced to recommend a full investigation – unless, Jon," he hesitated, "unless you're prepared to assist me with *my* enquiry." He coughed quietly as he concluded. Jonathan's eyes widened and met Norman's.

"I am prepared, in light of the progress Lizzie is making, to ignore that element of my discussion with Mrs Pritchard – if you can talk to Lizzie and try to establish whether there's any element of truth in what her mother's alleged. Lizzie trusts you and has, to the best of my knowledge, always been very open and honest with you."

Jonathan was speechless. His heart was pounding and he hoped that Norman couldn't hear it.

"And so Jon, can you find out for me please? I desperately want to disregard it as another of Mrs Pritchard's attempts to punish her daughter, but I do need you to agree to me handling the situation this way. I'm also fully aware that I'm contravening all the hospital's safety regulations, and could face disciplinary action if I'm found out. If *we* are found out."

Jonathan was thinking about earlier meetings he'd held with Lizzie, but heard every word that Norman had said. He also needed to consider the implications.

"Jonathan, are you listening?" Norman shouted. "Can you do this for me?"

Jonathan knew so much more about Lizzie than anybody else here, and nodded at Norman.

"Of course I will, Norm, but on one condition."

"What's that?" Norman enquired nervously.

"You shred that document right now," he ordered, looking at Norman's handwritten notes.

"I will," he replied. He straightened the crumpled piece of paper and shredded it. "I trust you implicitly, Jon," he said, offering his hand to the doctor, "and I know that you'll find out the truth."

Jon shook his hand and left Norman's office, knowing that Lizzie trusted him far, far more.

What had she said to him recently?

I trust you so much, doctor. Sometimes I feel that you're my only friend in the world and I can tell you everything. I can, can't I, Dr Davies? I know that you won't tell anybody about my little secrets, and they'll be safe with us. Thank you for understanding, doctor. If only more people did.

Trust was something that Jonathan had been recognised for during the whole of his personal and professional life and he was respected by many people for his honourable actions.

Right now, he didn't trust himself as he faced the biggest dilemma of his professional life. He closed his door and called Jen, who was a little chirpier than she had been and was heading off for work in a few minutes.

"Have a good day," she added, after reassuring Jon that she was fine.

"I will, Jen," he replied, not meaning it.

* * *

Despite the earlier disruption to her sleep, Lizzie awoke feeling refreshed and content. She opened her hand, in which she still held the delicate chain and locket, and smiled. She would thank Jason during breakfast and show her gift to Gloria later. She might even take it into her meeting with Dr Davies, as he always showed an interest in her life.

Sara stirred and rolled over to face Lizzie. Rubbing her sleepy eyes, she flicked her gaze towards her masterpiece and, realising that Lizzie hadn't hidden it, felt a huge sense of relief.

"Morning, Sara." Lizzie hung the chain around her neck, trying to secure it, without success.

Sara hopped out of bed and skipped towards Lizzie. "I'll help you, Lizzie," she said, lifting her hair out of the way of the chain and securing it easily. As she let go of Lizzie's hair, Sara stared, horrified, at her neck.

"Who did that to you?" she asked. Lizzie pretended not to hear her, and fiddled with the locket.

Sara returned to bed and tucked herself under the covers before continuing her interrogation. "Did you have an accident?" she asked, as Lizzie imagined the fairy breaking free and flying across the sky. She was distracted when Sara removed her bedding, revealing her chunky legs.

"Me too," she said, running her finger along a deep purple scar from just under her knee to halfway down her calf. "I don't really remember too much about how it happened, but it was enough to be put into foster care. My dad denied it all, of course, claiming it was an accident, but, even though I was only tiny, I remember the terror I felt every time I saw him and how scared my mum was of him." Her eyes glazed over; she re-covered herself and shuddered.

She now had Lizzie's attention, although, having hidden her painful memories for decades, Lizzie chose not to discuss how she got *her* scar. But, through Sara's simple declaration, she now had a greater understanding of why she had been acting so oddly and why she yearned to be popular.

"Did you have imaginary friends too, Sara?" Lizzie enquired as the fairy returned to her chain, following its lovely flight in the clouds. It was Sara's turn to be mute. She continued with her embroidery. She remembered the loneliest days of her childhood, playing tea parties with her pretend friend in Mrs Warner's back garden. She sucked the end of the green thread, knotted it and carried on stitching, deliberately avoiding Lizzie.

A familiar tapping on the door broke the awkward atmosphere as Gloria breezed into the room, smelling of roses and beaming. "Good morning, ladies," she said, opening the blind and allowing the winter sunshine to bounce off the walls. "And how are we both today?"

She placed their medication on the side table, then noticed a familiar smell – one that she had adored for years.

"How lovely," she commented. "Chanel No. 5! So who's the lucky lady, then?"

Sara continued to sew, concentrating hard on the fiddly leaves, but Lizzie, horrified at Gloria's words, reached for her hand for comfort. "You can smell it too?" she asked, believing that she had imagined the scent the night before. Her heart pounded as the realisation hit her. Gloria, surprised by Lizzie's actions, passed her the medicine, which Lizzie gulped down immediately.

"Are you okay, sweetheart?" the kind nurse enquired, before heading towards Sara with her pills. Lizzie felt nauseated but fought the desire to run into the bathroom.

"That smell," she whispered, remembering the endless times the perfume had been sprayed into her throat to sweeten her foul mouth, "is *her*."

"Her? You mean your mother?" Gloria enquired, passing the medicine to Sara. "It can't be, Lizzie; they wouldn't allow her into your room after all she's done to you."

Sara stopped stitching and looked for a reaction from Lizzie. Her eyes were wide and her hands trembling.

"I know I'm being silly, Gloria, but can you try to find out for me, please? It sounds really weird, I know, but I *think* I felt her presence here last night – and maybe I wasn't dreaming after all." Lizzie recollected her dream of hills and the countryside and the gentle whisper, like a breeze, in her ear. "If it wasn't her, I'm going mad again and will have to increase my medicine, won't I?"

Sara's eyes flicked from one woman to the other before focusing on the wall clock, which read 7 a.m.

Gloria said nothing as she left the room and stormed towards Mr Hillier's office. Sara reminded Lizzie that it was nearly breakfast time. The thought of soggy toast was enough to make

Lizzie bolt to the loo and vomit. She cleaned herself up before dressing.

"They're coming back, Sara," she said sadly as she brushed her hair and despised her bulimia.

"Your imaginary friends?" Sara questioned, pulling a small jumper over her head.

"No, my angry feelings," Lizzie snapped as she watched the stupid fat cow trying to squeeze into a ridiculously tight jumper, and slammed the door in her face.

* * *

The flowers were lovely and well worth the twenty pounds he had paid the local florist who, thankfully, had opened an hour earlier than normal to deal with the seasonal demand for wreaths and Christmas flowers. Jonathan filled the sink in his office with water and carefully popped the bouquet into the sink. The light scent of the lilies spread throughout his office and lifted his spirits. He would give them to Jen tonight in the hope that they might cheer her up. He knew how much she was hurting.

He opened his door to welcome the first of his clients. A number of patients dashed past, not wanting to be late for their one-on-one sessions before the community group. They giggled excitedly, having heard rumours about Mr Hillier and his strange new headgear, and looked forward to seeing whether they were true. Jon grinned as a familiar person slouched past his door, lifting her nose in the air and ignoring him.

"Lizzie? Have you forgotten about our extra session today? We have two, remember, and your first one starts in a moment." Lizzie chose to blank him, and headed in the opposite direction.

"I don't want to talk today," she replied angrily, and increased her pace to escape. Jon, used to her antics, caught up with her and suggested tactfully that she should join him, even if just for a few moments, unless she preferred to meet with Mr Hillier. It worked every time and Lizzie, although reluctant, dawdled towards his door and plonked herself on a chair before giving him a filthy look.

"How are you, Lizzie?" Jon asked. "You look well." He noticed that she had gained a few pounds over the past week or so. Lizzie felt bitterly disappointed with herself. She explained that, until this morning, she had managed to keep all of her meals down, but, as always, she had been a failure.

As she spoke, Lizzie studied the doctor, who was listening intently to her. He'd got a bit tubby, she thought, noticing a little paunch beneath his shirt. His blue eyes, although warm, weren't sparkling today and he looked tired as well. His fringe was far too long, as always, and Lizzie noticed a few grey hairs by his sideburns which were, as usual, way too bushy. She wished his wife would tell him how stupid he looked, but figured that she didn't care any more about her husband's appearance. After all, love was all that counted – although Lizzie didn't know the meaning of the word any more. She clenched her fists in frustration, and fought not to swear at the doctor.

"It's *her* again, Dr Davies," she exclaimed, wishing he would pull his fringe back so she could see his eyes properly. "She's still haunting me after all these years, and stupid bloody things, even perfume, set me off and make me sick again." Jon raised his eyebrows, allowing his client to continue.

"Like this morning. I have absolutely no idea who the hell was wearing the stuff and what the heck they were doing in our room, but just that smell, Chanel No. pissing 5, was enough to throw my mind into turmoil again. I'm terrified she's back. Am I going mad again?" she asked, looking sadly at the doctor. "Just tell me I'm not having delusions again, Dr Davies, please."

Jonathan felt Lizzie's anguish and recalled his conversation with Norman.

She trusts you, Jonathan.
I trust you implicitly.
Find out the truth.

He nervously shifted in his chair, dreading Lizzie's reaction when he told her that her mother *had* been in her room the night before. He hesitated. He met her scared eyes, delaying the moment by putting the kettle on for coffee. Lizzie watched him intently, wondering why his hand was shaking when he held the spoon; the coffee granules scattered across the work surface.

After clearing the mess, he handed Lizzie her usual and sipped his rather weak tea, wishing that he had also opted for coffee. He held on to the mug tightly with both hands, like a child hangs on to its security blanket. The warmth helped as he broached the difficult subject of her mother with Lizzie.

"Lizzie, you're not imagining things and, no, you're not having delusional thoughts." He stared at the weak liquid in his mug and wished it were vodka. "Following the assault on Mr Hillier, we had no choice, Lizzie, but to call your next of kin. After a number of attempts to telephone your first emergency contact, we were forced to call your mother. I'm afraid that she insisted on speaking to Mr Hillier personally, and after the meeting, she asked to see you."

Lizzie placed her mug on the doctor's desk and felt terror rush through her body. Jonathan looked at her sheepishly and continued, "Your father was concerned about you, Lizzie. Despite trying to dissuade them, Mr Hillier allowed them a brief moment in your bedroom while you slept. I can assure you that you were not in any danger," he added, doubting that Lizzie would agree with him. He looked for a reaction from his client. Her eyes had turned cold and blank.

Rage consumed Lizzie's mind, and thoughts of Mr Hillier became confused with her hatred for her mother. Both had to be punished. Lizzie threw herself onto the floor, thumping and scraping the hard carpet tiles with her knuckles, hoping the pain she was inflicting on herself would give her some relief from the hideous thoughts of revenge coursing through her mind. She had failed to notice the doctor, on his knees next to her, trying to console her and trying to force her fists away from the floor. He didn't matter to her, anyway – he was as bad as Mr Hillier. Her skin was raw, and blood seeped through the broken flesh, which throbbed with pain.

"Mummy's little angel will be punished!" she screamed hysterically, gouging the wounds with her fingernails, tearing the skin. Jonathan ran to his phone, but Lizzie was too wrapped up in herself to notice. Nothing mattered any more, and nobody – but nobody – would stop her this time.

The coffee cup was next. Grabbing it and pouring the boiling liquid over herself, Lizzie felt a burning sensation before a scalding pain. It was a familiar feeling, and gave her the relief she needed. Jonathan ran frantically towards her, begging her to stop hurting herself. He tore the wet clothes from her body; it reminded Lizzie of her childhood, and she howled as she remembered walking Alfie and then being punished by her mother for getting filthy.

You have been an extremely naughty girl, Elizabeth. What do naughty girls deserve?

The burning sensation on her chest reminded her of the caustic soap her mother had caked on her body, and, strangely, it comforted Lizzie enough to sit quietly as Gloria arrived.

Lizzie rocked backwards and forwards in her underwear. She imagined she was on a see-saw or a swing in her favourite park, then she was flying like a bird in the sky, its wings spread wide, looking down on the miniature girl in her tatty duffel coat, her dog playing by her side.

He'd always bark at the bird, hoping it would swoop down to play with him, but Lizzie knew that Alfie wouldn't catch the bird in a million years. He would need to grow wings too! She had laughed, imagining the floppy-eared creature flying with her on his back, hanging desperately to his collar as he soared through the clouds – away from that house, away from the torture, and into their very own little paradise.

Gripping her new necklace, Lizzie recalled Alfie's collar. It had been a tatty red-and-blue one which needed replacing. She wanted to find the money, somehow, to buy Alfie a new one – which is why she didn't go to ballet that day after school. The money Mummy had given her for the ballet lesson was nearly enough, and if she cleaned the kind teacher's car she would be able to afford the lovely green collar she had seen in the pet shop. It was two pounds, and Lizzie knew that Alfie would love it. His golden, silky fur would stand out against the green, and she knew he was worth every bit of the hard work it would take to find the additional money. The mud from the dirty car wheels didn't bother her, and nor did the fact that the soapy water had soaked through her coat onto her leotard. Mummy would understand the minute Lizzie told her how good she had been, and showed her the new sparkling collar. Mummy loved Alfie almost as much as Lizzie did.

The silver chain broke as the nurse and doctor carried her to her room, her fists still clenched, holding on to the chain for dear life.

The pet shop man was so kind. After Lizzie counted her pennies and gave him precisely two pounds for the collar, he threw in some doggie snacks for free. Alfie would love them, she thought, as she ran through the puddles, along The Avenue and straight through the back gate and to the back door, which was always unlocked.

Alfie knew Lizzie's voice well, and he also recognised her little whistle, which she had practised for months on end. She called him, but Alfie didn't respond. She pursed her lips and blew and blew and blew. The whistle, although quiet, would be enough to prompt him to jump off her bed, bound down the three flights of stairs and greet his little friend. Lizzie waited excitedly for Alfie, shuddering in anticipation of his delight when he saw his brand new collar.

The noise from the stairs sounded different today, and when she heard Daddy's car start and leave the drive, Lizzie wondered whether he was taking Alfie out for a walk or to see the vet. She tried to hide the little brown bag in her pocket while she desperately listened for the patter of Alfie's paws, but to no avail.

"Looking for something?" Mummy sneered, having magically appeared from behind the door. She glared hatefully at Lizzie, who knew how dirty she was after washing the car.

"How was ballet, Elizabeth?" she questioned, pulling apart the toggles on her daughter's coat and staring at the filthy leotard.

"Answer me, child," she yelled, yanking the brown paper bag from Elizabeth's trembling hand and examining the contents. She smelled funny again, and Lizzie retched at her breath.

"I see," she screamed. Lizzie quivered in front of her, terrified. "How did you buy this? Answer me now, or you will be punished even worse than the last time, Elizabeth." Mummy slammed the bag onto the worktop and lit a cigarette. Lizzie quivered as she edged closer to her, the look on her face that she knew so well.

Lizzie knew not to clench her teeth this time, and her terrified eyes met her mother's grey slits. "With the money I earned," she replied, shaking with terror. "I cleaned a car and I wanted Alfie to have a nice new collar and I…"

Mummy moved towards her thieving daughter and blew cigarette smoke into Lizzie's face, which always made her cough. She resisted choking in front of Mummy, though, and stood, silently awaiting a beating, knowing that she had overstepped the mark. Mummy just giggled, then laughed hysterically. She threw the collar at Lizzie. Grabbing her glass, she slugged the contents and moved her horrid, swollen face towards the confused child.

"Your precious Alfie won't be needing *that* in doggy heaven," she slurred.

Lizzie's eyes widened and stared deeply into the dark abyss of her mother's eyes. "What do you mean, Mummy?" she asked, desperately hoping that she had misheard the giant towering in front of her. Her voice trembled as she spoke, and her mother giggled loudly before taking another slurp from the glass.

"Oh, little baby," she sneered. "If only you had a brain in that hideous head of yours, you would know what I mean; take a look at your watch, Elizabeth."

Lizzie shuddered with fear. Her mother yanked the sleeve of her coat above her elbow. She lunged at Lizzie's hand then forced it onto the face of her little red wristwatch, pushing her fingers hard against the glass of the dial.

"What's the time, Mr Wolf?" she sneered at the terrified child.

Lizzie didn't understand this new game, but instinctively replied, "Half past five, Mummy."

Mummy glared at Lizzie. She checked the time to ensure that it was correct.

"Now pinch yourself, Elizabeth," she demanded, "and make sure that you do it hard."

Lizzie feared the worst. She forced her little fingernails into her skin as hard as she could.

Mummy appeared to be satisfied while she studied the red mark on Lizzie's hand.

"Good," she replied, taking a puff of her cigarette. "Did that hurt my little baby?"

"No, Mummy," Lizzie replied, not knowing what the right answer should be.

Lizzie soon found out. The monster forced her talons into Lizzie's hand, making it bleed.

"Did *that* hurt, little baby?" Mummy hollered hatefully at the child.

"Yes, Mummy," Lizzie sobbed, watching the globules of blood form. She hoped she had given her mummy the correct answer this time.

"Excellent," Mummy replied, smiling the contorted smile that Lizzie had grown to despise. "Because, my thieving little baby, I want you to imagine that the pain you feel now is the pain your stupid, stinking dog is now experiencing."

Lizzie's heart pounded with terror. She still didn't understand what this game was about and her mother howled with laughter as she dangled the green collar in front of her daughter's terrified eyes.

Forcing her contorted face towards Lizzie's, she ended the game.

"Alfie is dead. Do you hear, child? Dead."

Lizzie's heart felt as though it had exploded into a million pieces. She fell to her knees, clutching the collar her mother had chucked at her.

Mummy stared coldly at Lizzie who was quivering on the floor.

"He was becoming too attached to you, and the vicious animal bit me this afternoon, so your father is on his way to the vet, to put a little needle into the stupid dog who committed a sin."

Mummy continued to hum the tune that Lizzie had grown to despise, her words echoing through Lizzie's mind.

"Aah, crying, Lizzie, are we?" she screamed. Lizzie didn't care that tears were running down her face and into her mouth. She hoped they would drown her.

"Never mind, child, you'll be able to concentrate more on your schooling and your ballet now instead giving that ridiculous, stinking creature all your attention."

She lit another cigarette and bent down to face her sobbing daughter. Lizzie was too distraught to care anymore, and continued to sob loudly. She pushed the lighted end of the cigarette towards Lizzie's eyes. Lizzie stopped crying immediately. She could not face any more torture.

"Off you go now," she demanded. "You know the routine. Get yourself cleaned up before your father returns and before I change my mind about not punishing you on this wonderful evening. Oh, Elizabeth... if your father asks about your hand, tell him that Alfie bit you too. Good girl."

Lizzie didn't want to be yanked up by her hair, and obeyed her mother, knowing that if she did as she was ordered, she might escape more torture. Not that she cared any more. She stood up and held Alfie's collar close to her heart, forcing herself not to cry again.

Mummy bent down towards the floor tiles and grabbed the empty brown dog bowl. Laughing hysterically, she forced the bowl into Lizzie's trembling hand, allowing the collar to drop at Lizzie's feet.

"Here you are, Elizabeth, take this – you can eat from Alfie's bowl in future; it would be a shame to waste it. Run, child – off you go, back to your room, back to your precious little doggy."

The little girl gripped the brown bowl, remembering how Alfie had eaten, as Lizzie watched him in pleasure. She knew that Alfie, like everybody else she had loved, had gone to heaven. Her mummy wasn't finished, though.

"Oh dear, I forgot – he's not there anymore," she bellowed into Lizzie's ear. "He's *dead*, Elizabeth. D-E-A-D. Like you will be if you dare to lie to me one more time. Do you hear me, Elizabeth? Do you hear me?"

Lizzie didn't hear her mother. She ran up the three flights of stairs to her bedroom and threw herself onto the bed where Alfie had slept.

The front door opened and her father walked through into the kitchen, looking genuinely upset as he put his car keys on the worktop.

Meeting his wife's eyes, he asked how Lizzie had taken the news about Alfie.

"Oh, fine, darling," she replied, smiling warmly at her husband. "She was a little upset, but she understood."

"She really is Mummy's little angel, isn't she?" he added, helping himself to a gin.

"Absolutely, darling," she replied, hoping he wouldn't ask to see her bite, hidden underneath the plaster – because then he would find out she had lied.

* * *

176

Lizzie couldn't hear the voices surrounding her as she lay in her bed. Her hands had been tended to, and three faces peered anxiously at the woman, who was experiencing post-traumatic stress or one of her dreadful nightmares. Norman's eyes filled with tears and he loathed himself for speaking to Mrs Pritchard. He should have persevered with the first contact and he hated himself for sticking to the ridiculous rules and regulations. "I'm so sorry," he whispered to Lizzie. He closed her bedroom door and mentally prepared his letter of resignation.

"Me too, Daddy," said Lizzie in her dream-state as she stared at the blood on her hands and the scissors she had plunged into her mother's chest, before she collapsed onto the bedroom floor.

* * *

Norman sealed the white envelope and left it on his desk, feeling a great sense of relief. Cancelling this morning's meeting had been a sensible decision. Smiling, he retrieved the brown folder and studied the contents one last time. Switching on the shredder, he removed each meticulously written document, fed it into the machine and watched as it was destroyed. He pulled on his hat and studied his office before switching off the light and exiting the hospital. He knew he would be replaced within a matter of days, and didn't think he'd be missed.

He walked slowly along the high street, knowing he would have no need to pass these tatty shops ever again. The local shop around the corner would be fine for him and his mother, and the cat food was reasonably priced, considering it was just an independent store run by a middle-aged Jamaican man.

A woman pushing a pram passed him and grinned at the strange chap muttering to himself. Norman caught his reflection in a large shop window. Realising how ridiculous he looked, he tossed the hat into a nearby bin. It really didn't matter to him how he looked and he decided that, like so much else, other people's opinions no longer counted. After resigning, he would be content in his own private world. As he unlocked the door to his home, he welcomed the thought of sharing an evening with his mother, reminiscing about the good old days and flicking through some old black-and-white photographs.

After stirring the stew, he stroked his cats and, for the first time in twenty years felt absolutely shattered; the indigestion he'd suffered from since he'd eaten lunch hadn't lifted either. He would have a nap and continue dinner once his mother was home from the day centre.

The front room felt chilly, so Norman switched on one bar on the electric fire and almost collapsed from exhaustion into the armchair positioned close by. He reflected on the events of the day and felt, strangely enough, relieved by his decision. He and his mother would manage financially, he was sure, and she would understand why Norman had resigned, once he had explained everything to her. He closed his eyes, enjoying the silence and warmth surrounding him.

His heart struggled to maintain a steady rhythm and his breathing became more laboured. Norman felt a huge surge of energy jolt through his body. A sudden pain radiated along his left arm. He felt a searing pain in his heart. As Norman took his last breath, his worries about Lizzie, Gloria and Mrs Pritchard disappeared. He was free.

* * *

The sedatives Lizzie had been given were mild in comparison to those she had been given the previous day, and she awoke to find Gloria sitting by her bedside along with Sara, who clearly had been crying. Lizzie's hands were throbbing and she studied the plasters wrapped around them before gazing in Gloria's direction. Lizzie could remember everything, and needed no reminding of how she had injured herself or ended up being sedated once again.

Gloria smiled at the girls, pouring them each a fresh glass of water. She had discovered that Lizzie's parents had indeed been in the girls' room, and felt as angry and frustrated with the situation as Lizzie had. She hoped Norman would be reprimanded for his ludicrous actions – although, she knew, deep down, that he had been given no choice.

Lizzie had calmed down. Her memory of her meeting with Dr Davies had clouded over, just like her dream about Alfie and his death. In her life, most good things had been taken away from her, and she shrugged, getting out of bed and going into the bathroom. Studying her tired features, she noticed that she wasn't wearing her necklace from Jason. She couldn't remember where she had left it and burst back into her bedroom, fighting back anger, to thump the thief sitting next to her friend.

"You!" she screamed at Sara. "You saw it and stole it, didn't you, Sara? I know what goes on in that sad little mind of yours." She lashed out at Sara. Instead, her hand caught Gloria, who jumped in front of Sara to protect her. Lizzie stopped screaming immediately, mortified that she had hurt her friend.

Sara sobbed and ran towards her embroidery. Lizzie glared at the stupid girl then, realising the consequence of her actions, looked sheepishly at Gloria who, thankfully had not been hurt.

"I'm sorry, Gloria," she whispered, wishing she could control her temper when she was angry. Gloria, without saying anything, dug into her pocket and handed Lizzie the chain, which she had repaired earlier. Dropping it into her hand, she left the bedroom without saying another word. The strain was starting to affect her too. She went to Jonathan's office and told him all about Lizzie's nightmares.

Lizzie, in the meantime, apologised to Sara, who ignored her. Lizzie put on her slippers, left her bedroom and walked down the familiar corridor. As she passed Jonathan's office, she overheard Gloria's voice.

"She's had a terrible time, Jonathan. Her childhood was horrendous, but her nightmares are becoming more frequent and," she paused, "rather disturbing. She trusts you, doctor, and I believe it's in all of our interests to find out whether there's any truth in her mother's accusations." Gloria's heart was pounding as she faced Jonathan and recalled her conversation with Norman Hillier. "I am sure you can discover the truth, Jonathan; we all deserve to know what happened. I care for Lizzie. I want her to make a recovery and lead as normal a life as possible, but until she receives the correct therapy and faces her demons, she will never heal; she will never be free. You're the only one who can help her, Jon. I trust you, as Lizzie does. Help her to recover, please, Jon. She needs you. We all need you."

Lizzie hid as Gloria left the doctor's office and headed towards the staff room for a well-deserved cup of tea.

I trust you, as Lizzie does.

Help her to recover – please, Jon.
She needs you.
We all need you.

She had to tell him. She had no choice.

Lizzie burst through the door into Jonathan's office and ran into his arms. Jon, totally unprepared, was forced back against his desk and his cup of tea fell to the floor, the tepid liquid splattering over his trousers.

Lizzie moved away, remembering the no-touch policy, and apologised to Jon, whose pie was, once again overflowing with uncontrollable 'what ifs.'

Her eyes flicked to the corner of his office. There, Alfie sat, wagging his tail. He looked into Lizzie's eyes. He was wearing his wonderful new collar. However, she chose to ignore her pet.

Turning away, she sat in the lotus position on the floor and met the confused doctor's eyes. Jon smiled falsely at Lizzie and settled into his chair, ready to listen to his patient, although he just wanted to drive home to see Jen. That would, as always, have to wait.

Lizzie's eyes were vacant and her features drawn and tired. She spoke in a monotone.

"I'm here to confront my demons," she said, staring coldly at Jonathan, "and I need to confess what I did to my mother and how I ended up here." Her eyes were as cold as ice.

"And, doctor, as always, it will have to remain our little secret."

* * * * *

PART THREE

THE END

"If you prick us, do we not bleed? If you tickle us, do we not
laugh? If you poison us, do we not die? And if you wrong us, shall
we not revenge?"

William Shakespeare
The Merchant of Venice, Act III, scene i

21. MERRY CHRISTMAS BETH

1977

The radiator in her bedroom was, as usual, freezing cold. The bitter weather outside had eaten its way through the crack in the window and thick ice had formed on the inside. An icicle was growing, creating a magical sculpture behind the torn net curtain, and it had started to drip onto the flaking paint of the old wooden shelf at the foot of the window. At least that would hide the mould, which she was sure made her cough worse than ever.

Beth shuddered with cold as she tried to gather some warmth from her thin, army-issue blanket. She wrapped herself in the hard, itchy material, then realised that it would make no difference. A sheet would have helped, perhaps, but that little luxury, along with so much else, had been taken away from her. A spring from the mattress had broken through during the night and Beth rubbed her sore back where the sharp metal had scratched her skin. A few more were waiting to burst through the shell of the mattress, and pinged loudly as she moved.

Dragging herself out of bed, Beth blew into her hands for some warmth. Her breath formed steam when she exhaled and she followed the trail before it disappeared into thin air. She felt no warmer, though, and took a puff of Ventolin to make her lungs work better. Her cough was getting worse.

Leaving the relatively safe confines of her bedroom, she tiptoed down a flight of stairs and into the bathroom. By comparison, this room was like the Sahara Desert and, as she huddled close to the radiator, Beth's little fingers turned from blue to pink. After she thawed out, she yearned for the courage to run a bath. It would, for sure, help her blood's circulation, which she knew – despite being just six years old – was struggling to be pumped around her body. Her toes were purple and she wriggled them in an attempt to get the blood flowing again, but to no avail.

Her terror of drowning, however, forced her to run the warm tap into the sink and wash herself before getting dressed. Using the last of the soap, Beth foamed it in her hands and smothered the bubbles over herself. She'd got used to this way of washing and, although it looked safe to use the flannel, she knew it might hurt her again. It was so hard to resist, but she would ignore the innocent-looking towel dangling over the lovely warm radiator as well. She stood close to the towel, shivering while she waited to dry. The door opened. It was *her*.

"Happy Christmas," she said, tossing a small package towards the naked child. "Try not to spoil this. I've left the label in the back, and I'll return the dress to the clothes shop next week, but for today at least, child, try to look presentable for your grandparents – and stay clean." The door closed.

Beth tore at the brown packaging, which had obviously been wrapped by the shopkeeper, and excitedly held the item of clothing against her shivering body. The dress was bright red and had little green dots on the material and a jade-green ribbon that went around her waist and tied at the back. Beth looked closely for pins and was relieved to see that the dress was safe to wear. Running into her bedroom, she opened her drawer, grabbed a pair of tatty knickers, popped on a vest and dressed. There was no mirror in her room, as her mother had said that it would be cruel to torture herself every time she looked into it, and so Beth, once again, returned to the bathroom to examine herself.

Apart from her knotted hair and wishy-washy face, she looked quite nice. The dress was a perfect fit, although it was for a child two years younger than her. She was tiny for her age, but Nanny had told her that as soon as she hit '*puperty*' – whatever that meant – Beth would shoot up. Not that Beth was convinced, because Nanny was absolutely minute and so *puperty* obviously hadn't worked for her.

Grabbing a comb that had been left on the side, Beth worked her way through the tangles and finally her hair looked reasonably tidy. It was, however, dirty and needed a good shampoo – but after the last episode with the soap in her eyes, she had point-blank refused to allow her mother to touch her hair ever since. And so, two weeks on, and with all the shampoo hidden, Beth was paying the price, which she deserved, really, for being so rude and defiant to her mother.

She stood at the top of the stairs, awaiting permission to come down. Beth had learned that luxuries, such as entering the nice warm bits of the house, were forbidden. She had to wait to be invited. Sometimes, she would be lucky and was allowed down straight away; that was normally when Daddy was at home or relatives and friends were there. Beth always had to be perfectly behaved, though, or she would pay the price. She never played up when they had visitors, although she didn't think she was that naughty even when there weren't any.

Beth waited for her mother's permission to descend. Beth studied the white-painted door down the first flight of stairs. It had her name on a lovely white tile, with lots of butterflies next to it. Her nanny had bought it for her on a shopping trip. Beth recollected her old bedroom, with its pink wallpaper and flowery pink covers, and wished that she could, just for five minutes, play in there. It had real carpet and white matching furniture, along with all the toys she could wish for but, as with the remainder of the house, she was only allowed in her old room on extra-special occasions when she really deserved a reward. With Daddy being away so often and fewer people visiting, she slept in her lovely old room less and less often. She missed it.

Today was a good day. Yelling that Beth could come downstairs, her mother rushed back into the kitchen, muttering about stuffing the turkey and getting on with the frigging dinner. Beth's feet were still like blocks of ice. She thought she had been a good girl this year, and she hoped that Santa had bought her some nice new slippers.

The living room looked beautiful. Beth's eyes lit up as they flicked across the enormous, high-ceilinged room, noticing the bright decorations and the huge Christmas tree. Even though Daddy had to work abroad this Christmas, he'd gone to the trouble of buying a real tree. Although Beth had not yet been allowed to see it, she had smelled the pine needles from her bedroom and couldn't wait to see the real thing. Its branches boldly stood out against the soft cream of the walls, and almost danced as Beth jumped with joy. A fairy took pride of place on the top; it had gold wings and a magic wand. Below her, the sparkly baubles shone in bright colours as the fairy lights flickered on and off. There were even chocolates attached by golden string to the branches – although Beth doubted that she would be lucky enough to get one. Even so, they finished off, what she considered, to be the most beautiful Christmas tree in the whole wide world.

The fire was lit too, and Beth figured that her mother must have got up dreadfully early to do all of this. She'd gone to so much trouble to make this Christmas a special one after all, and Beth was very proud of her. She was glad she had made her mother a little present at school, which she would bring downstairs in a little while and hide under the tree as a surprise.

She rubbed her goose bumps and edged towards the open fire to warm up. Beth wanted to squeal with delight. Beautifully wrapped presents sat under the tree, wrapped in snowman paper and with great big red bows. Her heart skipped a beat as she admired the gifts and she realised excitedly that, despite the warnings and threats that *he* would not visit her house this year, Mother had been wrong. Santa *had* known how well behaved Beth had been after all, and he had been! He had come down the chimney before Mother had lit the fire and had delivered those beautiful parcels for her and her brother. She could barely contain her excitement when her mother walked into the room, followed by her younger brother.

Beth smiled at her brother as he toddled towards her, his dummy in his mouth. Mummy had bought him a special present too; he was wearing some Noddy pyjamas which were all fleecy and soft. Today, he also wore a bright red dressing gown which had a Santa hat joined to the top with a white fluffy border around the edge. He showed off his new reindeer slippers to his sister. Beth hoped he would stay clean – the lady in the clothes shop wouldn't take the clothes back if he got any dirt on them, so she opened her arms and cuddled him. He smelled lovely, all clean and soapy, and his hair glistened; she brushed her little fingers through the blond tufts and giggled with him.

The turkey was in the oven, Mummy had said, and Mummy would have a five-minute break before making breakfast. Mummy had cursed, and said that Nanny and Granddad would turn up early, as they had nothing better to do with their time, but Beth couldn't wait to see them. She loved them so much and they always, but always, bought her wonderful presents. She wondered what she had been bought this year, staring under the tree, then looking at her mother, who was placing the gifts in two piles.

Her brother must have been an incredibly good boy this year, Beth thought, as his pile of gifts from Santa almost reached up to the ceiling – which was nearly as high as the sky. He rapidly tore the paper away, revealing wonderful toys and magical delights inside. The wooden, child-sized train was Beth's favourite. It had been hand-carved and had little red wheels and a horn that went *toot-toot*. She sat on it, pretending to be the driver, and watched with pleasure as he played with the paper and sat in the boxes, ignoring the array of expensive gifts that Father Christmas had bought him.

Beth didn't care that her pile of presents was tiny by comparison. After all, she had, at times, been extremely naughty and she knew she would have to be punished. She looked longingly at her presents, and her mother allowed her to open them.

"This is from your father," she said, shoving a tiny box into Beth's hands. "Nothing to do with Santa *or* me," she added, looking disgusted. Beth tentatively removed the paper, trying very hard not to tear it; she would use it to wrap up her mother's gift in a little while.

The box was made of velvet and was light blue; it felt so smooth against her fingers. She opened the little gold catch on the side, and her eyes lit up when she spotted a silver bracelet with ornate charms attached to it. She held it up close to her eyes and noticed that there were four. A little love heart, a baby animal of some description, a four-leafed clover and a little angel. It was truly beautiful. She placed the bracelet around her wrist; she longed to cuddle her daddy and thank him for his wonderful present. Her mother didn't seem to be the least bit interested in Beth's happy reaction, and was putting together a toy garage with Weebles instead while her brother played in yet another box.

"Open the others, child," she demanded as she placed the fireguard round the fire. "I've got breakfast to do before *they* turn up."

There were two presents left, and Beth couldn't decide which one to open first. One was fairly small – *shoebox size*, she thought – and she imagined some pretty pink, warm slippers sitting among the tissue paper waiting to jump on to her feet. The other present, though, excited Beth the most. In comparison to the others, it was enormous – and so heavy. Mummy had struggled to pull it from under the tree, and Santa must have near broken his back lifting it down the chimney, along with everything else.

The box would have to come first. Resisting the temptation to rip the paper off, Beth delicately removed the Sellotape with her nails, tore it gently away from the paper and slowly pulled the paper away from the box. Folding it neatly, she lifted the top of the box away to reveal white tissue paper. Her heart was pounding with excitement... but, as she tore the tissue paper away, it sank.

"You need them for school," her mother hollered when she re-entered the room with a bowl of cereal for Beth's brother. "And whatever you do, do *not* wreck these, child."

Beth despised school and she hated these shoes even more. The girls would have a field day mocking her, and she dreaded the thought of wearing the stupid clunky things. Her legs were skinny enough and these hideous shoes would make them look even skinnier.

"What do you say, then?" her mother asked, tending to the fire.

"Thank you, Mummy," Beth replied, wishing she could chuck the ridiculous present in her face.

"You're very welcome. Now, open your other gift; this one is from Santa."

Although she was deeply disappointed with the shoes, Beth did understand why she had been bought them. She'd deliberately scraped the others on the pavement when she'd walked home from school, and they now leaked. Her mother was only thinking of her feet, really, and wanted them to stay dry. She forgave her in an instant.

Beth gazed at her mother, who looked excited. She suspected that she had, after all, passed Santa her list, although she couldn't work out what she had asked for that was this big!

"Hurry, child," she demanded. "I haven't got all day. Tear the paper now! Will you get a move on?"

Beth knew that her mummy had masses to do, and so she ripped the paper off, this time not bothering to save it. It was a huge, lumpy bag with yellow writing on a black background. Black powder was stuck to it and it smelled funny. Her mother's eyes gleamed as she watched the confusion on her daughter's face. Beth tore the black ribbon-like seal at the top. A lump of coal fell onto the carpet, leaving a filthy stain as it rolled towards her leg. Unaware of her mother's evil little trick, Beth picked up the lump and shook it, hoping there was a secret present hidden inside. After testing another six pieces, the harsh reality hit the little girl.

"Oh dear," her mother giggled. "You really have been a bad girl, haven't you?"

Beth fought back the tears as she watched her brother play with his wonderful new toys. Gathering the paper she had so carefully saved, she crumpled it into a ball and threw it onto the fire, wishing that Santa would fall into it and burn to death.

* * *

2014

She was burning up under the duvet. Beads of sweat formed across her eyebrows and she tossed and turned, waking Dave up with her screams.

He comforted his girlfriend. Beth's eyes opened wide and she tried to regain her bearings. The softness of her new bedding brushed up against her skin, and Dave's chest was warm as she hid her face in his soft chest hairs.

The warmth from the central heating radiated through the room and, as she escaped from the horrors of her dreams, she clung to Dave desperately, listening to his heartbeat for comfort.

He stroked her face gently and kissed her hair before looking at the time on the clock. 3.15 a.m. Beth moved away from him, her scared eyes staring back into his.

"They're back," she whispered, shifting to her side of the bed and dangling her feet over the edge.

"No, Beth, not *them* again?" he replied, petrified at her response.

"No, not the girls – the nightmares, Dave. The nightmares."

* * *

It would have been so easy to jump into the car and drive the twenty miles to her mother's house. He could break down the door or, easier still, run through the back door, which was always unlocked, and strangle her – but he knew that violence would not resolve Beth's problems. They were in her mind and, even if her mother was dead, Beth would still be haunted by her past.

She had been suffering from nightmares ever since starting her new medication. Each night, Dave knew that they were becoming worse. It was a catch-22 situation, though – the tablets eased the symptoms of her schizophrenia, and she really had made great progress over the past few weeks. However, the nightmares were making her tired and, more worryingly, frightened of everybody and everything.

He popped the kettle on. Beth tiptoed into the kitchen behind him. Although she wanted to stop him from using the tap, she resisted and, after watching the water trail down to the base of the kettle, she waited for Dave to be electrocuted as he switched it on. Thankfully, the red light came on and the kettle boiled normally. At least he would live to see another day.

She was tired: tired of the hideous nightmares she had been experiencing recently and their repetitive nature. For the past few nights, the Christmas one had been repeating like a 1980s series of *The Sweeney*, and each nightmare lasted longer than the last. She thought back to the nightmare she had just had, and how her Christmas dress had been covered in coal dust. Looking down at her fleecy white dressing down, she met Dave's gaze as he handed her a warm drink and shot back to reality once more.

"I know why, Dave," she whispered, blowing into the cup to cool the hot coffee. Dave led Beth into the living room, which was chilly. Lighting the gas fire, Beth sat in front of it, snuggling into her gown and holding her cup close to her chest.

Dave sat close to his girlfriend.

"Why what, Beth?" he asked confused by her statement.

"Why the nightmares about Christmas keep coming back," she replied, eyes huge and tearful. "It's my fault. I'm putting myself under so much pressure to make this one as perfect as possible. It's on my mind all the time, but" – she hesitated, looking deep into Dave's warm eyes – "I still have to do it, Dave. I have to prove to her that I'm better and that she won't control my every movement, my every action, or my life. I need to show her – *prove* to her – that I am over the horrors of my childhood; that I'm healed and free of her. I just wish that the nightmares would go." She fought the lump in her throat and resisted the desire to cry.

Dave took a sip of his tea and thought back to former Christmases. He shuddered, recollecting the arguments, then the tears that had followed, and how Beth slipped, once again, into deep depression.

"I know that you want to show everybody how well you're doing and how strong you can be, Beth, but why her – why your mother? She isn't important, really, Beth. If you look at the big picture, it would be a far more relaxed day if it was just us and maybe your brother. You don't need to prove anything to her. We're the ones who love you, and we're the ones who can see how well you're doing, sweetheart."

To Dave, it all made perfect sense, but he was missing the point. Beth had to prove everything to her mother once and for all. Her mother would no longer control her life – it simply had to end.

The wind blew something over outside, making Beth jolt. Collecting her composure, she realised that nobody was trying to break in to kill her, although she huddled even closer to her boyfriend as she went on, looking occasionally towards the window.

"I understand what you're trying to say, Dave, but—" Beth stopped suddenly, startled by a crash by the front door. It sounded like broken glass. Dave threw a jacket on over his pyjamas, and dashed out of the house towards the car.

I warned you, you filthy, defiant little brat. Now I won't be able to return that dress, will I? Do you have any idea how much it cost? Do you? No, of course you don't – you just scrounge off me and think that the money tree continues to grow and grow, don't you, child? Well, you'll learn. You will scrub and clean the entire house tomorrow, from top to bottom, and you will not stop until it's done. Do you hear, child? Do you hear me?

Her memory of her mother throwing the crystal glass at her head ceased as soon as Dave burst into the living room, shivering from cold.

"Bloody bin," he said, rubbing his arms in an attempt to warm up. "Blew over, so I've moved it to the side, which will be a bit more protected than the front."

Beth rubbed her eyes; she was tired and needed to rest. "Do you mind if I go up, Dave?" she enquired, finishing her drink and putting the cup next to Dave's.

"No, darling – rest now," he whispered, hoping that he too could grab some sleep. "Sweet dreams, Beth."

"Thank you."

* * *

1977

It had been a horrendous day and, when her parents finally left, she sighed with relief. With both children asleep and those idiots gone, at last she could have a decent drink and start to relax a little. Naturally, she'd had a glass of wine with her meal; that was acceptable, but the yearning for something stronger had gnawed away at her soul for most of the day. How she loathed her parents, who swanned around her home as though they owned the bloody place.

"You've done so very well, dear," her patronising mother had said after stuffing herself with the food that she had spent hours and hours preparing. And as for her father, he was as pathetic as her own husband. "Stand up to her," she had felt like screaming, but what was the point? He never had and never would; he was the second-weakest man she had ever known. The weakest was due to fly back home tomorrow.

She thought of her son. How she loved him. He was the only good thing that had ever happened during her miserable, godforsaken life. He was her precious, precious baby and nobody, but nobody, would take him away from her. But, as for the other brat, the unwanted one? She wished she would die from asthma – tonight. It was bitterly cold and she had smoked heavily all day, discreetly blowing smoke into the filthy girl's face in the desperate hope that her lungs would fail and she would finally die. She crossed her fingers and listened intently for the coughing from the third level of the house. It was persistent and sounded extremely chesty; she could always hope.

Her parents, despite her demands, had bought the children far too many presents. They had defied her when she had ordered them not to buy her daughter silly toys; she was growing up and needed to learn the value of money and have practical presents to aid with her education, which was suffering due to her ridiculous daydreaming and constant defiance. But no, as well as buying an enormous slide for her son, which would clutter up the garden, they had bought her – *the brat* – that ridiculously expensive walking, talking doll that had been advertised all over the place since its bloody release in November. She slugged back a glass of gin then lit another cigarette, enjoying the sensation of both as the chemicals entered her body.

Lifting the doll up by its hair, she studied its plastic face. Its eyes haunted her; they were dark brown with long eyelashes, and she felt uneasy looking into them. They belonged to her daughter – that monster upstairs. The dark wavy hair was real, she had been told, and, to her, it was life-like enough to despise it as she did her daughter's. Even the doll's pink tiny lips were similar. Every sodding feature of this toy reminded her of that child – the child she loathed more than her own pitiful life. The doll appeared to sneer at her as it took one rigid step after another towards her, blinking its eyes and giggling.

She had not considered the fumes. As the plastic melted into a molten mess in the fire, her mind grew confused and she dreamed of *her* fairy-tale with her beautiful angels. She suddenly grew wings so that she could fly away from this life and the horrors that she faced every day when her daughter woke and looked into her eyes.

"Those eyes," she whispered as she fell into a deep, unsettled sleep. "Those eyes are the work of the devil."

* * *

2014

Dave didn't bother going back to bed after all. Thankfully, Beth had crashed out straight away and, from the calm expression on her face, was at last sleeping peacefully. He opened his laptop. He realised that, despite his reservations over Christmas, Beth was right. She just wanted to face her mother in a stress-free environment, cope well and deliver a great meal. All she hoped for was a little respect from the woman who had controlled her life since the moment she had been born – it wasn't a lot to ask, really. But, despite trying to reassure himself that it would be okay, Dave had serious reservations. He still wanted to wring her mother's neck and was tempted to drive there right now. Or pick up the phone to ring her and wake the old bag up.

Fighting his anger, Dave clicked the spreadsheet he had been working on for days and played with the numbers again. Reducing his profit by another five per cent, he smiled at the final figures. If he actually won this contract, not only would Regency Furniture be saved, but his financial problems would be over, and he would have one less thing to worry about.

He prepared his final quotation, attached it to the email he'd written and clicked send. Now all he needed was a miracle. Well, two actually, but the miracle he wanted the most, he feared, would be impossible.

He thought back to his most recent meeting with Beth and Jonathan Davies, and recalled the medicines she'd had in the past. Some had eliminated both the delusions and the nightmares and so, picking up his mobile, he sent a text to the doctor asking one simple question. 'How do we eliminate the nightmares?'

Jonathan stirred in bed, feeling the vibration of his mobile phone, and focused on the message he'd just received. Leaving his warm bed and his sleeping wife, he drafted a reply.

'By eliminating the problem,' he texted. He then deleted his response and reluctantly agreed to see Beth the following day, during his lunch break.

Heading back to bed Jon took a sleeping pill, hoping to drift off to sleep again. Jen stirred and huddled close to him. He wrapped his arms around her and closed his eyes, hoping that his dreams would be of her and his beautiful daughters. Somehow he doubted it, as, once again thoughts of Beth's mother consumed his mind instead.

* * * * *

22. LET ME DIE

1994: Elise

Even though it was the middle of December, Ward 33 was so hot that it could have been located in the middle of Africa, rather than in Bedfordshire. Elise's hospital-issue pyjamas clung to her sopping body and her fringe stuck to her face. She was thirsty, and desperately needed a shower to freshen up.

The nosy lady in the next bed was already dressed and sat on the side of the bed, clinging to her suitcase and looking every so often at her wristwatch. Elise gazed in her direction, feeling envious as the lady checked, then double-checked, the wooden locker located at her side for any items she may have forgotten. Seeing Elise watching her, she stopped what she was doing and beamed at her.

"Well, you look a bit brighter today, young lady," she said, rooting into her enormous handbag and pulling out yet another chocolate bar. "Here," she went on, "take this and make sure you build yourself up before the little one arrives." Elise grabbed the bar and smiled back at the woman before lifting her covers to check that little Bump was still there. She felt relieved as she noticed the tiny bulge beneath her pyjama bottoms. Yanking them up, she left her bed.

"Thank you again," she said as she walked towards the bathroom, dragging her drip. "And I promise I'll look after little Bump too."

The lady smiled, and shortly after was greeted by her daughter. She hoped that the young woman would pull through, although she knew better than most just how difficult it would be.

Elise remained transfixed by her image in the full-length mirror in the wet room. The woman staring back at her was almost unrecognisable, and she shuddered as she gazed at the stranger's reflection. Apart from the eyes, she no longer knew herself. When she had been high, she had seen a happy-faced, young and beautiful woman who reminded her of an imp with her cute, short hair and beaming smile. She was alive and vivacious; she looked radiant and healthy with flushed cheeks and full pink lips. The woman standing there now in the oversized pyjamas scowled at the person staring back; *the stranger.*

"Who are you?" she asked, watching the mouth in the mirror ask the same question. Her pupils enlarged and she glared back at Elise. Her once long eyelashes had stuck to her swollen eyelids and, beneath them, dark trails ran down to the bridge of her nose, which was red and scabbed. The mouth that had spoken to her just a moment before was covered in sores and, as it tried to talk to the woman in the pyjamas, her lips cracked and droplets of blood ran onto her chin, which was covered in acne and matched the cheeks of the alien face.

Elise lifted her free hand and undid the buttons on the pyjama top, trying hard to avoid the drip. With the top dangling from her 'drip arm', the body in the mirror looked alien as well. Her breasts had disappeared; they were once full and pert but now, flaps of flesh hung like empty udders from a cow that had just been milked. The teeth marks around her left nipple jumped out at her, reminding Elise of the horrors of her prostitution days.

What's your name, bitch?

Her ribs protruded, like keys on a giant piano keyboard. She ran her fingers down one and felt the bump where a break had healed a few years before.

She continued to run her finger down towards her navel, then stopped. Her reflection's eyes moved towards her fingers and stared at the minute bulge under them. Her fingers stroked the bump gently, paused for a moment, then moved towards the waistband of the pyjama bottoms. Elise wriggled and they dropped, forming a crumpled mess at the reflection's ankles – which were attached to legs that looked like knotted ropes, grazed and bruised and so unbelievably thin. The reflection closed her eyes, too distressed to acknowledge the sight in front of her – the sight that she knew was herself.

She cried warm tears as she caught a glimpse of the scars. Trying to count them all, as she had in the past, she stopped at twenty-three. Twenty-three circular burns, twenty-three cigarettes and twenty-three years she had suffered – yet the other thirty burns, for now, she would ignore. From now on she had to focus on the present and try to eliminate the past. Turning round, she studied her back; her vertebrae poked out like an old cobbled path and the scar on her bottom looked raw and sore. Although the knife had slashed her skin at least a decade before, the scar was a constant reminder of the torture she had endured for most of her life. Once again, the eyes in the mirror turned away from the image they were presented with.

There wasn't a bath in this room. Instead a large shower head protruded from the clinical white tiles and two long cords were positioned nearby. The red cord meant danger, she figured, and so, pulling the white cord, she waited for water to rush through the shower head and bring her back to the present.

It was difficult to clean herself with the darned plastic tube protruding from her hand. It was so sore, and Elise was tempted to yank it out just so that she could feel semi-normal again. She resisted, however, and continued to mop her body awkwardly with the warm water, using hand soap from above the sink.

After a few moments, she felt a little cleaner and, avoiding the mirror, she dried herself, put on the pyjamas and re-entered Ward 33. Twenty-three years she had suffered. Right now, she didn't feel she could face another twenty-three seconds.

* * *

Jon was woken from his sleep by a key turning in his front door. It needed replacing, he knew that. No matter how many keys he had cut, they all seemed to jam in the lock, forcing people to shove the door to finally unlatch it. Jen, clearly, had been struggling for some time; when she entered the living room, she looked flustered and was rubbing her wrist.

"You must fix that flipping door," she yelled, dashing into the kitchen with an overflowing carrier bag, the contents of which were defrosting.

Jon cricked his neck in an attempt to see his wife, but realised that she was busy unpacking the shopping that he had promised to do the day before.

"Before you ask," she shouted playfully, "yes, there is chocolate ice-cream and yes, I did remember the biscuits!"

Jon smiled as he adjusted his boxer shorts and admired his torso in the full-length mirror. Holding his breath, he flexed his muscles, hoping to look like Mr Universe. Unfortunately, his reflection laughed back at him, he looked more like a beanstalk. Jen caught him at it and giggled as she stood in the doorway of his bedroom, holding a cup of tea.

"I take it you're feeling a little better today, Dr Davies," she laughed, flicking his flexed biceps playfully.

Grabbing his wife around the waist, Jon lifted her onto the bed and gazed lovingly at her. Her lips opened slightly and her pupils enlarged as she studied her husband's handsome features. Her breathing grew laboured; he knelt and tenderly brushed her lips with his. He could feel his heart beating hard and the hairs on his chest stood to attention as the bulge within his boxer shorts showed his desire for his wife. Pulling off her top, Jen placed Jon's hand on her left breast. He stroked it gently and, as her nipple stiffened, he replaced his hand with his mouth, covering her nipple through her satin bra and sucking passionately. He could feel Jen's heart thumping; her body tingled and she closed her eyes as her worries disappeared.

He undid her belt and pulled her jeans down her legs. Jon studied his wife's perfect body. Although the summer was long gone, she was still slightly tanned, which emphasised her perfectly toned figure. Moving his mouth to her navel, he flicked his tongue towards her pubis, making her moan.

"Make love with me, Jon," she whispered, opening her legs as he moved her panties to one side.

He didn't hear his pager the first time as he and Jen lay in each other's arms after making love. But when its vibration made his pager fall off the bedside cabinet and crash to the carpet, he was forced to read the message.

"Jon, call Ward 33. Elise is demanding an abortion. Can you authorise?"

"Jen," he whispered as his wife's eyes met his, "I have to go."

"That girl again?" she asked, pulling her sweater over her head and yanking on her jeans.

"I'm afraid so," he said, dressing hurriedly and combing his messy hair. "She's changed her mind, Jen; she no longer wants her baby."

After she heard the door close, Jen slumped onto the crumpled bedding. She imagined how it would feel to be pregnant, and desperately hoped that this time, the perfect time in her monthly cycle, she and Jon had, at last, created a new life.

Thinking of Elise, she shuddered at the thought of her terminating her unborn baby. For a brief moment, she wept. She would save that child if it was the last thing she did. Grabbing the carrier bag she had filled with the charity clothes, she ran to her Mini and started the short drive to the Luton and Dunstable Hospital, hoping to God she wasn't too late.

* * *

She wanted rid of the drip. She was hydrated enough now – heck, was she, going by the number of times she had dragged herself and that stupid contraption to the toilet. Although her nails were bitten, Elise managed to force the remainder of her index fingernail underneath the sticky tape and grip the corner just hard enough to lift it away from the fabric. Squeezing the edge with two fingers, she yanked hard and she could remove the cannula in her vein. She didn't care about the pain; her suffering over the past twenty-three years had enabled her to build up resistance to it. She forced the plastic away from her hand, closed her eyes and held her breath.

Hold your breath, little baby, under you go.

She watched the blood trickle out of her open vein. Elise held a finger over it to form a clot. Once again, her childhood experiences had served her well, and although she knew that this wasn't necessarily the best thing to do, Elise understood that she wouldn't bleed to death… although, if she did, it would do everybody a favour and she would be free. Moving her finger away, she allowed the blood to flow across her hand and to drip onto the cold floor tiles of Ward 33.

The wet room she had visited earlier would be the perfect place to end it all. They could mop up the mess in a few moments and all traces of her and her foetus would be eliminated in an instant. Disinfectant and bleach did the job a treat; she knew that too, but now she faced the dilemma of how she would do it. The pills she'd been prescribed were handed out one at a time so she couldn't overdose. She didn't have so much as a belt to strangle herself with, but there were cords for the shower and emergency call. They would do. It would be tricky, but she could do it, she hoped.

Placing the chocolate bar on the food tray by her bed, Elise closed the curtains, tore up her medical notes and walked towards the room that would finally release her from the years of pain she had suffered.

She didn't notice the young, auburn-haired woman dashing towards the nurses' station asking where Dr Davies's patient, Elise, was. Nor did she notice Jonathan who, after rushing back after treating a suicide attempt at A&E, had burst into the ward, to see his wife chatting to a nurse, who was pointing towards the curtained bed.

"I'm sorry, my little Bump," Elise whispered before taking one last peek at the alien reflection in the mirror. She forced the cord away from the plastic surround on the ceiling. "I wish that it could have been different, but I can't go on. Please forgive me." The powdery plaster from the cord's casing fell to the floor. It reminded Elise of the heroin she so yearned for. She kicked the powder, which formed a cloud of dust, then disappeared.

Ashes to ashes. Dust to dust.

The thin cord was tight and stung as it forced its way into the folds of her neck, constraining her breathing. She pulled hard, hoping that she would stay conscious long enough for her to finally end her godforsaken life. She gripped the end of the cord with both hands, pulling with all the strength she could muster. Then she closed her eyes and waited for darkness.

"Goodbye, my little Bump; heaven will look after you too. Goodnight, my little Bob. I will watch you every day from above and make sure that you are safe. I love you so much, my little baby, and I am so, so sorry that you got hurt. Bye bye, my darling David. I love you and I always will."

She forced her eyes to stay shut; a single tear escaped and flowed down her cheek. "I wish that you could have loved me, Mummy," she sobbed, wondering why her mother had hated her so much.

Can't you just hurry up and drown? Die, child, die – you even defy me now, and I need to go. Your brother's crying. Do NOT get out, child. Stay where you are: that's an order. I'll be back.

"Jesus, she's in the bathroom," Jonathan yelled. He burst into the room, forcing the door open with an adrenaline-filled strength. The woman on the floor hoped that this was a dream but, when she felt the warmth of his hand check her pulse, then remove the thin cord from her neck, she realised that her nightmare was real and she would, unfortunately, live to see another day.

A few of the nurses had followed Jonathan. They saw the crumpled body lying on the floor, fighting for breath. They stopped dead.

Her haunted eyes were confused and empty. They flicked across the room at the alien faces staring at her; none of them cared about her, really. And why should they? To them, she was just another worthless, addicted whore.

A stockily built nurse, and Jonathan, lifted Elise up and placed her in a wheelchair; she looked vacantly across the ward, then noticed a lady with auburn hair sitting by her bed. The lady was weeping and holding some items of clothing.

It was the little romper suit that hit Elise the most; it was yellow and the characters on the front shot straight through her heart. Thumper and Bambi were smiling. The lady by her bed folded the item and placed it back in the carrier bag. Elise jumped out of the wheelchair and ran towards her bed.

"No, please don't hide it, please don't!" she croaked, yanking the clothing from Jen and holding it against her chest. "My little Bump will look beautiful in that romper suit, won't you, baby?" she whispered quietly to herself. Stroking her tummy, Elise sat on her bed and studied the lady with the carrier bag and pretty face.

"Hello," the woman said, trying hard to hide her shock at the dreadful sight in front of her. "Jon asked me to get you these," she whispered. She pulled the clothes out and put them next to Elise. "I know they're too big but, if you want, you can have them for today and I'll get you some more for tomorrow."

Dr Davies watched the auburn-haired woman as she spoke. A nurse passed Jon some more medical records, which he placed in the holder at the end of the bed. Elise studied the woman's face again.

"I know that you don't know me," she said, wanting to stroke the woman's hand. "But Dr Davies is my husband and he has belief in you, Elise; that is your name, isn't it?"

Elise nodded, clutching the romper suit tightly in her hand.

"He believes that you can rebuild your life if you want to. I'm not forcing anything on you," she whispered, struggling to remain composed. "But if I can just help you a tiny bit by offering you some clothes and anything else you need, it would make me feel a little better, knowing you had somebody who cared, Elise. We care about you. Please don't be offended, and don't feel obliged to take them. It's just that..."

Elise had not expected this. It was clear that this woman was not judgemental. She really did seem to be concerned about her.

A nurse arrived a few moments later. She pulled back the bed covers before checking Elise's blood pressure. It was normal. She drew the curtains around her patient's bed.

"You must leave."

Before Jen had a chance to say goodbye, Elise took the clothing and folded it neatly into a little pile. Stroking the kind lady's hand, she met her pretty green eyes. Elise gently placed her lips on the lady's finger and kissed her wedding ring.

"I nearly got married," she whispered, her eyes downcast. "But that's a long story." She watched the nurse apply a plaster to her hand and give her a painkiller to ease the throbbing. "I told your husband, so he's allowed to tell you if he wants to."

Jen didn't let on that she knew far more about her than Elise could ever imagine, and before leaving, she handed Elise a leaflet. "It's a charity that helps people like you. If you're interested, talk to Jon and you can go from there." She said goodbye. Jon pecked his wife on the cheek and updated Elise's notes.

"So, this charity," Elise said. "Can we talk about it later or are you too busy?"

"Later, Elise," he replied reluctantly. "You should rest anyhow after the traumatic morning you've had. Take a nap and I'll be back after my rounds. It may be worth reading the leaflet," he added as he headed for the patient in the next bed.

Elise understood. She cuddled the romper and closed her eyes, hoping that, when she awoke, she might think her life worth fighting for after all.

* * *

Afterwards, Jen couldn't remember any details of her drive home, but when she arrived, she dashed straight to the bathroom and ran a cold shower. The icy cold water brought her back to her senses and she relished the chill as she shivered and studied herself in the small mirror above the sink. Her bright green eyes were alive and sparkled with youth and vitality. Her skin glowed and her hair shone, despite being sopping wet. The contrast between her healthy reflection and that poor woman was alarmingly distressing; Jen was only young, but the other woman had looked twenty years older than her. Elise's eyes were desperate and a vision of her, bashed and bruised, replayed in Jen's mind again and again. Her features were haunting and her appearance tragic. Jen could not erase the memory of the poor woman and how, after a simple act of kindness, she seemed to be genuinely moved.

Jen towel-dried her hair and dressed in a tracksuit before making the call. Unsure as to what she would say, she dialled the number and waited for somebody to pick up the phone.

"Joshua Charity Foundation," a woman's voice stated. Startled by the sudden response, Jen paused, then spoke. Her heart was thumping. "Hello, I'm sorry to trouble you but I wondered whether you could help me – or, rather, a friend of mine."

The woman listened to Jen's nervous voice, presuming that she was the 'friend' and needed help herself.

"She's a recovering drug addict," Jen said, "and she has nobody to turn to. She's alone and needs somewhere to live and to heal."

The lady listened intently. She knew this type of conversation well and had learned, just from the tone of voice, that the caller was genuine and really did want to recover. This caller certainly appeared to need help.

"I just wondered," Jen continued, "whether you would consider meeting her and her doctor, who will verify everything I've told you and explain her situation to you?"

The lady interrupted. "Her situation?"

"She's also expecting a baby. She has nowhere to go and nobody to turn to. Could you help her – please?"

The lady was, for the first time in her ten years at the charity, in a conundrum. She had set up the charity with her son, a reformed drug addict who, despite dying of an unrelated illness, had dedicated his life to helping others to rebuild their lives following drug or alcohol addiction. Every resident was encouraged to help the charity by working. The non-practical residents could learn to cook and serve coffee, while the more adventurous could restore furniture donated to the charity or learn to sell it. Over the past decade, over fifty residents had successfully completed rehab there, and some still remained at the charity, working as volunteers. However, none of the women had ever been pregnant or had a child. There were no facilities at the Joshua Foundation for expectant mothers, let alone a new-born baby.

Jen felt uneasy with the silence and cleared her throat. "Can you help my friend – please? She really is desperate."

The other woman could not ignore Jen's desperation and, after thinking of her son and his problems, she responded. "How far gone are you, love, and are you genuinely trying to stick to the methadone programme?"

"She's three months pregnant and, yes, I believe that she will try."

Studying the photograph of her son, the lady smiled as she checked her diary.

"Okay. Can you get her here for tomorrow with her doctor? We can interview them both and assess her suitability to the programme then. Say two o'clock?"

Jen agreed immediately.

"And her name?" the voice asked.

"Elise," she replied.

"Surname?" she questioned, writing in her diary.

"Hope," Jen replied, without considering why she had chosen that name.

"Well, we look forward to meeting her tomorrow. Do you have our address?"

"Yes," Jen said as she rechecked her notebook. "Thank you again for agreeing to see her."

"You're welcome," the voice on the telephone said. She smiled at the photo of her son on his graduation day.

"You would be so proud of me, Joshua," she whispered sadly. She closed the door to her private office and entered the communal dining area, which was overflowing with women and men who all hoped for a new beginning to their lives.

Jen placed the telephone back on the hook and shook with nerves. "Should I have done this?" she asked herself as she started to pack clothes into her overnight bag. She placed the last of her belongings in the case, and hoped that she had done the right thing. Her husband spent his life trying to help others, and it had rubbed off on her. She wrote a note for Jon before locking up and starting her journey home.

2 p.m. tomorrow darling. There is hope and the real pie is in the oven. I hope you enjoy it. Love you

Jen

xxx

For once, Jonathan found the time to enjoy his pie and, after he had scraped the plate clean and eaten the last piece of steak, he thought of Jen alone in her flat, then of Elise, alone in Ward 33. Putting on his coat, he jumped into his car, ignoring the ringing telephone as he left to meet his patient. He had some exciting news for her.

Jen replaced the telephone and headed towards her bedroom, wondering where her husband was and what he was doing right now.

The woman in the bed in Ward 33 knew the answer. Jon watched her intently as she drifted off to sleep. He tidied the clothes she had gathered into a neat pile and left her a message for her to see in the morning.

I want to help you, it said. He added his name to the bottom.

Jen was thinking of Jon. She lay alone in her cold bed reflecting on the past few days, and thought of the carefree young man she had met just a few years ago. She wondered whether he would ever return. Although she loved Jon with all her heart, she yearned for the laughter and happiness that had attracted her to him when they had met. She missed his carefree attitude and cheeky smile.

But as she drifted into sleep, her memories dissipated and, instead, thoughts of babies and Thumper the Bunny consumed her, along with the haunted face of the girl with no surname.

Jon also tossed and turned as he tried to sleep. He saw the green eyes of his beautiful wife, her perfectly moulded body in the throes of orgasm, then Elise screaming and writhing in pain, tubes attached to every vein, begging for help. 'I love you, Jon,' she cried, consumed with passion and desire for the man inside her. 'Let me die,' she screamed, staring into the blue eyes of the doctor who was saving her life. Her auburn hair had been shorn into clumps on her head, her green eyes haunted by the horrors of torture, scars all over her body.

"Jen," he yelled, pushing the covers off his burning body.

"No, doctor," she replied, her eyes turning to grey slits with red pupils bulging within them. "It's me, your nightmare, and you must stop now!" she bellowed, before her hair re-grew. Her auburn locks brushed over his face and her tender lips brushed his.

"Elise," he asked, "is that you?"

But the shadow loomed over him and the enormous body lunged towards his face. He knew who it was.

"Leave me alone," he hollered, rubbing his head and face frantically to eliminate the horrors of his dreams. Her green eyes turned to brown, then to grey. Her warm smile turned to a leer, and then the slender finger that stroked his chest turned into a fist and punched him in the ribs.

Breathless, he awoke, scrambling desperately for the light switch. Nobody was there; he was alone. He stumbled into the bathroom to run a cold shower, and realised that he was suffering from a nightmare. "Christ, Jon, think of Jen," he said loudly to himself. "Think of your wife, your future, and end this nightmare now."

"Good idea," the voice in his head said, and Jon imagined a giant walking through his wall and thrusting a knife in his direction.

"Jen," he sobbed, "I need you." But she couldn't hear her husband's cries. She slept peacefully in their flat, cuddling a teddy he had bought her seven years ago for her first day at university.

Elise, on the other hand, was wide awake, having had yet another nightmare about her mother.

"Get away from me," she ordered, her voice echoing through the walls of the ward, along the dark streets and into the bedsit, where Jon sat shaking violently.

He ignored the voice again, fighting the desire to scream. This was impossible; it wasn't happening. It was a figment of his imagination – he knew that, but as he felt the fear invade his body again, he responded to the girl's cries.

"I will help you, Elise," he replied, awaiting a reply from his patient.

Silence surrounded him. He sat naked and shivering on his bed. Holding his head in his hands, he came to his senses and knew it had all been a ridiculous dream. He was tired, that was all, and he was missing Jen. It would all be okay in the morning after a good night's sleep. He would ease off the vodka and maybe even do some exercise to alleviate the stress he was placing himself under.

"I'll be fine," he whispered before resting his head on his pillow and closing his heavy eyes, wishing to God that his wife was in his thoughts instead of those haunting images of death.

* * * * *

23. REVENGE

2004: Lizzie

Alfie had, at last, disappeared from her field of vision. Instead of her dead pet, Lizzie concentrated on Dr Davies, who had made himself another cup of tea and Lizzie, surprisingly, a fairly decent cup of coffee.

She was amazingly alert, considering her traumatic day. Jon, on the other hand, was exhausted and longed to be with his wife. Despite reassuring him that she was fine, he knew, from the quiver in her voice a few hours ago, that she had been weeping. How he needed to comfort her, and how he yearned to feel her heart against his; he too could do with a good cry, although he knew that wasn't the behaviour expected of a man. His dad had reminded him endless times that tears showed weakness but right now, Jon felt weak and frighteningly vulnerable.

Norman was right, though. Jon knew, reflecting on their earlier conversation, that he definitely needed to speak to Lizzie and discover whether there was any truth in Mrs Pritchard's allegation – and there was no better time than the present. The current personal pressures of his life seemed to be insignificant now. He studied Lizzie, who sat on the floor staring into space, and realised that she had to come first once again.

She'd been chewing her nails since she had entered his office and, having torn off the plasters, she picked at the scabbed skin which was forming over her wounds. Her chest, thankfully, had not been seriously burned, although it throbbed like crazy, and her sweatshirt, despite being fleecy and soft, made her feel dreadfully uncomfortable. Realising that sitting on the hard floor wasn't helping, she joined the doctor and sat close to him before she started to speak.

"I'm sorry, Dr Davies, for bursting in like that." She looked at the carpet, which was still damp and stained with the tea, and felt the urge to grab some tissues and clean it for him. Sensing her anxiety, Jon reassured her that it would be fine and wasn't worth worrying about.

"You mentioned your mother again, Lizzie." His eyebrows rose and Lizzie thought they looked too bushy, as well as his side burns. The bags under his eyes looked even bigger than they had this morning.

"Yes, I did, and I need to talk about stuff. I just don't know where to begin." She stopped picking her hand and resumed chewing a fingernail.

"Well, let's start at the easy part, Lizzie, if that's the correct assumption. We know why you're here, don't we?" Jon thought of Jen and the negative pregnancy test.

"Yes," she replied, removing her finger from her mouth and studying the deep scar across her right wrist.

"Suicide attempt, Dr Davies. The pills didn't do the job, and nor did the knife. Guess I should have done it somewhere in the middle of nowhere instead of at home, really."

Lizzie thought of her bed, smothered in blood. His face when he discovered her lying there, hardly able to breathe. The empty carton of pills. The horror of her loved ones slipping away before her very eyes.

Come back to me, don't die, princess. Please hang on. I love you. We can fight this together. Don't leave us — not now. Not after all we've gone though. Come back, sweetheart, please don't give up the fight.

"So that's how I ended up here," she added coldly, "after they released me from hospital, of course. But what I need to tell you is not so obvious. Why do you think I wanted to kill myself?"

"Your history?" he guessed.

"Your history," she mimicked, watching his face for a reaction. Lizzie shifted back to the floor and adopted the comforting lotus position before meeting Jonathan's tired eyes once again.

"You mean the abuse, the mental torture, the murder of my Alfie, the starvation and the other awful things my mother did to me, Dr Davies. Is that the history you refer to? Is it? Or is it the fact that *my* history has tormented my mind and caused me endless mental issues, resulting in me trying to kill myself and ending up here, in a sodding nut house? Which history do you refer to, doctor? Mine, hers or both?"

Lizzie felt anger pulsate through her veins as Jonathan shifted uncomfortably in his chair. He had asked the wrong question and, considering his years of expertise, felt ashamed and rather embarrassed with himself.

"Lizzie, I didn't intend to offend you. I know you better than most, and of course I understand the horrors that you have suffered, both physically and emotionally. It's just that," he paused while thinking of the correct words to say, "I believed that perhaps you wanted to escape from the history of your past and, despite having the love and security of your own family now, the demons in your mind took over and you felt that the answer was suicide?"

"Demons?" she questioned.

"Memories, Lizzie, sorry; your painful memories." Jon's tiredness was starting to show and Lizzie picked up on it immediately.

"You're not your usual self today, doctor, are you?"

Jon couldn't reply. Even though he was struggling to cope, he knew that he could not share his personal issues with a client – although, as her eyes warmed and studied his face, he could have weakened and told her everything about the baby that he and Jen so yearned for. She would have laughed and told him how pathetic and weak he was. Right now, that's exactly how he felt. He decided in an instant to keep his private life just that – private.

"I'm fine, Lizzie," he replied, smiling at his client. He gulped down his tea, hoping that the caffeine would keep him going for a bit longer.

Recapping on his question, Lizzie answered. "No, doctor, it's not the demons, it's not my abuse, and it's nothing to do with memories. The reason I wanted to end it all was due to my guilt."

"Guilt, Lizzie? You must never blame yourself for any of the events that have happened in your life. You are not at fault – your mother—"

Jon stopped himself from saying what was in his mind, knowing that he was not permitted to express his personal opinions, despite having known Lizzie for years, and having seen the irreparable damage her mother had caused her.

"Dr Davies, you need to understand something. I couldn't live with myself knowing that she would seek revenge for what I did to her. Whether it is in a year or ten years away, she won't forget. She'll hunt me down and destroy everything I love and so, when I took the pills and slashed my wrist, I was doing it to free my family from her evil and her anger. *I* am the catalyst for her evil – so, if I was gone, then my loved ones would be free and, more importantly, safe."

Lizzie's heart pounded as she thought of her family and hoped to God that they were okay.

Don't go, Mummy, please don't go.

The doctor was more confused than ever and tried to understand what Lizzie meant. "Lizzie, why would she want revenge? Revenge for what exactly?"

You hopelessly pathetic little bitch. You can't even get that right, can you? CAN YOU? Is there anything you can do without failing? No, of course not. You can't do anything right.

She thought of the long-bladed scissors hanging from the kitchen wall.

"Trying to murder her, doctor," she replied coldly.

* * *

The children burst into the hall and threw their rucksacks onto the wooden floor. Lizzie's boyfriend didn't notice the answer phone flashing. Time was never on his side and as his kids changed out of their school uniforms and switched on the TV, he started to prepare their evening meal.

"Dad, we're starving," they yelled in unison. "How long till dinner?"

He didn't have a clue, really; being a chef was not his forte in life. Give him the garden to landscape, or anything practical, and he'd be perfectly competent, but since Lizzie had gone, he hadn't mastered the art of cooking.

Reading the instructions on the packet, it seemed simple enough. One pack of mince, one onion and the mixture, added to some water. He knew that there was some rice somewhere, so their chili con carne would be ready in no time at all.

The stroppy teenager was the first to slouch into the kitchen and raid the food cupboard. Grabbing three packets of crisps, he grunted and threw his half-siblings a packet each before moaning about their dad's meal choice and wishing that he could have pizza like his mum always gave him.

"We don't want crappy chili con carne," he complained, in a semi-squeaky voice.

His father snapped. "Shut up, Tommy. If you don't like spending time here, then go back to your mother. For God's sake, son, I have you two days a week and all you do is whinge."

Tommy's voice trembled as he stuttered an apology and scoffed his packet of crisps, glaring in his father's direction.

Tommy's father chopped the onion and fried the meat. He took a moment to study the kids' itinerary for the next day. PE for two and cookery for the other. The latter horrified him when he suddenly realised that the mince and the onion were meant for her next day's lesson, not for their darn evening meal. He'd rush down to the superstore once they were in bed – if he didn't fall asleep first.

He scribbled down the reminder and resumed preparing their meal, chucking it in the oven with the mixture and hoping for the best.

It would be at least an hour until dinner. He broached the subject of homework. His daughter was the only one to grab her bag and pull out her homework diary for him to read. She held her reading book and read four pages to him perfectly. He smiled as he listened to his little girl trying to pronounce the words correctly. Bless her, she had a lisp but she fought it and was working extra hard to learn to speak properly. She was a tough little cookie, he thought, just like her mum.

As for the boys, he couldn't face yet another battle. The ten-year-old had spellings, and failed miserably when tested. He laughed with his brother when he deliberately misspelt *liaison,* and tossed the spelling book onto the carpet, appearing to be satisfied with his mark of three out of ten. "That's not good enough," they mimicked before switching on the TV and watching their dad burst into the kitchen to switch off the blaring smoke detector.

He'd set the oven to completely the wrong temperature. Rather than following the recommendation of 180 degrees, he had hoped that, if he turned it up to 240, dinner would cook faster. However, once he had rescued the blackened remains of the chili, he realised that had not been such a wise idea.

"Okay, kids," he yelled, heading for the phone, "pizza it is."

"Yay, Dad," they replied. "You're the best!" After they had fought over which flavours they wanted, he agreed that they would have pepperoni and that there would be no more arguments. The boys finally settled down after setting up their Xbox 360 and starting a football game. The little girl hated football, so went upstairs to play with her dolls, who were all lined up in their bed waiting for their mummy to come home from school.

The phone continued to flash as he made the call. He knew that it couldn't be that important; the kids were with him and he'd spoken to his mum earlier. Work was fine too, so the message could wait.

He grabbed his jacket, telling the kids not to let anybody in or answer the phone as he would only be a couple of minutes. The pizza place was local so on the way he'd pick up the ingredients for cookery from a shop nearby. The children ignored their dad; they were too preoccupied with their game and the dollies were having fun as their 'mummy' brushed their hair and changed them into their sleep suits.

"Night night," she said, skipping down the stairs and looking for her daddy. Bursting into the living room, she asked her brothers where he had gone.

"Pizza shop," they replied, playing their game.

"I miss my mummy," she sobbed. She stood on the sofa, looking for the familiar headlights of her daddy's car. Her little pigtails wriggled as she looked for Mummy; she wished that she would come home soon.

"We all miss her," they replied, and one turned off the TV and gazed at the family photograph of them all in Spain the year before. It had been the best holiday ever, and in the photo the five of them smiled, standing on the beach without a care in the world.

"Will she ever come home?" the little girl asked, grabbing the frame and placing it on her lap. She looked at her mummy's pretty smile and her slender brown arms which were around all three children.

Looking sadly back at her, they lowered their heads and went back to their game console.

"Hurry up, Dad," they grumbled. "We're starving."

* * *

Jon studied Lizzie. She stared once again across the room towards his filing cabinet. There was nothing there, yet she kept looking, almost as though she was expecting something to magically appear. He double-checked, but all he could see was a cobweb and a few crumbs from the biscuits he regularly ate instead of a healthy lunch. Thinking of his biscuits, he retrieved a packet from his desk drawer, took a couple of them and offered Lizzie one. Lizzie was too preoccupied to notice his offer. When he had finished eating his biscuit, Jon approached Lizzie again, speaking softly in order not to cause her distress. He needed to understand fully what she was admitting to.

"Lizzie," he asked tenderly, "are you sure you're okay to continue?"

This one's for my scars.

Alfie had gone; he'd probably given up waiting for his owner to walk him and had left the doctor's office to find somebody else to look after him.

She remembered everything that had been wonderful about her beloved pet. She still missed him, despite knowing deep down that he was dead and she was imagining his presence. Gazing back at the doctor, she reminded herself why she was in his room.

"It had been years since I'd seen her, but I'd never forgotten what she had done."

Jon was relieved to see that his patient was back in his world, and settled down as she continued. He nibbled his second biscuit after realising that he hadn't eaten anything all day other than a few soggy cornflakes.

"I'd taken the children to school and had intended to go shopping – just for food and bits. Then, as I drove, I saw what I believed was my dog, Alfie. It was a large golden retriever and he was walking along a busy road with no lead and, apparently, no owner. I slammed on my brakes, put on the hazards and ran towards the dog, calling his name. Of course, he didn't stop, although his owner – who was jogging behind – gave me a filthy look and leashed the dog straight away."

This one's for Alfie.

"It shook me up, Jon. I know it sounds ridiculous; he was only a dog but something inside me at that point flipped. I realised that even though it had been years since she'd played that evil game with me, I still missed him and I was still suffering. Then, after a few more miles of driving, I saw a young mother pushing a pram; the same as the one I'd had all those years ago. She was only young, and I guess she'd bought it from a second-hand shop but, again, it reminded me of *her* and what she did to us all so long ago."

This one's for my baby.

Jon moved his chair close to Lizzie. She continued to tell her story and he no longer felt self-pity. He knew that Jen would be okay. He'd treat her to a meal out later to cheer her up, and they would be fine – unlike the young woman in front of him, whose eyes were empty and her face so incredibly sad.

"I was so consumed with hate that I frightened myself, doctor. I had to concentrate so hard on driving; my mind felt like a whirlpool and I was forcing my foot down on the accelerator, speeding through country lanes and not even caring about my safety or anybody else's. I had completely lost my mind, I know that now, but, at the time, I wanted to make *her* suffer for all that she'd done to us. I wanted her out of my – *our* – lives once and for all. I wanted her dead, Jon – *dead.*"

This one's for starving me.

"I arrived in no time at all and parked my car at the edge of The Avenue, not even sure how I'd got there. I'd forgotten which roads I had taken, everything about the journey, but none of that mattered at the time. So I locked up my car, tried to avoid being spotted by anybody, and stood by the back gate, waiting."

"Waiting for what, Lizzie?"

"For the kitchen light to go out."

Lizzie knew her mother's routine well. Her first drink would always be at 10.15 a.m. This had started when Andrew had been little and she'd dropped him off at nursery and returned home. Thereafter, the routine had stuck. She'd clean the kitchen, mop the floor, and then the gin would come out. After the first drink, she'd make the beds, vacuum upstairs, have another shower, then reward herself with her second drink of the day, reminding herself to have no more until precisely 12.30 p.m., which was after she'd picked Andrew up from nursery.

"It was 10.56 a.m.," she continued, looking directly into Jonathan's eyes. "The light went out and I knew where she'd be. She would have finished her drink, washed the glass, put it back into the cupboard then gone to bed for a nap."

I hate you, you evil cruel bitch.

"And so, knowing where she would be, I ran into the back garden, down the path and went in the kitchen door. It was never locked, you know." Lizzie shrugged and smiled at Jonathan, who was starting to feel a little uncomfortable.

This one's for every evil thing you've done to us all, Mother.

"And then I saw the scissors, *those* scissors. Revenge, Dr Davies, can be so, so sweet."

And this one, you evil tyrant, is for my hair.

"And, hell, did I want revenge."

* * *

His children picked at the pineapple and pretended to choke on the ham. Dave held his head in his hands and counted to ten to avoid losing his temper. "Okay kids, I'm sorry. The bloody pizza shop got the order wrong; please just eat your meal."

He knew that none of this was their fault – they missed their mum as much as he did but sometimes, like tonight, he struggled to cope with everything, and felt close to despair.

Leaving them fighting at the table, he ran to the phone. Thankfully, she was home. "Mum, sorry to bother you at tea time, but you couldn't come over for a while, could you? The kids are giving me hell and you know how lousy I am at coping when all three play up. I just need a bit of support for an hour or so."

His mother completely understood. Life had been so difficult for her son since Lizzie had been admitted to hospital, and the fact that she had refused to see him and her children since her admission had brought the poor man close to a breakdown. She pecked her husband on the cheek and headed out of her cosy home for the short walk to her son's.

The flashing on the phone was getting on his nerves now. He cleared the mess from the dining room and ordered the kids to get showered, and decided to finally play the message. It wasn't a sales call, nor was it from an automated machine with a robotic voice on the end. Instead it was from a Norman Hillier at St Thomas's Hospital.

It was related to Lizzie. Mr Hillier asked for a return call or a meeting, whichever was the easiest.

His mother's timing was impeccable. She arrived and he took the chance to go to Lizzie. He ran to his car and started the engine. "It's Lizzie," he yelled as he wound down the car window. "I don't care what she says this time, I'm going to see her. I want my princess back home."

* * *

The biscuits had done absolutely nothing to alleviate his hunger. Jon's stomach rumbled loudly and he felt more exhausted than ever. The odour from the canteen, which normally turned his stomach, smelled inviting, and he imagined all the patients chomping on their pork chops with apple sauce and mash. God, he was starving.

Lizzie was hungry too. She'd eaten nothing all day and feared that after all the good work she had done with keeping meals down, she would lose weight and be reprimanded by the staff.

"Did you have lunch, Lizzie?" Jon asked, desperately hoping that she too wanted a break and some sustenance.

She thought back to the earlier events of the day and realised that she had also missed breakfast. Her tummy rumbled and she blushed.

Jon smiled and left his office to see what remnants of food were left in the canteen. He just hoped that the catering staff had not cleared it all up: he felt he couldn't last another hour without food.

Thankfully, there were a few bits and pieces remaining. The chops had gone, but half a dozen dry sausages sat in their own grease and there were a couple of yoghurts left. Grabbing two plates, he took the remaining food along with some cutlery, back to his office.

Lizzie must have been hungry. She had pulled a chair against his desk and positioned it next to Jonathan's. It reminded him of a dinner table. She downed the small portion he brought in just a few minutes. Jon was delighted to see her enthusiasm as she enjoyed her meal; when she had been admitted she would only eat a minuscule portion of food, then regurgitate it when nobody was watching. She was making progress and he was proud of her. Until he remembered what she had just admitted...

He scooped the yoghurt onto his spoon. Lizzie watched him intently. Despite everything she had said to him in the past, she really liked this doctor. He was a nice man. She thought of her dad. He too was nice. She could do with him now.

Jon felt a little more human after eating his snack. Moving his chair away from his desk, he sat back with his hands behind his head. Lizzie moved her chair away too, hoping that she would feel as relaxed as the doctor looked. The thudding of her heart stopped any chance of that, and she knew it would be difficult to explain the rest of her story.

"Revenge," Lizzie stated in a cold, uncaring, almost sinister manner, "isn't always so sweet."

You will rot in hell – even the devil will hate you.

"She was asleep as always. I counted the stairs like I always had – there were thirteen to her room, which was on the first floor. I stood at the opened door where she slept, and I hated her, Jonathan. I despised the image in front of me, snoring and stinking of that disgusting perfume which she'd smother over her clothes to hide the smell of cigarettes and booze … and sometimes spray down my throat."

That will sweeten that foul mouth of yours, child.

"My hand was shaking like a leaf, though, and I thought that the blades would clatter loud enough to wake her. I have never been so terrified in my life, but …" Lizzie paused, then stared coldly at the doctor, "or as determined. This was my chance to pay her back for everything, and chances like that don't come very often, do they?"

Mummy's little angel hates you too.

"She had always loved cushions. Everywhere in the house, she would scatter them; they were on the floor in the living room and she had giant ones which she would collapse into – when she was happy, that is. I'd always have to drag her up, though; she was so fat, but, on those occasions, I knew that I'd be safe. She'd either be drunk or high on pot and she would just laugh and dance to her old hippie music, dragging me around with her, or Andrew, or sometimes, the pair of us."

We all hate you.

I recognised the large purple cushion on her rocking chair. She had tried to smother me with it a few times. Thankfully, she would stop once I started to have an asthma attack, because she knew that if she really did kill me, she would lose everything, including my brother, who she loved so much."

Why can't you be him, Elizabeth?

"She was still snoring. I tiptoed towards the chair, which I held with my left hand when I lifted the cushion, knowing that it creaked. It didn't move and so I stood over her, scissors and cushion shaking, studying the monster in front of me, willing her to stay asleep and not open those hideous, evil eyes of hers. Do you believe in angels, Dr Davies?"

Jonathan was deeply engrossed in Lizzie's story; he pictured her mother lying there and tried to imagine the tiny woman sitting in front of him with a huge cushion and scissors. Although it was a despicable thing to even consider, he admired Lizzie's courage.

"Sorry, Lizzie – I missed your question."

"Angels, doctor, do you believe in them?"

"I'm not sure, Lizzie," he replied honestly. "I've never seen them, but I don't discount anything paranormal. Until it's proven or disproven, I really cannot say."

"I do, doctor. At that moment, mine were watching over me. She didn't hear a thing and she hadn't sensed me either. I knew that she was twice my size, and I'd have to knock her out first. She had a large brass lamp on her bedroom cabinet and so I grabbed it and slammed it into her head."

"Heavens, Lizzie!" Jon's eyes widened as, once again, he tried to imagine Lizzie lunging at her mother. It was impossible.

"Not yet, doctor, let me continue." Lizzie's eyes shone. She smiled at Dr Davies. He felt uneasy.

"She must have been stunned – she woke and held her hand up to the huge gash on her head, which was pouring with blood. But she didn't move, doctor, she didn't move, and the adrenaline was bursting into every vein of my body, and I was excited that I might finally succeed. It was as though I really was being protected by them – my angels," she added. "So I jumped onto her, forcing my body against the cushion which I was holding over her face, and with the other hand, as she struggled, I stabbed and I stabbed and I stabbed those long blades into her body, not caring where they were going, not caring which organs I had punctured, and not caring whether I saw another day. Because," she concluded, her eyes wide and excited, "just for a brief moment, I had controlled her. 'Mummy's little angel' had flown away with her own little angels and instead, 'Mummy's little killer' was lying on that bed being punched and bitten – but not stabbed."

Daddy, is that you?

Once again, Jonathan was speechless. He shifted nervously in his chair. He watched the cold expression on Lizzie's face.

Leaving the safety of his seat, he turned to face the window. There was no sun, just clouds, and the car park was starting to empty. Normal folk were driving home now to have their dinner and spend time with their families. One young nurse hopped onto the rear of a motorbike after embracing a tall man in leathers. She looked so happy.

He watched the clouds thicken in front of his eyes. Droplets of rain fell, and ran down the window like tears. His crimson blind wobbled as he leaned against it, the crimson turning into blood, the window latches into blades. In the darkness the clouds had created, his own reflection formed a shadow against the cold glass, its silver slit eyes looking hatefully back at him.

A Range Rover appeared and a man sat staring up at him. In his hand was a case; some lucky person would be going home today, back to normality. Jon yearned to be that person. He turned to face the wide-eyed woman who was weeping and rocking backwards and forwards.

"And what happened next, Lizzie?" he asked, finding it difficult to meet her eyes. "How did you escape?"

Rising from the chair and joining Jonathan by the window, she spoke gently as she studied the people and cars below.

"My dad, doctor, he took the scissors away from me. He had seen the whole thing."

* * * * *

24. RECOVERING

2014: Beth

It was a clear, crisp day. Even though it was the middle of December, sunshine drenched the bedroom walls. He felt cosy. He turned to cuddle Jen, but was shocked to find her side of the bed empty.

The penny dropped when he caught sight of the red digits on his bedside clock. It was daylight because he had overslept by two hours. Throwing the covers off his bed, he burst into the shower room and within five minutes, had showered and was drying himself off, while trying to find something to wear. The washing basket was overflowing with dirty linen as Jen had been so busy over the past few weeks with school nativity plays and the girls' extracurricular activities – and Jon? Well, he wasn't allowed to touch the washing machine after the … incident … with the muddy trainers.

He grabbed a pair of half-clean chinos and a creased shirt from the day before and ran into the kitchen. There was a note for him on the fridge, a large Mickey Mouse magnet securing it.

Jon, I left you sleeping after your dreadful night. Called the secretary in your office who said she would reschedule your first two appointments. I hope you managed to grab some rest.

Love you.

Jen

xxxx

His heartbeat resumed a healthy rate. Jon put the kettle on and a couple of slices of bread into the toaster. Although he'd managed to snatch a few hours' sleep, it hadn't been deep enough to enable him to re-energise; he still felt drained physically. He studied the calendar that hung on the inside of the door where the cups were. Eight days until Christmas.

He'd decided to take three days off this year, which he had never done before. Christmas, although quieter regarding client meetings, was an ideal time for Jon to catch up on paperwork and get organised for the year ahead. But he didn't want to miss these magical years when the girls were young and believed in Santa, and so – much to the girls' and their mummy's delight – Daddy had booked three whole days away from the office to spend with them.

He'd planned to take the family to London on Christmas Eve to see the lights and to take the girls around Hamleys. It was something that he'd been lucky enough to do as a child, and he wanted the girls to have the same happy memories. He also still adored the toys in the famous store, especially the miniature cars, which cost almost as much as his old Volvo.

The toast had burned. He scraped the blackness away and recollected the message he'd received earlier from Dave Lewis. He had sent it at an unholy hour and Jon figured that, once again, Beth was having a tough time. Hastily eating the toast, he dashed upstairs and grabbed his mobile.

He had received a message from Jen. It was blank other than a screen full of kisses, and he smiled, replying with the simple word, 'ditto.' He knew that she'd smile too: *Ghost* was one of her favourite movies and she cried every time she watched it – which was often!

It was now 9.15 a.m; he figured that Dave would be around to take his call. As he dialled, however, he decided to call the office first. He knew that he had two more appointments before lunch and needed to make sure that his daft secretary hadn't cancelled those, as well as the earlier two.

It was obvious from the tone of her voice that she had been preoccupied. Jon imagined that she was caking yet more makeup on, or even plucking her ridiculously thin eyebrows; he found this repulsive. She had, not surprisingly, cancelled *all* his appointments for the morning and giggled while apologising for being ditsy. That was an understatement, he thought but, deep down, he was quite chuffed. He'd have a decent breakfast instead and, if Dave and Beth were available, he'd fit them in earlier and actually enjoy a real lunch break. He put some eggs on to fry, and rang Dave.

Dave was at work when he called, and was relieved to see Jon's name on his screen.

"Oh, Dr Davies, thank you ever so much for calling me back. I'm so sorry for texting you at that ridiculous time. I just didn't think for a moment that you would read the message at four in the morning; I just sent the text while Beth's nightmares were fresh on my mind. I forget things so often now – it has to be an age thing!"

"Tell me about it, Dave," Jon laughed, having forgotten that he'd left the eggs frying for the past four minutes and they would no doubt be like bullets.

He scraped the eggs from the pan and threw them out, then offered Dave an earlier appointment. Unfortunately, Dave had a meeting with a potential client and could not risk losing the possibility of, what could be, a business-saving contract.

"How about I call Beth," he offered, "and see whether she's up to seeing you alone?"

Jon agreed, thinking that she might well feel strong enough, since, during her last meeting, she had managed to remain reasonably calm and composed without Dave being there.

Dave thanked the doctor and went back to preparing his presentation for the meeting. His PowerPoint skills were very basic, but he'd taught himself how to attach photographs and add text, and that should be enough. Along with his sales patter and a tour of his – pretty empty – workshop, there wasn't much else he could do. At the end of the day, his estimate and the quality of his workmanship were the critical elements and, if the client liked them, then maybe Dave would seal the contract. He crossed his fingers as he saved his presentation and thought of Beth.

* * *

Beth's mother reached for the bottle, then resisted the temptation and closed the cabinet door gently. She had been dry now for three whole weeks which, to her, felt like thirty years. It was only 9.30 in the morning and she dreaded the thought of being conscious for at least another twelve hours before she could end the misery of yet another sober day.

Lighting her eighth cigarette since waking up, she slouched into the living room and stared at the fire. The burned remnants of yesterday's logs sat on the hearth, and she needed to clear it out, lay it and get the coal in. It was too much to cope with, and so she turned up the thermometer dial for the heating, hoping that the ridiculously small radiator in the enormous room would offer her a little more warmth.

The sunshine, despite throwing light into the room, exaggerated the filth of the place. Thick dust sat on the antique cabinet, which was adorned with nicotine-encrusted photo frames. The glass on each family portrait was a dingy yellow. She picked up one from many years ago, and licked her finger, wiping away the sticky film to study it. It had been taken some twenty years before, in her back garden. It must have been summer time: the trees were in full leaf and apples were hanging from the branches, some of which were bent with the weight of the ripe fruit. *September*, she figured. *Oh, how time flies.*

Her son had been oblivious to the camera lens focusing on him, and she studied his sturdy little body in a pair of blue swimming trunks. He was splashing in a circular paddling pool and she smiled, remembering his excitement as he watched her blowing the pool up, and then running in and out of the kitchen with buckets of warm water to fill it up. The red bucket in his hand was still in his former bedroom, along with an enormous Tonka truck, which he'd played with in the water. How she missed him.

Placing the frame back on the dusty shelf, she sat down and closed her eyes, hoping to sleep for a while and forget her emotional torment. The memories flashed back when she recollected her last conversation with him.

You leave her alone, Mother, do you hear me? Just let her run her life as most normal people do – I'm warning you, you touch her one more time, or cause her any more pain, and I will kill you. Do you understand, Mother? Do you?

How could he? she questioned. After all the love she had shown him for the whole of his life. She wished that he'd listened to her, or even tried to understand her reasons why, but he'd disappeared out of her life and ignored her calls and letters for ten years now. Her heart was empty; she would do anything to win him back, even if it meant letting go of her past and finally accepting her daughter for who she was.

But her daughter's eyes still haunted her, along with the painful scars that she'd hidden so very well.

Could she ever forgive?

Could she ever forget?

* * *

Beth wiped the screen on her mobile phone and removed her latex gloves, relieved that she would be seeing Dr Davies today. It was only eight days before her family meal and she had planned to prepare some of the food today, then, if there was room, to freeze it.

She'd decided to cheat on the actual Christmas cake, having overheard an elderly lady speaking to her husband in the supermarket earlier in the week. *No point in faffing about with all that mixture,* she had said. *I'll buy the fruit cake, then marzipan and ice it at home. Nobody will know.* Beth had laughed when she added the cake and a number of boxes of mince pies to her trolley. It made perfect sense to Beth too, and she felt reassured, knowing she had one less thing to worry about.

Her OCD and nightmares were, however, causing her great concern. Although she was managing to cope with some aspects of her life, especially with 'the girls' no longer hanging around, she was still finding it so hard to manage without believing that germs would harm her. Logically, she knew that she would be fine without her gloves, but now that her friends had gone, she still had to hold on to some of her security blankets, such as the gloves and bacterial wipes.

When she picked up her pen, she resisted wiping it and held it between her quivering fingers. She knew that only *her* germs were on it and that the pen, so long as she didn't put it in her mouth, would not cause her any harm. The drawer from which she had removed it was sterile; she cleaned it daily, and so, for once, she would write with it, glove-free. She applied the same sense of logic to the notepad as she placed it on her immaculate worktop.

She began to write her shopping list. The phone in the hall shrilled loudly. Since her recent decline, she had been unable to speak to anybody on the landline as the sales calls frightened her. She shuddered remembering the last call she'd taken, when she'd thought the caller was a potential killer.

But today, she realised that if she was ever going to lead a semi-normal life, she would have to face and conquer many of her fears. Leaving the notepad behind, she ran to the phone and deliberately avoided wiping it before answering.

"Hello," she whispered nervously.

"Hello," *she* said. "How are you?"

The voices in Beth's head returned, ordering her to terminate the call immediately. She resisted the urge to run away, like she had for most of her life; in eight days she would be facing the woman on the end of the line and this call was the beginning of the rest of her life.

"I'm fine, thanks," she replied, her voice shaking as she spoke. "Dad said that you will be coming for Christmas. Are you calling to cancel?" Beth half hoped that her mother would; after all, her dad had now left her and she hoped that her mum wouldn't want to spend any time with him. Secretly, she was still petrified of her.

You stupid, stupid child.

"No," her mother replied. "I just wanted to make sure that you were still able to manage with us all, considering how sick you've been recently."

Beth would not rise to her mother's snide comments; she thought of the amount of work she had to do, but resisted the temptation to panic.

"I'll be fine, thank you, just fine. I'm doing so much better now, and Dr Davies is really helping me to get everything into perspective. Did Dad tell you that I'm going to restart my art course this week?"

Her mother did not respond.

Beth continued to speak, her voice becoming louder, gaining more and more courage and confidence with every passing second.

Suddenly, she thought about her brother. "He won't be coming for Christmas. Despite everything I've told him, he still won't budge, although Kirsty reckons she might be able to persuade him. You know how she can be, don't you?" Beth thought excitedly of her daughter, who would soon be arriving for a whole two weeks.

Are you out of your head? She will never change; why don't you get that, sis? her brother had said.

"Well, whether he does or does not decide to partake, your father and I will be joining you all. I am pleased you are benefiting from the sessions with that doctor but, dear, you need to stop depending on him to make your decisions. He will naturally choose to carry on booking sessions with you – but purely for his financial gain. Don't believe for a moment he is interested in your wellbeing; all he cares about is his bank balance."

Beth looked at her watch, again trying to ignore her mother's nasty comments about her friend. She only had a few minutes to tidy herself up before leaving for her appointment.

"Talking of Jonathan, I have to go now as I'm seeing him soon," she replied sternly.

"Oh, well, I won't keep you any longer. Do you have to drive far?"

"No, just a few miles to Dunstable."

"Well, goodbye. Your father will be in touch to discuss timings for Christmas."

"Goodbye, Mother."

Beth replaced the receiver and collapsed onto the bottom stair. Her heart thudded and sweat ran down her forehead. She studied her shaking hands. She desperately needed her friends right now and looked behind her in the hope that they would be there. The cream carpet and banisters were all that greeted her, however, and, after regaining her composure, she realised that she had taken the first major step of her recovery and had done it all by herself.

"I don't need you anymore," she shouted, knowing that nobody could hear her shaking voice. "I can – and I will – do this alone."

With that, she threw on a jacket, tossed her latex gloves into the bin and pushed down the lid with her bare hand, which she then scrubbed with soap and dried with a paper towel.

After polishing the living room, Beth set off on her short trip to tell the doctor everything.

* * *

Jonathan finally decided to abandon the idea of preparing a half edible breakfast at home and went to McDonald's instead, only just arriving before they finished serving breakfast. It was worth the drive. He finished his hash brown and egg McMuffin and smiled, thinking once again of his girls, who also loved McDonald's Happy Meals. He would try to get a few hours' shopping done at lunch and buy the women in his life a few surprise Christmas gifts, he figured, racking his brain for some original ideas for them all. Last year had been a disaster, and he reminded himself not to buy Jen anything practical again – although privately he still felt that the Jamie Oliver saucepans had been a great idea.

When he reached the car park, a car barged in front of his, making Jon slam on his brakes and spill the coffee he was sipping all over his half-clean shirt. He'd taken the lid off to cool it down and realised, once again that it was daft. This really wasn't his day.

The secretary, for once, was doing some work, updating the computerised diary system for Jon's colleagues. She entered the client information, then raised her eyebrows, shrugged her shoulders and looked at her watch.

"Afternoon, Jonathan," she said, resuming her typing and grinning at the messy, flustered man in front of her.

"Morning, Joanne, and how are you today?" he replied, wiping his shirt with a handkerchief. "Any messages?"

"Nope. I've sorted out the new appointments with the clients from this morning. Won't be till after Crimbo," she said, saving the calendar online. Jon nodded, gathering a few handwritten notes from her desk.

"Oh, some sales reps popped in." She handed Jon a large calendar for the following year, which one rep had given her. Jon was disappointed that he hadn't received his usual case of wine.

"Was that it?" he asked, disappointed.

"Yep, that was from the supplier – and the strange woman who visited shortly after didn't leave a thing," she added while she fumbled through her handbag looking for her e-cigarette. She'd tried quitting endless times and this time had managed to abstain from smoking for precisely forty-seven hours and three minutes. She was now addicted to the plastic stick with a blue light, but at least she could smoke indoors.

Jon smiled, then watched Joanne puffing on the electronic cigarette. "What was her product, Jo?"

"Dunno. She just waltzed straight into your office when I said you were out and left a few minutes ago. Didn't leave a card, although she did say she would call you later."

Jon shrugged and gave up trying to clean his shirt. Bloody sales reps drove him potty. His argument was that if he actually needed anything, he would call them first. And now that his stationery supplier only gave him a crummy calendar instead of wine at Christmas, he would buy his supplies online instead!

He cheered up as the large portrait of Jen and the girls welcomed him into the warmth of his office and, after settling into his comfy chair, the familiar face of his client peeked around his door and smiled.

"Beth, hello, and thanks so much for bringing the appointment forward; it's really helped me out."

£2.50

Beth closed the door behind her and made herself comfortable in the old green chair to which she was so accustomed.

"How are you doing?" Jon asked. He noticed that her nails were bitten again. Beth picked up on his disappointment immediately; she'd learned to read his facial expressions very well over the years.

"I know, I know. I chipped one, abandoned the thought of killing myself with the germs, and then nibbled it instead of filing it. Then I started to chew the others and here I am back to square one." She formed fists with her hands to avoid looking at the ugliness of her fingers.

£5.00

"Never mind, Beth, you have proven you can kick the habit once and so, when you feel ready, you can grow them again. How's everything else? Dave mentioned that your nightmares are back."

£7.50

Without moving or meeting Jon's eyes, Beth spoke. "It's the Christmas ones again," she said in a whisper, recollecting every precise detail of that terrible Christmas when she had been a child, down to the hours she had been forced to scrub the fire hearth the following day and scrape the strange melted stuff from it. "But each one is longer than the last, and they're so vivid."

Where's my dolly, Mummy?

Beth's eyes met Jonathan's as she spoke. "The good thing is, doctor, I understand completely why these nightmares are back. The closer Christmas gets, the more anxiety I have and, naturally, with my history, I'm frightened, of course I am. But I'm more determined than ever to prove to her that I am capable and that I'm on the mend. Does that make sense to you?"

Jonathan completely understood; however, from the knowledge he had of Beth's relationship with her mother, he still feared the worst.

Beth sensed this. "I spoke to her, just before I came here, and, for the first time in my life, I didn't throw up afterwards or have an episode. I stayed pretty calm really." She thought of her friends not being with her and smiled proudly at her achievement.

£10.00

Jonathan was impressed; Beth really was showing very positive improvements.

She continued. "It was only a quick call, mainly about Christmas, I think, and even though my brother says he won't be coming, *she* still is. Perhaps, after everything that's gone on, she really is changing."

Beth, she's evil; she will never change.

Jonathan hoped that Beth was right, and that her mother could finally extend a little kindness to her daughter. He doubted it, however.

"Do you believe that, Beth? That she really is starting to accept who you are – that she is, as you say, changing?"

Don't put yourself through this, sis.

"My dad says that she's been off the drink for almost a month now and, although she can't concentrate very well and the house is starting to become neglected, she is apparently coping. It's part of the deal he set with her when he walked out. Stay dry and you can stay in the house. Start drinking again, then you're out! He's also paying for her to have some counselling as well – like mother like daughter." Beth smiled at the doctor, who was studying his client's body language. She was sitting up straight; her posture was good, which demonstrated that her confidence levels were increasing. She'd also removed her boots and tucked her feet under herself. He found this very endearing, especially as his daughters did exactly the same when they were watching TV.

£15.00

"How much are your sessions, Dr Davies?" Beth asked suddenly, after realising that a quarter of an hour had passed.

Surprised by her sudden change of tack, Jonathan smiled warmly again at his client.

"Beth, I don't charge you. It's only if you fail to attend an appointment that costs are incurred. You've always been, and always will be, an NHS patient. Why do you ask?" he enquired, watching Beth. She slouched in her chair and put her boots back on.

"Oh, it was her again, Jonathan. I should have known. She mentioned that you weren't interested in my wellbeing, only in your bank balance." Beth chewed her nails and Jon looked frustrated. Why the hell wouldn't her mother leave Beth alone?

"Thank you," she added, pushing her chair against the large desk in front of her. She studied his features and noticed that he looked shattered.

"You're welcome, Beth. So, did what your mother say affect how you feel?"

"No, Jonathan. I should have expected it, and I am not under any illusion that Christmas Day will be all fun and games. She'll be sober, at least, and I guess that she'll hopefully be quiet and just let the rest of us enjoy ourselves."

Jonathan hoped that Beth was right.

"I need to talk about my OCD," she added, noticing the brown stain on his shirt. She desperately wanted to clean it, but resisted the temptation to rush to Jonathan and remove it from his back. The germs would be okay on him.

"Are you managing to deal with it in a more logical way, Beth?"

She thought of the pen and paper this morning and also the fact that she had been able to start doodling once again with some new pencils Dave had bought her.

"I'm starting to improve," she replied, remembering that she had some half-finished Christmas cards to complete later. "But it's not easy. I don't worry so much about other people dying from germs and poisoning, though," she added. "Like your shirt." She pointed and giggled. Jon blushed. "The old Beth would have torn it off, worrying first about you, and second, about the germs from the stain entering the air and polluting my body." She threw her hands in the air and laughed loudly. "How insane is that?"

Jon smiled thoughtfully at his client. She really was improving.

"So, now, rather than get myself in a terrible state, I hold my breath and think things through. Let's face it, if there really were harmful germs from everything, we would all be extinct! And so, every day, I set myself a new little challenge and try to face it." She thought of her mother. "Like, for example, the call from *her*. I resisted the temptation to wipe the telephone first and also, I had enough courage to pick the call up, despite my terrible fear of it being a stranger who wanted to kill me."

She thought back to the recent episode with the cold caller once again and shuddered. It had seemed so real, and the girls really had protected her that day.

"Well, Beth, you're showing real determination to overcome some of your issues, and I am so proud of you, as I am sure Dave is too. But I am concerned about the nightmares so, although your current medicine is helping to alleviate your other issues, I may need to change it again."

Beth's eyes widened and she stared at the doctor. What if the nightmares went and *they* came back? She was getting used to not having them around and, over the past few days had not even missed them.

"No," she replied sternly. "I believe that once Christmas is over, the nightmares, like so much else, will go. It's only eight days. I can live with it, doctor, and then, if they still haunt me, we can look at changing the medication."

"Beth, sometimes you leave me almost speechless! I am so impressed with your attitude and yes, I completely agree. But, Beth, please don't suffer in silence. If you find you can't cope, please call me immediately. My mobile is always on and I don't charge."

Beth returned the smile, then a look of anxiety overtook her emotions.

"Even on Christmas Day, doctor?" She was still so nervous at the thought of facing her mother after the last time.

Jon imagined how his Christmas would be. The girls, no doubt would wake up at an unholy hour, squeal with excitement realising that Santa had been, and they would take their sacks into bed with him and Jen. They'd tear off the paper, play with their new toys and share one of Jen's superb festive breakfasts – with bucks fizz for the adults and a pretend one for the girls. How he adored Christmas.

"Beth, I know that you won't need to call. You can do this; I absolutely know you can. But, yes, I am always available for you. You know that, even on Christmas Day." He hoped to God that she didn't have to call him – for more than one reason. He wanted to treat his wife this year to a romantic gift, as the set of saucepans the year before had gone down like a lead balloon. *Diamonds,* he thought. *Yes, diamonds are forever.*

Beth understood. She studied the clock on the wall, then rose from her chair and moved towards her friend.

Pecking him gently on his cheek, she looked deep into his eyes. "I don't know what I would have done without you,

Jonathan," she whispered. "Other than Dave, you know me better than anybody else; I will always be eternally grateful to you. Jen and your daughters are very lucky to have you in their lives."

"And Dave, Kirsty and Robert are lucky to have you too, Beth," he replied, having gone crimson with the embarrassment of her little kiss. Heck, if the authorities were to find out, he'd be struck off, but Beth was different from all his other clients – she really was special.

Beth, after moving away from Jon, thought of her Dave and his meeting which was happening right this very moment with the American customer who liked his furniture designs. She smiled, thinking of her shy, handsome son. How proud she was of him. And her Kirsty, her little princess who, despite everything, was always chirpy and had such a zest for life. Beth was one lucky woman.

"Thank you again," she said, heading for his door. "Oh, and if I don't see you before the big day, have a great Christmas, doctor."

"I will," he replied, opening the door for his favourite client and feeling the butterflies rush through his stomach at the thought of spending time with his own family. "And Beth, you too. I know you can do this. Should the worst come to the worst, remember your saying."

"Yes, Jonathan," she replied, completely understanding what he meant.

"Third time lucky, Beth."

"Yes, Dr Davies," she replied, waving. "Third time lucky."

25. HOPE

1994: Elise

For the first time in years, Elise had woken up with an appetite. Whether it was because she hadn't eaten properly for months, or because she was pregnant, she enjoyed her cereal and even the burned toast that had accompanied it.

The bed next to her, which the nosy lady had been in the previous day, now belonged to a young woman, similar to Elise's age, who had left all of her breakfast after turning her nose up at everything placed in front of her. She was dreadfully skinny too, and Elise hoped she wasn't suffering from anorexia or bulimia, like she had in the past. It was a terribly hard battle to force food into your body but, when she looked down at her bump, Elise realised that she could never allow herself to slip into her old ways. She had two lives to consider now.

She was becoming used to the methadone too, although she still missed the buzz that the heroin had given her. She figured that, as with everything else she had fought previously, the addiction would pass and, if she kept herself occupied and focused on her baby, the cravings would diminish in time.

After showering and dressing in the clothes that Jen had kindly brought her, she sat down on a hard plastic chair by her bed. The charity leaflet jumped out at her. She read the case studies of some former residents, and Elise felt a glimmer of hope grow inside her. The Joshua Foundation appeared to be the perfect solution – perhaps she could, in time, learn a trade. In the past, she had shown a creative flair, which she thought she could apply to the furniture element of the charity. She knew how to strip wood and smiled as she recollected Bob's bedroom and the little cabinet she had painstakingly stripped and repainted for him. Perhaps the charity would allow her to buy one for her Bump if she earned some money for them in the cafe. Everything depended on them liking her, and she hoped that Dr Davies would find the time today to chat with her. She liked him and trusted him. Elise smiled at the skinny girl in the next bed, and crossed her fingers and thought of her future. It was going to be tough without David and Bob, but now that she had a chance to move on, she could aim for the toughest goal of all and finally gain closure on her past.

* * *

Jonathan's nightmares had not subsided. As well as feeling physically and emotionally drained, he now had a hangover from hell.

After calling Jen and offloading his worries, she reminded him that he had a meeting with the Joshua Foundation at 2 p.m. He showered and left for his shift at the hospital, dreading the thought of reawakening the nightmares of *her* when he next met Elise. She was the link to his suffering, he knew that, and her pain had radiated into the depths of his own soul and was tormenting every waking moment of his life. He felt reassured that he had analysed the cause of his problems, although he knew that he could not escape them. The next few months of his training would lead to better things and form the basis of his career as a psychiatrist. Two months left, then all would be fine, he reassured himself, dashing into the staff room and helping himself to his fourth coffee of the day.

Although his work schedule never panned out as it should, Jon had a reasonably quiet day ahead: twelve hours on shift, but most of it was relatively straightforward. He would do his rounds in the psychiatric ward then hold a number of one-to-one sessions in the peaceful confines of his interview room. Elise was second on his list and he figured that he would focus more on the charity side than reopen the very raw wounds that Elise was suffering from. He would discuss her rehab, keep it short, and then move on to the next patient. It would be fine, he reassured himself, fighting the urge to run away and never return to the Luton and Dunstable Hospital.

* * *

Another downfall of not using drugs was that time dragged. Elise had read the charity leaflet and was now bored stiff. After studying the patients in Ward 33, she tried to work out why they were all there, which killed about a quarter of an hour. She watched the nurses as they checked the patients' blood pressure, took their temperature then fed them their pills – that killed another thirty minutes. The nurse then spent ten minutes with Elise, checking all of the usual things, re-dressing her hand, and giving her the medication she needed in order to stay clean. She had no abdominal pain, her blood pressure was still fine and she had eaten well. With all boxes ticked on her chart, Elise shrugged hoping that the girl in the next bed would notice her and respond. She did neither.

There were no books in the ward either, and Elise wished that she had some money to buy one – or even a newspaper. She had no idea what was going on in the world anymore and needed to be in touch with reality; something that she had lost touch with the moment she had been forced to run away from home.

She hobbled back onto her bed, and tried to relax, in the hope that she would doze for a few hours. She blanked out the surrounding noises in the ward and closed her eyes, concentrating hard on Bob and David, smiling at her, full of love. Her former life.

Smile for the camera, Elise. That's it, just as you are – perfect.

Now, hold Bob close to your chest and kiss his head. Fab! Oh you should see this photo, Elise – quick, come here.

Smile for the camera, child; show everybody what a sniffling little brat you really are. Say cheese.

She never did see the photograph her mother had taken that day. It was taken on her birthday and that's all that she could remember; she had no idea how old she was; her mother chose not to celebrate her birthday, and refused to allow Elise to remind her of the fact that she had been born.

The idea of the birthday cake had been her nanny's, but Elise could never own up to that as she had been forbidden from seeing her, and dare not let on that she had been playing hooky from school again. Nanny had given her a surprise gift, a cute teddy bear, which also had to stay at her house. She'd made Elise a cake too, with chocolate butter icing and a candle, but she had warned her not to eat too much of it as her mother would punish her if she failed to eat her evening meal. But Elise wanted to celebrate her special day and felt that a simple request for a tea party with a birthday cake was not too much to ask. Clearly it had been.

Her mother had refused, and, after she had shouted at Elise, Elise had broken down and sobbed. The photograph had been taken as her mother sneered at her before forcing her to eat her meal. It was cold meat and soggy roast potatoes from the week before, which had been left in the fridge uncovered. Elise had gagged when she tried to chew the meat, which had turned bad – and, having forced it down, had thrown up over her school uniform and her mother.

"You filthy, disgusting child," her mother had screamed, tearing off her daughter's clothing and roughly stripping her naked. She forced Elise, by her hair, up to the bathroom, she ran the bath, closed the door behind her and pushed the shivering girl into the icy cold water.

Under you go – hold your breath if you want to make another birthday.

Elise had taught herself how to hold her breath for over a minute. Having spent most of her time locked in her room with no toys or books, she had learned to meditate, which involved taking deep breaths. Sometimes, she would count how many seconds she could go without breathing and, despite having asthma, had trained herself to hold her breath for as long as a hundred seconds. That had, she was sure, saved her life that day.

She suddenly awoke from her nap; Elise noticed that an hour had passed. A number of visitors had appeared in the ward, some with books and others with bottled drinks and snacks. The skinny girl in the bed was smiling as a young chap with more earrings than a jewellery shop window entered the ward and waved at her.

"Hey babe," he yelled, "I got you these!" He waved a box of chocolates in the air and sped towards the woman, who turned away when he presented her with the Milk Tray. Elise figured that she had an eating disorder – she could recognise the signs.

As the visitors pulled their chairs closer to the patients' beds, a tall Jamaican woman entered the ward and approached the nurses' station. Pointing in Elise's direction, they directed the woman to her bed and spoke quietly to her. She walked over to Elise and stood at the end of the bed.

"Hello, Elise, you won't know me. I'm Leroy's Auntie Vera."

Elise's eyes widened and the softly spoken lady sat down. She wheezed as she lowered herself to the plastic seat, and studied Elise closely. Shocked by Elise's haggard appearance, she gazed down at her hands, which were shaking nervously, and stuttered a few words.

"I don't know where to start," she said softly. "Losing Leroy has been absolutely devastating for the whole family, especially his mother." She wiped her eyes with a pink hanky as she continued. "Such a waste, losing our precious boy to the evil of drugs. Where did we go wrong?"

Elise studied the lady, who wept loudly. She wore a St Christopher's cross on a chain and was gripping it tightly with her left hand. Her features were drawn and sad and her eyes were empty – a sight that Elise was all too familiar with.

"I'm so sorry," Elise replied sadly. "It's nothing you or your family did." She tried to reassure the stranger, knowing that Leroy's family was so different to her own. "Leroy just slipped into the habit, Vera, and, from one joint, he ended up needing more and trying the harder drugs. Trust me, it wasn't you, – he loved you all and spoke so highly of you." Elise thought back to her trip to church with Leroy and how every member of his family was full of life, love and laughter. How she had yearned to be part of his family.

"But why?" the lady asked. "Why did he need to do that stuff when all he had to do was pick up the phone and talk to us?"

Elise felt like a psychiatrist as she tried to formulate an explanation. Her circumstances had been so different to Leroy's, and she had started taking heroin out of desperation. But Leroy? Well, Leroy just wanted to live life to the max. How ironic, she thought, since she had lived, and he had died.

She thought back to the good times she had shared with her friend.

"Leroy, like most young people, didn't worry about tomorrow. He lived for today and before he started on the heavy stuff, he just enjoyed the kick of a joint. Then, I guess he tried the stronger stuff and before he knew it, he was an addict – like I am." Elise lowered her head in shame, knowing that despite her rehab programme she would always be a drug addict.

The woman smiled at Elise, who huddled beneath her bed covers. Passing Elise her dressing gown, she wrapped it around her shoulders kindly.

"Were you close to my nephew?" she asked.

"He was a good friend to me. He offered me shelter, warmth and protection when nobody else would so, yes, I cared deeply for him." She thought of their first meeting, when Leroy had taken pity on her and had bought her a coffee. "But we were never involved as boyfriend and girlfriend, if that's what you mean. We were just friends – good friends," she added tearfully, realising afresh that she would never see him again. "I wish that I could go to his funeral to pay my respects."

Vera cleared her throat and looked uncomfortable. "That's why I'm here," she replied, lifting a large red handbag from the floor. She unzipped the bag and rummaged in it before pulling out a brown paper bag.

Handing the bag to Elise, she continued. "After Leroy's death, we had to go to his flat. It may sound ridiculous to you, but we wanted to dress him in smart clothes for his final journey. It was a horrendous experience for me and his mother."

Elise listened intently and sympathised deeply. Although both her Bob and David were alive, she had grieved for them every day since she had left. They may as well have been dead; the suffering she constantly felt was painfully similar to a bereavement.

Vera continued, "We were standing in his living room when there was a knock at the door. Believing that it could be the police or somebody connected with his passing, I opened it. I was frightened to death; the man standing opposite me looked terrifying. I'll be honest, he didn't look like the type that Leroy would have associated with, but anyhow, he handed me this bag and said that it belonged to Leroy's girl. He asked me to return it to her, and that's why I'm here." Elise stared at the woman in shock; it sounded like Craig, the thug who had beaten Leroy the day before he had died. Or his henchman Duke.

"Did he say anything else?" she asked, petrified that Craig would hunt her down and demand the rest of his money. She was also terrified that he knew where she was.

"Just that he didn't mean it to come to this," she replied looking directly into Elise's frightened eyes. "I have no idea what he meant, but he left soon after and said that I should say no more about our meeting after handing you the bag. He looked deadly serious about it, and so, as far as I am concerned, I've kept my part of the deal – and you must too. He didn't look like the type of person you should mess with, and I won't be telling anybody else about this visit." She stood up and moved to the side of the bed. "I'm sorry for you, dear," she said kindly. "Whatever brought you to this bad place, you can trust in our Lord. Pray when you feel the need and ask Jesus to guide you through – he is our saviour and he can be yours too."

Elise smiled, wishing she had faith too. But God had never protected her from evil, despite her praying to Him every night as a child. Fighting the desire to snap at the woman, she politely replied, "I will, and thank you for all you've done. Please pass my condolences on to the rest of the family. Oh, and your God will reassure you that it's nothing you have done wrong. Leroy is in heaven now, along with all of the other angels, looking down and smiling at you."

The woman fought back her tears. "I'm glad I found you," she whispered, smiling sadly at Elise.

"How did you find me?" Elise questioned.

"When we identified Leroy's body, they said that you were rushed into hospital too. You were the lucky one."

She exited the ward without saying another word. Despite everything she had told the poor girl, she had started to question her own faith. Elise clearly needed a miracle to help her, and without God, who could do this?

* * *

Jon's first meeting of the day had been an absolute disaster. His client was a middle-aged man suffering from cirrhosis of the liver due to him drinking two bottles of whisky a day. He had attempted to take his life after his wife had rejected him – she had left him for his best friend. Jon simply was not in the mood to be sympathetic, but his client was desperate to hear a friendly voice.

His yellowing eyes met the doctor's. "I feel so tired all the time. And although I know I have to eat, I'm never hungry these days and feel so weak. Now that she's gone as well, I feel like going back to the booze. What have I got to lose, doctor? Nothing, that's what I say. It's not as though I'll ever meet anybody else, and even if I did, I'm bloody impotent now, so she'd chuck me the minute she found out I can't perform in the bedroom."

Jon, although he was suffering from a hangover, disliked the man in front of him. He thought of Elise and the pain she had suffered at the hands of an alcoholic. Looking coldly at his patient, he asked, "Were you violent when you were drinking?"

The man looked shocked and replied instantly, "No, never. Why on earth would you ask that?"

"Because often the two go hand in hand," Jon replied sternly.

"Have you never heard of the saying *a happy drunk*?" the man replied defensively, shifting his chair as far away from the doctor as possible. "Well, just in case you haven't, I was that type of drunk. Comatose most of the time, actually, but before that, I was very happy with everything." He thought back to his days as a pub landlord and how work had formed his association with drink. How he missed those happier times.

Jon continued to fire questions at the man. He had no idea why his patient expected him to resolve his issues – only *he* could do that and, by the state of him, he didn't have that long left, so what was the point?

Standing up and walking towards the doctor, the man looked at him sadly.

"I can't believe that you of all people have judged me because of my addiction. As you know from my records, I've been off drink for two years and not once – *not once* – have I touched a single drop. I've lost everything through alcohol – my business, my wife, my health, my home – but now I'm asking for help. My suicide attempt was a call for help, doctor. I'm frightened of dying and I'm lonely, and, to be honest, I just needed to talk to a professional. I guess I was asking too much."

He headed for the door. Jon felt riddled with guilt, realising the despicable way he had treated the man. He hated himself and silently questioned whether he was really cut out to be a psychiatrist.

"Please, John, do sit down. I'm so sorry – I have no excuse for my behaviour other than I am tired and haven't slept properly for a few nights. Please forgive me."

The man studied the doctor and figured that he too needed a shrink. Forgivingly, he nodded and sat down again to face Jonathan.

"So, where would you like to begin?" Jon asked, smiling at his patient.

His client began to explain his life history to Jon, and felt a little better just for sharing his feelings with a professional. None of it registered with Jonathan, though, who was too preoccupied with thoughts of Elise and the Joshua Charity Foundation just a few miles down the road – and, of course, Jen, who had arranged so much for his patient.

* * *

She'd known almost as soon as she felt the crumpled bag what was inside. Resisting the temptation to open it, Elise ran her fingers gently over it and imagined how it would look. She hoped the diamonds were still intact, and that the tiny hands still moved across the delicate glass face. Visions of her nanny came back to her. Perhaps, Elise thought, this was a message from her angels. Perhaps, after all, somebody was indeed looking out for her.

Her thoughts were interrupted when Jon strode along the ward and offered her a tired smile. Her heart fluttered at the sight of her friend and, after placing the bag on her bed, she beamed at him. Jon's heart warmed as he studied her. Although she still looked exhausted, her eyes were brighter, and the scabbing on her face was healing.

"Oh, Dr Davies," she exclaimed. "Am I pleased to see you! I've been so bored, and now that I've read everything about that charity, I really want to ask your opinion – and a huge favour too."

Jon looked worried.

"Oh, nothing major or anything," Elise added, picking up on Jon's anxiety. "Shall we chat here or in your office?"

She threw off her bed covers; Jon grinned at the sight of her. The pink tracksuit bottoms hung below her underwear and the top swamped her.

"It'll be fine for when I'm nine months pregnant," Elise chirped, guessing what the doctor thought of her oversized clothing. Jon led Elise towards his office, feeling better than he had all day. After turning on the heater, Elise plonked herself into a chair and faced the doctor.

"So, today has been the best! Firstly, I am doing really well with the methadone, secondly I got my watch back and thirdly, I want to go to this place – that's the favour," she added, smiling at her doctor. Elise handed the charity leaflet to Jonathan and then showed him her watch in the crumpled bag.

Studying it closely, Jon realised that it had some value. His mum had a similar one, which his dad had given her for their twenty-fifth wedding anniversary – and, as he had constantly reminded her, it hadn't been cheap.

"Gosh, Elise," he enquired, "who gave you that?"

"My nan left it to me, doctor. It was her dying wish that I had her watch and, although for a short while I thought I had lost it, I've got it back." She held out her hand and Jonathan placed the watch back on Elise's palm, which closed firmly around it. Jon considered asking how she had lost it, but refocused on the purpose of his session with Elise.

"So Elise, how are you feeling today?"

"Good, doctor, thanks," she replied. "I'm hungry all the time and am kind of getting used to the methadone, which is another good thing. Can we talk about the charity and when I can move there, please?"

Jon was encouraged by Elise's attitude, and his earlier anxieties about meeting her, and reliving his nightmares, subsided in an instant. He also had some encouraging news for Elise about her forthcoming visit to the Joshua Charity Foundation. The adrenaline rushed through his body in anticipation of breaking the good news to her.

"Of course you can, Elise," he replied, smiling and returning the leaflet to her. "In fact, I've set up an appointment for you to visit the project later today and to meet some of the staff. I will also be there to represent you and, all being well, they may agree to allow you to move in." He crossed his fingers behind his back, hoping they would see the good in the woman.

Elise excitedly jumped out of her chair and hugged the doctor. "Thank you so much, Dr Davies!" she cried, feeling optimism burst through her. "I don't know what I would do without you, I really don't."

He subtly moved away from Elise. Jon replied tenderly, thinking of the beautiful auburn-haired woman he adored so much. "Don't thank me; it was all down to my wife, Jen. Oh, and by the way, staff at the charity believe that your surname is Hope."

Elise's eyes widened; she smiled once again at her friend.

"Hope," she repeated. "I like the sound of that."

She skipped out of the room and headed back to the ward for her lunch, beaming happily.

"Elise Hope," she said over and over again, counting down the minutes until they reached one o'clock.

He arrived precisely sixteen minutes and thirty-one seconds early. As she secured the seatbelt in his battered old Volvo, Elise's heart pounded with excitement. Jon smiled too. He left the car park and headed towards the motorway, wondering whether Elise would touch their hearts as she had his.

"You'll be fine," he reassured her when he exited the motorway and headed down a winding country lane. At the home, she spotted a friendly-looking woman smiling warmly at them and, as they walked towards the entrance, Elise felt that too.

"Hope," she whispered as they were led into a brightly lit office. "We have hope, little Bump, we really do."

Right now she had a job to do, and getting better and gaining strength depended on this charity taking her in. After that, she could finally seek closure.

Crossing her fingers, she smiled at the thought.

Retribution was going to be such a pleasure.

26. SOMEBODY CARES

2004: *Lizzie*

His heart was thudding with anxiety as he approached the entrance of St Thomas's Hospital. It had been so long since he'd seen Lizzie, and the past three months had been the toughest of his life. The kids had adapted reasonably well, considering, but he knew that they were missing their mummy desperately and blamed themselves for her being so poorly. "Was it because we had lots of fights?" his youngest son had asked him shortly after Lizzie had been admitted to hospital. It had broken his heart seeing the anguish his child was suffering. They had continued to blame each other when their mummy didn't want to see them, and, again, despite all the reassurances he had tried to offer them, they had punished themselves time and time again for something they had not done.

Of course it wasn't their fault; only one person was to blame, and *she* still had the freedom of a life of luxury and relative normality. He shuddered, picturing her evil eyes and huge hands, which had caused so much harm to so many. But, worse still, she had hidden her evil from society, her peers and even her husband, and was considered to be a respected member of society. Life was so unjust. Lizzie should have pressed charges against her mother, he knew, but her terror of her mother's retaliation had prevented her from doing so. Her answer had been to try to end her life.

Memories of her suicide attempt consumed his every thought, and he shuddered, recalling the sight of Lizzie lying on the bed, bleeding from her wrist and suffering from violent convulsions. She had simply stared at him as he had tried desperately to stop the bleeding. The tourniquet he had made from his shirt sleeve had, no doubt, saved her life, but the vision of her fighting for breath and shaking violently when the paramedics rushed to her aid still haunted him, along with the suicide note she had left on the bedside cabinet.

I need to set you free, darling.

As you know, I have done something dreadful and she will seek revenge. She won't care how long it will take, or who she will harm in the process to gain revenge, but I know that, until I am gone, she will never stop torturing us.

I love you all, please remember that, and I promise to look over you all from heaven.

Goodbye my love. Please forgive me.

Your Lizzie.

xxx

He pressed the buzzer on the entry pad, and lifted his head; he caught sight of a shadow at a window above. The hair was familiar and he recognised the profile. He had stroked and caressed it a thousand times.

"Lizzie," he yelled, hoping to attract her attention. But it was too late and the shadow moved away.

* * *

It was late. Although he had no idea of the exact time, Jon had had enough. He entered the staff room, and a few weary faces greeted him before updating him on the day's events. He wasn't listening, nor was he interested. He had just been a witness to a confession of an attempted murder, and so their ridiculous comments about a patient throwing their meal at a member of staff, or another refusing to take his medication, really were irrelevant. Guilt weighed heavily on him. Should he tell his supervisor? Should it remain a secret? How far did the Hippocratic oath go? He didn't even manage to smile as he left to go home.

At home, Jon parked his car and slipped into the hallway, hoping to surprise Jen. He'd forgotten her flowers, after dashing away from his office, but had stopped on the way to buy her some more, and a box of chocolates. As he entered the kitchen, a craving for chocolate and a hug overtook his despair, and his wife's beaming smile melted his heart.

"Hello, you," she smiled, wrapping her arms around his waist. "I've been worried about you, love. I tried five times to catch you today, and every time I rang, that snotty woman in reception said that you were tied up in meetings."

Jon grimaced, recollecting his horrendous day.

He embraced Jen, and met her eyes. She looked tired and he knew from the redness and smudged mascara that she had been weeping.

"Hey Jen, less about my day, how are you?"

Jen lowered her head and walked towards the kitchen worktop before grabbing a vase and filling it with water. She arranged the flowers, smiling at her husband as she did so.

"I visited my GP this afternoon after school and he's referring us to a fertility clinic. I'll have my eggs and tubes checked and you'll have a little plastic cup and some dirty magazines," she added, looking for a reaction from her husband. "What do you think?"

Jon returned his wife's smile. Although the thought of masturbating into a pot really did not appeal to him, Jon desperately longed to be a father and knew that Jen would have to suffer many more invasive tests than he would. He faced Jen and held her close once again. "Anything for you, Jen, you know that."

"That's my line, Dr Davies, and, anyway, this is for us!" she replied, passing him the box of chocolates to open. "Help yourself to the coffee creams, I'll have the nuts," she added before Jon passed the box back to her. She opened the lid and studied the contents before selecting a chocolate with a nut in the centre. Jon couldn't help but remember the movie *Forrest Gump*. Life really was like a box of chocolates, and he sure as hell had no idea what would be coming next.

* * *

Lizzie knew that, this time, she had definitely overstepped the mark with her doctor. Although she had felt an overwhelming desire to confess to him, she now realised the implications of her confession, and the possible impact it could have on her – *and* Dr Davies.

He was, after all, a professional and, despite being kind and compassionate towards her, he could never really be her friend. She had taken the easy option. Should the doctor tell the police about her confession, she could always plead insanity or something like that – she'd get off and, considering her history of being abused, would probably walk away. But what would the doctor do if he was found out? He didn't have a choice; he'd have to stay quiet too. Lizzie knew that all doctors swore to uphold some special oath, including Dr Davies, and so Lizzie's little secret would have to remain just that.

Her roommate Sara was nowhere to be seen and Lizzie felt disappointed; she really needed somebody to talk to. She thought of the twat Mr Hillier, and hoped to God that Jonathan hadn't told *him* about their chat. She shuddered at the thought and swung off her bed, leaving her room and heading towards the communal area, where the other patients were watching TV and talking.

A familiar voice called her name. She headed towards the pile of books in the reading corner. Jason ran towards her. "Lizzie, hiya, I've been looking for you all day – where have you been?"

Lizzie struggled to smile at her friend, but, as he pulled out a chair for himself, then for her, she welcomed his company and managed to turn the corners of her mouth so that he didn't become upset. Jason, despite making great progress, was still extremely sensitive and often misinterpreted body language, perceiving it as a sign of aggression. He was reassured by her smile and excitedly asked her if she had liked his gift. She had completely forgotten about the fairy on the chain after her traumatic day. Wrapping her fingers around it, she thanked Jason warmly.

"I'm glad you like it, Lizzie," he replied, studying the little figure, which was now wobbling on the chain. "I asked my mum to get you an angel, but her friend only did fairies. So I thought that a fairy was similar, with its wings and everything, and the magic wand might actually work and help you fly away, like you do in your dreams."

Lizzie smiled warmly at Jason, who she thought was stupid but also incredibly sweet. "You never know," she replied, wishing that right this moment she could fly into her boyfriend's arms. She imagined herself swooping through the clouds and landing in the garden where she had played so often with her family. How she missed them, and normal family life.

"Jason," she whispered, moving closer to him so as to avoid prying ears and eyes, "I really am going to miss you when you leave. Could you come and see me once in a while if you have the time?"

Her eyes saddened as she thought of the emptiness she would feel once he was gone; she now had nobody to talk to here, except Sara, and she desperately regretted hurting Gloria and telling Jonathan her dreadful secret.

"Of course, Lizzie. You and me are good friends and I will never forget you. Perhaps when you escape too, we can meet up and maybe perhaps even have a date or something." He blushed as he gazed into Lizzie's huge brown eyes with their long eyelashes.

Lizzie was almost speechless and replied nervously, dreading her friend's reaction. "Oh, Jason, if only we could, but there's something I've never told you. I have a family outside of this place, and I also have children. They need their mummy to get better so that I can go back home and look after them. And so, as much as I want us to be friends, I can't be your girlfriend, Jason. I am so sorry."

His eyes filled with rage and he stared hatefully at her. She had misled him with her pretend kindness and had made him believe that she had genuinely cared for him. Fighting the urge to lash out, he turned on his heel and headed towards the corridor leading to his bedroom, resisting the temptation to thump every patient he passed. He had learned a great deal from Dr Davies over the past few months and could manage his anger issues much better now, but, as the old familiar voices crowded into his head, he was frightened once again. Was he really cured, or had the doctor been lying to him as well as Lizzie?

* * *

Richard stood motionless by the telephone waiting for a sign that she was asleep. She'd had a number of drinks now and, following her usual rage, had slammed the bedroom door in his face, ordering him to leave her in peace.

He was relieved to hear the snoring and now knew that the coast was clear to call Norman Hillier. Seeing Lizzie had rekindled the love he had always felt for his daughter, and he desperately needed to hear that she was okay.

A woman answered the phone and, after trying to transfer the call three times to Mr Hillier's office, told Richard he must have left for the day. "Can I take a message?" she enquired, tutting as she did so. Richard presumed that she'd had a tough day, replaced the receiver and retired to his study. He poured himself a whisky, then retrieved a key from his pocket and opened the drawer to his large wooden bureau. Inside, there were numerous handwritten cards, along with a pile of photographs. He blew the dust off the top photo, and studied the little girl in the background. She looked so sad standing alone by the garden shed. Her huge eyes were empty and she was painfully thin. Her little grey pinafore dress hung from her body and she had no shoes on. How had he failed to notice this when he asked her to smile for the camera on that lovely September afternoon? He should have noticed.

How blind he had been. How incredibly naive, trusting and ignorant he had been. Why had he believed his wife all the time, even though he had never quite understood why his little girl was always in her room 'reading'? He had believed *her,* whom he had adored more than life itself, until that day, when he had discovered her dark secret and the torturous life his precious little Lizzie had suffered at her mother's hands. How he loathed that woman – and how he wished he was brave enough to seek revenge.

Placing the photograph and a few others in his jacket pocket, he retrieved another large, sealed envelope from the drawer.

He planned to change his will. He would leave his entire estate to his children, and the woman lying upstairs in a drunken stupor would pay a hard price – all she had ever wanted him for was his money. Richard, for once, would have the last laugh, and regretted the fact that he would not be around to see it.

But first he had something more important to attend to. He would speak to Brenda and offer her the ultimatum he had been considering for many days now: be kind to his daughter or lose everything – including her son, her home, her status and finally her freedom. The threat of imprisonment would terrify her, but not as much as the thought of never seeing Andrew again.

He dialled his son's number, and Andrew answered. "Dad – how are things?"

"Andrew, I need to see you urgently. It's about your mother and Lizzie. When can we meet?"

"Now, Dad," Andrew said, fearing the worst. "Is Lizzie okay, Dad? Please tell me she's alright."

"She will be," Richard responded, welcoming the support he would receive from his son and relaxing a little. "After your help, Lizzie will be just fine." He arranged to meet his son at the local pub just a few miles away.

He heard his wife's snoring bellowing from the bedroom at the top of the first flight of stairs, and Richard smiled for the first time in years.

He just hoped that it wasn't too late to save his daughter and make up for the pain she had endured for so very long.

* * *

Lizzie's boyfriend had been pressing the button for over a minute and was becoming very agitated. The receptionist finished her telephone call, then yelled into the speaker, demanding an explanation for such a late visit.

"I'm here to see Mr Hillier," the voice replied, sounding as frustrated as she felt.

"Hold on," she said, checking the shift rota. Norman was still on shift, so why he hadn't answered his phone earlier baffled her. He was normally so efficient.

Replying to the voice again, she asked him to wait while she checked Mr Hillier's office. She knocked on the door and, after receiving no response, opened it gently. The room was in darkness and there was an envelope on the desk. He'd obviously had an emergency and, knowing how old his mother was, she hoped that she was okay.

Running back to reception, the out-of-breath receptionist explained that Mr Hillier had left for the day, and refused to allow the visitor entry.

"I need to see somebody in authority then," he demanded, banging on the door. "My girlfriend is in there and Mr Hillier left me an urgent message to see him or call him about her. I demand that you let me in."

"And *who* exactly is your girlfriend, sir? What's her name?"

"Elizabeth Pritchard; you know her as Lizzie."

She only had ten minutes left on her shift so the receptionist reluctantly allowed him in, knowing that she would be going home soon. Somebody else could sort this out in her absence.

"Sit here," she demanded, pointing to a red plastic chair as she ran a finger down the list of available personnel. Most were tied up for the remainder of the day so she rang Norman. There was no reply, which she had expected. The next number rang and was answered immediately.

"Jonathan Davies," he replied, hoping to God that it wasn't work again. Hearing what the caller had to say, his expression changed. He got up and kissed Jen goodbye. She abandoned all hopes of conceiving tonight and switched the TV on to watch a soap opera.

"Don't wait up," he said, dashing towards his car, dreading what was to come.

"I won't, Jon," she replied, eating another chocolate and becoming engrossed in the world of Albert Square.

On his way towards the hospital, Jonathan made his decision. If Lizzie's boyfriend was determined enough to take Lizzie on, then he would allow her to leave St Thomas's. Armed with the right medication and support infrastructure, she would eventually resume some form of normality in her life. To be honest, Jonathan was tired of it all now. He'd heard enough and was in far too deep already. It was time to let Lizzie go. Locking his car and running towards the entrance, he sighed with relief when he saw a grey-haired man, who he assumed was Lizzie's boyfriend, in the reception area. He smiled at him.

"Nice to meet you," he said, shaking the man's hand. "Come through to my office, where we can discuss Lizzie's release and her after-care plan."

Lizzie had not expected to see the doctor again, let alone her boyfriend and was hiding underneath her bed. She knew that she couldn't trust that doctor, who had obviously told him everything. But what was he doing here at this ridiculous time?

"Sara," she whispered from beneath her bed, staring in the direction of the bedroom door. "If anybody asks, you don't know where I am, okay?"

"Okay," Sara replied, cricking her neck to study Lizzie more closely, and wondering who she was hiding from. "But why are you hiding, Lizzie? Is it the one who hurt you, the one who did those scars on your neck and your legs? Have they come to hurt you again?" She shuddered, imagining her terror if her father ever found her.

Lizzie shuffled further back, then curled into a ball towards the rear of the bed. "No, Sara, it's not. It's my boyfriend and he wants to take me home and look after me, but I can't go – I can never go, never. It's just too dangerous and he can't protect me and my children forever." Lizzie's blood pressure rose and her heart thudded with the fear of her mother terrorising her again.

The girl's eyes widened as she listened to her friend. "You're a mum?" she enquired, finding it hard to believe that her roommate had children. The boyfriend bit had shocked her enough. Lizzie had never had any visits from them.

"Yes, I am," Lizzie replied sadly, thinking of her babies back home. "I have a son, Bob, a stepson, Tommy and a little girl." Tears welled in her eyes as she thought of little Kirsty. How she missed them all. "But I can't go back to them – it's too dangerous. My mother will hunt me down after what I did to her. She will never forget or rest until she's got vengeance on me. I have to hide from her forever – which means I can't ever leave this place."

Sara hopped off her bed and crouched down close to see Lizzie. "You can, you know – there's protection out there for people like us. I should know, I have a restraining order against my dad, and if he comes within a mile or something of me, he could go to prison."

Lizzie studied the girl, who seemed to know what she was talking about. "I'll help you, Lizzie," Sara added, "with all the paperwork and stuff, if you want. I kept copies of everything. When I get out of here, I could show you, if you want."

Lizzie uncurled herself and shuffled towards her friend. "Do you mean that, after all the horrible things I've done to you?"

Sara stood up and walked towards her embroidery, which was almost complete. Turning to face Lizzie, who was brushing herself down, she smiled. "I'll never forget how you helped me with this," she replied, running her finger over her colourful stitches. "I know, from your nightmares and your scars, what you've gone through. But, despite the pain you've suffered, and despite all your abuse, you were kind to me once and so, it's my turn to be kind to you."

Lizzie smiled at Sara, amazed at how articulate she could be. Perhaps she wasn't that dumb after all. Lizzie hopped onto her bed, inviting her friend to join her. Sara placed her embroidery carefully on the window sill and joined Lizzie. The two sat hand in hand, no longer caring about the rules and regulations, and they made a pledge.

"To happiness and freedom," they said in unison.

Next moment, the door to their room opened. Jon, Dave and Gloria smiled at the girls warmly.

"Lizzie," Dave whispered. Lizzie sat on the bed, wide-eyed, and huddled closely to her friend, shaking nervously as she met his eyes.

"Hello," she replied, gripping Sara's hands tightly. "I'm so sorry for everything. I promise to be—"

He lifted her into his arms and stroked her face, and she knew then, that perhaps, despite her fear, everything would be just fine after all.

"I'm taking you home soon, princess," he promised. "The kids are fine and can't wait to see you again. They will be so excited to hear the news when I get back. I promise you, Lizzie, it won't be long now, and you will be safe. It's all sorted. I mean it, sweetheart; she can't hurt you anymore."

Lizzie and her boyfriend followed the doctor into his office to discuss her forthcoming release. Although it would be impossible to obtain the clearance today, Dr Davies had briefly reassured Dave that, if all went to plan and he managed to obtain the relevant signatures, Lizzie could go home within the next week or so. She would, of course, need to continue her sessions with a psychiatrist, but those would also become less frequent in time as Lizzie continued to improve.

Passing Sara her medication, Gloria tenderly stroked her arm. "You'll be next, Sara, I promise you," she whispered, knowing how much Sara had cared for her roommate and how much she would miss her company.

Sara just stared into space as Gloria's words echoed through the emptiness of the stark bedroom she had become so accustomed to. She didn't even bother with her embroidery, which Gloria had placed by her side.

"But Gloria, where do I go?" she replied sadly. "I have nobody and nothing," she whispered, fighting the urge to cry, but failing miserably.

Once again Gloria's heart wrenched with the pain and suffering she was observing. She knew that, just like she had befriended Lizzie, she would have to care for Sara, as she had her own daughter before that dreadful August evening when she had taken her own life after hearing voices in her head.

"Don't worry, Sara," she replied tenderly, closing the blind and turning back the bed covers for her. "I'll be here for you, rest assured."

With that, she left the room and sobbed before entering Dr Davies's office to discuss the release of the woman she had grown to love.

* * *

The Rose and Crown was almost empty. Other than a middle-aged man in a tweed jacket chatting to the barman about politics, Richard and Andrew were the only other people there.

There was an open fire at the far end of the room, and the barman looked relieved when Andrew sat close to it in a comfortable armchair. The barman headed towards the fire and tossed a large log on it, causing the flames to flare up. Andrew nodded politely and rubbed his hands together, welcoming the warmth.

Richard smiled as he ordered a couple of pints of Strongbow and a bag of peanuts for Andrew. He'd always loved them and, despite his paunch, Andrew could never resist the temptation of snacking. Quite a contrast to his sister, who could hardly manage a single nut without becoming poorly, Richard thought as he tossed the packet towards his son.

After paying, he settled down on another comfortable armchair and felt enormous relief at being with Andrew, who took a mouthful of cider. "Heck, I needed that," he said, smiling at his dad. He placed the pint glass back on the coaster. "So Dad, what's all this about? It's not like you to be so impulsive."

Richard had rehearsed his lines as he drove the short distance to the pub but now, like on a first night in a school play, his nerves had got the better of him and he had completely forgotten everything he had intended to say. He tried hard to retrieve the perfect sentences, but to no avail. Taking a sip, he shook his head in frustration.

"Gosh, Andrew, this age thing is not so good. I'm so forgetful these days," he laughed, knocking his head gently with his fist. "I'd worked out everything I wanted to say to you before I came out, and now, when it comes to the crunch, it's gone – the whole lot!"

Andrew looked bemused while he studied his father. He'd aged over the past few years and what hair he had was thinning. He should shave it all off, he thought, but then, looking at his thin face and narrow lips, Andrew realised that his dad would look ridiculous with a shaved head. All the same, his eyes were kind. Andrew had his dad's eyes too; bright blue with little flecks of green in them. They were unique, and in his younger days had attracted numerous women. He wasn't so sure that his dad had benefitted from that, though, as he was very short. Andrew was six feet four with blond wavy hair. The height, he thought, had come from his mother's side.

"So, Dad, come on, don't worry about the eloquence, what's up? Tell me the worst first."

He thought of the last time he had seen his sister and shuddered at the memory. She had been so sick then, and he believed her suicide attempt was something to do with her former drug addiction. He hoped to God that she would never return to that awful lifestyle.

Richard shifted nervously in his chair and looked directly into his son's bright eyes. "It's your mother," he said, trying not to show any emotion as he spoke. "Despite appearances, Andrew, she is not the woman you believe her to be."

Andrew stared at his father, wondering what he meant.

"Think back to your childhood, Andy. Where was Lizzie in all of that?"

Andrew remembered only good things about his childhood, like his lovely bedroom painted with bright colours, his massive toy box full of Action Men and train sets, the best dinners on earth, and loads of love. Even boarding school had been fabulous; all in all, he had enjoyed every moment of his childhood and youth.

"Not sure what you mean, Dad," he replied, remembering the happy times.

"Lizzie – where was she in your childhood? Andrew, can you remember?"

Andrew thought about his big sister, who at every opportunity when he was tiny, would carry him and pretend to be his mummy. She had long hair, he remembered that, and always smothered him in kisses. When he was small, this had been fine, but when he got a bit bigger it had been very embarrassing. He wiped his cheek subconsciously before replying.

"She was there, Dad, I remember. She never stopped fussing over me, though," he said.

"And at mealtimes, Andrew; did she share meals with you? I need you to think hard, son, and to be honest with me."

Andrew recalled the large dining room with the enormous teak table which seated twelve people. Christmases when the house was full of family and friends had been the best. Yes, Lizzie was always there too and always had a new dress. But everyday dinner times had been different, he recollected now. Lizzie was allergic to most foods, and so she had to eat different meals to Andrew. Mummy had told him that, to avoid upsetting his sister, rather than watch him eat his normal meal, Lizzie had chosen to eat upstairs in her room.

"It was a bit weird, now you mention it. I just never questioned any of it, due to Lizzie's allergies and stuff."

Richard stared in disbelief at his son.

"What allergies, Andrew? Lizzie had one health problem, which was asthma. Nothing else was wrong with her." He fought the desire to blurt out everything. Shifting nervously in his chair, he took another mouthful of cider. "Andrew, I believe your mother starved Lizzie. Don't you remember how very tiny she was, and how your mother would blame her build on your gran?"

Andrew thought back to his nan who had been tiny, but never particularly thin. Lizzie, on the other hand, due to her allergies, was often sick. His mind spun as he remembered meal times with his mother, laughing and chatting as they ate. He couldn't handle the thought of his sister being alone in her room, near starving.

"No, Dad. Mum would never do that. I would hear her singing to Lizzie when she bathed her and got her ready for bed. Then Lizzie would skip down the stairs as soon as you got home. You must remember that, Dad, surely?"

This was going to be so difficult. Richard downed the rest of his pint, knowing that he would be over the legal limit for driving if he had another drink. However, he had to finish what he had started. Studying his son's hurt face, he reached out to touch his hand but Andrew pushed it away.

"Dad, what the hell is this about? I can't handle what you're saying. This is Mum, *my* mum, you're talking about. She loved me and she loved Lizzie too. What the hell has got into you?"

Flagging down the barman, Richard ordered another two pints.

"Andrew, I'll give you a choice. You'll either believe me, or you won't. It's as simple as that. She had me hoodwinked too, you know." His eyes filled with tears as he spoke to his son.

"It happened not so long ago," he whispered, staring out of the window as he spoke. "It was raining – just for a change! I'd always believed that you both slept on the first floor close to our bedroom. After all, I'd decorated both of your bedrooms and bought the matching furniture for you which, God knows, took me long enough to assemble."

Andrew smiled, recollecting his dad's efforts to build his wardrobe.

"Go on, Dad."

"It was winter and the bloody wind was howling through the attic window, which I knew had been cracked for some time. The draught was driving me potty. I'd planned to call somebody in to repair it, but lost track of the months, then summer came round again and I'd forgotten about the repair. It was only a small crack but the cold finally made it smash … and it was then, Andrew; Jesus, that was when I found everything out."

Richard had his son's attention now, and Andrew's heart thumped with nerves.

"Found what out, Dad? What the hell are you trying to say?"

"The room, Andrew. That awful attic room had been your sister's bedroom for years."

"What?" he exclaimed. "How do you know?" Andrew thought back. His mother had always told him never to enter the attic room. She had said there were mice in there. He had never disobeyed her and studied his father, who fiddled nervously with his watch strap.

"The windowsill had etchings in it, Andrew. Lizzie had obviously found something sharp and she had inscribed dates and years into the wood. It started when she was just four years old and went on … well, until she ran away from us."

"But Dad, that doesn't mean anything. You know what she was like, running off in her imaginary world. She probably played up there with her toys and stuff. That doesn't mean she was sleeping there."

Richard shuddered and looked directly into Andrew's eyes. "Oh yes she did, Andrew. There was a bed up there – an old wrought-iron one, with a stinking mattress. It was stained with urine and, worse still, blood. Then underneath, I found *proof* that Lizzie had been a prisoner all her life – right under our noses!"

Andrew downed his pint in just a few mouthfuls and studied his dad, who looked desperately unhappy.

"It was a box. A shoe box with a painting of a dog on the front. Lizzie had obviously hidden it there and, when she ran away, she left it – until I discovered it when I was fixing the window."

"What was in it, Dad?" Andrew was finding the tale incredulous.

"Her life. She'd made a little diary from scraps of paper and had written a daily account of what her mummy had done to her and what she had forced her to eat."

Richard recollected the drawings he had found. Lizzie had obviously drawn them before she could even write; there were pictures of a little girl with red on her body and a huge monstrous figure close by. It didn't take a rocket scientist to interpret the meaning of the images she had scribbled. He shuddered as he continued his account of events.

"Alfie's collar was in there too," he added sadly, remembering the love that Lizzie had felt for her little pet, "along with some locks of hair and some photographs of your nan and … oh God, Andrew, of herself. But the worst thing was," he paused, trying to remain composed, "there were numbers against each entry. The numbers represented injuries, Andrew – from knife wounds to cigarette burns. Lizzie, by the time she left, had over a hundred wounds, all at the hands of your mother – *my wife*. Oh Andrew, if only she'd found the courage to tell me, or even the police, the abuse could have stopped. I can only presume that she was terrified of the consequences – petrified that her mother would seek revenge and murder her. Whatever her reasons, Lizzie was tortured for her whole childhood, and she was too frightened to tell anybody."

Andrew struggled to remain calm as he faced his father, who was sobbing. The man in the tweed jacket stared at him and whispered to the barman, who headed in their direction. He tapped Richard's shoulder and pointed to the room at the rear of the bar.

"It's all yours, mate, if you need some privacy."

Andrew thanked the man and held his father's hand. Father and son gazed at one another, the silence almost impossible to handle.

"I'll be fine," Richard replied, wiping his eyes with his shirt sleeve. "Andrew?"

Andrew was unable to say a word. The impact of what he had just been told had hit him like a sledgehammer. Memories of his mother singing to him and bathing him and playing with him swept through his mind, which refused to believe anything his father had told him. She had loved Lizzie; he had seen her brushing her hair, he had seen her talking softly to his sister. No, it couldn't be true. None of it. Absolutely none of it.

"Why are you lying, Dad?" he asked, trying hard not to raise his voice. His anger was rising, and he wanted to scream at his father or even hit him.

"I wish I was," his father replied, trying to meet his son's eyes. He fumbled in his jacket pocket and pulled out a small envelope. Placing it on the table in front of his son, he gestured for him to open it.

"Please, Andrew, just take a look."

"What is it, Dad?" He just wanted to end this evening, go home and get drunk; forget about what he'd been told.

"It's something that was in the box – you need to see them, Andy. Then you might believe me. Please."

Andrew's hand shook. He pulled the envelope open and removed several photographs. He studied the backs of the photos; they had been taken by a Polaroid.

"Turn them over, son," his father said softly.

Smile for the camera, baby.

"Dad, I can't," he replied, feeling anxious and terribly nervous. "Whatever they are, just tell me."

"No, Andrew, you need to see them for yourself, then perhaps you'll believe me. Do it now, son – you must understand why I am here and why I need your help."

Say cheese to Mummy.

They were taken inside the house, most of them in the hallway or the bathroom. Despite the discolouration, they were well preserved. All were of his sister.

Her eyes looked haunted and her eerie smile terrifying. Clearly, she had been forced to look into the lens by the photographer, as nobody would want to have their photograph taken in that dreadful state.

Dried blood covered her chin, and her hair had been stuck in clumps with something that looked like clay. In another, she sat in the bath. Her ribs were all visible, and her red eyes stared into the camera. He moved the photo closer and noticed tiny marks on her naked legs.

"Christ, Dad, what the hell is that?" His hand shook as he handed the photo to his silent father.

"They're burn marks, Andrew. From cigarettes."

Holding his son's hands, he passed him the photograph again, which Andrew returned to his father immediately.

"I don't need to see the rest, Dad." His stomach heaved. He feared he would throw up.

"Are you sure it was Mum?" he asked, hoping that someone else could be blamed for doing this to his sister, and that *he* could be banged up for life after Andrew had battered him.

Richard removed another photograph from the envelope. This one was of Lizzie scrubbing the fire hearth in nothing but her pants and vest. His fingertip stopped at a smudge in the corner. He held it towards Andrew.

"I'm sure," he whispered sadly as his son focused on the blurred image at the side of the photograph.

The diamond was the evidence. It was his mother's ring. *Her* hand had taken these hideous photographs of his precious sister. *Her* hand had caused all the injuries Lizzie had listed in her little notebook.

His stomach heaved. Andrew ran out of the pub, slamming the door behind him. He ran to his car and got in, slumping against the steering wheel.

Trying to calm his son, Richard removed his keys from the ignition and flagged down a passing taxi. He forced his son into the back and slammed the door shut before giving the taxi driver directions to Andrew's home. Thankfully, there was a glass barrier separating the driver and his passengers so the driver was unaware of the scene behind him.

"I'll kill the fucking bitch," Andrew bellowed as his father held his son's hand and fastened his seat belt.

"Lizzie's already tried that, son," he replied sadly, hoping the taxi driver couldn't hear what he was saying. Andrew could not take any more and simply held his head in his hands. His head thudded and his stomach was churning.

"That's why I need your help, Andrew. Only you can stop her from hunting Lizzie down and finally killing her."

Andrew was oblivious to everything his father was saying. As they passed a rain-swept wood, and rain cascaded down the roads like a frantic river, all he could hear was his mother's voice singing the all-so-familiar lullaby to his sister.

Cry baby bunting
Daddy's gone a hunting
To fetch a little rabbit skin
To put the little baby in.
CRY BABY BUNTING.

27. THREAT

2014: Beth

Kirsty felt a rush of excitement burst through her when the aeroplane wheels hit the runway, and the flaps descended. She hadn't been home for eighteen months, and just the thought of seeing her mum and dad was enough to make her quiver with anticipation. Kirsty smiled as she ran across the runway towards the arrivals lounge; she desperately hoped that her mum was better now, which was all she wished for this Christmas.

Beth was already standing by the front door awaiting the sound of an engine, knowing it would be her daughter. She was so very proud of herself because, for the first time in many years, she had braved the filth and danger of the loft. It hadn't been an easy feat but, dressed in her old decorating overalls and armed with extra-thick gardening gloves, she had pushed herself to her limit and worked up the courage to retrieve the Christmas decorations alone.

It had been tricky fighting the cobwebs and realising that they weren't going to harm her. After carrying the tree and lights down the loft stairs, she had a shower, changed into fresh clothing and started to transform her home into a spectacle of festive colour.

Realising that Kirsty could be a while yet, Beth rearranged the tree, bending some of the branches at strategic angles to line up with the rest of the furniture in the living room. The angel on the top was wonky and so she stood on a chair to straighten it, smiling as she did so. She'd been given the angel by her nan years ago after the old lady had admitted that she couldn't be bothered with Christmas decorations any more. Beth had treasured it ever since. Despite a few blemishes, it was still her favourite Christmas decoration and, she figured, it always would be.

She studied the neatly wrapped parcels beneath the tree, tempted to tidy the pile once again. Some of the boxes were nice and straight, but the more awkwardly shaped items just didn't look right. No matter how many times she had turned them and repositioned them, they hadn't fitted in, but somehow, Beth thought, this year she would stop worrying about things like that. She reassured herself that once the paper was torn off, the gifts put away and the carpet beneath the tree had been vacuumed, all would be tidy once more.

She felt better already and headed for the stereo to put on a CD; her favourite. It was cheesy and childish, but somehow, every Christmas, when she played this CD, she felt content. She had purchased it eighteen years ago in her son's favourite toy shop. Although every Christmas song was a children's number, sung by various choirs, she adored every track. Humming along to 'Rudolf the Red-nosed Reindeer', she headed for the kitchen and checked the icing on the Christmas cake for the fifth time.

It was still in one piece and despite her earlier concerns about the icing being too runny, the little tree and snowman hadn't slipped off. In the centre of the cake, she had placed a gold star and, nearby, tiny silver balls had been scattered randomly. Although she knew they didn't resemble anything Christmassy, she was delighted with the end result and congratulated herself on this achievement too.

The table in the formal dining room had been laid perfectly already, even though it was only the twentieth of December. As 'Away in a Manger' played in the living room, Beth studied the intricate detail of each place setting. She had set eleven places. Despite having to borrow some odd chairs from neighbours who were away for Christmas this year, the cushions she had made for them blended perfectly with the cream fabric from her existing dining suite. The gaps between each place mat had been measured to the centimetre and the hand-decorated crackers were perfectly positioned to the side of the mats. Three sets of cutlery had been placed in the right order, along with name cards and beautifully fanned napkins. She had bought these especially from a terribly expensive shop in town but, as she admired her work of art, Beth realised that it had been worth every penny. She'd decided to leave the wine glasses until the actual day, though, as dust could settle in them, and that would be very unpleasant for the guests and, possibly, harmful.

Beth rechecked the drinks cabinet to ensure for the umpteenth time that she had bought enough wine and champagne. After straightening the bottles, she was satisfied. All she had to do now was hand-deliver a few of her cards – and wait.

Five days to go.

* * *

Jon was so pleased that he'd booked half a day's leave from the practice. Not that he was missing much; this time of the year was always dead, and he only had a few clients to see before he finished for Christmas.

After struggling to find a parking space, he took the long walk past the modern cathedral towards the main shopping centre of Milton Keynes.

The decorations this year were stunning, and piped music echoed through the centre as he passed the old oak tree and headed towards a fine jewellery shop. He had seen the bracelet a few weeks before and had resisted spending the £3,000 it cost. But, following a great deal of consideration, and sacrificing the upgrade of his car, Jon had decided that Jen was worth every penny. They had also celebrated their wedding anniversary earlier in the month and, having forgotten again, Jon figured that this gift would go some way to Jen forgiving him.

Purchasing the bracelet had been relatively painless, and Jon was surprised at how much money some folk spent at this time of the year. To him, £3,000 was a ludicrous sum to spend but, to others, he observed, it seemed to be nothing out of the ordinary. He obviously wasn't charging anywhere near enough for his private clients – although, to be honest, he still didn't care what his partners thought about his company's bank balance.

He thought of his daughters and how quickly they were growing up. Although only at infant school, they were confident enough to leave Mummy in the car park and walk to the school gates independently. They were also very athletic: Rebecca, the second-born twin, was an aspiring gymnast, and was constantly practising her backwards rolls on the front room carpet, or on Jon and Jen's bed. He thought that she would like something to do with her favourite pastime and headed towards the Nike shop, which was located next to the Disney Store.

After buying her a bright pink leotard and a bar contraption that would fit against the door frame so she could practise, he entered the Disney Store and headed straight towards the princess range of dresses. Chloe loved dressing up, and so, after selecting a My Little Princess outfit and a couple of cuddly toys as stocking fillers, Jon headed back to work, making sure he kept the expensive bracelet in his jacket pocket, and not in the boot of his Volvo.

The secretary looked daft today, Jon thought. He felt incredibly old compared to her, and he thought that wearing a tiny red dress, with silly flashing antlers, at work, in a psychiatry practice really was unprofessional. She beamed at him; the silly headpiece flashed.

"Happy Christmas, Dr Davies," she yelled, skipping to his door and opening it for him. She was obviously hoping for a bonus or Christmas tip – but the only tip she would be getting, Jon mused, would be on appropriate office attire.

Women, he thought, realising that in the not too distant future, his little girls could be just like his secretary! He decided that he would take up golf or snooker at that point – and buy his daughters chastity belts for Christmas. *Thank heavens they are still little*, he thought, grinning at their cheeky smiles in the photograph on his wall.

He switched on his coffee percolator, which Joanne had prepared earlier, and poured himself a coffee. His telephone extension rang.

"I've got a woman on the phone for you. She wouldn't give her name, but says it's important that she talks to you."

If this was another bloody sales rep, he did not want to speak to them. Reluctantly, he accepted the call, expecting to hear a sales pitch.

"Hello, Dr Davies," the voice said. Jon didn't recognise the tone and racked his brain from previous meetings. Nope, it wasn't a client or a supplier of his.

"Who's calling?" he said curtly.

"You will stop seeing a long-term client of yours. You are not helping her, nor are your stupid recommendations assisting her with her personal life."

Jon was flabbergasted and tried to interrupt. He wondered who the hell she was, and was appalled by her audacity.

She continued. "I am warning you, Dr Davies, if you do not cease all contact with Elizabeth, I will take action against you. I have many contacts in your field, and could easily destroy your career. Do I have your attention now, Dr Davies?"

Jon's heart rate trebled, and his face flushed. How dare this woman call him and try to dictate who he should or should not see! He snapped. "Get off my line now and keep your nose out of my private affairs or I will call the police; do you understand?"

"You have a lovely family, Dr Davies," she sneered, knowing she had his attention. She thought of the family portrait on his office wall, and smiled deviously before continuing. "It would be a tragedy if anything happened to your daughters, wouldn't it, doctor?"

Jon's blood pressure immediately shot through the roof. He stood up and tried to stay calm.

"Who the hell are you?" he demanded, wanting to call the police immediately and trace the call.

"That is irrelevant, Dr Davies. Your client will no longer require your services, do you understand? Her name, Jonathan, is Elizabeth Pritchard. You call her by one of her ridiculous nicknames, which is an insult to her and myself. You will refuse to see her again – or I shall be forced to use alternative methods to dissuade you. I hope that I have made myself perfectly clear, doctor."

She hung up. Jon stumbled towards Joanne, no longer caring about her flashing antlers. His hands were shaking and he was seeing double again.

"Jo," he whispered, "trace that call – now."

Hearing the urgency in his voice, Jo removed her head attire and retrieved the customer services number for their telephone supplier. Jon stormed out of the office, and ordered her to refuse all future calls until he was back from the police station.

He headed towards the town centre. The woman got out of her car and set out on foot, towards the school that she now knew very well.

* * *

Dave could not believe his eyes as he read, then re-read, the letter that had arrived only five minutes earlier. His eyes focused on the wording, and the numbers, along with the purchase orders attached to it. There was enough work here for the next three years! Rather than lay staff off, he would have to recruit people instead. The miracle of Christmas had come true, and to his delight and enormous relief, Regency Furniture was saved.

Dave dashed into the workshop, and grabbed Mike and Charlie's attention by sounding a fire horn. The men almost jumped out of their skins and, bemused, stared at their boss.

"Guys, I have some fabulous news for you both."

The men stared at their boss.

"You okay, Dave?" Mick asked.

"Okay? Well, chaps, that has to be the understatement of the century," he replied excitedly. "Come with me," he ordered, grabbing both staff by their arms and leading them into his office. He passed Charlie the purchase orders, and handed the official letter to Mick. Both men opened their mouths in shock.

"That American bloke, the one who came here a while ago; is it him?" Charlie asked, finding it hard to absorb the numbers on the paperwork in front of him.

"That's him!" Dave replied, rubbing his hands together with glee. "And he wants Regency Furniture to supply bespoke furniture to all of his apartments over the next three years – all one hundred and fifty of them," he added, beaming at his men. "Which means, chaps, you will have an enormous pay rise each, and a new title – project manager. Mick, you will be responsible for recruitment and Charlie, you will need to help train the new staff. Are you okay with this, guys?"

Charlie and Mick were more than okay with this, as they had realised recently that the dwindling order book would have eventually resulted in them losing their jobs.

They replied together, accepting their new roles with pleasure, and wishing Dave the best of luck with his new client. Within a few minutes of leaving his office, Charlie was on the phone, speaking to a recruitment agency, and Mick was already drawing up a training schedule.

Beth was busy cleaning the bathroom when Dave rang her mobile. She removed her gloves, and breathlessly took the call in her bedroom, wondering what was wrong – Dave rarely called her at this time of the day.

"Beth," he yelled excitedly. "We've done it, princess, we really have!"

"What's happened, darling?"

"You believe in angels, don't you, Beth? And you also believe in miracles too. Well, your angels are looking down on us both – I've just won that tender – the huge one that I didn't believe we would win in a million years."

Beth sat down on her bed with shock. She caught her reflection in the wardrobe mirror. Her eyes shone with excitement.

"Does that mean we keep this house, Dave?" she asked, hoping that, at last, they could clear the credit card bills and pay off their debts.

"More than that, Beth," Dave replied. "We can do that, and then some! How do you fancy an art studio being built on to the back of the garage?"

Beth's heart was thudding loudly and she jumped up and down with delight – she had always dreamed of having her own little room to paint in.

"Really, Dave?" she asked, pinching herself to ensure that she wasn't imagining the conversation.

"Really, Beth," he replied, picturing her in her overalls with her watercolours.

"Oh, Dave," she replied, weeping with happiness. "I can't believe how clever you are, and how kind you are to me, despite everything." She recollected the last few months and the horrendous stress Dave had endured as a result of her illness.

He smiled as he listened to his girlfriend. "Beth, I've never stopped loving you, and never will. And perhaps, after Christmas, you will finally agree to marry me?"

She thought of fairy-tale princesses and her prince, and this time, hesitated before accepting his proposal. "But Dave," she whispered quietly, "what if, you know, what if *she* spoils it all for us again?"

"She won't, Beth," he replied firmly. "She has too much to lose this time round. After Christmas, when you've finally faced her and forced her to accept that you're better, she will never try to control your life again. And, remember, this time you won't be alone. You have our support, your brother's and, of course, your dad protecting you. So, Beth, I'll ask you again; will you marry me, please?"

She paused before responding, picturing the church with her children all dressed up and smiling at their mum.

"Yes, Dave, I will. I love you so much."

"I love you with all my heart, Beth," he replied.

And he really did.

* * *

The police were hopeless. Unless Jon could provide them with proof that he had been threatened, they suggested that he pursue the matter initially with his telephone supplier. Due to him not having any recording equipment on his phone system, he had no evidence to prove that the call had even occurred. It would be unlikely that the police would take Joanne seriously, although she had offered to support Jon if he needed a witness that the call had been made.

He'd explained that the woman had made threats against his family, and the police's advice was to be extra-vigilant and to keep an eye out for anything unusual. Other than that, they couldn't do a thing unless, of course, the threats continued or he managed to track the call.

Jo had been extremely efficient, having followed the correct protocol and discussing the situation with a very sympathetic lady in a call centre. The call had been traced to a mobile telephone number, and they would investigate whether it was linked to a major network, and whether it could be tracked. It would, however, take some time and she would have to be patient.

Jon wanted an answer now, but knew that he had to see his clients before he could take any further action.

He left a message with the school secretary, asking Jen to call him back urgently. Jon then took his next two sessions. Both clients just needed simple guidance and advice. He was grateful for small mercies, but still felt anxious about the earlier call.

Finalising his notes, he thanked Jo for her assistance and smiled warmly at the young woman. She had been terrific today, and Jon realised that he had been wrong to judge her by her clothing and makeup. Her heart was in the right place, and that was all that counted in life.

She smiled sympathetically at the doctor, who started his car and headed for home. He would speak to Jen as soon as the girls were in bed, and then await contact from the telephone company to see where the call had originated. As for cancelling his future appointments with Beth, he was in a dilemma. She was making exceptional progress, and Jon, along with Dave, had become one of the most important men in her life; he couldn't just abandon her. She was a real person and, over the years, had become a friend. However, on the other hand, if that woman was serious – and, heck, she sounded it – he could never threaten his family's safety. They had to come first and Beth would have to come second. He would speak to one of his colleagues tomorrow and ask whether he would be prepared to accept her as a NHS client. Although Jon very much doubted it, he hoped that, for once, his colleague would show compassion before thinking of his finances.

Jon was surprised to see Jen's car on the drive – normally she got home around five o'clock. He double-checked the time, then grabbed the carrier bags and burst through the front door, dashing straight upstairs to hide the surprise Christmas presents he had bought.

"With you in a mo," he yelled, trying desperately to hide the tension he had felt since the earlier call.

"No worries," Jen replied quietly, passing the girls some paper chains to finish.

When he entered the living room, the twins ran excitedly towards their dad, opening their arms and hugging him tightly. "Daddy," they squealed, "look what we made."

They dangled the multi-coloured paper chain from their little hands, and their eyes lit up. Jon gave them an enormous, very proud, smile. Grabbing them both, and swinging them around, he winked at Jen as he told them they were the best girls in the world. They resumed making the chain; Jen looked at her children, who were concentrating so hard, and smiled weakly at her husband.

"You okay, love?" he enquired, noticing that she was quiet and not her normal chirpy self.

"Oh, you know," she replied, "just tired and stressed after the day at school. I always find this time of the year exhausting; thank God I finish in a few days and can have a rest."

Jon put his arm around her waist and faced his wife. He knew Jen far too well. Even though she could lie convincingly, he knew she was hiding something. "Jen," he enquired, tilting his head and meeting her eyes, "come on, spit it out. What's up?"

"Nothing, Jon," she replied, storming out of the room. The girls failed to notice, and continued to stick the chain together. It was now almost as tall as Jon.

Following his wife, Jon stopped her in her tracks. "Please Jen, tell me."

He recalled previous occasions when Jen had been unable to confide in him about her innermost worries. It had seemed to be ironic, considering his job, that she, of all people, felt uncomfortable speaking to Jon about personal issues. He thought of their struggle to conceive, and how Jen had reacted when she had been informed that she was suffering from premature ovarian failure. At the time, she had become a shadow of her former self, and had, initially, rejected the idea of egg donation. Thankfully, Jen changed her mind. They had made a trip to a Spanish fertility clinic, and the egg donation treatment had worked: Jen and Jon had been blessed with their daughters, who had been worth every single penny of their investment.

Jen's bright green eyes met Jon's and she sat down on a stool close to the worktop.

"Oh, it's probably me," she said, fiddling with her necklace nervously.

"Come on, Jen, just tell me," he said.

"Oh, there's just been something odd going on, and I really can't put my finger on it."

Jon tried desperately not to switch into psychiatrist mode, and watched his wife as she spoke. Jen blushed as she faced her husband, realising that she was being paranoid. He didn't react when her face flushed; in fact, he found it sexy, but he couldn't let on right now.

"Carry on, Jen," he whispered, fighting the urge to whisk her off her feet and take her to the bedroom.

"Well, over the past few weeks, I've been on playground duty and a couple of times I've spotted a car driving slowly past the school gates. I didn't take any notice at first, but after I'd seen it a couple of times, I made a point of watching it and trying to spot the driver. Whoever it is wears sunglasses, and doesn't want to be seen."

Jon's heart pounded as he recalled the woman on the telephone earlier.

You have a lovely family, Doctor Davies.

"Jen," he asked sheepishly, "did you manage to see whether the driver was male or female?"

"I don't know, Jon. As soon as the driver could see me watching, they sped off. The car hasn't been back for a few days now. But, something, don't ask me what, something triggered an alarm in me, and I guess, with all of the talk and publicity about paedophiles, I am really worried. I wish I'd taken down the registration number, but by the time I'd found a pencil, it had disappeared."

Jon wished that too, and Jen read his anxiety immediately.

"Jen," he replied, closing the kitchen door so that the girls couldn't hear him, "I don't know whether this is connected, but I had a threatening call today from a woman."

Jen's scared eyes opened wide; she stared at her husband.

"What do you mean, Jon?" she said, her voice shaking with fear.

"She ordered me to stop seeing a client and although she didn't directly threaten to hurt you, she did mention my family."

Jen shuddered and chewed her thumbnail frantically before replying.

"What did the police do, Jon? We need protection. Christ! Do you think it's the same woman driving past the school? Oh my God, what the hell are we going to do?" She thought of her daughters playing hopscotch in the playground earlier; that would stop immediately.

"It's all under control, Jen," he tried to reassure his wife, grabbing her hand and holding it tightly. "The telephone company is working on tracking the caller and, so long as I cancel all appointments with this client, we will be fine, I am sure. Tomorrow morning I will speak to Geoff at work and ask him to see Beth."

"Beth?" she replied coldly. "*The* Beth?"

"Yes, I'm afraid so, Jen," he replied, worried, avoiding eye contact with her and staring at the kitchen floor.

"Oh my God, Jonathan, you don't think – Jesus, you don't honestly believe that the caller was *her* – her mother, do you?" She recalled the young woman in the hospital bed after her overdose, and Jon's horror at her injuries.

Jen's words repeated in his mind, he felt giddy and had to sit down. Meeting his wife's scared eyes, he nodded. She glared at him.

"I told you years ago that you were in too deep, Jon," she screamed, slamming the kettle onto the worktop. "And you promised me, *remember*, you absolutely promised me that you would refer her to somebody else. But you lied, Jon, didn't you? You lied to me again!"

Tears flowed down her cheeks. Despite all the secrets he had shared with her, he had broken the one promise she had asked him to make.

Staring at her husband, she wiped her eyes with kitchen roll. "How could you, Jon? If I can't trust you, I can't be your friend. And if I'm not your friend, I can't be your wife. I can love you, but you've deceived me and your daughters. For that, Jon, for that, I don't think I can ever forgive you." She joined her children. Jon stood alone in the kitchen. An eerie silence once again surrounded him, and the dripping of the tap reminded him of blood dripping from one of Beth's wounds.

Hearing footsteps running down the hall, he had to resist the temptation to warn Beth of what was to come. Instead, he followed his wife and daughters to the playroom.

Jen wouldn't let him in and, once again, he was scared.

* * *

She had waited for nearly an hour for a bus and wished that she had changed some euros into sterling before entering the UK, so that she could have afforded a taxi instead. Nevertheless, when she walked along the main road to her parents' cul-de-sac, Kirsty was bursting with excitement, absolutely desperate to tell her mum her great news.

The house looked just as it had when she left, which was very reassuring. In the past, her mum had liked to change everything on a regular basis, from the plant pots to even the style of the front door, but this time, other than a pretty winter hanging basket full of colourful pansies, everything looked normal.

She rang the bell and saw the familiar outline of her mum run towards the front door. Opening the door, she threw her arms wide to welcome her daughter. Kirsty reciprocated, leaving her suitcase and bags on the driveway.

"Mum, it's fab to see you looking so great," she chirped, noticing her mum's new hairstyle and more natural makeup.

Beth smiled lovingly at the pretty woman standing in front of her. Her blue eyes shone and, despite her hair being pink and braided down to her bottom, it suited Kirsty too. She had always adored bright colours, and it was natural for her to apply such boldness to her personal attire. Although Beth would never be so brave, she admired Kirsty for being able to express her individuality so well.

She removed her Dr Martens and pulled off her socks, then realised that she'd forgotten her bags. Knowing that her mum would struggle coping with the germs, she headed for the front door, but her mum stopped her. "No, Kirsty, I can do this."

Watching Beth lift the heavy suitcase and the carrier bag into the hall, Kirsty was amazed. She had never seen her mum carry, or even touch, items without her sterile gloves, but now, in front of her very own eyes, she had seen a miracle.

After washing her hands and drying them with a normal hand towel, Beth smiled proudly at her daughter. "Well, Kirst, what do you think then?"

Kirsty hugged her mum again and beamed. "Mum, you always have been the best but, wow, you really are doing so brilliantly. I bet Dad is so, so chuffed and proud of you – like I am."

"Oh, I have your dad to thank for so much, but really, without my doctor – you know him, Jonathan Davies – I could never have got this far. He has, like Dad, saved me so many times and so I have the two of them to thank for my progress."

Kirsty smiled again and headed up the stairs to her old bedroom, struggling to lift the heavy suitcase. "Back in a minute," she yelled. Beth filled the kettle and prepared the coffee.

"Still two sugars, Kirst?" she asked, but Kirsty was too busy texting her boyfriend to hear her mum.

He had texted her:
Have you told her yet, Kirst? xxx
She replied:
Nope, but will soon ;-)

Beth was dying to tell Kirsty about her dad and how well he was doing at work, but first she had a few bits and pieces to finish, including the delivery of her Christmas cards. Although there were a few days to go, Beth had planned to deliver the last of her cards personally and she knew that her doctor would be finishing work very soon. She could go now, or tomorrow morning. Beth toyed with the various options; she decided that it wasn't worth worrying over. She had learned that deadlines often caused her undue stress, and she was battling hard to fight this minor issue which really, she reassured herself, wasn't that important.

Kirsty skipped down the stairs, joined her mum in the kitchen and grabbed her coffee. "Well, come on, then," Beth said. "Tell me all your news!"

Kirsty blushed as she thought of Paris and her boyfriend's recent text. She wriggled nervously and stuttered as she replied. It was always when she was anxious that her speech impediment flared up, and despite overcoming her lisp following speech therapy, she had never fully eradicated her stutter.

Beth held her daughter's hand and smiled warmly into her bright eyes.

"Have you got something to tell Mummy?" she giggled, knowing that her daughter was dying to tell her something, but was a little embarrassed.

"Sort of," she replied, going as red as a beetroot and moving Beth's hand towards her stomach.

Memories of Beth's first pregnancy flooded back to her as she recalled doing the exact same thing with Dave when she had discovered she was expecting a baby. She stroked her daughter's tummy, and met her eyes again; hers filled with emotion.

"You're expecting, Kirsty?" she whispered, stroking her daughter's cheek gently.

"Four months gone, Mum, and counting," she replied, unsure how her mother would react to becoming a gran.

She didn't need to worry. Beth rushed into the hall and called Dave's mobile straight away. The answerphone kicked in, but it didn't matter in the least. After leaving a garbled message, Beth ran to the drinks cabinet and went to open a bottle of the champagne she was saving for Christmas.

Kirsty placed the bottle on the table and reminded her mum that she was teetotal for the duration of the pregnancy – and yes, the cigarettes were history as well. Beth simply hugged her daughter and stroked her tummy once again.

The front door opened unexpectedly, and Dave stood there. He removed his shoes, while the two women waited in the hallway beaming at him. He could tell that something great had happened.

"Hello, Granddad!" Kirsty squealed, running to her bemused dad and throwing her arms around his neck. "I'd like you to meet Blob."

He and Beth stared at each other in disbelief, then the warmth of their smiles radiated throughout the room and towards their daughter.

Beth's angels really were looking out for them after all.

This was going to be one hell of a Christmas.

* * * * *

28. SUPPORT

1994: Elise

Although not the prettiest of buildings from the outside, the interior of the Joshua Foundation Charity was very homely and welcoming. It was laid out like a large family home; each resident had their own private bedroom and the luxury of an en-suite bathroom. The rooms were small but comfortable, with central heating; something Elise relished the thought of.

The kitchen was a hive of activity. All meals, although supervised by a member of staff, were prepared by the residents, who were encouraged to provide a healthy and balanced diet to everybody residing there. With a weekly food budget, the more senior residents were able to purchase the fresh produce from local farms and village stores and there was a car so that they could drive to the supermarket a few miles away for the other essentials. Elise loved the idea of being independent, and the more she observed the modern living arrangements of the charity, the more she wanted to live there.

There was a large communal room with a TV and DVD player. Mrs Mullins led them through and a number of residents nodded at Elise as she nervously smiled at them. She was shocked at the difference in ages of the people, having expected a majority of them to be young. However, an older woman with scars on her arms approached Mrs Mullins. She passed through the room, smiling at Elise, before limping by. Elise noticed she had a prosthetic leg and for the first time in an age, realised that she may not be the worst off. She wondered what had caused the lady to lose her limb, and watched her sympathetically as she hobbled out to the patio and lit a cigarette.

"That's our Lilly," Mrs Mullins explained, pointing to the woman outside. "When she first came to the project, we really didn't think that she'd pull through. We found her on the streets of Bedford, in a desperate state. She was an alcoholic. It was too late for the doctors to save her leg, though, but we're thrilled that she's stayed on at Joshua's. Now she assists other recovering alcoholics on the programme."

Elise studied the woman, who had realised she was being watched. Stubbing out her cigarette, she opened the patio doors and walked slowly towards them.

"Welcome to our project," she said, holding out her hand to Jonathan, then Elise. "I'm the longest-serving member here, so if you have any problems or questions, just yell. And, despite appearances, I don't bite," she laughed, chewing her bottom lip and making growling noises.

Another resident, a man in his thirties, smiled at the woman, then joined another younger man and set up a game of dominoes. Elise felt comfortable there, and was reassured by the relaxed attitudes of the residents. After ordering Lilly to give up the fags, the man resumed his game with his friend.

After a two-hour interview with Elise and Jonathan, Mrs Mullins had made up her mind. Despite never previously considering an expectant mother and recovering drug addict, she liked this young woman and had decided to accept her as a resident – should she meet all of the entrance criteria.

Taking drugs was never permitted. If a resident was ever found in possession of illegal substances, including weed, they would be removed immediately.

Alcohol was also banned. Although Mrs Mullins heartily disliked smoking, residents could smoke within their own bedrooms, or outside the home in designated areas.

Elise nodded frantically in agreement and rubbed her bump to remind herself why she was being such a good girl.

"What about the Methadone?" she enquired. "That's still a drug, isn't it?" Her eyes met Mrs Mullins', who said that the project would administer Elise's medication in the same way as the hospital had, and this would continue throughout her pregnancy. Elise felt a surge of relief, knowing that she would be supported with her drug rehabilitation, as well as being given a roof over her head.

She smiled at Jonathan, who was preoccupied with some paperwork he'd been asked to complete on Elise's behalf. He reached the next of kin section and looked at Elise, who was daydreaming about her bedroom and where the baby's crib would go.

He distracted her from her thoughts.

"Elise, they need your next of kin information here; who should I write down?"

Elise studied the blank section of the document and shrugged. She had nobody left in her life other than the man sitting next to her: she looked longingly into his eyes.

"I don't have anybody, doctor, other than you." She blushed, lowering her gaze to the pen in his hand.

Feeling awkward, Jonathan met Mrs Mullins' eyes. She responded on his behalf.

"Elise, although your doctor is a representative, that is all he can be, I'm afraid. Is there nobody else we can add as an emergency contact? A boyfriend, a sibling; your parents, perhaps?"

Elise discounted David, immediately recollecting his last angry words to her: *Get out, you cheap little bitch. Get out and never, ever come back.*

Looking sadly at the thin woman in front of her, then at Jonathan, she replied, "I'll leave it blank, if you don't mind. There's nobody left who cares."

Jonathan did care, but he knew that he couldn't dispute Elise's statement. He reminded himself that he was just her doctor, and nothing more than that, although his heart wrenched as he added the words *'no next of kin'* to the document and returned it to Elise to sign.

* * *

David had heard rumours during his searches that Elise had been seen hanging around the streets of Luton and getting into strangers' cars. The last sighting had been just over a week ago, close to the local market, where somebody matching Elise's description had allegedly stolen some boots, but had managed to escape from the owner of the stall. "If you find her before I do," he yelled at David, "tell her she owes me £20!"

David thanked the man, although he felt that he could have been a little more polite when he'd explained that his girlfriend could be in deep trouble.

He handed the crumpled photograph of Elise to numerous other stallholders and shop owners, most of whom shrugged. Nobody recognised the fresh-faced, attractive woman in the picture. David realised that she might be a little thinner now, but her features would be the same. Where on earth had she gone? Jesus, if the rumours were correct, what had become of his little princess? He shuddered as he exited the Arndale Centre and walked across the main road towards the police station. Crossing his fingers, he headed for the reception desk, and hoped that she'd been arrested and was safe in a cell.

A friendly police woman smiled at David when he showed her the photograph of his pretty fiancée. The WPC had been based at Luton for five years and had experienced endless requests from desperate mothers and fathers, husbands and wives, all hoping for the same end result – a sighting of their loved one. This woman was no different to the rest, and she knew that she was more than likely safe and well. Nevertheless, she took the details David gave her.

"What were the circumstances of her leaving?" she asked after taking down Elise's basic details. David grimaced as he recalled the last conversation he had had with Elise, forcing her to leave with nothing but the clothes she had been wearing.

The police officer raised her eyebrows after he had explained the situation to her, and immediately changed her opinion of the well-presented man in front of her. Although he looked decent enough, he was obviously very callous; however, as always, she could not vocalise her private feelings, and continued to listen intently to him while he explained what had happened.

Elise had not been arrested for solicitation or anything else. After taking David's contact information, she wished him luck in finding her, although she doubted that he would. If it had been her, she certainly would have stayed away, she thought, as she filed his paperwork and logged the case on her computer.

David had one final call to make, and he headed for the Luton and Dunstable Hospital. Although he dreaded the state that he might find Elise in, had she been admitted, it was a better option than never finding her – or, heaven forbid, discovering her body in a morgue.

* * *

What a fool she had been believing that David was as stupid as her daughter. She should have realised that he would have eventually found out what she did to her grandson.

Studying her enormous hands, she cursed the fact that she had pressed the baby's backside so hard. She could have used an object to hurt him rather than her own thumb, or could have *accidentally* bruised him with a hairbrush, like she had done in the past with her daughter, but the impulse to act had taken over and, once again, she had been caught out. She was losing it, and would have to take more care in future if she ever wanted to see her daughter again – and finally have revenge on her. Carelessness was getting to be one of her major flaws, and as she grew older, she paid less attention to details; a very foolish mistake.

Hiding her hands in the pockets of her dress, she headed for the lounge and slumped into a large leather armchair. She needed a drink, but had promised Richard, once again, that she would stop. For now, he seemed satisfied, although as each day passed, the harder it became. Drink was her escape from her life: the harsh reality of who she was and what had happened to her, and who her daughter was. Although the effect of the alcohol was short-lived, at least it dulled her pain.

Trembling, she regretted hurting the little boy. Although he was partly created by her idiotic daughter, he did have some decent genes in him too. Although David had threatened to press charges against her once he had established it was *her* thumbprint on the child, he was a decent man and, she had liked him. His kindness had attracted her to him from the start, along with the fact that he was not judgemental. Not only had he accepted her hideous child and learned to love her, he had not questioned *her* either or stared at her, as so many did.

Her peculiar features had blighted her life and, from the tender of age of five, when she had towered over every other child at school, she had been bullied. She despised her parents for creating her, and loathed the fact that they were blind to her constant sadness. She had felt invisible ever since her twin sister had died of meningitis. Her parents had found it hard to even look at her after that day, avoiding conversation and any warm gestures, instead investing their time and energy into fundraising for medical research and treatments for the virus that stole her sibling's life. When alone with her surviving daughter, her mother cried constantly. "Please bring back my angel – Mummy's little angel." She seemed to have forgotten that her other little girl was still alive. Nobody, it seemed, cared.

She hated everything about herself, especially the reflection in her bedroom mirror.

Her wild hair was uncontrollable, her narrow eyes made her look evil – even before she had felt that way inclined. Her teeth were yellowing and uneven, and she was grossly overweight. She wished that she could travel back in time to the happy days of her youth when, just for a very short while, she had, for once, fitted in, and had been accepted by all of the members of her group. If only she had not left them that day; her life would have been so different and *the monster* would not have been born.

Rising from her armchair, she opened the drawer in a side unit and gathered the photographs into chronological order. She smiled, recollecting every member of the group, each of whom had their own individual hippy identity. They were all named after bands that played at music festivals in the seventies.

She wanted to be known as the Black Widow, after a cult band formed in Leicestershire in 1969. The name seemed appropriate and mirrored how she felt following the loss of her sister. She had never questioned the meaning, although some of her friends had tried to dissuade her from using it.

It wasn't until she hitchhiked to Portsmouth, then took the ferry to the Isle of Wight in the summer of 1970, that she wished she'd listened to them.

But the effect of the drugs and the lyrics from Jimi Hendrix's song 'Purple Haze' had swept her away into another place, with a new crowd of friends, who relished the fact that they had met a new Black Widow fanatic.

She had, indeed, kissed the sky, as Jimi Hendrix had sung – and numerous men – that evening. She cringed when she remembered the lips of one of the other cult members, who had forcefully kissed her. There had been others, too, who fed her more drugs before sadistically torturing their latest victim or, as they called it, 'their newest cult member'. They had called it their satanic ritual.

She had called it hell.

Throwing the photos into the fire, she lit a firelighter, tossed it into the grate and watched them melt, and fade away, as she hoped that the nightmare of that festival would as well.

* * *

She didn't recognise her signature; the surname hadn't matched to the name she had been given. Mrs Mullins asked why Elise had not signed her surname as 'Hope'. Elise blushed when she realised her mistake and, after explaining that she often used aliases for her own protection, she crossed out *Elizabeth Pritchard* and re-signed the document with her other surname. Satisfied, Mrs Mullins smiled warmly at Elise and thanked her for being so honest.

"I do understand, Elise, trust me, but from the moment you join this project, I ask that you never lie. We try to encourage honesty here, along with abstinence, and, although we won't enforce religion into your life, we would appreciate it if you could accept our Christian values."

Elise looked closely at the woman, who was wearing a large gold St Christopher pendant on a long chain. She thought back to Leroy's auntie and the church she had attended with him, and realised that God played an enormous part in so many lives. And, although she questioned why she had suffered all of her life from dreadful abuse, she understood the meaning of religion a little better. God gave these people hope and they, in turn, forgave those who had sinned, and allowed them the chance to redeem themselves too. She had much to learn from God, and hoped that He would find it in His heart to forgive her for all that she had done in the past.

"Can I come to church with you some day?" she asked softly. "I guess that I could do with somebody in my life who won't judge me," she added, glaring at Jonathan, who she had not yet forgiven for refusing to be her emergency contact.

"God forgives everybody, Elise," Mrs Mullins replied, smiling back at the young woman, fingering her pendant.

"Everybody?" Elise enquired, thinking of the torture she had endured at the hands of her evil mother so many times.

"Yes, Elise, He does – or at least that's my belief." She thought of her son and how, despite him stealing from her to feed his drug habit, and eventually costing her everything she possessed, she forgave him in the end.

Elise had no way of knowing what the other woman was thinking. Thinking she didn't want God to forgive her mother, Elise decided she wasn't meant to be a Christian after all and decided, there and then, to abandon her ideas of attending church with Mrs Mullins. Changing the subject immediately and cheering up a little, she then asked the woman the obvious question. "Am I accepted here, Mrs Mullins? If so, when can I move in?"

Mrs Mullins nodded at the young woman seated in front of her, and handed her a leaflet detailing the moving-in arrangements and in-house rules.

"We'll provide you with a month's worth of sanitary provisions, some clothes and, of course, all of your food. Then, once you've started working for us, you will continue to earn your privileges as the others do. How does next Monday sound, Elise?"

The young woman jumped out of her chair and swung her arms around Mrs Mullins' neck. "Perfect," Elise replied, beaming from ear to ear. Turning towards Jonathan, she threw a weak smile at him.

"Can you thank your wife too?" she added coldly, yanking up her baggy tracksuit bottoms and opening the door.

The journey back was silent but, as she watched normal people going about their normal days, Elise knew that she too would soon be joining that group, with or without the help of the doctor driving her.

Jonathan was relieved that Elise had a future at the charity. Although he knew that she would forgive him soon enough, he felt a twinge of sadness, knowing that he wouldn't be seeing his patient again. He hoped she would make a full recovery and that perhaps, once she had given birth to her baby, he and Jen could visit her at the Joshua Charity Foundation.

Breaking the awkward silence, he addressed Elise, who was still staring out of the car window. "That went well, Elise, didn't it?"

She studied a woman struggling to strap her screaming toddler in his buggy, and turned towards Jonathan before replying. "Yes, I guess it did, but can I ask you something before we go back to the ward, please?"

Jon raised his eyebrows before nodding. "Sure, what do you want to ask me? Go ahead."

"Will you be my baby's godfather, please? It's just that he or she won't have anybody if anything should happen to me and I, well, I just wondered whether you would agree. Please, doctor, please say you will."

Once again Jonathan's mind reeled as he searched for yet another excuse to make. She looked pleadingly at him. "That means that you will have to go to church, Elise; the place that forgives everybody, remember?"

She remembered alright.

"Okay," she said, focusing on the large park to the right of the car which was filling with school kids and dogs as they drove past. She thought of her baby and how she too would, someday, be one of those women who seemed so content with their lives and their little ones.

"I'll just have to make sure that nothing happens to me, then," she concluded, realising how critical it was that she never touched any form of drug again. She would also have to abandon her other ideas of revenge to avoid getting injured – or, she shuddered, even worse.

And, although she felt disappointed, she no longer felt anger, just resolved to continue with her rehabilitation and make a fresh start for her and her baby. If it was a boy, she would name him Jonathan after the man who had made such a difference to the way she felt right now.

* * *

The staff at the hospital were remarkably helpful and within a matter of minutes of David making his enquiry and showing them a photograph of her, they had been in touch with the admissions department.

Although nobody with the surname, Pritchard had been admitted, an Elise was indeed present; however, for data protection reasons, they could not reveal exactly where she was and explained tactfully why.

"But she's my fiancée," he explained, looking desperately at the fraught woman behind the desk. "And she probably didn't mention me – we parted on bad terms."

The woman agreed to speak to her supervisor to establish whether they could do anything more to help. The Elise on their records had been admitted after a drug overdose and had given no address or surname. David had, however, unbeknown to the woman, overheard her telephone conversation and details of the ward where Elise was located. After finishing her call, she said, "As far as we are concerned, this particular patient is of no fixed abode and so the address and surname you have provided don't help, I'm afraid. Unless you can prove that she is your fiancée and she would agree to see you, I'm afraid there's nothing more we can do to assist."

David shook his head in pretend disbelief. He thanked the woman and exited the building, but smiled, secretly knowing Elise's location. As he walked along the side roads of the main building, he took note of the ward locations and spotted a large sign leading to various wards. Ward 33 was just a few yards away. He walked in with some other visitors and did a double-take at the woman in the oversized tracksuit speaking to a doctor. *That can't be my Elise*, he thought, remembering the healthy, vivacious woman he had adored, but when her brown eyes met his, then opened wide, he knew immediately that it was her. He walked towards her bed.

She had not expected to see David ever again, and had resigned herself to that fact. As David introduced himself to the doctor, he studied Elise. Her normally flawless skin was dull and scarred from what, he guessed, had been a severe crop of acne, although he had never seen a single spot on her face before. She looked exhausted, and had puffy eyes, and her lips were chapped. She spoke quietly, not quite believing he was there.

"Dr Davies," she whispered, "this is David; the knight in shining armour I've told you so much about."

The doctor looked shocked. He shook David's hand and examined his features. David was far older than he had expected, with greying hair and a slightly weathered face. However, his warm blue eyes shone when he smiled at him and held his hand firmly while shaking it. "Nice to meet you, Dr Davies," he replied politely, still shocked by Elise's appearance.

It seemed the ideal moment for Jon to make his excuses to leave and continue with his day-to-day duties. After agreeing to meet David in an hour or so to discuss his patient further, he left the ward and the couple in peace. Elise shook as the realisation of David being in the ward hit her. Meeting his eyes, she once again spoke softly. "I thought that you hated me and that you never wanted to see me again."

Her head lowered. David sat on the side of the bed and stroked her thin hair. He felt more remorse than he had ever experienced before; guilt washed through him as he studied her bruised hand where the drip had been, and noticed how terribly thin she was.

"Oh God, Elise, how can I ever ask you to forgive me? I can't even begin to say how incredibly sorry I am for not listening to you and for letting you take the blame for Bob's injury. What a fool I was believing *her* instead of you, my princess; she is what you said she was, Elise, evil through and through, and I'm so, so sorry."

He desperately wanted to cry, but, soon realised that he was being watched by a number of other visitors and patients. He fought the urge, swallowed hard and spoke in a near whisper. "I don't know what got into me. You had told me all about her, I had seen what she had done to you, yet still she managed to manipulate me. She somehow turned me against you before my very eyes, Elise. Please forgive me."

Elise stared towards the wall as he continued. She wanted to run away from the man who had abandoned her, yet her heart still overflowed with love for him.

"We talked about so much when you were asleep. Your mother told me about her unhappy childhood and how she grew up believing she was worthless. She told me about her twin sister dying and how her mum yearned for her 'little angel' to come back and ignored your mother constantly. She explained how she turned to drink, claiming that it hid everything she hated about herself and the past. Before I knew it, I was confiding to her – telling her about Tommy and how – since I broke up with his mum – he had started wetting the bed. She even spoke of you and your emotional problems; she seemed to understand, Elise – due to her own childhood issues and, at the time, showed pity towards you and some remorse.

"That's when I made the fatal mistake. Your mother had won my trust; I believed that she was a reformed person and, oh God, Elise, that's when I allowed her to feed and bathe little Bob."

Elise moved forward and gazed into David's eyes. They looked empty and desperately sad as he spoke in a near whisper.

"It was early evening. Bob was chortling away as your mother dried him after his bath. It was lovely to see, Elise; there seemed to be a real bond forming between them." He paused; tears welled in his eyes. "It was when she was putting the barrier cream on his bottom that I noticed it – the bruise. She was completely unaware of what I'd seen – the indentation of her thumb matched the shape of little Bob's bruise perfectly. I almost threw up."

Elise's eyes widened. She stood up and moved towards David, who was sobbing.

"What happened then, David?"

"I was nervous. She was holding Bob and I feared that if I lashed out at her, she may hurt him again. I asked her to fetch a clean romper suit and she passed Bob back to me – thank heavens. She followed me downstairs; that's when I told her to get the hell out of our house and to never return.

"Of course, she didn't leave quietly. She screamed abuse at me, claiming that I had no evidence or proof that she had injured our little boy. She even had the audacity to threaten me, and said she would sue me for slander. I was too shocked to fight back – all that mattered to me at the time was little Bob and, and finding you – my princess. I should have gone to the police, I know that now. But you were my number-one priority; you still are, Elise. Please try to understand."

Elise studied David's face. Thinking of the life she had led for the past three months, she wanted desperately to scream at him and order him to leave. But the love she still felt for him, her baby boy and the unborn child in her belly, overwhelmed her with a stronger emotion than the hate she wanted to feel, but knew that she never could.

"Do you have any idea of how I felt, knowing that you had believed my mother over me – your so-called princess? I was so desperate, David; my heart shattered into a million pieces and I felt I had no choice at all ... but to start taking heroin and ... do some really bad stuff as well."

She thought of her brief, but awful, stint of walking the streets and some of the clients she had entertained. Her eyes widened. She faced David. It was her turn to shudder with the memories. "Let's try to find somewhere a little more private," she said, feeling eyes on her.

David nodded in agreement and Elise informed the nurse that she was seeking some privacy; she kindly offered her a spare office, close to the one in which she had spent many hours speaking to Jonathan.

The radiator in the small room was actually working and the warm air welcomed the couple as they continued their conversation.

Elise had dealt with so much pain over the last few weeks that another few moments would be easy and so, without emotion, she explained how she had been forced into prostitution. David loathed the fact that so many men had forced themselves inside his fiancée; he took a deep breath as Elise explained each encounter in detail; she had nothing to lose by being honest.

"The bites were the worst," she concluded. She pushed up her tracksuit top and moved her bra to show David the now fading bruise. He studied Elise's chest while she spoke and noticed he could see her ribs.

"Did you eat anything, Elise?" he questioned, shocked at the image in front of him and trying hard to disregard the fact that she had been bitten by some filthy slob.

She adjusted her clothing before replying. "A little, once in a while. I made a friend, David, he was kind to me and, from time to time, he took me in and fed me." David shuddered at the thought of a pimp owning Elise and repaying her with a few morsels of food in return for selling her body.

"Where is he?" he demanded. He imagined the filthy pimp exploiting his vulnerable princess. "I'll track the bastard down and get him arrested for encouraging solicitation; tell me where he lives, I need to sort this out once and for all." Elise shifted from her chair and moved behind David, massaging his shoulders as she replied.

"It's not like you think. He really was just a friend to me, but he died." She felt a lump form in her throat and fought back the tears. "We both overdosed, David, on bad stuff. I was the lucky one and they saved me; Leroy wasn't so fortunate." She recollected the image of her friend lying on the living-room carpet, lifeless, and the paramedics trying in vain to save him.

David stood and turned around to face Elise. His eyes were riddled with guilt, pain and sadness yet, when he studied Elise's large brown eyes, they looked empty; vacant, almost.

"What have I done to you?" he whispered. He brushed her fringe away from her eyes. "Can you find it in your heart to ever forgive me, Elise?"

She moved his hand away from her head and held it tightly in her own small hand. "God forgives everybody, David," she replied, thinking of her earlier meeting at the Joshua Charity Foundation.

He was confused by her statement but smiled anyhow.

"And do you?" he asked, looking deeply into her eyes and gripping her hand even tighter than before.

She broke away from his grip, and smoothed her hand over her stomach, pointing to the tiny bulge there.

"I have to," she replied sadly, looking at the man she still adored with all of her heart. Brushing her fingers over the bump, she imagined her baby eventually growing up in a secure and happy environment.

"We're having another baby, David," she whispered, "but this one will be so different to Bob; he or she will be a drug addict. We'll need to be strong, David – very strong, for the child's sake. And, before you ask, I was pregnant before you threw me out. You can ask the doctors here if you don't believe me."

David initially felt ashamed, then the anger and hatred he felt for her mother escalated. Now she had inflicted pain on four innocent people. He wanted to scream aloud or thump the wall, but knew that it would achieve nothing. It appeared that no matter how much evil that woman delivered, she would always get away with it scot-free. But Elise was right; they both had to be strong and, this time, they had to remain united.

"We can do this, Elise. No matter how tough it is for you and our baby, we will get you both better in time." He clenched his fists in an attempt to hide his anguish, but still felt bitterness for that woman surge through his veins.

Elise felt exhausted and slumped into the chair again. Although her desire for revenge had dissipated, she realised the impact of her mother's actions and dreaded the thought of her new baby suffering. Could she ever repay her for what she had done?

Gazing sadly at David, she appeared to read his thoughts as well.

"How do we get revenge on her, David?" she asked, knowing that he despised the woman as much as she did.

"All in good time, Elise," he replied coldly. "She has a short memory these days, thanks to the drink frying her brain, and sometime in the future, when she believes that we've forgotten all she did to you and Bob, we can repay her for everything she has done and stop her once and for all."

David smiled as he planned his revenge; he would destroy Brenda's outstanding reputation within the local community by informing both the WI and the Lady Taverners of her *other* activities and, perhaps, even tell her precious son about her evil tendencies. Yes, she would pay alright. Her pride and status were so incredibly important to her.

Elise, on the other hand, closed her eyes and recalled her failed attempt to murder her. That had been the practice run. Next time, she would succeed.

"Shall we go back to the ward, David? I'm a bit tired now."

"Sure, princess," he replied, holding her hand.

Elise sat on her bed. Jonathan approached David and offered him the chance to talk about his girlfriend in his office.

"She's one amazing woman," he confirmed before leading David towards the chilly room. "To have survived all that she has, and to still have a positive outlook on life is quite something." David nodded in agreement and smiled at him.

"She certainly is," David replied. He helped himself to a seat and rubbed his hands together, hoping to warm up. The doctor switched on the heater; he looked more serious as he thought back to the last few days and the nightmares he had suffered as a result of his meetings with Elise.

"There's just one thing that I must ask you, David, before we discuss Elise's medication and her release from the hospital." He paused, then took a deep breath to give him the courage he needed. "Is it really true that all of Elise's injuries were caused by her mother?"

He still found it impossible to believe that somebody could inflict so much harm on their own flesh and blood. David nodded sadly and left the chair to face the window.

"I'm afraid so," he replied, feeling his blood pressure rise again. "But, despite everything she did to Elise, Elise has always dreamed of her mother being part of her happy family." Lowering his head as he continued, he studied his shaking hands. "I guess that she just needs to hear the three words from her mother that most people have been privileged enough to grow up with and take for granted."

"What do you mean?"

"I love you," he replied sadly. "And until Elise hears those words from her mother's mouth, I don't believe she'll ever feel whole or complete."

Jon recollected the number of times his mum and dad had shared those simple words with him and his siblings; he'd lost count.

"But, David, how can Elise expect her mother to say those words when all she appears to feel towards her daughter is hatred and contempt?" He thought of the cigarette burns on her legs and the scar on her buttocks and shuddered.

David agreed and had questioned the very same facts on numerous occasions. "I don't understand that either, but Elise said that after her mother had beaten her, once she had cried, and once she had begged her mother for forgiveness, her mother would change for a short while. Elise said that her eyes would sparkle and she'd stroke her back, and she'd be kind to her. She'd mutter to Elise, too."

Jon was completely absorbed in the story David was telling him; Elise had never told him this before.

"What did her mother mutter?" he questioned, intrigued by David's statement.

"Something to do with Mummy's little angel," David replied, never having quite understood why she quoted something that had caused her so much pain following the death of her sister.

Jon was confused; the contrast between the anger and violence, then the gentleness of the warm words made no sense; he would explore this scenario later in his textbooks.

David studied the doctor's features and finalised his statement.

"Then her mother would disappear into her own bedroom and cry, asking for forgiveness and mercy, and wishing that she could find it in her heart to love her little girl and to simply accept her for who she was. This would carry on until her husband came home from work, or the childminder returned her son from nursery. And so, Dr Davies, this is why Elise yearns to hear those words; she feels that somewhere, deep within, her mother wants to love her or even *does* love her. It beats me," he concluded, "how somebody can hurt their child so dreadfully, yet yearn to love them too. But I'm not the shrink here … that's down to you."

It baffled Jon too: this was far too complex to understand after his limited exposure to psychiatry, but he was sure that, in time, following more experience and further studies, he would, someday, understand Elise's psyche – and perhaps even what had driven her mother to treat her as she had.

But that would take many years, and his belief that a textbook would answer all his questions pleased him as he wrote his discharge notes and handed them to the nurses on Ward 33.

"She'll be just fine," he concluded, before explaining the methadone dosage and writing details of the nearest rehabilitation centre on the notes.

How wrong he was. Little did he know that he would learn every reason for Elise's mother's actions and play a major role in finally ending it all, with no involvement whatsoever from a textbook.

Actions were to speak far, far louder than words.

He just didn't know it yet.

* * * * *

29. CHILDREN

2004: *Lizzie*

It was very cramped in Jon's small office. The four people present – Lizzie, Dave, Jon and Gloria – had just enough room and they settled down to discuss a release date for Lizzie.

Jon filled up the kettle and made everybody a drink, smiling as he did so; he felt a huge surge of relief wash through him, knowing that despite his initial reservations, Lizzie would be going home soon. He thought back to the stress her confessions had caused him and, although he knew that she had trusted him and felt comfortable with him, he still felt uneasy with the knowledge he had acquired during their most recent session.

He studied the tiny woman sitting hunched up with her knees pressed to her chest. Lizzie raised her head and, for a short moment, stopped chewing her fingernail. She spat out the remnants of her nail and threw it onto the carpet, then resumed chewing on the next finger, causing the skin on the side to tear and bleed. It looked sore and Jon wished she would stop; it was one of those habits that showed a person's stress and anxiety and it made him feel uneasy about releasing the young woman so suddenly.

Gloria was speaking softly to Dave, who had agreed that she could visit Lizzie once she was better. She felt elated, knowing that she could still see her friend once in a while, and was already planning which books she would buy her next from the book stall on the market. She'd known the owner for years and she always kept the best books aside for Gloria, especially the thrillers, which she knew Lizzie enjoyed the most.

Once everybody had finished their drinks, Jon tried to control the meeting and exert his authority by standing up and facing them all. After asking for a moment's quiet, Gloria and Dave stopped chatting, but Lizzie remained preoccupied with destroying her fingernails one after the other. Sucking the blood from a finger, she lifted her head and stared at everybody in the room. They were all talking about her, yet, as she had encountered on so many occasions, she felt that she was outside of the group and that their words were mere echoes in a non-existent world. Her head spun and she felt giddy. In the corner of the office she saw *him* again. He was curled up in his basket, sleeping peacefully. Her precious Alfie was back at last.

She wiped the blood from her finger on her tracksuit top, and gazed at her dog. The others in the room followed her with their eyes as she knelt down and stroked the air. Lizzie then proceeded to lie down close to the wall and rub the carpet beneath. She relaxed, smelling the animal's familiar scent and felt his body's warmth against her own.

The silence in the room created an awkward atmosphere. Gloria and Dave looked at Jon, who had now sat down and was writing some notes. It suddenly felt chilly and he rubbed his arms in an attempt to warm up; it didn't help.

Dave was the first to talk and, after observing Lizzie for a painful few more moments, he dreaded the response to his question.

"She's not ready to come home, is she, doctor?"

Lizzie was oblivious to everything and everybody else in the room. She was happy in her peaceful world, which consisted of her and Alfie. Suddenly, all her worries about being a mummy and a girlfriend had disappeared. It was nice here, and she would be looked after and safe here as well. She wouldn't have to worry about cleaning or shopping or washing and ironing, and nor could she get injured by *that* mummy. Alfie wouldn't be any trouble either, she reassured herself as she rubbed his tummy and smiled at the dopey expression on his face. She was pleased with her decision and patted his head, leaving him to resume his doggy dreams. She smiled at the alien faces in front of her.

"Alfie and me are staying here," she declared, sitting down cross-legged.

Jonathan knew that she was far too sick to discharge, and the relief he had felt just a few moments previously turned to anxiety as he observed Lizzie rocking backwards and forwards. Gloria turned to face Dave, who was wiping his eyes with his shirt sleeve. He swallowed hard before moving towards Lizzie and stroking her face. Her confused brown eyes met his and filled with tears. She whispered softly to him. "I don't want to go home; she will kill us all. Please don't let them take me away, please don't."

Gloria was the first to leave the room and politely smiled before saying goodbye and promising to return once she had finished her evening rounds. Lizzie stared vacantly in the direction of the door, got up and headed towards the exit, hoping to see where the friendly nurse was going. It was medicine time and she must take her pills or she would become very poorly again. Dave's hand gently stopped Lizzie as she held the door handle and pushed it hard to open it.

"Lizzie, stay here for a moment longer," he asked kindly, guiding his girlfriend into a vacant chair. Lizzie robotically obeyed then spoke quietly to him.

"I have to take my medicine, doctor," she said. Jonathan, exhausted and demoralised, agreed and got up, opening the door for the confused patient.

"You're right, Lizzie," he replied. He walked her towards the security of her bedroom. Dave trailed behind, and with the empty suitcase in his hand, agreed to leave and get back to his family.

"I'll speak to you tomorrow, Dr Davies," he said after he had kissed Lizzie tenderly on the lips and tucked her into bed. Closing the door softly behind them, the doctor and Dave headed towards the car park, aching for the comfort of their own homes.

* * *

Sara beamed when her special friend pulled off her bed covers and raised her thumbs in the air.

"I fooled them, Sara," she giggled, jumping off the bed and joining her pal to continue their girlie chats.

"You sure did, Lizzie," Sara squealed in delight, knowing that she still had some company to enjoy while she was still here.

"I'm just not ready yet," Lizzie added, hugging her friend tightly. Sara cuddled Lizzie back as she replied cheerfully, "I'll miss you, though, when you do go but I'm so pleased you're staying for a bit longer. How long do you think it will be until you really do want to leave?" she questioned, hoping that her friend would say 'forever'.

Lizzie gave the question some serious thought before responding. She had her children to care for and a home to run, in addition to staying healthy and strong. She also had her final objective to achieve which, she considered, would take the longest to sort out. Dismissing the latter action temporarily, she finally replied.

"About four weeks, Sara. Then, as for the final matter – well, that'll take as long as it takes."

Sara completely understood and hugged her pal once again.

"Third time lucky, Lizzie," she said giggling loudly.

"Yep, indeed Sara," she replied crossing her fingers as she hopped out of bed and waited for Gloria to join the girls with their medicine and bedtime drink.

* * *

The bloody boiler had packed up again. Jon had bled the radiators only the week before, believing that was why they were only half warm, but the noises emanating from the boiler should have warned him that the problem was a little worse than trapped air. He checked the pilot light, which was out. He pressed the button to restart the boiler, but nothing happened. He knew he'd have to call a plumber to fix it. All he fancied was a hot bath and a nice sit-down in front of the TV, but even that simple request couldn't be met; was anything going to go well before he finally went to bed?

Hoping to find Jen asleep on the sofa, he discovered an empty living room with an empty heart. It was freezing despite the double glazing, and the electric fire had also packed up some time ago. Abandoning all hope of warmth and relaxation downstairs, Jon went upstairs, had a quick wash and joined Jen, who was reading a book.

"I thought you were asleep," he snapped at his wife, annoyed that she hadn't even had the courtesy to welcome him home.

Jen placed her book on the bedside cabinet after popping a bookmark into a page and scowled at him. "Jon, I can't always be giggling and laughing, you know. If you took the time to notice, I've also had a shitty day, I too am tired and maybe, just maybe, you could have said no to returning to that place, knowing how low I've been all day, and how I needed *you* to comfort *me*. I don't ask for much, Jon, but just once in a while, I need you to be my pillar of strength. It's not a lot to ask, considering how many times I'm your crutch."

She glared at her husband, who stood open-mouthed and mute.

"Well, do I get an apology or are you just going to be an arse all night as well as all day?" She had completely disregarded the box of chocolates Jon had bought her, and the pretty flowers displayed in the kitchen, and continued to scowl at her husband.

Jon was not going to bite. Although he accepted that Jen had failed to conceive a baby yet again, she had absolutely no idea whatsoever of what his day had entailed, or indeed the repercussions of what might or might not happen as a consequence of Lizzie's confession. Storming out of the bedroom, he assembled the camp bed in the guest room and slammed the door shut.

"You have no idea what goes on in my world, Jen," he bellowed, not caring if the whole street could hear him. "You swan into your classroom full of little kiddies, teach them a bit of this and that, then bugger off home to mark a few pathetic sums. Tell you what, Jen, I'd swap with you any day! In fact, to hell with you, woman, I'll quit my sodding job tomorrow and be your house husband if that's what you want. Then we can have dozens of kids and be absolutely broke but hey, you'll have your crutch then. How about it, babe; you up for that?"

Jen had rarely heard her husband shout, yet alone swear at her, and was shocked by his tone. Jumping out of bed, she opened the spare bedroom door, shivering as she did so, and immediately calmed down.

"Whatever is the matter, Jon?" she asked, shocked at the sight of the white, angry face belonging to her once cheerful husband.

"How long have you got, Jen, because this isn't going to be quick. I feel like resigning."

He pulled on a thick jumper and jeans and led his wife down the stairs and towards the kitchen. "We'll need a strong drink," he added, pulling the kettle away from her hand and replacing it onto the worktop. Jon poured them both a glass of vodka and added some ice. He downed his in a single mouthful.

"My pie is so full of crap," he whispered, pouring another drink, "that I can't manage it any more, Jen."

Jen just stared at her husband when he explained what had happened over the past day.

"As if the confession wasn't bad enough, Jen, I honestly believed that when her boyfriend came to collect her that at last it would be over. I thought that she would be just fine with the right support infrastructure, but how wrong I was. I'm faced with not only a moral dilemma but also an extremely sick patient: how far does the Hippocratic oath go? Yes, I should do my utmost to protect Lizzie, but what if she really did attempt to kill her mother? And how on earth can I release her into society when her schizophrenia is controlling her every move? I just can't deal with this – it's far too much pie."

"What on earth are you going to do, Jon?" she questioned before taking a sip from her glass.

"I've got no choice," he replied, placing his glass on a coaster. "I'll resign tomorrow and set up my own practice; that way I'll be free – at least from St Thomas's and that bloody patient."

It was a huge step to take, and an enormous decision for Jon to reach in such a short period of time. She stroked his arm, then after rinsing her glass, headed back to the bedroom.

"Sleep on it, Jon, then if you still feel the same way after a good night's sleep, then go ahead and quit."

Following his wife into the bedroom, he agreed with her sensible advice and kissed the back of her neck before turning over.

"I'm sorry for lashing out, Jen," he whispered before closing his eyes. But she didn't hear. She was already falling asleep. She'd spent an exhausting evening at the hospital following a suspected miscarriage. Jon hadn't answered his phone when she had tried to call him. She had lost her tiny embryo; the baby that they had so yearned for. But once again it seemed that Lizzie had come first and Jen second.

That girl was trouble and Jonathan was playing a very dangerous game by continuing his sessions with her. Jen just hoped that he could see that too, and would finally let go of his precious Elizabeth Pritchard and the horrendous baggage that came with her. Because, sooner or later, that woman could destroy Jonathan's life *and* the marriage that, once upon a time, had been so incredibly perfect.

And that really would be too much pie.

* * *

Dave drove home silently. He couldn't face the radio or even listening to his favourite band, Coldplay. He just needed to clear his head after what he had seen in the hospital, and he had to think about how ill Lizzie still was.

He should have expected it, really, having had so many similar experiences before. Although not medically trained, he had observed Lizzie's delusional behaviour numerous times previously and he realised that, under pressure, she reacted badly. That had been evident tonight and he should have warned her that he would be visiting her at least, instead of bursting into the hospital and expecting the fairy-tale ending he had dreamed of.

Reversing the car slowly onto the paved driveway, he locked up and was welcomed by three pairs of bright eyes gazing through the window. The children looked towards the car hopefully, then their heads lowered and the outline of the three children's bodies stood out boldly against the glass of the front door.

His mother led them away from the hallway. She let Dave in and sensed immediately that all had not gone to plan.

"Don't ask, Mum," he said softly, removing his shoes and joining his children in the front room. Following her son, she gently picked up her granddaughter and placed her on her knee as their father finally spoke.

"Mummy's still very poorly," he said sadly. Four sets of eyes studied him intently. They remained silent as he continued to speak softly. "She needs to get completely better before she can come home, and Daddy's seeing her doctor tomorrow to talk about how long it will be, then I'll be able to tell you more."

Robert's eyes met his dad's. He was the first to speak. "Did she ask about us, Dad?" He tried to recall the last time his mum had tucked him into bed or had read him a bedtime story. He honestly couldn't remember.

Dave thought back to the brief time he had spent with Lizzie. She had been in no condition to ask about her children, but he lied as he responded to his son.

"Of course she did," he replied, smiling at all three children, "and Mummy said that she can't wait to come home and see you all again." His voice trembled and he stopped speaking; his emotions were taking over and his mother picked up on it immediately.

"So, kids, let's get you off to bed now and, tomorrow, we can all draw Mummy a get well soon card, so Daddy can take it with him when he next visits her."

They reluctantly ran up the stairs, apart from the little girl, who clutched her nanny desperately. "I want my mummy," she sobbed, not caring that her two brothers were laughing at their sissy sister with their gran.

"And Mummy wants you too, sweetheart," she replied, holding Kirsty tightly as she carried her up the stairs and towards her princess bedroom. Her dollies had all been lined up perfectly in her bed, along with a photograph of Lizzie in her younger days, which had been precisely placed in the middle of her toys.

"Why do Mummy's eyes look so sad in this picture, Nanny?" Kirsty asked, carefully placing her dollies in their crib.

Studying the picture, she too recognised the pain written across the woman's face; her smile was fake and her eyes were almost dead. It had been taken the night Dave had met her at a friend's party. She had moved in with him soon after.

Replying honestly, she shook her head, unable to offer an explanation to the little girl, who had tucked herself into bed and was already sucking her thumb.

"Perhaps, just sometimes, we all feel a little bit sad," she replied before kissing the child warmly on her cheek.

"Do you think that we make Mummy sad, Nanny, and that's why she won't come home?"

"Of course not, darling," she replied, hoping to God that her granddaughter would never find out the true reason for Lizzie's sadness. "Mummy loves you all so very much and she will be the happiest mummy in the whole wide world when she comes home for good. I promise you that, and she will be back sooner than you can count to ten."

Kirsty's eyes were heavy. She heard her nanny leave her bedroom and say goodnight to her brothers, and started to count, timing each second precisely:

Ten

Nine

Eight

Seven

Six …

She was asleep. In their room, her brothers coloured in a card they had made for their mum, also counting down the time.

They wanted Mummy back too, but unlike their sister, they didn't believe that she would be back in a measly ten seconds. It had been obvious from their dad's expression that it would be a while before Mum came back, but there was no reason why *they* couldn't visit her first.

They hatched a plan to see her the next day, straight after school, then they could hand her the card that they had just drawn for her. It had a golden retriever with a bright green collar on it. She had started to tell them her story about her pet numerous times, but had never quite finished it, and so, the boys hoped that this would jog her memory and that she would finally tell them the ending to her tale, which was bound to be a happy one.

* * *

Jen awoke to the smell of burning from her icy cold bedroom. Although masked by the aroma of filter coffee, she sensed that, out of guilt, Jon was attempting to produce breakfast in bed for her. She was absolutely right.

Jon looked weary. He was wearing what looked like a picnic blanket around his shoulders. He entered the room with a tray and a burned thing on a plate; she forced a smile. Jon was shivering so much that he spilled the orange juice onto the carpet as he handed it to Jen and placed the tray on the carpet before jumping back into bed to thaw out.

"Before you say anything, Jen, I am so sorry about last night and, after shivering my proverbials off for most of the night downstairs, I've decided to make a compromise."

Jen placed the empty glass on the bedside cabinet and waited for her husband's declaration.

Yanking the blanket up to his shoulders and almost smothering Jen, Jon continued.

"I'm quitting, Jen; today I'll resign from the hospital, but I will continue with the psychiatry – just in a less stressful environment. I've been thinking very seriously about everything we spoke about and, I believe I'm more suited to working in a little practice with maybe a small team of other psychiatrists, or even independently. What do you think; do you reckon it's a good idea?"

Jen thought that it was a fantastic idea and threw her body on top of her freezing husband, kissing him frantically. Sitting up on his lap, she beamed and nodded wildly as she blurted out how happy she was and how incredibly proud she was of him.

"I need to sort the boiler first, Jen, so after I've made the call to the gas board, I'll go straight in and resign. I'll have to give a month's notice, but who cares? I'm just so relieved to be leaving that place and starting afresh." Jon's tired eyes showed relief. He held his wife and smelled yesterday's perfume which was still on her neck.

"You smell lovely, Jen," he whispered, aroused. His erection brushed against the top of her leg. Under normal circumstances, she would have adored a long, carefree lovemaking session; however, after the previous evening, she could not, and avoided touching her husband, despite her pounding heart. She would tell him about the miscarriage later, feeling that he was already under far too much pressure, and not wanting to add to it.

"You do too, Jon," she replied, shifting to her side of the bed and attempting to chew the cremated offering on her plate, which also had something closely reassembling an egg next to it. The crumbs lodged in her throat, and she coughed, causing her to drop the plate onto the bedcovers, which made them both laugh. Grinning as she picked the black clumps away from the sheets, Jon offered to cook some fresh breakfast for his wife before calling the gas board.

She declined his kind offer and, instead, showered before facing another day at school. Jon had left before she had even applied her makeup but had, this time, left her a note on the fridge.

Have a good day at school, darling. And remember, I will do anything for you, Jen, absolutely anything.

She smiled, combing her wet hair. This time, she genuinely believed her husband.

"Me too, Jon," she replied, hoping that his boss would accept his resignation, and that he would never have to see Elizabeth Pritchard again.

* * *

Early next morning, Lizzie was up and dressed and, as she and Sara headed for the canteen, they laughed happily like the best friends which they had now become.

Lizzie, of late, was responsible for getting the drinks, and Sara, the breakfast cereal. Both knew each other's precise requirements; Lizzie liked to take three sugars with just a dash of milk in her coffee. Sara, on the other hand, was trying to diet and, therefore, took hers black with just a few grains of sugar to take away the bitterness. After adding an eighth of a teaspoon's worth to the mug, Lizzie stirred them both and headed for their favourite table at the rear of the canteen, close to the window. They liked it here and faced the window seated together, so they could study the staff and visitors when they arrived or left the car park. Both girls enjoyed the people-watching element of their breakfast far more than the soggy toast but, as always, they would eat in order to stay in the staff's good books.

Although she still loathed eating at such a ridiculously early hour of the day, Lizzie had progressed to managing sixty-eight cornflakes in a morning's session. Each day, for the last few weeks, she had increased the number she ate which, she added, aided Sara with her mental arithmetic. Sara found it annoying, but if it made Lizzie happy, she was happy too. She wished that Lizzie would try Weetabix, though, as these were so simple by comparison. That would come in time, she hoped, and, as they munched on their cereal, the girls spotted Dr Davies walking towards the entrance, with a very serious look on his face.

"Oh, he doesn't look too happy," Sara confirmed, finishing her cereal and pulling out her chair to fetch the toast and marmalade. Lizzie didn't respond when he disappeared and a few more staff joined the covered section of the main entry door, which she could no longer see.

Jason had joined the breakfast queue for the very last time. He was due to go home later today and, although nervous, couldn't wait to leave. He shoved himself against Sara, who looked surprised. Jason had always been quite kind but she knew, along with so many others in this place, that the best thing to do was to keep quiet and just smile.

"That don't wash with me, fatty," he said angrily, pushing his way in front of Sara and helping himself to the last of the toast. "And as for her, the slag over there, tell her from me she can rot in hell and that I want my necklace back now."

Sara was shocked, but not alarmed; she knew this boy's history and the fact that he had tried to kill someone. Abandoning the hope of getting any toast, she replaced the plates and headed towards Lizzie, who had observed the whole episode, having got bored with people-watching.

"Leave it to me, Sara," she whispered, heading for the table close to the far side of the canteen. She joined Jason. He ignored Lizzie and slurped the milk from the bottom of his bowl, then lifted it to drink the remaining sugary liquid. Adding a clump of marmalade to his toast, he chewed noisily, deliberately avoiding eye contact with her.

Lizzie did not want what had been a lovely friendship to end like this and smiled nervously at her ex-friend. His eyes lowered as he continued to decimate his toast, and then swallow loudly.

"Jason, I know what you think and I am sorry that you feel I misled you into believing that I wanted us to be boyfriend and girlfriend."

He spread the marmalade on the next piece of toast slowly and tried to ignore her. He failed miserably.

"But I really like you as a friend," she added. "You're kind, thoughtful and have a great sense of humour, but more than any of that, you never judged me, Jason." Lizzie thought back to the numerous times she had lashed out and had been drugged. Not once had Jason shied away from her. Not once had he abandoned her.

Jason stopped chewing and placed the remaining toast back on to the plate.

"Jason, you were – *are* – a true friend to me and I would like nothing more than to stay friends with you forever."

Jason stared at Lizzie then went to respond. However, he resisted, thinking she was probably manipulating him again.

"In fact," she continued, "I value our friendship so much that when I get out, if you want to, you can meet my boyfriend and our kids and we can all go to somewhere like Alton Towers together. But only if you want to, Jason."

Lizzie recollected the endless magazines and books she had read to Jason, which included the fastest and scariest roller coasters in the world. He had only ever been to Blackpool, but hoped that once he was better, he could go to one of the big parks in the UK with his mum on a bus or something. It had always been his biggest dream, she recalled him saying, to go on the super-duper Oblivion coaster. She so hoped that she could help to make his dream come true.

"We can pick you up and take you there," Lizzie added, knowing how scared Jason could be of public transport. "What do you think, Jason, do we have a deal?" Lizzie crossed her fingers. His eyes met hers, then lit up. She knew immediately that she had succeeded in winning him back.

Jason excitedly nodded, responding to his friend. "Really? Do you really mean that, Lizzie?"

"Absolutely, Jason, and you'll love my children too." She thought of her sons, who also adored fast rides at funfairs, and her little girl, who became so excited that she squealed at the sight of a merry-go-round.

"How old are your children, Lizzie?" Jason asked as he finished the toast and gulped down his tea.

"Well," Lizzie replied, "let me think. Tommy, my stepson, is thirteen, Robert is ten and my baby, my Kirsty, is nine."

"Cool," he replied as he thought of the great games they could all play together once they got there. "I'll ask my mum to get your phone number and you can give her yours, then, once you are better, we can all go together with a nice picnic as well."

Lizzie's heart jumped with excitement. The perfect memories she had of her childhood with Nanny and Granddad picnicking here, there, and everywhere, returned. She remembered the tatty red blanket they would always sit on, the curled-up sandwiches with warm squash, and yearned to make more memories, this time, with her own family.

"A picnic sounds perfect, Jason," she replied as she left the table and joined her friend who was standing behind her, waiting patiently for their one-on-ones.

He followed Lizzie and joined the women, then apologised to the tubby girl, who actually had always been quite nice to him.

"Will your friend be coming as well?" he asked, hoping that she could. He thought that she was quite pretty really, despite being fat.

Lizzie smiled happily, and walked towards Dr Davies's office for her morning session. "Absolutely, Jason – yes, Sara and me are best friends, aren't we, Sara?"

However, Sara had already entered her psychiatrist's office and was busy telling him all about Lizzie's naughtiness, but how she still was and always would be her very best friend.

* * *

Neither man had slept a wink, despite them both feeling mentally and physically exhausted after their terrible evening.

Andrew had tried to sleep by downing half a bottle of whisky once he had returned home, but had, instead, thrown up, then suffered from a pounding headache all night long.

Richard, on the other hand, had retired relatively early to the spare bedroom, but failed to get a moment's rest as he recollected their earlier conversations and studied the photographs of Lizzie over and over again. Blaming himself for being ignorant of his daughter's suffering for so long, he swore to his son that he would make his mother pay for all that she had done to Lizzie. Andrew had been too tired to ask what exactly his father had meant, and had finally collapsed into his own bed at 3 a.m.

By eight o'clock, both men were showered and dressed. Richard entered the large, homely kitchen. Natasha welcomed her father in law and passed him a cup of coffee before laying the large oak table for breakfast.

The Aga threw out some heat and Richard warmed his hands on the mug, thanking Natasha again. Ten years younger than Andrew, she was a nice enough girl and, despite his wife's initial reservations that she was only with him for his money, Richard knew she was wrong. Natasha was good for Andrew, who had always been rather brash and cold. Natasha, on the other hand, was tactile and kind and had brought the best out in his son over the years. Progress had indeed been slow but, as Andrew brushed his father's shoulder with his hand when he entered the kitchen, Richard felt reassured that his son's heart was in the right place.

After pecking Natasha on the cheek and helping himself to a croissant, he joined his father, asking her to allow them some privacy. She left the room, quietly closing the door behind her.

Andrew didn't hang around. The subject had been on his mind all night.

"Dad, I need to ask you something about last night's conversation. It didn't register at the time, but, when I said I would kill Mum, you said that Lizzie had already tried it. Are you serious? Did Lizzie really try to kill her?"

Richard also needed to cover everything he had intended to the night before. Meeting his son's eyes, he responded. "Yes, Andrew, Lizzie did; in fact, she tried to poison your mother with some pills years ago, but I failed to acknowledge how serious it was, believing that your mother was exaggerating."

"She lies, Dad," Andrew replied coldly. "Please don't protect that bitch with your kind words."

"Okay, lie, Andrew, she lied all the time, as I've learned, but the second time was years after, just before Lizzie's suicide attempt, actually." Richard pictured his daughter when he had last seen her, sleeping peacefully and muttering as she dreamed. He had avoided looking at the deep scar across her wrist where she had slashed it with a kitchen knife before taking an overdose of Nurofen.

Andrew studied his father's face. He looked even more drawn than he had the night before. He had deep wrinkles on his forehead and along his cheeks, and tiny blood vessels had burst, causing a red latticework to form above his eyebrows.

"Dad, what did Lizzie do?" He didn't care why his sister had tried to murder his mother. Jeez, he thought, she had good enough reason to do it, with the torture the bitch had subjected her to over the years.

Richard thought about that day. He'd left for work but had forgotten his briefcase and had needed it for a later meeting in

London. He got home and heard a thud from his wife's bedroom. He had checked to see whether she had fallen out of bed, which was common. Instead, he had found Lizzie smothering her mother with a cushion and stabbing her with the kitchen scissors.

He explained the details to Andrew, who sat in disbelief. Richard added that he had watched it happen, then, when his wife had regained consciousness, he had removed the scissors from Lizzie's hands and allowed Brenda to hit her back.

"You did *what*, Dad? Why on earth did you let her hurt Lizzie again?"

"Simple, son. So that Lizzie could plead self-defence, and get away with what she had done. Let's face it, who the heck would believe your mother? All Lizzie had to do was show her injuries and scars to somebody who believed her and your mother would have been charged and sent to prison, not Lizzie. I allowed your sister to get hurt in order to protect her from her mother, Andrew, and although I hated to watch her suffer again, I knew that it had to be done."

Once again, Andrew was horrified at his father's account of what had gone on in his sister's life. He poured himself and his father another coffee before sitting down again, dreading what was to come.

Richard sheepishly thanked his son before drinking his coffee. His stomach rumbled; not with hunger, but with anxiety. Andrew watched his father's body language; he was shifting uncomfortably in his chair, clearly finding it difficult to continue.

"So, Dad, bearing in mind what you've just told me and, knowing Mum as I do now, how the hell did you get out of this one? Surely she was badly injured and you had to get help. You didn't just leave her, did you?"

Although he wanted to despise the woman, Andrew still felt some compassion towards her; after all, despite all the shocking things she had done to Lizzie, she had never so much as smacked him as a child.

Richard lowered his gaze and studied his wedding ring as he replied. "I took her to the hospital and they treated her. Thankfully, most of the injuries were superficial, and she just needed lots of stitches."

This was ridiculous. Andrew punched the table; his coffee cup wobbled and the coffee spilled onto the polished surface.

"For Christ's sake, Dad, do you really expect me to believe that you just waltzed into A&E with your wife suffering from multiple stab wounds and near bleeding to death, for them to just bloody fix her without asking any questions? What do you take me for? I'm not Lizzie, and I'm not an idiot!"

He slammed his fist again on the table in frustration before storming out into the back garden. Richard's eyes remained transfixed on the warm brown liquid which was running down the table leg. He took a hanky from his pocket, stood up and wiped the coffee away, before following his son, who was leaning against a tree, smoking.

"I'd thought you'd given up, Andrew."

Glaring at his father, he exhaled smoke before trying to brush it away with his hand. "I have an emergency pack," he replied, stubbing the cigarette out and tossing the butt into the flower border. "They help me in times of stress, Dad, and, Jesus, don't you try to stop me from having another one. I can't handle this shit any more, Dad – it's too much to cope with."

He lit another, then turned to face his father, who was shivering. Andrew realised that his father was also suffering; in fact, his stress levels must have been near hitting the roof.

"Dad," he added softly guiding his father by his arm towards the kitchen door, "I'm sorry. I'm just being selfish. Jesus, how inconsiderate I have been, bearing in mind what you must be going through."

Closing the door gently after him, he ran the smouldering cigarette under the cold tap, threw it in the bin and sat next to his father.

Richard was so tired. If he'd had a choice, he would have left his son's home straight away. However, he had to finish his story and he had to ask for Andrew's assistance; he felt more anxious than ever as he continued.

"I'll be honest with you, son – it wasn't that simple, it really wasn't." Richard recalled the amount of blood he'd had to remove from the leather seats in his Jaguar and how, despite washing the bed linen three times, the stains had never lifted.

"Your mother, once she had regained consciousness, demanded that I call the police and have your sister arrested for attempted murder. Judging by how much she was bleeding, she also knew that she needed medical attention urgently and so, without even considering the implications, I dragged her into the car and took her to the hospital – as soon as I had attended to a few essential matters. I daren't leave her as I had no idea what internal injuries Lizzie might have caused, and she was bleeding dreadfully." He closed his eyes, recalling the horror of his wife's stomach wound and picturing the red mass of blood spreading from her breasts to her abdomen. "But, equally, I knew that *we* controlled the situation, Andrew, and that your mother, for the first time in her life, would follow my orders."

Richard shifted in his chair uncomfortably as he remembered what he'd said to his wife on the way to hospital. The sun beamed brightly through the large kitchen window, making him squint.

"I knew she'd dispute everything I told her to say; after all, she had been stabbed, but, after I threatened her with Lizzie showing the doctors *her* injuries and bruises, I forced your mother to accept my account of events."

"Which was?" Andrew asked, still finding it hard to grasp his father's tale.

"That she was attacked in her own home – by a stranger. It was as simple as that."

Andrew stared disbelievingly at his father and pulled out another cigarette from the crumpled pack in his pocket. He lit it, and recollected the photograph he had recently seen of his sister and the burns on her legs. Holding the cigarette end in front of his eyes, he studied the burning ember and tried to imagine the pain she had felt as it had been forced into her flesh. He shuddered at the thought and resumed smoking it, studying his father for a reaction.

"I'd taken away the weapon, and put the bedding in the wash. She always left the back door open and Lizzie ensured that she hadn't left any footprints anywhere; thankfully she'd removed her shoes before she'd entered the house. The police asked whether she wished to pursue the matter further, and your mother declined."

This really did baffle Andrew, and his confusion was written across his face as he gazed at his father.

"She blamed herself for everything, son, and begged the police not to take any action. It was her fault for leaving the door open; it was her fault for drinking in the day, and she felt the police would be wasting their time trying to find her attacker. Of course, they ignored her request. After all, as far as they were concerned, a potential killer could have been on the loose. But the lack of forensic evidence and the fact that I'd *stupidly* washed the bedding, eliminated practically everything other than the fact that she'd been attacked by someone with a large pair of scissors in a frenzied and unprovoked attack. They figured that the motive was robbery, which seemed to be the case, as some of your mother's jewellery had been stolen."

Richard wondered what Lizzie had done with the gold necklaces and diamond rings; he hoped she'd sold them and bought herself something nice with the money.

Andrew still found it incredibly difficult to believe, and, as he pictured the crime scene, he questioned his father again.

"Dad, what about Lizzie's fingerprints?" "They must have been all over the place; surely they checked Mum's room for evidence."

Richard was amused by his son's naivety. He really knew so little about his big sister.

"Andrew, Lizzie has OCD, and rarely does anything without wearing latex gloves. This occasion was no different."

Andrew finished his cigarette and grabbed a loaf of bread from the larder. He cut through the soft dough, speaking quietly, studying the sharp, serrated blade as he did so. "So, Dad, what do you want me to do for you exactly?"

He hoped to God that it didn't involve murdering his mother. Despite everything he had been told, and as shocked as he was, he would never harm a fly, yet alone attempt to kill somebody.

"It's simple. I need you to talk to your mother and tell her everything I've just told you. Threaten to never see her again unless she leaves Lizzie alone. That's all I am asking from you. Will you do this for Lizzie?"

Andrew felt the relief flood through him as he absorbed his father's request. He nodded and agreed, suddenly feeling a terror he had never experienced previously. He now feared for his life too. If his mother hated his sister so much, then surely she too could hate him equally.

Only time would tell. He'd have to ring her now, before he lost his nerve and refused to ever see her again. He grabbed the telephone on the kitchen wall and dialled the number. She replied almost immediately, wondering whether it would be her husband, who hadn't come home the night before. Instead it was her son.

"Andrew! Hello darling, are you okay, and is Dad with you?"

"Yes, Mother, we're both fine. Can I see you today? We need to talk."

"Of course, dear, of course! How lovely to hear your voice. I look forward to seeing you. Drive carefully, and see you soon."

He shook as he strolled back to the pub and collected his car to drive the few miles to his parents' home. Richard followed him, picturing his wife polishing and vacuuming in preparation for her guest of honour. He dreaded her response.

She already despised *him*, which he could accept, but he worried about how his son would cope after threatening his mother. He was about to witness her evil side, and Richard hoped to God that his son was strong enough to handle it.

* * * * *

30. BREAKING HEARTS

2014: Beth

The twins didn't understand why Mummy wouldn't allow Daddy into the playroom; after all, it was a fun place to be and he had always been involved with their toys and games. Although only six years old, they sensed that something was wrong as they watched their mum standing against the door, not smiling. Daddy was tapping on the door, quietly asking to speak to Mummy, but she was pretending not to hear him.

"Daddy, we're in here," Becca giggled, hoping this was a new version of hide and seek. But her mum gave her a stern look, and she heard her dad run downstairs again. Becca soon realised that their game would not involve him after all.

"Why can't Daddy come and play?" the girls enquired, reorganising the bedrooms in their wooden doll's house. Lowering her back against the door, Jen joined in with their game and adjusted the beds, moving them against a miniature window which was framed by tiny net curtains. Jen didn't want to drag her girls into her argument and simply smiled at them before offering a very simple explanation.

"Sometimes, just like you have arguments with one another, Mummy and Daddy do as well." They looked at each other before continuing to dress their dolls in their new outfits. Jen watched them.

Becca was the first to respond. "But when me and Chloe don't like each other, we don't do *that*, Mummy."

"Do what, Becca?" she questioned.

"Shout really noisily, like you did at Daddy."

Jen felt ashamed and heartbroken, realising that her daughters had heard far more than they had initially let on. She lowered her head in embarrassment, acknowledging that she should have kept quiet and spoken to her husband once the girls were tucked up in bed and asleep.

"And," Chloe added, "I still love Becca when we fight. Do you still love Daddy?"

Jen's eyes welled up. Her daughters sat silently, cross-legged on the carpet. She crawled closer towards them and hugged them, smiling weakly at them.

"Oh, babies, of course I still love Daddy; but sometimes mummies can get cross and say nasty things when they're angry, which they don't always mean." She thought of her row with her husband just a few moments ago. Jen had meant every word she had said to him.

The twins seemed to be fairly satisfied with her reply and continued to play happily in their land of make-believe, where everything always worked out just fine.

Sensing that Jon would be sulking, Jen opened the door and headed downstairs, then towards the kitchen to start tea. She could hear him on the phone. His voice was warm as he spoke. "Eight thirty it is. Great, see you then and thanks for helping me out."

Standing in the doorway, she glared at Jon before speaking, this time very quietly, to him.

"So who was that?" she asked accusingly, before turning her back on her husband.

Running towards his wife, he grabbed her waist and forced Jen to face him. His eyes were wild. He gritted his teeth before replying angrily.

"For your information, Jennifer, it was Geoff. I'm handing Beth's notes and records over to him tomorrow, first thing, and need to see him before he starts his 9 a.m. appointment. I hope you're bloody satisfied now." He stormed out of the room, grabbing his car keys and slamming the front door. Soon after, she heard his car loudly accelerate off the drive.

The twins burst away from their world of miniature people and stood, hand in hand, at the top of the stairs. It was their turn to cry now, and they returned to their bedroom sobbing loudly. Jen ran upstairs to comfort them and discovered a neatly written letter:

Deer Santa

All that we want for Cristmas is for our Mummy and Daddy to be frends.

Pleese make our wish come troo.
Love Becca and Chloe Davies

* * *

After the initial euphoria of realising that they were to be grandparents had eased, Dave settled down with his girls and excitedly shared *his* wonderful news with them.

A nearby disused workshop and factory were being converted into luxury apartments and the owner wanted bespoke, hand-made furniture within the million-pound apartment specifications. Dave enthusiastically scribbled rough illustrations of the design choices each purchaser would be given, along with details of the kitchen designs and the choice of units. Dave's eyes were bright as he chatted enthusiastically. Kirsty and Beth smiled at him as he spoke faster and faster and scribbled new ideas down. Finally, he stopped for breath and was met by two very amused faces grinning at him.

Laughing, he stood up, headed towards the drinks cabinet and grabbed a bottle of bubbly. Beth didn't mind at all; she had intended to crack it open earlier, until Kirsty had stopped her. He opened the fizzy liquid, which bubbled over the champagne flute and fell to the carpet after she and Dave had chinked glasses. Beth no longer cared about the germs, or the stain. She was on the mend and, for once, life was being so kind to them all. She couldn't wait to tell her son about Dave's new contract and, of course, the wonderful news about his sister having a baby, but first she would tell her second-closest ally, Dr Davies, if she could get to him before five o'clock.

Dave had agreed to fetch them all a Chinese takeaway later on to celebrate, but he had a few loose ends to tie up with his new client first. He made his phone call. Kirsty headed for her bedroom to call her boyfriend and share her news with him about her dad, and Beth finished writing the last of her Christmas cards. She licked the seal on the envelope, and held her breath, fighting the desire to worry about the bacteria, then placed the small cards into her handbag.

"I may as well deliver these," she whispered to Dave, who was preoccupied, but acknowledged her as he spoke to his client.

She delivered most of the neighbours' cards in just a few minutes, then, knowing that she had at least an hour to spare before dinnertime, jumped into her car and headed towards Dunstable. The traffic was absolutely solid when she hit the high street, but Beth didn't mind as she edged her way forward into the queue, passed the traffic lights and parked her car in the doctors' car park. She was surprised to see that the lights were on: it was well past five o'clock, and she knew that the practice closed promptly at five every day. It was probably the cleaners, she figured.

Removing the small envelope from her handbag, she walked to the post box, which was located on the exterior wall close to the main entrance. She tapped on the door, hoping that Jon was working late. There was no answer.

The blind in his office opened and, from behind it, he saw her. She slipped the envelope into the box and headed back towards her car, swinging her handbag as she did so.

"Beth," he yelled as he ran out of his office and stopped her from leaving. "I must talk to you, please don't go yet."

Her bright brown eyes met his and she was alarmed to notice that three of his shirt buttons were undone and he wore scruffy jeans with holes in the knees. Beth liked her doctor looking so trendy, and smiled when he led her into his office and locked the door behind him. He also had a cute backside, she thought. Jon offered her one of his infamous coffees and she politely declined, still enjoying the aftertaste of the champagne.

Sitting on the edge of his desk, Jon faced Beth. Despite his casual appearance, he spoke seriously and his eyes were distant when they met hers. "I'm not sure how I should deliver this, Beth, but I need you to understand one thing; this is not personal." Jon shifted on the slippery surface before speaking again. Beth was baffled; she had no idea what was to come.

"Unfortunately, due to circumstances beyond my control, I can no longer be your psychiatrist, Beth, and so, from tomorrow, you will need to consult with Geoffrey Pilkington. He's just as experienced as I am, and will be just as effective in helping you to continue with your recovery."

Beth studied him, dumbfounded by his statement. Her feeling of euphoria disappeared immediately and she felt an overwhelming desire to cry. A deep pit formed in her stomach and, despite trying to fight it, she allowed the tears to flow down her cheeks, without caring about smudging her makeup. Her hands shook and she felt nauseated and giddy. She tried to comprehend the statement her doctor, *her friend*, had just made. It didn't make sense.

After blowing her nose and wiping her face on a tissue from her pocket, her sad eyes met the doctor's. "Why, Jonathan? What have I done to upset you so much? Is it because I wasn't paying? I can pay now and, if you need the money, I'll pay you as much as you want just so that you can carry on being my doctor."

Her voice trailed off; she recollected the conversation she'd had with her mother on the phone. Staring into his tired eyes, she questioned him again. "Is that what this is about, Jonathan, is it the money?"

Jon felt emotionally drained and longed to hold Beth in his arms and reassure her that she had done no wrong, and that it was absolutely nothing to do with financial reward. How he needed to feel the warmth of a woman's body against his; how he longed to feel the gentle touch of a female's hand within his own. How tempting her tender lips looked. If only he could close his eyes, kiss Beth and imagine that it was his Jen; the Jen who had once loved him with all her heart but had, in just a few cruel words, broken his.

If I can't trust you, I can't be your friend. And if I'm not your friend, I can't be your wife.

The room was drenched in silence. Jon studied the beautiful woman sitting in his old green chair – *her* chair. She had come so far since he had met her so many years ago in hospital yet, despite all that she had suffered and all that she had survived, she still had an air of innocence – and extreme beauty – about her. He disregarded the scars on her fragile body, he eliminated the psychotic tendencies she had shown on so many occasions, and he tossed aside his eleven years of training and twenty years of marriage as he slipped his body away from the edge of the desk and fell to his knees in front of his favourite client – his favourite friend – begging with his eyes for forgiveness and holding his hand out to her in desperation.

"Please, Beth," he pleaded, as tears flowed down his cheeks. "Forgive me, my friend. This is the hardest thing I have ever done; please don't be angry." His head fell into Beth's lap. He continued to sob. She sat, stunned at the pitiful state of the man she had respected for as long as she could remember. Gently placing her hands on his face and lifting his head, she met his eyes.

It all made perfect sense now; over the past twenty years of treating her, Jonathan had become attached – far too attached to her. She wiped the tears away from his cheek, she understood it all. Pushing his body away from hers, she stood up and adjusted her coat before passing him a tissue and heading towards the door.

"I can't love you back, Dr Davies," she replied distantly, thinking of her precious family back home and her knight in shining armour. "And you must stop loving me too," she added before running out to her car.

He watched the car disappear into the distance and, as the red lights faded away, he left his office and grabbed the key for the mail box. Holding the small, handwritten envelope in his shaking hand, he closed his eyes. He imagined Beth's fingers holding the pen and guiding it over the paper. He envisioned her delicate lips being half open as she gently licked the seal before securing it and delivering it to him. He pictured her smiling as she slid the envelope into his mail box; the breaths she took when she walked back to her car, and the skip of her heartbeat when she unexpectedly heard his voice calling her name.

Locking the main door once again, he cautiously opened the envelope and felt the dampness of the seal from her saliva as he held it closely. Trying not to tear it, he carefully removed the card before studying it closely in the dim light of the room.

The hand-painted illustration was a beautiful artistic portrait; four people perfectly replicated, but, instead of being in a cold faceless studio in London, they were in a winter scene with snow, ice-capped trees and a frozen pond with a reindeer in the distance.

There were children skating on the pond and four faces smiled out of the card – as they did from Jonathan's photograph on his office wall.

Opening the card, he read the simple message before closing it and replacing it in the envelope.

Dear Jonathan,
From one happy family to another.
With my thanks and best wishes for a wonderful Christmas and New Year,
Beth x

* * *

Having finally organised a planning and design meeting with his new client for the second of January, Dave settled down with his daughter and the takeaway menu, selecting his and Beth's favourite dishes, along with some special fried rice and noodles. Kirsty chose her meal, beef with green peppers and black bean sauce. The phone rang, and she dashed to answer it.

"Oh hi, Nan, how are you?"

After a brief chat (and having decided to keep her good news a surprise for Christmas Day), Kirsty yelled for her dad to take the call after agreeing to ring the Chinese from her mobile.

"Hello," he replied sternly. Despite feeling happy at Kirsty's news, Dave still loathed the woman on the end of the line and resented the fact that she was holding up his Chinese feast and wasting precious seconds of his life by just being on the phone.

"David? I told Kirsty that I wanted to speak to my daughter, not you. Is she there?"

Dave's skin crawled at the tone of her voice and he responded curtly. "Nope, she's delivering cards at the moment and won't be back for hours."

He knew that Beth would only be a few more minutes, as she'd been gone for a while, but heck, why the hell should Beth have her life dictated to by this horrible woman?

"Cards?" she exclaimed. "Surely there's very little point in doing that, considering how close we are to the actual day, or has the stupid woman forgotten the date?"

Dave could feel his blood pressure rise; he bit his tongue before finally replying. "She wanted to hand-deliver them. Beth has started painting again and has made some very special cards this year; she wanted to see their faces as they opened them."

Her mother scowled. She studied the cheap boxed card she had received from her daughter, and felt the urge to slam down the phone on David.

"And who exactly would those special people be?" she demanded, wondering who the hell would be remotely interested in her daughter.

Oh, he had really annoyed her now! He knew that Beth had painted her father a card for the actual day, but had sent a boxed one to her mother to wind her up.

"Oh, some kind neighbours, her best friend and, of course, Dr Davies," he replied, a broad smile on his face. He waited for a reaction; the line was cut off, which cheered him up once again.

"That shut you up, you old battle-axe," he said before placing the spoons and forks on the kitchen worktop. He cracked open a bottle of wine.

Kirsty was confused as her dad beamed at her; she knew that he hated her nan, but had never understood why. Although she hadn't seen her very often, she had always been kind to her and her brother, and she didn't know why her dad was so horrid to her.

"Dad, why do you hate Nan so much?"

Now was not the time. Or was it? Dave had tried his best to shield the horrors of Beth's torture from his children for long enough. They were now adults and needed to understand why their mum had been so sick for most of their lives. He cleared his throat.

"Sit down, Kirst."

Obediently, she sat on the kitchen stool, her eyes enormous.

"It's not easy telling you this, but, with Christmas looming, I need to explain some things to you." He pulled away a stool and joined his daughter.

"Your nan abused your mum, Kirsty. She hurt her so badly – physically and mentally – for as long as your mum can remember." His eyes closed. He remembered the first time he had met Beth – her hair had been sheared away from her scalp that night, yet he hadn't known why until she had told him the full story once they were dating. He shuddered before continuing.

"She hid it well, Kirsty. She was so brave, but…. but the price she paid was horrendous."

"You mean her illnesses, Dad?"

"Exactly."

Kirsty stood up and moved towards her dad. She held him tightly and tears flowed down her cheeks as she sobbed loudly.

"My poor, poor mum. Oh God, Dad, how could Nan do this to her? Why, Dad? Why?"

"We don't know, Kirst. But Mum hopes to find out soon."

"On Christmas Day? Is that why Mum's making such a big deal of it this year?"

"Exactly. But, Kirsty, we must be brave for your mum. She needs us all to be strong for her. The courage this is taking is incredible. Can you do that …please?"

Shrugging her shoulders, she blew her nose and wiped her face before nodding to her dad. "I love her, Dad. I'll do anything for her – you know that."

Dave smiled and pecked Kirsty on the cheek. "You're an amazing young woman, Kirst, don't you ever forget that."

"I'm like my mum," she replied as she got the bowls out of the cupboard and wrapped the cutlery in a sheet of kitchen roll. She heard the front door open and welcomed Beth with a warm hug.

"Oh Mum, Dad told me about Nan and what she did to you. How could she hurt you, Mum? Why?"

Beth smiled sadly at her daughter. She walked straight through the hall without wiping her feet or removing her boots first. Slamming her handbag down on the worktop, she poured herself a glass of wine, which she gulped down.

Her pretty eyes met Kirsty's before she lowered her head and studied her wrist. The scar, at last, was almost gone.

"I'm glad your dad told you; I was going to before Christmas, I promise." She lifted her head high and smiled warmly at Kirsty, then Dave.

"I'll find out why on Christmas Day, Kirst; then it will all be over and I'll be able to finally find peace and closure."

Kirsty moved closer to her mum and held Beth's hands tightly. Her eyes filled with tears.

"Don't cry, Kirsty. Look at me – I'm not crying. In fact, I'm elated!"

Kirsty and Dave looked at Beth, confused, as she continued to talk confidently.

"You're not going to believe it," she said, recalling her awkward encounter with her doctor. "I don't think I need a shrink any more. I think I'm finally healed."

She popped a pill in her mouth and swigged down another mouthful of the sweet wine, and smiled at her loved ones.

"So where's that Chinese?" Beth asked, as she washed her hands then sat on a kitchen stool. "I'm starving."

* * *

She hadn't cooked her husband an evening meal. Instead, she'd eaten a light tea with the girls before snuggling down in her and Jon's bed, the twins either side of her, finally falling asleep herself.

The comfort of her daughters' scent and gentle rhythm of their breathing eased the anxiety in Jen's tired body and she slept very deeply, awaking refreshed and far more positive than she had felt the evening before.

After the girls were washed and dressed, she braided their hair and left for school; today she would walk them to their classroom before officially reporting the suspicious car. Then, at least everybody would be aware of it. Thankfully, it was the final day of term.

Jen looked forward to the two weeks' break, although she also felt anxious about spending time with Jon. The way she felt about him at the moment was far from affectionate and she dreaded the thought of any more rows in front of the girls. She would have to plan days out and about to kill the time with Jon, and maybe she could spend some of the holiday with her parents in Kent. The twins loved it there and Jen really did need some time away from Jonathan. She planned to call her mother later and arrange the visit for after Christmas Day.

Jon, on the other hand, despite swallowing two sleeping pills, had not slept well. The wafer-thin mattress on the short camp bed had been uncomfortable, and he now had a chronic backache as well as a thumping headache.

He was, as always, ravenous and, having calculated how long it had been since he had eaten, he headed towards McDonald's again and ordered two breakfasts and a large black coffee, in the hope that the food would make him feel a little more human. The sustenance didn't ease the aching in his stomach he had felt since speaking to Beth, however, and he loathed himself for being so pathetic with the woman who was supposed to be the needy one. He was supposed to be the professional! But he had turned out to be weak after all. Returning to his car, he realised just what a mess he had made of his life and of his marriage.

He still adored Jen, but at the moment he was still angry with her. Yes, he had hidden the truth from her about continuing to see Beth, but who the hell did Jen think she was, ordering him around and telling him who he could and couldn't see as a patient? Beth had been one of his very first clients and their relationship had always been strictly professional. On the other hand, though, Beth had also shared her innermost secrets with Jon and that, in turn, had affected his personal life which had subsequently affected Jen. It had been a real problem for as long as he could remember. He knew that he shouldn't have let himself get too involved. Beth was his patient and he was governed by strict rules. Now he had completely screwed up by falling apart in front of his client, who now believed that he loved her!

Holding his head in his hands and swearing, he wound down the window, hoping that the crisp December air would clear his foggy head before he went to work.

He drove with the freezing air blowing against his face, and finally reached his office. He greeted Jo and asked whether she had any news from the telephone company.

She told him they hadn't yet called back, but she promised to report any developments to Jon immediately.

Jon, in the meantime, went through his years of case notes on Beth and gave Geoff a thirty-minute overview of where she was in terms of progress. Geoff yawned and checked his watch twice within a few minutes before filing Beth's records into his empty NHS folder and assuring Jon that he would continue to treat her with compassion. Jon wasn't so sure, though, and worried that Geoff lacked the sensitivity Beth required.

"Treat her as a friend, Geoff," Jon asked as he closed the door to his office. Deep down Jon knew that his colleague couldn't care less about Beth – unless, of course, she chose private sessions with him which, at £75 an hour, would ensure that he was friendly and warm towards her.

Jo was busy talking to one of the phone company's customer service agents, who had confirmed that the mobile phone number wasn't on a contract and was from a 'pay as you go' mobile phone. Unfortunately, they had been unable to trace the caller. Jon thanked Jo for passing the message on to him. He entered his office and noticed the envelope on his desk; the one he had opened the evening before. Placing it in his desk drawer, he thought of Beth once again before picking up his phone and dialling Jen's mobile number. The answerphone kicked in immediately, despite it being before the start of her lessons, and he left a brief message.

"Jen, I'm sorry; please call me."

Jen replaced the phone in her handbag after deleting the message, and headed for her first class of her day. Although it was supposed to be English, as it was the last day of term, all children had been allowed to bring in a board game to play. After placing the kids in groups of eight, she let them get on with their games and Jen sorted out the Christmas cards from the cardboard post-box the children had made and had painted the week before.

This, along with exchanging gifts in the afternoon, was her highlight of the last day of term, and she loved the fact that the children were getting so excited at the thought of Father Christmas coming. Thinking of her own children, she sadly recollected how they had stood at the top of the stairs the evening before, crying. Their dad had now dragged her babies into his miserable state of affairs, and she felt her anger flare up again. If he had listened to her and stuck to his promise, this would never have happened.

* * *

She had parked her Jaguar a few streets away from the school this time, knowing she had been noticed by the auburn-haired woman who she knew as Mrs Davies.

It was odd, she mused. Despite having their father's smile, his daughters had no other similarities to either parent. Dr Davies had wavy black hair, the wife was a redhead, yet the girls had straight blonde straight hair. How peculiar, she thought, adjusting her scarf and pulling a woolly hat over her wiry hair.

It was a lovely day despite the cold and she was having a wonderful time this morning, despite the news Dave had given her the previous evening about her daughter hand-delivering a Christmas card to her interfering doctor. Why did everybody defy her? Didn't they understand that she never made idle threats? It was such a shame that she always had to go to such extremes to prove a point, and today was a classic example of how far she was prepared to go.

Richard was, at least, calmer these days, and delighted with her progress. The gin bottle was still sealed. He checked her breath every evening before returning to his flat; and he congratulated her on remaining alcohol free. How hilarious it was to see his pride in his good little wife – and how stupid he was. Vodka had very little odour. Mixed with cola or orange juice, it left no trace. And so, unbeknown to Richard, she'd started enjoying her carefree days again, drinking as often as she so desired but, this time, careful not to pass out or give anything away.

The break from drinking had taught her well, though, which was a positive on days like today. Although she fancied a drink, she didn't actually *need* one.

She held the small carrier bag in her gloved hand and started to hobble. She entered the school foyer, walking towards the desk where some women were giggling like stupid school girls.

She fought the desire to lash out at them – her husband's tax was paying their salaries! With her large sunglasses covering her grey eyes, and a white stick deliberately tapping the walls and floor, she struggled to find her way. The noisy women stopped chatting immediately and ran to assist her.

"I hope you don't mind, but I have a small gift for the Davies sisters," she said. Her hand was shaking as she held it in the air.

The women didn't think of asking the poor lady any further questions; they were embarrassed and felt pretty ashamed.

Thanking her for the gifts, they led her towards the door and asked whether she needed any assistance in getting home.

"No, thank you," she replied, struggling to keep her face straight. "My husband is waiting for me in the car and I will be fine in a moment." She breathed heavily, threw a weary smile, and hobbled away from the school, tapping the white stick frantically as she did so.

Her laughter bellowed out when she sat in her car afterwards, having thrown the hat and white stick into the same bin she'd dumped the mobile phone previously.

"Merry Christmas, Dr Davies," she sang while driving home. She couldn't wait for the big day now either, when she would destroy all the good work that pathetic man had done over the past twenty years in just a few moments.

Revenge was going to be so sweet – and, with an audience, it would be even more spectacular. Then, at long last, they would understand why she hated the monster she had been forced to call her daughter, and they would despise Elizabeth as much as she did.

* * *

The day had dragged. Despite having left Jen a further three messages and a text, Jon had not so much as received an acknowledgment from his wife.

Although it was only four o'clock, he'd decided to call it a day. He gathered his Christmas cards from suppliers into a pile, opened his wallet and passed Jo a fifty-pound note. Her bright eyes almost burst out of their sockets, and she jumped out of her chair and gave him a big kiss before thanking him half a dozen times.

Jon smiled, knowing that at least one woman still liked him. Popping his head around the door to his colleagues' offices, he wished them all a nice break and reminded them that he had three days' holiday. They waved at Jon, who couldn't help but notice a large calculator on the desk. He guessed that they felt their profit margins were still lower than they wanted them to be. He tried not to worry about Beth; she was their only NHS patient. He shook his head, dismissing his concern, and started thinking of Jen.

Checking his mobile before he got into his car, Jon realised that he was still in serious trouble with his wife. There were no messages. He could try the old charm offensive by buying her some chocolates and flowers, or just face the music and apologise once again to her. Realising he had no cash, and unable to face the queue at the cashpoint, he opted for the latter, drove home slowly and parked his car next to Jen's. He realised she'd broken up from school today, along with his little girls.

They burst into the hallway when they heard his car engine, and stood by the front door.

"Guess what, Daddy?" they squeaked excitedly. "We played games today and look how many cards we got given." They had at least thirty little cards each; some were hand-drawn, others were bought, and one had so much glitter on it, it sprinkled onto the carpet when they waved it in front of him. Jon smiled at his daughters, then at Jen, who was busy organising the numerous gifts she'd been given from her students, and the twins' piles of presents. There were two identical boxes, with no labels on them, and Jen studied the bright wrapping paper, wondering whether a friend had handwritten a message to the girls. Passing the packages to Jon, she asked him to double-check for a message, but he just shook his head and asked the girls where the presents came from.

"Don't know, Daddy," Chloe replied. "The Santa sack gave the presents to us all after the cards, and we gotted lots of others as well as this one." She pointed to the pile of boxes by the tree, which Jen was trying to sort into some order. She hoped that they weren't all selection boxes – as they had been the year before.

"Oh well, I'm sure you can find out, then thank whoever it was, once you return to school," Jen said, placing the boxes with the others. She stood up to close the living-room curtains.

The girls looked tired. As they sucked their thumbs and switched to their favourite TV programme, Jon gently touched his wife's arm and led her towards the hall. "I tried to call you, Jen – please tell me we can sort this out."

"Jon, not now," she whispered, checking that the girls were okay. They were both engrossed in a cartoon, thankfully, and she felt some relief, at last; they appeared to have forgotten the traumatic events of the previous day.

Jon didn't want an argument either; he was worn out. But, before putting on the oven to start dinner, he faced Jen, who looked as shattered as he felt.

"It's dealt with, Jen; Geoff has taken over and I'll never have to see Beth again. So, hopefully that's the end of the threats and we can all move on now."

Oh, how simple life was to her naive husband. Everything was either black or white; there was never any grey in that stupid pie of his. As with everything else, the enormous lump of pie that Beth had been twenty-four hours ago had now diminished and been compartmentalised into a little closed segment, so life could resume with the perfect normality and synchronisation he had planned.

Resisting the desire to scream at him, Jen glared at him before whispering a reply. "It's not quite as simple as that, Jon; it's the trust part I'm struggling with."

He gazed into her eyes. He thought back to just a few years ago when he was so self-assured and confident in his role. But now, he had become somebody else; he was weak and vulnerable. He had almost begged Beth to hold him and comfort him, and he understood perfectly what his wife meant. He couldn't be trusted any more. "I understand Jen," he replied sadly as he took some pizzas out of their packaging and put them in the oven. "But, in time, do you think you will trust me again?"

Jen desperately wanted to. She loved Jon so much, but the pain she felt at his deceit was still so raw. She brushed her fingers against the roughness of his unshaven face before moving away.

"I hope so, Jon, but only time will tell."

Grabbing her by her waist and holding her close to his chest, he kissed her fresh-smelling hair.

"Jen, I love you so much, please give me a second chance. I'll do anything for you, Jen, absolutely anything."

She placed her lips against his wedding ring finger and kissed it lightly before heading towards her daughters; Becca was now fast asleep on the sofa.

She couldn't reciprocate their little saying, though – it no longer felt right and she no longer believed anything her husband said.

Turning towards him, she replied sadly. "But you won't, Jon, will you? Or, rather, you didn't when I begged you all those years ago to give her up. I don't believe you any more when you say that to me. It's just not true. You won't do anything for me, Jon. Please stop lying."

Once again, he knew she was right. How he longed to turn back the clock to his days before psychiatry, when life had been so amazingly simple and happy. But it was too late now, and all he had left was hope. Jon knew from his endless meetings with Beth, hope was a positive emotion and, as she had proved to him only the night before, life could turn out just fine.

He kissed Becca's face as she slept and headed upstairs to gift-wrap their surprise presents before studying the beautiful bracelet he'd bought for his wife.

Placing it in a gift bag, he wrote a simple message to Jen before securing it with tape and adding a tiny silver bow.

I mean it, darling, really I do.
Anything for you, Jen, absolutely anything.
Today and always,
Your loving husband
xxxxxxxxx

31. HOME SWEET HOME?

1994: Elise

It didn't take long for Elise to pack her few belongings into a plastic bag and, as she sat on the side of the bed swinging her legs impatiently, she reflected on the past few months of her life and started to look forward to her future.

It wouldn't be easy, she knew that much, but having survived life on the streets *and* a heroin overdose, she figured that life back home would be a far nicer option than the dreadful existence she had recently endured. She smiled, watching Dave walking towards her with an array of paperwork and prescriptions tucked under his arm, and a smile as large as Elise's. Dr Davies was speaking to the nurses and would formally discharge his patient in a few minutes' time.

Dave spoke warmly. He sat beside Elise and held her hand tightly. "Well, princess, it looks as though we're almost ready to go. Dr Davies has arranged for you to attend a clinic to continue with your drug rehab, and he's just sorting out some psychiatry sessions on an outpatient basis for you to attend until you're better. Then that's it – we can head home and you can hug Bob all day and all night, while I wait on you hand and foot!"

Dave's fingers gripped Elise's tightly as he excitedly planned the next few days in his mind; he'd already called into the office to say he'd be taking some leave, and his mother was en route to his house with Bob. He would try to make the following days as stress-free as possible for Elise, although he knew moving back home would be difficult for her to deal with, and a huge transition for her.

Despite her initial excitement at the prospect of leaving Ward 33, Elise's heart sank when Dr Davies strode towards her, a number of clinic cards in his hands. She realised that this could be the last time she saw him. He had become one of the most important people in her life over the past week or so and, without his wife's kindness and Jonathan's compassion, she might not have survived. She fought the urge to weep, and dug her fingers tightly into the palm of her hand to distract herself from crying.

Her sad eyes met Jon's when he passed the appointment cards to her. "So, Elise, this is it! You're ready to leave and, as you can see, I've booked you in to a clinic near your home for your methadone treatment and your psychiatry appointments."

Jon looked at the foreign name on the card and didn't recognise it. Meeting Elise's eyes again, he smiled reassuringly at her, sensing her anxiety as she tried to read it. "I'm sure that he'll be fine, Elise," he added, signing the last of her discharge letters and handing them to Dave.

Elise was nervous. She now feared her future without Jonathan. Hugging her fiancé tightly and gazing at the doctor, she shook nervously. "Can't you still see me Dr Davies?" she begged. "I feel that I've got to know you so well recently, and it's so hard for me to trust people." She doubted that she could trust this Dr Kozlowski, and dreaded the thought of confiding her history to a new doctor.

Jonathan, although relieved that his patient was leaving, shared Elise's anxiety. He replayed their meetings in his mind and recalled the details of the nightmares she had shared with him. His blood pressure rose. He felt her nervousness.

He needed to free himself from her pain, but had become emotionally involved in this young woman's life. Scribbling his telephone number onto the corner of her discharge letter, he finally said goodbye to Elise. "I know that you'll be absolutely fine, Elise, but, if ever you need to speak to me, please call."

Elise broke away from Dave and stood in front of her friend, tears flowing down her cheeks. "Thank you, Jonathan, for all that you and your wife did." She rubbed her tummy, and then smiled sadly at the doctor, who was clearly upset as well. "Although I promise not to bother you, I will ring you once little Bump is born and, if it's a boy, I'll name him after you. I hope you don't mind, doctor."

Dave and Elise thanked Jonathan one last time and left Ward 33. Jon didn't dare look back; his emotions were taking over again. He wiped his cheeks dry and headed towards his next patient. He was already missing his friend, despite privately wishing he had never met her.

* * *

Elise chewed her nails frantically for the short journey home, but Dave didn't interrupt her or try to distract her from thoughts. He couldn't even start to imagine the terrors she had experienced and the fears she felt now that she was returning to a place where her mother had been made welcome and where her little boy had been injured. His stomach was churning with nerves when he reached his driveway and opened the door for Elise. She stood completely motionless in front of the house that she had missed so much, but now wanted to run away from.

It all looked so alien to Elise and, despite the familiar décor and the welcoming smell of percolated coffee as she entered the hallway, she turned back and headed for the car.

"Take me home, please," she cried, frantically trying to open the locked car door. Dave held her hand gently. He moved it away from the door handle and placed it in his jacket pocket, his hand firmly gripping it. He could feel it trembling as he gently restrained Elise.

"This is home," he whispered before guiding Elise towards the hallway again and calling his mother's name. A grey-haired woman smiled at Elise and gently placed a little boy in blue dungarees on the wooden floor. He stood up for a moment then flopped onto his bottom before shuffling towards the old woman's ankles and grabbing her stocking. Elise stood transfixed as he pulled his little body up and wobbled before falling onto his bottom again, chortling as he did so.

Bob was the first person she had dreamed of seeing again. As the tiny boy with the curly mop of blond hair and huge pair of brown eyes turned around and studied the strange person standing with his daddy, Elise tiptoed towards him. She noticed that he now had some little teeth and, judging by the amount he was dribbling and his flushed cheeks, he was still teething.

Bob had grown over the past few months, and Elise wanted to measure him immediately and add a new mark to the growth chart, which she had drawn on his bedroom wall close to the door frame, next to Thumper. But that could wait. Scooping the child into her arms, she smelled his hair and kissed his cheeks before smiling at him with all the love she could find in her heart. His body stiffened. He screamed loudly, startling Elise.

He sobbed, struggling against Elise's grip, holding out his arms for Dave to rescue him. Dave's heart sank as he witnessed the sadness and desperation on Elise's face. She handed Bob to him and then fell on the floor close to where he had sat.

Bob was crying loudly and, as Dave rocked him, the child pointed towards Elise as though she was a frightening monster. Recollecting her hideous reflection, Elise jumped up, ran up the stairs, and hid herself in the bathroom before plucking up the courage to look in the mirror. She now understood why her son had been terrified, and shielded her reflection with her hand, before stripping naked and taking a hot shower in the hope that she would eradicate the sores and bruises that she had accumulated before being admitted to hospital. Fighting the screams echoing through her mind and from the little child downstairs, she scrubbed frantically in an attempt to erase everything bad and start again with a clean slate. The soap helped and, as she rubbed her body harder and harder, the scars seemed to fade, along with the germs she had started to worry about recently.

She dried her skinny body and looked sadly into the full-length wardrobe mirror. Elise studied her pitiful reflection again. She had a tiny bump, and her breasts were today, she was sure, starting to fill out, despite her only weighing about seven stone. She opened the wardrobe door and examined her clothing which was neatly hung on numbered coat hangers. Checking the sizes against her new figure, she selected the smallest item of clothing there, pulled the dress over her head and zipped it up from the back. Although baggy, it concealed her scars and the bump nicely, and she looked quite presentable, she thought. All she had to do now was apply lots of makeup and she would look like a brand new woman, who could face the world with a happy, pretty mask that would hide all her pain.

* * *

After calling the Joshua Charity Foundation to cancel Elise's forthcoming placement, Jon resumed his paperwork and felt an enormous sense of relief as he closed Elise's file and handed it to the Medical Records Department who would file it somewhere, hopefully never to be seen again.

He slowly headed through the numerous corridors towards the staff room, selected a weak cup of coffee from the vending machine, and collapsed into a tatty chair, closing his eyes. The chatter of the staff bounced across the walls. He ignored their conversations and focused on more important matters.

Thinking of Jen and then of Elise, he wondered what the women were doing now. Jen, of course, would be teaching English; he knew her timetable like the back of his hand. Would Elise be okay back home and how would she cope? He crossed his fingers and made a private wish that she would remain strong and focus on her recovery and, of course, her unborn child. She so deserved a lucky break – and Dave finding her had been just that.

Recollecting his conversation with Dave, he tried again to work out why Elise's mother behaved as she did. As before, he abandoned all hope of trying to understand her bizarre actions. He just hoped that she would finally leave Elise and her family in peace, although he somehow doubted it.

* * *

She didn't recognise her bedroom any more. The bedding had been changed from the embroidered white range from John Lewis which she had put on the bed just before she had run away. It had been replaced with a cheap beige quilt cover which hadn't been ironed. It wasn't to her taste. It looked as though it needed a good hot wash or, even better, thrown away with the rubbish.

The cream carpet had shoeprints on it too; large ones. Obviously, Dave hadn't wiped his feet on the doormat downstairs, then removed his shoes and placed them on the mat outside. It would take hours to erase the stains, let alone the germs. Falling to her knees, Elise ran her finger over another dark stain. She smelled it fearing that Alfie had found his way to the bedroom. It was only mud, thank God, but she would insist that it was cleaned immediately, as the germs could spread and hurt her son, which would be catastrophic.

She tiptoed down the stairs and stood silently when she reached the bottom step, trying hard to regain her bearings. The doors leading to the other rooms were open and the kitchen at the end of the hallway was messy. The sterilising unit she had used for Bob's bottles was where she had left it all those months ago, although she knew that he was on normal food now and could also drink cow's milk. She would clean it and put it away soon, before giving the room a good scrub. She remained transfixed on the door; somebody, she was sure, was hiding behind it. She blinked and the person had disappeared; it was probably the light reflecting from outside, playing tricks on her eyes, but somehow, like the incident when Leroy had died, it seemed very real.

Dave swept past his fiancée with his son, who had calmed down and was dangling from his daddy's hip playing an 'upside down little boy' game. "Elise," he whispered after settling Bob down with his gran, "come and sit down for a moment, you look exhausted." Elise followed him robotically and settled in a leather chair positioned far away enough from the baby to avoid upsetting him again.

Dave studied his fiancée's confused features. Her eyes flicked from the dining-room glass doors, to the living room's, then stared into his. Perspiration ran down her forehead and cheek, and sweat had already formed on the armpit of her dress, even though she had just taken a shower.

"I'm scared," she stuttered. She slumped into the deep chair. She had never felt so strange, and suddenly everything that she had been so comfortable with felt peculiar, alien and very dirty. Even the baby studying her had a grubby face; she'd have to wash the chocolate off soon, or it could poison him.

Heading towards his fiancée, Dave reassured Elise that she would be just fine. The medicine would continue to ease her away from her heroin addiction and, once the baby was born, they could get back to some form of normality. She was disorientated and confused, but soon, he reassured her, everything would be perfect once again, as it had been before her mother had wrecked it all.

"You're right," she replied, as the alien room transformed into the cosy and friendly place she had formerly called home. Even her son seemed to recognise her now, and happily crawled in Elise's direction, clutching her knees and dragging himself up to smile at his mummy.

"I'll be just fine, Dave," she replied, feeling a huge sense of relief that she really was back home and nobody was ever going to hurt her again. She knew that she was only suffering from the side effects of the methadone and classic symptoms of stress; everything would be wonderful soon. She smiled at Dave and hugged her precious son. They really were going to be one big happy family.

"I'll protect you, Elizabeth Pritchard," her friend whispered quietly, hoping not to disturb Bob, who Elise was bouncing on her knee.

"Who was that, Dave?" Elise asked, confused by the woman's voice in the room.

"Probably Mum talking to herself again!" he replied. Dave pecked his fiancée on the cheek and headed towards the kitchen to make some lunch. Elise followed him, hugging Bob close to her chest, and kissed the back of Dave's neck while he prepared the toast and opened a tin of beans.

"I hate beans," the shadow yelled before storming upstairs, but Elise chose to ignore her this time. She was too preoccupied with planning the design of little Bump's nursery, which would have teddy bears painted on the walls this time.

After popping Bob into his high chair and tucking a bib around his neck, Elise sat on a kitchen stool and pushed it closely against the worktop. She was too happy to worry about the crumbs on Bob's hands and watched him as he munched his toast. She smiled, counting each bean before spooning them up and feeding them to her son.

"You not joining us, Elise?" Dave enquired, studying Elise's peaceful expression as she fed their son.

"I'm not hungry, Dave," she replied, fighting the urge to throw up at the thought of the food hitting her stomach. "In fact, can you take over with Bob so I can start cleaning?"

Dave nodded and smiled; he watched Elise head towards the kitchen sink and wash her hands. She was doing so well, considering what she had gone through. How very proud he was of her.

"So much to do, Dave, and so little time," she whispered, pulling the rubber gloves over her fingers and starting to frantically spray the windows.

"You've got forever, Elise," he replied tenderly, wiping his son's mouth then feeding him a yoghurt. But Elise was too engrossed with the pretty little girl smiling at her through the kitchen window. "I'm sure I know you," she whispered, hoping that Dave hadn't heard her.

But he had. Excusing himself and going into their bedroom, he dialled the number on her release notes, hoping that Dr Jonathan Davies would answer the phone – and, more importantly, his questions. What was wrong with Elise? What could she see and hear that nobody else could?

The answers to these questions scared him so.

* * * * *

32. MOVING ON

2004: *Lizzie*

Jon sealed the envelope which contained his resignation letter, then smiled in relief. Although still a month away, he looked forward to his unknown future with enthusiasm, and pictured himself in a small practice in a nice rural area, with Jen at home and, hopefully, a baby to tend. His stomach fluttered with excitement at the thought of finally leaving St Thomas's Hospital and the baggage associated with it. He wrote the name of the hospital director in neat handwriting on the envelope, and jotted down some names of fellow students from Oxford; he would contact them later to find out where they were and what they were doing these days. Perhaps one would be in a position to form a partnership with him.

His thoughts were interrupted by a tap on the door; a noise he was familiar with and a patient he looked forward to never seeing again once he had left the hospital. Leaving his chair, Jon headed slowly towards the door, dreading his meeting with Lizzie. She had been so poorly the day before, and her delusional behaviour had disturbed him dramatically. He made a mental note to increase her medication, which would reduce the symptoms of her schizophrenia and help her to cope when – or if – she finally went home.

Lizzie looked far brighter than she had the previous evening. Her eyes shone and she had tied her hair into a short ponytail and wrapped a red ribbon around it, forming a bow at the top. Noticing the direction of his gaze, Lizzie wriggled her head and laughed. "Sara gave me it," she giggled, helping herself to a biscuit from Jonathan's desk. She hinted that he should put the kettle on.

Jon was used to his patient's antics and knew that, despite appearances, Lizzie was still desperately sick. She just hated the medication she'd been prescribed and would fight the voices in her mind to create an illusion that she was 'normal'. She would do anything to avoid being forced to take yet more drugs; a pitiful state to be in, but one that Jon was not going to ignore. He was tired of Lizzie's games and, no matter how hard she tried, she would never win this game of hers.

Filling the kettle, he studied Lizzie's facial expression for a hint of pressure. Her smile did not falter, her brown eyes still sparkled and, for once, she was not chewing her nails – not that there was much left to nibble. He was not, however, fooled.

"So Lizzie, how are you this morning?" he asked, placing a mug of coffee next to his client and sipping his tea.

Curling her feet under herself, she smiled warmly at the doctor before settling on the carpet. "I'm very good, thank you, doctor," she replied, fidgeting in an attempt to get comfortable; Lizzie knew that she had to come clean about her acting the night before, but dreaded his reaction to her deceit. She met his eyes and continued. "Last night, Jonathan, I didn't see Alfie and … and the rocking? I did that on purpose too."

Jon raised his eyebrows but, other than that, failed to react to his patient's confession. Lizzie continued, although she was surprised that her doctor had not shown any form of surprise or shock at her statement.

"I was scared, Jonathan, that's all. After everything that has gone on, and the fact that I'm still terrified of my mum, I wasn't prepared for Dave's announcement that I could go home. I need time to adjust and to prepare myself mentally and emotionally; can't you understand that?"

She raised her head, hoping to read her doctor's body language; once again, Jon did not move.

Two can play at this game.

Lizzie stood up and faced the doctor who was fumbling nervously with the envelope on his desk. He just wanted to hand in his resignation now, and hoped that he would be asked to leave immediately; he no longer cared about his four weeks' bloody notice.

"Doctor," she yelled. She dropped her trousers and forced her skinny body into his line of vision. Jon blinked in an attempt to avoid studying her scars. Lizzie edged closer to the doctor, forcing him to study her half-naked body; he scrunched his eyes closed, hoping to eliminate the image before him. She moved even closer and placed her hand into Jonathan's. It was trembling as she guided his fingers over the mottled scarring on her thighs. His eyes opened and followed the latticework of injuries his patient had suffered at the hands of her mother. His nightmares returned.

"You see these, don't you? Don't you remember what and how you felt when you first met me in hospital, when you wanted to quit the medical profession and your wife talked you into staying – for me, Jonathan? You wanted to save me, didn't you? Thanks to you, I am still here – suffering and struggling to deal with my life – or what's left of it. It's all your fault, you know. If you had let me die in hospital, none of this would have happened. I would never have had to hide from my mother, I would never have tried to kill her again; I'd have remained a junkie, died in the streets, and Dave and Robert would have forgotten me by now. Is it any wonder I'm scared, doctor? Can't you even try to acknowledge how terrified I am at the thought of going home and her finding me, hunting me down and seeking revenge? Look at these scars again, Jonathan – try to imagine how much pain I've suffered at the hands of that woman and how much I will suffer once I am out of this place. And look at my face too. Look beyond my eyes, into my mind, and imagine taking a journey within it. Feel what I've been forced to feel!"

Lizzie fell to her knees and her head faced Jon's chest, which was heaving as he breathed deeply. His eyes remained transfixed on Lizzie. She opened hers wide and stared deep into her doctor's blue eyes.

"My mind has been abused, too, Jon," she whispered. "It is tortured with the memories of my life; you would call yours nightmares, but mine, mine are *real*. Mine cannot be eliminated with a strong cup of coffee. My life, my soul, my mind, my body are all tortured by her, and I'm still so frightened. Please, for one moment, Jonathan, try to empathise."

He did. He always had and, despite fighting with his emotions, he could no longer hide how much he cared for this woman; his patient; his friend.

"Oh Lizzie," he whispered, stroking her ponytail and holding her head in his lap. "I do empathise, how can I not?"

Lizzie wiped her cheeks and, realising how compromising a position her head was in, moved away, towards the window.

Turning his chair to watch his patient, Jon continued. "I'm sorry for everything, Lizzie, really I am. But let me assure you that you will not be bothered by your mother ever again; Dave has taken out a restraining order against her and he has arranged to sell your house so that you can all move away and she can never trace you. He's even sorted for the estate agent to handle it as a private sale, meaning no board and no advertising; just in case."

Lizzie continued to study the sky as she replied quietly. "So when do I leave, Dr Davies?"

"Soon, Lizzie. Very soon."

* * *

Nothing had changed. The large wooden door still needed rubbing down and repainting, and the antique urn still contained the five umbrellas it had at least fifteen years ago. Even the doorbell was the same, chiming loudly in the large hall with its uneven wooden floor and flickering light. She looked no different either, as she opened the door and welcomed her son with a warm smile and a hug.

"Andrew, my darling, how delightful to see you. Do come through."

He stood motionless in the hallway, thinking about the photograph which was sitting in his jacket packet. The mud on her face, the sadness in her eyes. The parquet flooring beneath her bare feet. The blood. Her agony.

Richard wiped his boots on the doormat and tapped Andrew's back gently, managing a weak smile before heading towards the living room and the warmth of the fire, which smelled lovely.

"Pine," she said, tending to the fire, smiling as she did so. "I gathered them the other day when I was walking through the park. Lovely, aren't they, Andrew?"

Andrew failed to acknowledge his mother's statement; her voice bounced through the recesses of his mind then disappeared into oblivion as he studied her face and her grey eyes gazing lovingly into his.

Ignoring her husband, she offered her son a drink. He accepted robotically. His fingers fumbled in his pocket, stroking the edge of the evidence, shaking. Her smile still haunted him. His poor, darling sister. Tortured by *her*, the woman standing in front of him *pretending* to be normal.

I'm not stupid. My pathetic husband has been poisoning my precious Andrew's mind; that's where he was last night. It's so bloody obvious, but I won't let on that I know.

The large mouthful of vodka helped a little. She filled the kettle with cold water and watched the birds feeding on the fatball in the garden while she waited for the kettle to boil; her tension lifted and she realised that she was being paranoid. Andrew still adored her as much as she adored him; of course he did.

From the moment she had given birth to her son, her heart had burst with the love she felt for him; it ached with emptiness when she wasn't with him and she missed his voice, his smell, everything about Andrew since he had met that dreadful wife of his. *She* had taken her son away from her and would have to be dealt with at some point. But not yet, not now.

"Andrew, my love," she said tenderly, placing his cup on the coaster and offering him a biscuit, "it really is wonderful to see you again. So what brings you here at such short notice? Are you alright, dear? Do tell me, my darling, please tell Mummy."

* * *

Dave couldn't concentrate. It was no good; he had to see Lizzie again but, this time, it would be planned; no element of surprise for his little princess. No frightening her any more. Just an informal visit with no pressure. Just him and her.

Norman Hillier still was not available. After leaving a message for Jonathan Davies to call him urgently, Dave dropped the kids off at school then returned home, unable to face work, unable to focus on anything other than the disturbing image of his girlfriend rocking backwards and forwards.

They were back again. He held his head in his hands, sobbing loudly, knowing that *they* controlled everything in Lizzie's mind and influenced so many of her decisions. It was *them*, she had said upon her admission to St Thomas's Hospital, who had told her to commit suicide. Of course, he knew that *the girls* were a figment of Lizzie's imagination, as was Alfie, but the realisation of what he was about to take on when she was eventually discharged finally hit him hard. Was he strong enough to cope with her, or should she have her own way and stay, indefinitely, in hospital?

The ringing phone brought Dave back to reality. He grabbed the receiver, relieved to hear the warm and friendly voice of Dr Jonathan Davies.

"Thank heavens it's you, doctor; can I see you or Mr Hillier later to discuss Lizzie, please? I'm so worried about her."

Jonathan hesitated before responding. *That's funny,* he thought. *I haven't seen Norman again today.* He made a mental note to call Norman at home, before agreeing to meet Dave after lunch. He too was worried about Lizzie, but that could wait. His personal feelings towards a patient were unimportant. He had to hand in his letter of resignation first. He knocked and entered the hospital director's office, smiling as he greeted her.

"Do take a seat, Jonathan," she said, sending him a strained smile. "I wanted to speak to you as well; it's bad news, I'm afraid. Norman Hillier has passed away – he had a suspected heart attack, his mother says, although it's unconfirmed at the moment."

Jon almost collapsed into the hard wooden chair by the director's desk. Her words spun through Jonathan's mind: a heart attack? Norman? Christ.

His heart thumped. He passed her the letter, knowing that he was making a wise decision to leave this godforsaken place. The stress had killed his colleague; it would destroy him in time too and, before explaining his position, he studied his boss's strained features as she scribbled down some notes, then met Jonathan's tired eyes.

"Please tell me some good news, Jon," she whispered, before closing her notebook. He lowered his gaze to the envelope he had left on her desk. "I'm sorry, Laura. I'm giving you four weeks' notice from today. I will help you to recruit replacements for me and Norman, if you want me to; it's nothing personal against you or this place. I need you to understand that, Laura. Nothing personal at all. It's just my time to move on."

She didn't care about it being personal. Within a few minutes she had lost her two most valued members of staff. It sounded pretty personal to her.

"Then, Jon," she yelled, edging towards the wooden door of her office, "what the hell is this about then if it's not bloody personal?"

He couldn't tell her the truth. Despite all that had happened, he cared desperately for his patient and would protect her from her secrets. Lizzie deserved that much. As did Jen.

He turned to face his boss once again. She was leaning against her windowsill and clutching a packet of cigarettes. She removed one from the packet and placed it in her mouth without lighting it. She glared at her colleague as he tried to explain his reasons for resigning.

"I need to escape from this environment, Laura, that's all. I've worked in hospitals for too long now and I want to work in my own practice, with set hours and my own clients. Jen and I also want to start a family. It seems like the perfect time for me to leave and to start afresh."

Laura understood. At the age of fifty-nine, she too had endured too much pain and stress at work but, with just a year left until retirement, she would hang on to the bitter end. If her heart could stand it, that was.

She brushed down her jacket and lit a cigarette defiantly, after opening the office window in the hope that the air would eradicate the smell of the tobacco. Grinning at Jon, she exhaled the smoke before speaking.

"Well, they're hardly going to sack me for this little offence, are they? There's far worse than a little bit of smoking going on in this place, I know that for sure."

Jon did not react; he left Laura's office and ran towards the safety of his own, feeling his heartbeat increase and his palms starting to sweat. Dialling Jen's number, he took deep breaths in an attempt to calm down. The line was engaged and so, after leaving a brief message on her answerphone, he went to see Lizzie. She smiled warmly at him as he entered her bedroom.

Lizzie had to know; he owed her that much, but he knew that telling her would be far, far harder than resigning had been.

* * *

Andrew couldn't drink the coffee. He didn't want a bloody biscuit. His father was just sitting in the sodding armchair staring at him.

Jesus, Dad, you could help me out with this, for Chrissake.

The atmosphere was so tense, you could have cut it with a knife. Even the warmth radiating from the fire felt artificial; like his mother's love and his entire superficially happy childhood.

Andrew forced himself out of the comfortable armchair and tossed another log onto the fire. It ignited immediately, and the warmth it produced gave Andrew a new inner strength. Gulping down his coffee, purely for the caffeine boost, he strode towards the wooden display cabinet and picked up a framed photograph. Blowing the dust away, he rubbed his thumb across the glass and studied the image of the tubby child splashing in his paddling pool. He remembered that day well. How happy he had been, and how much he had adored the woman taking the photograph. She had been his world; the centre of his universe.

His sister's torturer.

His mother's eyes sparkled and she joined her son, placing her arm around his waist. "You were such a beautiful child, Andrew," she said.

Placing the picture face-down on the cabinet, he faced his mother; his eyes bored into hers. The atmosphere froze.

"Strange isn't it, Mother?"

She studied her son's cold features, her mouth half open.

"It's strange that, despite you having an endless supply of photographs in this home, there is not one of Lizzie. Why is that?"

He grabbed another frame, then another – all of which were of him – and forced the images in front of her face. She backed away automatically, horrified at the sight of her son.

Disturbed by his mannerisms.

Confused.

Scared.

Her heart was thudding; she felt sick and she desperately needed a drink. Richard had poisoned her baby's mind – it was obvious now. She glared in her husband's direction. He studied his son, whose eyes were wild and his face flushed as he continued to shout at her. She tried to head for the door towards the hallway; her son's large frame stopped her in her tracks. He gripped her wrists tightly. He screamed at her: "Where was my sister when all of this was going on, Mother?"

He lowered his gaze to the kitchen floor. Shadows appeared to lurch out from the tiles, their long bony fingers pulling at his ankles, as he dragged his mother into the kitchen and forced her to sit on a kitchen stool while still restraining her by her wrists.

"I know where Lizzie was, and I know what you did to her," he said coldly. His mother's eyes welled with tears; a lump formed in her throat when she saw how angry Andrew was.

"I know that you tortured Lizzie mentally and physically, Mum; I know absolutely bloody everything now, and I'm here to finish it. It will end now, Mother, once and for all. Do I make myself clear?"

His fingers forced their way into the folds of her skin; he gripped harder, fighting the desire to hurt her. He understood what rage could do; he was feeling it now, yet she was as quiet as a mouse and shivering, sobbing in front of her son. The shadows disappeared beneath the floor tiles before she spoke. Even they were scared.

"You have no idea, Andrew," she whispered, forcing her hands away from his and running towards the kitchen sink to throw up.

Hold her, you fucker; tighter, man. She can't get away.

He studied his mother as she retched into the sink before reaching for a bottle of vodka which she'd left on the worktop. Her eyes closed for a second; she gulped the liquid, and then swallowed hard. He hoped she would choke to death.

"I have a few things left to say, Mother, and you will say nothing."

"You don't understand, Andrew – please let me explain."

"Do you hear me? This is your final warning, Mother; if you interrupt me one more time, you will never see me again. Do I make myself clear?"

Wow, man, that was one hell of a ride. D'you want a turn now?

She understood. Nothing could destroy the love a mother felt for her son. Absolutely nothing. This would pass; Andrew would get over it and learn to love her again. Of course he would – once he knew the truth about his sister. He was, after all, her life and she, his mother, was his. She sat down on the oak chair and nodded obediently.

Good girl. Stay still now.

His hollow eyes stared directly into his mother's grey slits. He spoke in a monotone and stood motionless as he concluded his statement.

"You will leave Elizabeth alone. If you hurt her one more time, emotionally or physically, I will kill you."

Her mouth opened; she needed to speak. Andrew threw his body forward and lunged his fist towards her mouth, stopping it just centimetres away from her lips. She shook with terror, closing her eyes to hide the fear, to eradicate the memories, the nightmares.

"No, Mother, you will not speak; I know about *that* too. The scissors, the stabbing. Lizzie. Nothing has been hidden from me. I know it all. Everything, Mother. Absolutely bloody everything. I need you to agree with my terms, and say that you understand what I have just said."

She nodded.

"You agree to leave Lizzie alone," he demanded.

She nodded again. Her eyes filled with tears as she studied the stranger giving her unfair and unreasonable demands.

"You're evil, Mother; I realise that now. But if you stick to my terms, you will at least see me when I visit Dad; that's as far as our relationship will go, though. Do you understand what I'm saying?"

She nodded frantically. The tears flowed down her cheeks and into her mouth. Her mind clouded with memories of the festival, thumbing a lift home to Hertfordshire, her clothes torn, crying salty tears, her bruised and battered body.

"Help me."

"It's too late for that, Mum," he whispered, tossing the crumpled photograph of his naked sister in front of her. "It's too late for tears. You can't be helped, but hopefully Lizzie can."

"Mummy's little angel," she sobbed, as Andrew stormed out of the kitchen and said goodbye to his father.

He had gone. Her darling, her reason for breathing and staying alive every painful day. Without him, there was no point. She loved him so much.

"I'm so sorry," she whispered, holding the crumpled photograph close to her chest. "My poor little Lizzie, please forgive me."

But the haunted eyes in the image just stared coldly back, grinding deep into her soul, as they had so many years before.

They were the devil's eyes. That devil was named Damien. He had loved the number six. He thought that she would too.

His Black Widow.

But she hadn't.

* * *

Lizzie knew that something was bothering her doctor. She'd got to know his mannerisms over the years and, over the last week or so when he was under pressure or uncomfortable with a situation, he'd started to suffer from a little tic in one corner of his eye. Lizzie could tell that it was bothering him, and tried not to giggle as he blinked in an attempt to stop it, but she couldn't help it.

Jonathan was not amused. He studied his patient and wondered whether this was another of her little antics to confuse or annoy him. Despite him having practised psychiatry for over a decade now, Lizzie's behaviour continued to baffle and sometimes, like now, irritate him. Someday, he would find the time to write a case study on her, but not today.

"Lizzie," he said firmly as she rolled on the carpet, giggling. "Will you please sit up and listen to me for a moment?"

She composed herself just enough to sit up in the lotus position, but dare not look into the doctor's eyes – just in case.

"Yes, doctor," she whispered, trying hard to keep a straight face.

Jonathan settled into his chair before making his announcements. He cleared his throat and rubbed his eye again. Lizzie fought the desire to giggle once more.

"Two things, Lizzie," he said. He had her attention now, and she lifted her head and opened her eyes wide as he spoke.

"Firstly; Dave. He wants to visit you again – are you okay with this?"

She didn't respond and picked at her thumbnail instead, before putting it into her mouth and chewing on the quick. The sweetness of the blood comforted her a little, but not enough. She wasn't sure whether she could face Dave so soon; she needed to give considered thought to the question before she could reply. She stared back into the doctor's eyes, which no longer sparkled, and looked terribly serious.

"Secondly, I am leaving St Thomas's Hospital, Lizzie. I handed in my notice this morning and, four weeks from today, I will be gone."

Lizzie stopped chewing her thumb immediately and removed it from her mouth. Her huge eyes studied the doctor's face for a hint of playfulness and jest; he was joking – he had to be. She smiled and waited for a reaction from her friend. His eyes were cold. His smile did not follow. Hers disappeared in an instant.

"You're leaving, Jon? What will I do without you – how will I cope?"

Lizzie felt the urge to rock backwards and forwards as she so often did in times of desperation. She clutched hold of her buttocks and forced herself to remain still as she tried to gain some composure.

Jon fought the desire to show any form of emotion; this time he had to remain professional with his client.

"You have two options, Lizzie," he replied. "You can let Dave continue with your care at home, with support, or you stay here and attend sessions either with Dr Bailey or my replacement."

Lizzie shuddered at the thought of attending sessions with Dr Bailey. Sara liked the man, but he gave Lizzie the creeps big time. His eyes were horrid; grey and small like her mother's, and his frizzy hair reminded Lizzie of *her* too. No way would she see him. Never.

"Who is your replacement?" she asked, shuffling on her bottom across the carpet, then leaning against the wall.

Jon had absolutely no idea, and answered Lizzie's question honestly. Leaving his chair, he faced his client, who was frantically chewing her fingernail again. She looked lost and vulnerable and, as before, he felt the desire to hold her and comfort her, knowing that he could never do so.

Jen would never understand.

It would be morally wrong.

He was a professional.

Lizzie was his reason for leaving.

Lizzie had caused his argument with his wife.

Lizzie was trouble.

"I don't know," he snapped, turning his back on Lizzie and heading towards the large, familiar window at the rear of his room. "But I do know that Dave adores you, Lizzie, and is willing to take you on – *home*, I mean. If I were you, I would choose that option over this place, I really would."

The car park was filling up again. It had to be close to lunchtime or the afternoon shift, judging by the number of cars arriving. Jon was hungry.

Sensing his distress, Lizzie got up and walked slowly towards her doctor. He was watching a woman in the car park with a buggy and a toddler. He smiled as he watched the toddler pointing to a bird in the sky and grabbing his mum's coat for attention. What a simple, carefree world he lived in. Jon wanted that lifestyle back, and soon.

"If only our lives were that simple," Lizzie whispered. She brushed her hand along her doctor's arm and turned away. His eyes met hers briefly and, as she reached the exit, she smiled sadly at her doctor.

"I understand, Jonathan, I honestly do. It *is* time for me to move on, and you too. I will tell Dave that I am ready to go home and we can get the wheels into motion for my discharge if you like. If you are happy to do this for me, that is?"

Jonathan nodded. The door gently closed behind his patient, and he took a deep breath to regain his composure and fight the desire to weep. What was it about this woman that touched his soul so deeply? Why did he care so much about her?

He was distracted by a knock on his door. It was Dave who wanted to discuss Lizzie's release. Jon sighed with relief, knowing that soon he would be free from this woman, which, surely, was for the best.

* * *

Robert and Tommy had decided to visit their mum during their lunch break, rather than after school, as previously arranged. Granny had agreed to meet them and, after she welcomed the boys at the school gates, they took the short walk across town, through the small park and towards the main entrance of St Thomas's Hospital.

Their friends had talked about the place at school, but the boys had never dared to admit that their mum was a patient there; their peers would have teased them if they had ever found out. Hence, they had said they were going with their granny to visit the dentist at lunchtime.

Surprisingly, the hospital looked quite normal from the outside. The windows didn't have bars on them, which both boys had expected, and there was glass too; it must have been strengthened though – it had to be, as so many of their mates said that they had seen the *nutters* jump out last year. In fact, one boy in their year reckoned that three mental patients had apparently escaped through the windows as the staff were beating them up and drugging them with poisonous pills.

Robert gazed at the chimney billowing with smoke at the rear of the building. He hoped to God that they hadn't set fire to his mum and dumped her body, which he also knew happened in this place. It was full of murderers and crazy people. The rumours were that some of the patients had killed the staff, stole their uniforms, and still worked in the hospital, killing the mad people one by one. He was terrified. What if the boys at school were telling the truth? What if his mum had turned into a freak like some of the others here had?

Tommy was petrified. He wanted to go back to school – even physics sounded appealing now. Perhaps he could visit his step mum another time.

Robert was too frightened to say a word, and held on tightly to his granny's hand, despite feeling like a real sissy.

At the door, Granny said who they were and a woman who looked quite ordinary pressed a button and the door buzzed, allowing all three to enter the asylum. No screaming mad people were in this room; it seemed to be safe – for now, at least.

"I'm here to see Elizabeth Pritchard," their granny said and, after signing herself and her grandsons into the visitors' register, they sat patiently in the red plastic chairs. Tommy thought they were red to hide the blood of people who had been stabbed by the staff or residents here.

"This place gives me the creeps," Tommy whispered into his brother's ear. His brother nodded and focused on the main door, which took you into the scary bit of the hospital; where *they* were – the mad people, the lunatics, and their mum.

"You can go through now," the woman said, pressing yet another button and leading the grey-haired woman and two boys along numerous corridors, towards an area that looked very similar to a canteen. "She's just finishing lunch," she said, pointing at Lizzie and a rather fat woman who was slurping her drink very noisily.

"Is that Mum?" Robert whispered softly to his gran, gripping her hand even more tightly than before. He crouched low and tried to hide behind Gran in the hope that the crazy people wouldn't see him. It was too late. One had.

The sandwich slipped out of Lizzie's hand and fell to the floor. Her mouth gaped, yet she could not speak. Her eyes focused on the two boys and the elderly woman, yet she did not recognise them. How she loathed her lunch-time medication.

"Who are they, Sara?" she asked, pointing towards the three alien faces, who were all staring in Lizzie's direction.

Sara recollected the conversations that she and Lizzie had had over the past few days, and she also recognised the haunted expressions on her family's faces. She knew that look well too.

"Your sons, Lizzie," she replied, having lost her appetite in an instant. "Your babies are here to see you."

Lizzie regained her bearings and finally recognised the blurred images in the distance. Another two familiar faces entered the picture: Dave, and, of course, Dr Jonathan Davies.

It was time to go home.

* * * * *

33. CHRISTMAS DAY

2014: Beth

It had come.

It was the twenty-fifth of December.

The day of reckoning had arrived.

She was terrified.

The bedroom was warm, yet Beth shivered as she edged out of her warm bed and padded towards the bathroom. Her stomach churned and her head felt foggy; similar to how she had felt in the earlier days when she'd first been introduced to her medication.

Fighting the desire to throw up, she filled the sink with cold water and rinsed her face. It didn't help. Her dark eyes studied the reflection in the mirror – she looked exhausted. She hadn't slept well. Dave had been right. Dr Davies had been right. She was putting herself under far too much pressure, far too early, but it was too late to change her plans.

She had so much to do.

Too little time.

* * *

Brenda, too, had been restless. She'd believed that by drinking a bottle of vodka earlier, she'd sleep well; however, after collapsing into a drunken stupor, she was abruptly awoken by Richard who was calling to remind her to wake up early the next day or he wouldn't give her a lift to Beth's. Sleeping off the booze, then eating an evening meal far too late, had meant she'd found it virtually impossible to sleep at bedtime. She was exhausted.

The enormous house was bitterly cold. Money was tight these days; or at least Richard was, rationing every single penny he earned since he had left her. She, his loyal and wonderful wife, now had to literally beg for an addition to her measly allowance; it was a pathetic existence and she vowed she'd do something about it in the New Year.

She walked carefully down the large, wooden staircase, holding tightly to the banister as she did so. Her balance, of late, had been poor, and she'd fallen down the stairs a couple of times recently. It hadn't been the drink – she'd been sober at the time. Probably stress. That was more than likely the reason why. She would go to the doctor after Christmas to have some tests, though. Just in case…

After boiling the kettle, she made herself a strong cup of tea, added two sugars, and entered the living room. The radiators creaked when the boiler burst into life and she rubbed her arms frantically before throwing a log onto the still smouldering fire.

There was no Christmas tree this year, but, in line with the usual Pritchard traditions, he had bought his family gifts and she, hers. He had increased her allowance this year so that she could buy an extra-special present for the hostess. She smiled, studying the large, square package which had been beautifully gift-wrapped the day before; she'd paid particular attention to not creasing the paper and, having managed to wrap the awkward gift so beautifully, despite packing it in bubble wrap first, she had felt very proud of herself that afternoon. Dave would welcome the gift too. She'd done well this time.

Of course, Richard would never approve of her gift choices. His were never practical. In fact, ever since the children had been born, he would spend ridiculous sums of money on unnecessary extravagances, such as extortionate toys when the children were tiny, to jewellery and perfumes when Elizabeth had got older, and expensive aftershaves for Andrew. He'd also felt the need to purchase the same perfume for her, year in, year out. She swore that if anybody ever bought her another bottle of Chanel No. 5, she would throw it down the toilet. She despised the stuff – almost as much as she despised Richard.

She sorted the remainder of the gifts into neat piles and smiled as she gently brushed her hand across the foiled gift-wrap on Andrew's present. This was an extravagant gift; something that she had given considered thought to for many months. It was her only way of telling him how much she loved him. How much he had always and would always mean to her. It had been her future, her retirement fund – it was his now. She was bequeathing him everything she possessed; the envelope contained a legal document she'd had drawn up. Her parents' home was no longer being rented out to provide her with a monthly income. She had decided to give it to her precious son. Her wonderful baby. And he would now love her back, as he had done before; before Richard and, of course, Elizabeth, had wrecked it all.

"Please be there, Andrew," she whispered, placing the gift carefully on the top of the pile.

"Please come today Andrew," Beth whispered, as she struggled to compose herself before entering the filthy kitchen and pulling latex gloves over her hands.

* * *

Although it was only eight o'clock, Jon and Jen had been wide awake for the past four hours. Despite tiring the girls out on Christmas Eve with a trip to London and even some ice-skating before tea, it hadn't made an ounce of difference. Like an alarm clock, they had woken up at precisely 4.01 a.m. and had excitedly burst into their mummy and daddy's bedroom ten seconds later.

Thankfully, Santa had completed his rounds on their estate early and Jon had suggested that they go to bed early too. Jen, although shattered from her day out, had declined. It seemed that, despite it being the season of goodwill, she would not be giving much to Jon in *that* department. He hoped that things would improve once he had given her the beautiful bracelet he had so lovingly selected and gift-wrapped. He smiled, pecking all three girls on the cheek, and dashed downstairs to see what Santa had left underneath the tree for Mummy and Daddy.

"Daddy, Daddy," Becca squealed, "can we come too? Then we can all open our presents together." Jon smiled as he studied his little princesses' excited faces. Their eyes shone and, despite having tangled hair and wobbly (and in Becca's case – missing) teeth, to him, they were the most beautiful girls in the world. That was, until Jen stood behind them and stroked their hair, before kissing their heads. Her green eyes met Jon's and, for a brief moment, they remained transfixed on her husband's as he stood in his boxer shorts, motionless and in awe of his wife's beauty.

"Looks like Santa's been for you, Jen," he whispered, holding a rectangular gift-wrapped object in the air. Becca and Chloe ran down the stairs and joined their dad. "Look, Mummy, look," Chloe hollered as a mountain of other gifts, all brightly gift-wrapped, met her excited eyes. "And they're nearly all for you," she added, knowing how to spell 'mummy' and 'Jen'.

The number of presents Jon had bought her this year made no difference to Jen although, for the girls' sake, she would make an attempt to be positive.

"Wow, how good has Mummy been?" she replied before joining her family.

"The best mummy in the whole wide world," Chloe giggled, before Becca nodded in agreement and gave her parents a toothy grin.

"And the best wife too, Jen," Jon confirmed, before handing her the gift and running upstairs to fetch the girls' Christmas sacks from Santa.

"Wait for me, everybody," he yelled breathlessly, coming down the stairs with two enormous plastic sacks. But it was too late. The diamond bracelet sat in Jen's palm and tears flowed down her cheeks as she met her husband's eyes.

"But why Jon, why now?" she whispered softly, wishing she wasn't so desperately sad.

"Diamonds are forever, Jen. Just like our love for one another."

Jon watched the twins, who smiled and hugged each other excitedly.

Yet again, Jen could not reciprocate.

"Thank you, Jon," she replied, placing the bracelet on the sideboard. "Now let's start with your sacks," she added, before passing the sacks to her daughters and beaming at them. "Let's see what Santa has brought you both."

* * *

Kirsty awoke before her father. She'd heard a noise downstairs and, alarmed, she'd investigated it further. Beth was on her hands and knees, frantically scrubbing the already immaculate floor tiles.

360

"Mum," she whispered, kneeling down next to Beth and tenderly stroking her arm. Beth's tired eyes studied Kirsty, before she resumed scrubbing. Work had to be done. There was so little time. She was panicking.

Kirsty had seen this before and knew, like her dad did, that under times of strain, her mum's condition would flare up again. She grabbed the packet from the kitchen cupboard, filled a glass with water and passed the Abilify to Beth, who stopped scrubbing immediately and stared coldly at her daughter.

"No, Kirsty," she yelled, standing up and removing her gloves. "I'm taking enough pills already, for God's sake – I don't need more. I hate that one. You know I do."

Kirsty recollected her mum after she had left St Thomas's Hospital, and the drugs she had taken for months. Abilify had been one of them – the one that helped to hide Alfie, the girls and the germs.

"Just one, Mum," she replied as she caressed Beth's back. "Today is so important to us all and, once it's over, you will be cured completely. Please, just swallow. This is for you. This is to give you strength for today. This is your future, Mum – your freedom."

Beth smiled at her daughter. She knew that Kirsty wouldn't try to poison her like the others had tried to in the past, and placed the pill on her tongue. Gulping a large mouthful of water, she swallowed hard, hoping it would kick in soon.

Dave awoke alone. He'd expected Beth to be sleeping after the horrendous night she'd had. The repetitive Christmas nightmare had haunted her for most of the night and, once again, she had awoken sobbing, sweating and terrified. Terrified of the woman haunting her in her nightmares, terrified of the monster who would be arriving at their home in just a few hours.

Dave hoped that today would finally give her closure. She'd been so strong until now, the crunch time. And he was as determined as Beth was to make today a success. He slipped on his dressing gown and saw Beth and his daughter embracing in the kitchen; he crossed his fingers behind his back.

"Merry Christmas, ladies," he whispered before switching on the CD player. Beth smiled as 'We wish you a merry Christmas' began to play.

"Your favourite CD," Dave laughed, holding his hands over his ears, in jest.

"Mine too," Kirsty added, remembering the trip to the Early Learning Centre with her mum and Robert so many Christmases ago. Beth recollected that day too and, as the medicine absorbed gradually into her bloodstream, the memories of her precious children flooded back and the germs jumping up at her ankles and scrambling across her legs fell away, one by one, and disappeared into the grout of the kitchen tiles.

"Happy Christmas," Beth replied before opening the fridge and placing the huge turkey on the worktop. "Better prepare this before we open our gifts," she added. She washed, then stuffed the bird with the sausage-meat stuffing she'd made the previous day.

Beth and Kirsty peeled and prepared vegetables, wrapped the pigs in their blankets and added the final touches to the dining-room table.

* * *

Andrew, his baby daughter and beautiful wife hugged each other before heading to their car. "Be strong, Andy," she whispered before planting a kiss on her husband's cheek. "This is for your sister, remember. It will be fine."

And as he kissed his wife back and secured his little Lizzie into her baby seat, he agreed, although he feared what might happen.

This wasn't just for his sister; it was for him too.

* * *

Despite their tender age, the Davies girls were excellent mathematicians – or at least that's what they thought as they counted their 'two million' presents, before asking which one they could open first.

Although Jon and Jen were pretty lenient parents, they had set a new Christmas rule for this year: the girls would not rip the paper off their presents all at once as they had previously; instead, they would open their gifts one at a time. This would prevent a repeat of the embarrassment they had experienced the former year, when they had had to guess who had purchased what for their daughters and, in most instances, had got it completely wrong. Jennifer's parents were far from amused. They had bought each girl a trike and had been thanked for a doll instead.

The large presents had to be opened first. Becca squealed excitedly over her new pink bike with stabilisers, a bell and a basket, before calming down and opening some of her other presents from Santa. He'd been very kind this year and the Minnie Mouse cuddly toy fitted perfectly into the basket of her bike.

"Did Santa really get us all these presents?" Becca asked as she reached selection box number nine and added it to the pile of other chocolates under the tree. Even at six, Becca had a good sense of logic - something that she had, no doubt, inherited from their father.

Jen laughed at her question; how perceptive her daughter was at such a tender age. Although it hadn't been her eggs that had created her little darling, she had *her* blood in her smart little body. She had definitely inherited that trait from her.

The atmosphere had transformed from one of tenseness to one of enormous happiness. Somehow, the innocence and the excitement of their precious daughters had brought the family together again. They giggled, laughed and cuddled as Jon put on his Santa hat and went into the kitchen calling 'ho ho ho', promising to prepare the best ever Christmas breakfast for his family.

Chloe settled down to watch some Christmas TV cartoons. "One million presents already opened, the other million can be opened after breakfast!" Chloe said, snuggling in between her mummy and sister, sucking her thumb.

This year, Jon was absolutely determined not to burn breakfast. He warmed the grill under a medium heat, pierced the chipolatas several times with a fork, and popped them under the grill. As they cooked, he warmed the oven, poured the girls some orange juice and opened a bottle of bucks fizz, before pouring it very carefully into a champagne flute for him and Jen.

The table was easy to lay and, after turning the sausages, he neatly positioned the bright red place mats on the table, grabbed four Santa paper napkins, placed them next to the mats, and retrieved some clean cutlery from the dishwasher.

It was almost time for the bacon. Using oven gloves for the first time in years, Jon removed the tray, turned the sausages, and added the thick rashers of bacon. "Smells delicious, Daddy," Chloe yelled as he turned the grill up a notch, retrieved the frying pan, and warmed some oil.

"Watch out, Jamie Oliver," he called, hoping to impress his wife with his new-found culinary skills. He didn't even break an egg yolk, and after frying each one to perfection, he called his family and placed their breakfast proudly in front of them.

"Wow, Daddy," Becca giggled, stabbing her chipolata onto the end of her fork and dipping it into her still runny egg yolk. "This is the bestest!"

Jen giggled. Her auburn hair brushed against her shoulders and her bright green eyes opened wide as they met Jon's. "Thank you, darling," she said before tucking in to her delicious meal and smiling warmly at her husband.

"You're welcome, Jen, anything for you!" he replied, raising his champagne glass and clinking it with all three of his girls', and then throwing one of his cheeky, but irresistible, grins at his wife.

"That's my line," she giggled before knocking back the bucks fizz in a couple of gulps and finishing her breakfast in record time.

Jon's heart melted as he carefully watched the three most wonderful people in his life. He couldn't help, however, but wonder how Beth was coping. It was, after all, such an important day for her too.

After mopping up the egg with his bread, Jon went back into the kitchen and put the turkey in the roasting pan. "Jen, you take it easy today. Dinner is also on me. After I've showered, we'll open the rest of our gifts."

Jen's eyes widened. He really was trying hard.

"Yippee!" Chloe replied, devouring the last of her bacon and egg. Jen smiled again. She watched Jon trip up the stairs, before entering the bathroom whistling 'Jingle Bells'.

Happy Christmas, Beth. Thinking of you, he texted after showering. He *was* thinking of her, and it broke his heart to delete the evidence – especially her reply:

Thinking of you too, Jon.
Happy Christmas.
Love, Beth x

* * *

The Lewis household had been absolute chaos for the last few hours, but chaos in the best possible way. Robert had crawled to his parents' home suffering from a 'hangover from hell', after spending the night with his old school pals whom he hadn't seen since starting university. His red eyes tried to focus on his sister, who was darting around the kitchen, moving things around and preparing some weird-looking starter.

"Is your hair really pink, Kirst, or am I imagining it?"

Kirsty scowled at her big brother before thumping him on the arm. "Stoppit," she replied, giggling. Robert burst into laughter, despite his ghastly headache, and mocked his sister. "Okay Kirthy, I'll stop being howwibal to you if you pwomise to keep the noise down for a while. My head kills."

This time, she giggled with her brother. He *was* funny, and he had made her laugh so many times when she'd been little. He'd made everything better so many times too.

"I wuff you, Wobert," she said, after basting the turkey and popping it back into the oven. He smiled again. Hearing her son's request to turn down the music, Beth selected another CD rather than the kiddie one, and softly hummed along to the Christmas carols while she uncorked the red wine and poured it into the crystal decanter Dave had bought specially for today.

"Thanks, Mum," Bob said before shifting on the comfortable sofa. "When can we do the gifts?"

Beth met her son's large eyes and smiled. He looked so like his Mum, it was uncanny. "After dinner," she replied, grinning at Dave as she did so. "I want everything to be just perfect today and, once the meal is done, we can all open our presents, and enjoy the rest of the day afterwards."

She'd planned everything meticulously and, despite the tiny mishap first thing, all was now working out perfectly. Dave hugged Beth as she added the final touches to the table, a beautiful candle centrepiece – with a beautiful price tag from John

Lewis to match. But that didn't matter. She was worth every penny, and he quivered with excitement at the thought of her face when she opened his three gifts to her this year.

* * *

Although she knew that there was no such thing as Father Christmas, this year Sara had received everything she had ever wished for in every single letter she had written to Santa when she'd been a little girl.

For her entire life – twenty-eight years of it, to be precise – she had yearned to be wanted. Sara had never been cuddled as a baby, kissed, tucked into bed or, as Gloria had explained to her on their weekly shopping trips over the past decade, loved. But this year, when she opened an endless array of thoughtful presents, all with huge love hearts and affectionate, simple messages, she realised that, after all her years of yearning to be wanted, her dream had finally come true.

She slipped out of bed and smiled at him. Her perfect man. Her wonderful husband, her Jason.

"I love you, baby," she whispered before retrieving a small envelope from her bottom drawer, which had been hidden for months. She'd been bursting to tell him about the surprise for ages, but Gloria had reminded her that the best part of any surprise was keeping it a secret. And Sara had done just that – until now.

She shook with excitement as she jumped back onto the bed then slid under the covers in between the numerous teddy bears and sexy pairs of knickers she had been given. Jason held the small envelope in his hand, trying to guess what was inside. It could be a gift voucher, or a love letter, maybe?

"Open it," she demanded, after planting yet another kiss on her husband's mouth.

He tore open the seal nervously. What if it involved reading? He couldn't let his wife down and just guess what the words said. He would tell Sara later that he needed to learn to write and read properly as he was going to be a daddy very soon.

He didn't need to worry. There were two tickets; he could at least count, and he recognised the Virgin logo from the television adverts with that fast runner man, Bolt. Sara had also printed out an A4 sheet of paper with lots of pictures of roller coasters and fun fair rides on it, along with a photo of Jason and her glued next to the images.

Jason's hand shook as the realisation of what the gift was hit him.

"Is that you and me, Sara?" he questioned, running his finger over the photograph of his wife's face and kissing it gently.

"It is, Jason," she replied, finding it virtually impossible to compose herself. "We're going to Florida in the spring – it's our wedding present from all our friends and family put together. It's our delayed honeymoon, Jason, and me and you are gonna have the most brilliant time ever. Gloria even gave us some spending money, and guess what? She's gonna take care of the baby when we're there as well!"

Jason wept with joy and held Sara close to his heart before making love to her for the third time in just a few hours.

Then, after tidying their bed and tucking the teddies in so that they wouldn't feel the cold, they left the safety of their sheltered accommodation and headed towards their best friend's house to pick her up before going to their other best friend's for a wonderful Christmas dinner.

"Did you remember Lizzie's gift?" Sara asked, skipping in between her husband and Gloria.

"Of course, Sara," Jason replied, clutching the package carefully. It had taken Sara over a year to complete, but the tapestry was so worth it. It was of a golden retriever with a green collar. It was named Alfie.

* * *

Beth looked absolutely stunning. The rich auburn lowlights and blonde highlights of her silky hair complemented each other even though, today, most unexpectedly, she'd worn her hair up. Kirsty had helped her mum, of course, creating the French plait before twisting it and securing it with a sparkling, yet subtle, hairclip. Beth smiled in appreciation of her daughter's hard work; her eyes sparkled in her daughter's direction. How proud she was of Kirsty; her little angel.

She'd not spent too long on her makeup today as, once again, she wanted to look natural, not like the 'painted doll' they had all grown to recognise as 'Beth' or 'Mum'. She applied just a touch of translucent foundation, then lightly powdered her face with loose powder and a brush, adding a little blusher to her already finely defined cheekbones. Her eyes, although tired, were bright; again, after applying just a dusting of light gold eye shadow and some fine mascara, she was satisfied with the reflection in front of her. Finally, she retrieved some baby pink lip-gloss and applied it to her lips. She smiled warmly at her husband and daughter, who had watched Beth as she so delicately transformed her already beautiful face into one of an absolute princess.

"You're beautiful, Mum," Kirsty whispered, after adjusting a strand of her hair which had fallen out of her plait. Beth nodded at her daughter as Dave said the same. He ran his finger along the scar at the rear of his fiancée's neck then bent slowly before kissing it.

"I am so proud of you, Beth; you've come so far."

Beth thanked them, before retrieving the little black dress from the wardrobe. Dave had arranged for it to be dry-cleaned the week before and, after removing the fine plastic sheet and safety pins from the coat hanger, Beth held the precious item of clothing against her body, seeking a reaction from her audience.

Kirsty studied the dress closely, running her index finger along the plunging neckline, stroking the diamante stones, imagining her Mum's perfect figure hugging every inch of the fabric. Sensing Kirsty's urgency to see her in this amazing dress, Beth dashed into the bathroom, slipped off her dressing gown, and pulled it, extremely carefully, over her head, then down her torso.

She avoided looking into the bathroom mirror. Instead, she opened the bathroom door and faced Dave with a nervous smile.

"Beth," he whispered as he edged towards his fiancée. "Are you sure about this?"

She had never seen herself in the dress, but had known from the moment she had set eyes on it that it was 'the one'. She had to buy it. It was perfect for Beth's big day. Not for reasons of vanity; it was designed perfectly for her for another reason: Beth's determination to show everybody how proud she was to be herself; how comfortable she now was living in her own skin. How accepting she was of her scars that were, as Dave and Jon had reminded her on so many occasions, part of her. Part of

Elizabeth Pritchard who, for the first time in her life, now agreed with them both.

Kirsty and Dave stood motionless. They studied Beth's expression when she caught sight of her back. The dress plunged not only to just above her breasts, but to the base of her spine. Her eyes widened, and then twinkled with pride as, despite the purple scar running along her vertebrae, she was still attractive; pretty, even. The slit at the side of the garment showed off her slender legs. Kirsty gasped in shock when she saw the circular scars, too numerous to count, running down the inside of her mum's legs.

"It's okay, darling," Beth replied, opening her bedroom drawer and fishing out a pair of sheer tights, "even I know where to draw the line." She met her daughter's tear-filled eyes and moved towards her, holding out her arms for her daughter to fall into.

Despite Dave telling Kirsty about her mum's abuse the night before, answers to every single question she had asked herself as a child fell into place now. Why, as a little girl, she had never been allowed to spend time alone with her gran. Why the visits were always supervised. Why Daddy hated her gran so much. Kirsty's heart pounded with the stark realisation of the abuse her mum had suffered – it had all been at the hands of her gran.

"How could she do this to you, Mum? Why on earth did she hurt you so badly?" Kirsty sobbed, gripping tightly on to her mum's frail body. Wiping the tears away and then stroking Beth's face, she asked the most obvious question in the world again. "Why, Mum, why did she do this to you?"

Beth's previously warm features turned cold. She gazed into her daughter's sad and confused eyes.

"I don't know, Kirsty, but I sure as hell intend to find out today and finally close this horrific chapter of my life," she whispered, before sitting on the edge of her bed and pulling up the tights carefully.

"*Our* lives," Beth corrected herself, realising how much her entire family had suffered as a result of her mother's evil and scheming actions.

It was too much for her young daughter to contend with and she ran out of the room and to her own, where she threw herself on her bed and sobbed until emotional exhaustion finally took over.

The butterflies in Kirsty's tummy distracted her from any form of rest. She stroked her minute bump. She pictured her innocent, tiny baby growing within the safe and protective confines of her womb.

"How could a mother do this to her own flesh and blood?" she sobbed, imagining the horrors her own mum had suffered at the hands of *her* mother.

"That's what we'll find out later," Beth replied before joining Kirsty on the bed for a cuddle. "But please don't say a word to anybody else, as I don't intend asking her until the end of the day, when everybody else has left. Until then, Kirsty, I genuinely want today to be perfect. That's part of the plan too – to show your nan how well I'm doing, despite all that she's done to me in the past. And I want her to see this scar too. Just to remind her of what she once did to me but, more importantly, just how beautiful I still can be to everybody else, despite my injuries."

Kirsty had nothing but pride in her veins now; her mum was an amazing woman to overcome all that she had, and to be proud of herself.

"I love you, Mum," she whispered, before getting ready for the guests arriving shortly.

"And I love you too, my little angel," Beth replied, fighting the lump in her throat and the desire to sob. "Be strong, sweetheart, today and I'll be strong too."

"Cross your heart and hope to die?"

"Cross my heart and hope to die – yes."

"Not yet, though," Dave laughed, before grabbing Beth by the waist and holding her close. "Come on, you, there's champagne downstairs and I don't want it going flat."

Nor did Beth, and as she counted the minutes down before her guests arrived, she felt relieved already.

Not much to do now.

And not long left.

* * *

His daughters distracted him immediately when they hammered loudly on the bathroom door and insisted that Daddy hurry up and come downstairs.

"Come on, Daddy," Chloe demanded in her squeaky voice. "We've got a million presents left to open and Santa has bought you some too." The girls giggled, nudging each other playfully. They laughed as they remembered their recent trip with Mummy to the shops, when they had chosen Daddy's present so very carefully.

Jon towel-dried his hair, wrapped the towel around his waist, and headed for his bedroom. "Two minutes, ladies," he replied cheerfully, throwing on a pair of boxers, his favourite tatty jeans, and a fairly clean shirt.

"You don't have to worry 'bout your top, Daddy," Becca giggled before her sister scowled at her disapprovingly, knowing that surprises should always be a secret. But Jon, thankfully, hadn't heard – he had felt the vibration of his mobile phone in his pocket. Switching it off, he scooped his daughters into his arms, dropped onto his bottom and very carefully slid down the stairs one at a time, enjoying their hilarity.

Jen was sitting cross-legged on the carpet between the four piles of gifts. "Hurry up, Daddy," she giggled; she threw a soft parcel in his direction. The girls bit their tongues and fought the desire to blurt out what was inside the bright Santa paper. As the T-shirt fell out of the wrapping and the two little faces beamed at him from the fabric, his heart melted.

"Look at the back, Daddy," Becca demanded, fidgeting excitedly as her dad turned the shirt over. On the back two little hands were printed and their names, along with a heart and the date.

"We did it with Mummy," Chloe said proudly, not noticing the tears in his eyes.

"Thank you, babies," Jon whispered. He yanked off his shirt and pulled on his new, soon to be cherished, T-shirt.

"Is it the best present in the whole wide world, Daddy?" Chloe asked proudly.

He studied his daughters in their fluffy pink pyjamas with their perfectly formed toes and their flawless features. His gaze turned to his wife, sitting with their girls, glowing with beauty.

"Almost the best present in the world," he replied before concluding his response. "My three girls are the best gift I could ever wish for, and now that I have the perfect T-shirt, I am the happiest man on earth."

Jen smiled warmly at Becca, at Chloe, then back at Jon. She did love him with all her heart, which she so hoped would, in time, heal.

"Thank you again for my beautiful bracelet," she whispered before passing the girls the remainder of their gifts to open. "I shall cherish it forever Jon, it really is perfect."

Jon's heart fluttered as he studied his wife's face. He was blessed to have such an amazing family. She'd forgiven him, he knew that now, and nothing upon nothing would get in the way of their perfect lives.

Nothing could spoil it now.

Nothing and nobody.

* * *

Despite the shocking revelations of earlier, Kirsty had, in her usual positive manner, bounced back and produced the eleven starters of smoked salmon with avocado pear and king prawns.

Robert had sobered up a little and, despite still feeling a little fragile, he was the first to jump up and answer the door. Three damp, bedraggled people stood shivering outside – Gloria, Jason and Sara. After removing their shoes, they approached Beth, who looked, as Jason had said, 'like a million dollars'.

"Lizzie, you look beautiful." He had never got used to calling her Beth – not that it mattered. His friend – whatever her real name was – was one of the most important people in his life. He smiled once again at her.

Beth blushed at her friends' compliments and passed their coats to Robert to hang up and dry in the airing cupboard. "Shhhh," she giggled, feeling her cheeks burn with embarrassment. "Now, look at you two," she added, pecking all three of her guests on the cheek and stroking the enormous bump beneath Sara's maternity dress.

"Two weeks to go," she proudly replied, "before we are a mummy and daddy and Gloria is a granny."

Beth was sure that Gloria had blushed too. Having unofficially adopted Sara as soon as she had been discharged from St Thomas's Hospital ten years before, Gloria was indeed going to be a nanny, and an extra-special one at that. Gloria smiled tenderly at her girls; how proud she was of them both.

"You've come through, sweetheart," she said, stroking Lizzie's face with her chunky fingers. "I knew you would. And as for you, Sara, and you too, Jason, I can't say how proud I am of you as well. It's taken a lot of hard work and effort, and I'm so proud of you all."

Tears streamed down her wrinkled cheeks and she smiled warmly at her friends. "You have made an old lady very happy."

Kirsty witnessed the emotional scene in silence. They were part of her mum's world that she had been protected from when she'd been tiny, yet, when she tiptoed shyly towards the door, and the black woman threw a smile in her direction, she knew that these people were kind, and genuinely loved her mum for who she was.

"Kirsty, poppet, don't hide from Auntie Gloria, come on over and give this old lady a cuddle."

The five people embraced tenderly before an extra two joined the group hug. After all, Dave and Robert were part of this gang as well. Very soon, the next three members would be joining them as well.

"To happiness and freedom," they toasted as the circle of people opened and they all held hands. Beth and Sara broke away as they recollected the first time they had made that statement. It felt like an eternity ago. They guessed that it was.

Kirsty was the next to move, as dinner, she knew, had to be perfect. She'd assured her mum a few days before that she would manage the meal on her behalf, so long as Beth did the clearing up. That statement, despite being said tongue in cheek, had made Beth howl with laughter. Even though it was, indirectly, mocking her OCD, it had delighted her too! She adored cleaning and, having been relieved of the cooking duties, she had been able to relax and enjoy the countdown to Christmas – well, almost.

The first of her guests were shown into the living room and given a welcoming drink. There was a loud knock on the front door. Beth froze. She knew that it was *her*.

Beth's mother never rang the doorbell. She thought it was a common, cheap chime and she loathed it. Beth's eyes flicked across the room nervously. There was no dust, her existing guests were dressed smartly, nobody was drunk, the lighting was soft, candles were lit, the presents were neatly wrapped. Everything was perfect.

Dave opened the door. Richard brushed down his coat and burst into the hallway with a pile of gifts and numerous carrier bags. "Ghastly weather," he said, as he returned to the car, dragged out yet another bag, and closed the boot.

She stood on the doormat and glared at the man welcoming her into his home. "Take my coat," she demanded, unfastening the buttons and almost throwing the coat in Dave's face. Robert dashed into the lounge, welcomed his grandparents, and hung his gran's coat in the airing cupboard along with the others.

"Happy Christmas, Brenda," Dave muttered before he and Richard made light conversation about the weather and headed straight for the drinks cabinet.

"Whisky, Richard?"

"Large one, if you don't mind," he replied, already planning to book a taxi home. He'd been good enough to collect Brenda this morning; she could walk back home as far as he was concerned and he needed a drink if he was going to survive a full day with her. Since he'd walked out on Brenda, she had been a bitch from hell. Maybe she could today, as it was Christmas, just have one drink – or ten.

He didn't need to ask his wife, who towered over him as he turned away from Dave. "A large vodka, son," she ordered, before deliberately brushing the soles of her muddy shoes onto her daughter's beautiful cream carpet. Beth didn't seem to notice. She faced her mother. "Mum, welcome. And happy Christmas to you; I'm so pleased you decided to join us all."

The CD in the background played a cheery Christmas tune from the 1970s, which Brenda had loathed from the moment it had been released.

"Do you have anything more tasteful than that trash?" she asked bitterly before slugging back her vodka and glaring at Beth.

"I'll change the CD if you like," Beth replied calmly, proud of her ability to handle her mother's catty comments.

"Not the music, you stupid child, the dress, Elizabeth. That hideous dress you are wearing. It is highly inappropriate for Christmas; I suggest that you remove it immediately."

Dave's mouth opened in disgust; he started to respond on his fiancée's behalf. Beth stopped him in his tracks. "Of course, Mother," she replied obediently, "if that's what you want."

Sara covered her eyes with one hand and Jason's with the other; she knew the old Lizzie from St Thomas's Hospital very well and completely understood how her mind worked. This was going to be so embarrassing.

Beth lifted the dress over her head. She faced her mother, staring defiantly into her grey slits. Although they had faded, the scars were still there; over a hundred of them, along with the crooked bones, which had re-set themselves after endless breaks. Her mother fought the desire to stare at the injuries and, instead, held her hands over her eyes to avoid seeing the scars she had caused on her daughter's skinny body.

"Put it back on!" she screamed, resisting the temptation to hit Beth. She needed another drink.

"Yes, Mother," Beth replied. She slipped back into her beautiful black dress and smiled at the others who, despite feeling a little awkward, felt proud of Beth and her response to her mother.

She'd been victorious. She was winning, and she had the support of everybody in the room with her. Oh, revenge was going to be so, so sweet and it didn't need to be physical at all.

No need for third time lucky.

She was almost there.

* * *

The turkey smelled so good. Jon's tummy rumbled as the delicious aroma from the kitchen wafted through the living room and deep into his lungs. Despite enjoying a hearty breakfast only a few hours before, he was starving – again!

He watched Jen, who was plucking the chocolate decorations from the Christmas tree. Jon begged with his eyes for her to throw one his way. She smiled before tossing one in his direction. "Just one though, Jon," she giggled as the girls tucked into their early morning treats. He chomped the chocolate reindeer in a single mouthful, then, when Jen wasn't watching, took another. He caught Becca's concerned expression as her eyes flicked from him to Jen. He held his finger to his mouth in an attempt to stop her snitching on him. Becca did; she'd been taught never to lie, and even Jon with his cheeky smile wasn't getting away with this one.

"Daddy just had another chocolate, Mummy; I want one too."

Chloe was the quieter of the twins and never told tales on her daddy. She chose the largest selection box from her pile of gifts and gently placed the box on Jon's lap. "You can have this, Daddy," she whispered into his ear. Jon's heart melted again, like the chocolate on his tongue.

Jen smiled lovingly at her husband and passed him a small present, wrapped in bright red foil, with a big bow, which the girls had clearly made from a ball of ribbon.

"From me to you. I know it's not much but it's the words, Jon. Just listen to the sixth track. You'll know what I mean."

Jon carefully removed the paper and examined the cover of the CD. He'd not heard of John Legend, but thanked Jen before placing it with his small pile of unopened gifts. "It's from the heart, Jon, like this is."

He'd never been one for sentiment; other than with his girls and Jen, Jon had always found it difficult to explain just how he felt. It had been the same when his father had passed away; unlike his siblings, who'd sobbed loudly at his funeral, Jon just held his mum's hand and fought back the tears when the vicar paid tribute to his dad. Jon didn't need to tell his dad how much he loved him; his dad had known, from the simple gestures and quality moments they had managed to find as father and son, alone. Rare moments of solitude for them both but, all the same, special, private times when no words were necessary.

The package was tiny and hard. He closed his eyes, trying to imagine what it could be, and the girls watched eagerly as he finally weakened and tore off the paper. It was a golden heart on a key ring. The heart was jagged in the centre and was engraved. The words were simple. "Don't break mine again."

He was unsure how to react. On the one hand, it was beautiful, but on the other, the bitter message reminded him just how painful the last few days had been and how dreadfully he had behaved.

Jen held his hand, removing the heart from her husband's. She gently pulled it apart; the heart broke into two sections. Becca was mesmerised by this magical gift and held hands tightly with Chloe as she watched her parents' strange reactions. Jen smiled and held on to her half. "This is mine, Jon. I'll keep it with me forever, so long as you hold on to your half. Cherish it, please; it's my heart, remember."

He gripped it tightly, then tucked it into his trouser pocket before tapping it with his hand. "I'll cherish this, as I cherish you all," he replied, before beaming at his girls and handing them each a parcel to open.

They were almost there; one million, nine hundred and ninety-nine thousand and ninety-nine presents had been opened, according to Chloe.

They'd forgotten all about the last parcel and so had Jen, then it dawned on her that these were the gifts that had come home from school, with no labels attached to them. Becca was bored now and simply wanted to play with some of her new toys, especially the trapeze that Daddy had bought. Tearing off the paper rapidly, the twins were confused as they studied the picture on the box. It was of a pair of binoculars.

"What an odd gift," Jen said, turning the box over to study it. They were decent ones. Chloe took the box back and prised it open.

Her blood-curdling scream echoed through the room. Becca had also opened her box and was shaking like a leaf. It contained a photograph of a giant wolf with enormous teeth and hideously curved claws, lashing out at a superimposed child who was playing hopscotch. She was the child. Chloe's was the same, except it was her face in the photo, with the scary wolf behind.

Sobbing, Chloe dropped the photograph and ran up the stairs to her bedroom. Jen ran behind her as Jon hugged Becca tightly. His daughter was screaming hysterically as she watched her mummy hug Chloe and stroke her hair, wiping her face, reassuring her that it was only a nasty, wicked trick.

Becca gripped her photograph tightly, confused as well as scared. "What is this, Daddy?" she sobbed, passing the photograph to her dumbfounded father. He turned it over. Tiny italic print jumped out into Jon's face like a fist, thumping him time and time again:

Watch out, watch out, there's a big bad wolf about.
Your daddy wouldn't listen and now you'll scream and shout
As the big bad wolf will find you and hunt both of you down
Then force you into a freezing bath and watch you slowly drown
Your daddy could have stopped this – he put her before his wife
And now, my little angels, you will pay for it with your lives.

* * *

The tension from the earlier episode between Beth and her mother lifted after they had enjoyed a few more glasses of champagne and Kirsty had announced her pregnancy. Even her grandmother had congratulated her granddaughter when she had shyly announced her news. Of course, there would have to be a wedding, she had ordered, to which Beth laughed and said that *she* ought to get married first. Her mother's smile faded; she glared at Beth before downing yet another drink.

Andrew was, as always, late. He rang the doorbell, carrying baby gear and baby Lizzie, and Beth's heart jumped. How she loved him, and how grateful she was that he had eventually agreed to come.

He kissed her gently on the cheek before passing the baby chair to 'Auntie Beth' and popping the bags and bottles on the hall floor. Beth ignored the temptation to move them; it could wait.

Little Lizzie was asleep. She had a mop of dark hair and long curly eyelashes. Her lips pouted as she slept peacefully; she looked like a tiny princess. Beth ran her finger across the baby's cheek before planting a kiss on her finger, then placing the finger on the baby's mouth.

"Uncanny resemblance, eh, sis?"

"Like looking in the mirror," Beth replied, although it wasn't quite. This little one would not be scarred for life, and she was loved by her mum, who proudly smiled while hugging her sister-in-law before taking Lizzie upstairs to sleep.

Brenda was too inebriated to get out of the armchair. Instead, she listened intently to the voice she had yearned to hear for so long. The voice of her precious son. The very reason for her coming here today. Her Andrew.

After hugging his favourite niece and spending a few minutes chatting about university with his nephew, Andrew held his father close to his strong chest. "Dad – good to see you. How's it going?"

"Terrific, son. You were right – face up to the bully and she backs down – you should have seen the earlier show with Elizabeth. It was, how do I put it…?"

"Entertaining, Dad?" Andrew replied, having been updated already by his nephew on the earlier, and rather unexpected, events.

Richard laughed. Heck, it had been, although he wasn't so sure that his daughter had needed to stand in the living room in nothing but her underwear. That had been rather risqué; nevertheless, she had proved her point to her mother and ever so clearly.

"Very," he replied, before grabbing a beer for all the men. "You'll need this," he added as he shepherded his son towards the living room and introduced him to the other guests.

Her heart melted when she saw him enter the room. None of the others mattered; even the baby could wait. She wasn't interested in meeting his spawn, or rather the spawn of that awful wife of his. Andrew was the one that mattered. He *was* here, after all; he *did* love her, of course he did, and all he had said before had just been poison from his father, his sister and his wife. Not her Andrew.

She finished her drink before speaking.

"Andrew, darling, how lovely of you to come. How wonderful to see you again after so many years. You look so handsome, my darling; to think that it's been ten years since we last spoke. Tell me everything that's happened, my son. How are you, my love? How's my precious baby?"

He could not meet her eyes. She tried to meet his, but he looked down at the carpet as he nodded. "Mother," he replied coldly before turning towards the rest of his family, and holding them close to give him strength. Natasha stood silently, watching her husband. She'd been his protector since that evening ten years ago when he had learned the truth about his mother's abuse of Elizabeth; she had been Andy's strength and saviour ever since.

His nightmares had been the worst. Nightmares that continued to torment the very soul of her precious husband, nightmares where he blamed himself for his sister's injuries, nightmares that had left him questioning the worth of his own life.

She also looked down at the carpet, avoiding eye contact with his evil mother. The tyrant. The grandmother of her baby who would never, ever be allowed to touch her.

* * *

He had burned the turkey. It was cremated – like his soul. The potatoes remained in the saucepan, covered with cold water. There was no need to cook them now. Even the Brussels sprouts, which he adored, looked unappealing; revolting clumps of green vegetation which would have turned to mush once cooked.

Who the hell was he kidding when he said that he'd cook Christmas dinner? He failed at everything.

The pigs in blankets squealed as they entered the cold and smelly confines of the stainless steel bin next to the discarded parsnips. The champagne no longer fizzed as it glugged down the sink plughole. Jon vomited in the sink. Washing with a cold cloth didn't ease his temperature; he was now standing in the pits of hell. Burning up. He belonged there – it was his choice. It was his fault. He failed at everything.

The heart in his back pocket throbbed against his buttocks. Beating hard, erratically, the noise echoed through the kitchen like a heart attack. Pounding like a million drums in an empty arena; with only him there, holding his hands over his ears to silence out the noise. Failing miserably to do so.

Paddles.
One.
Two.
Three.
Stand clear.

His heart, tragically, was still beating. He kicked the living room door in anger. It swung open and slammed against the wall. It was cracked and broken. Like his heart.

The other half of the golden heart key ring that his wife had held only an hour before was there, embedded in the living room carpet. Trampled on in anger. But still there. He bent down, and placed it in his back pocket where it belonged. Next to his half. His shattered half.

Jen had only taken a small number of the girls' gifts; all of his had been tossed aside, like he had been – unwanted and unloved. Not needed.

The diamonds, torn away from the bracelet, sparkled as the Christmas lights flickered on them; they were mocking him, reminding him, every time they glistened, of the words he had said to Jen as he handed her the gift.

The colours from the lights bounced onto the diamonds, then formed a minute rainbow against the cream wall. He wailed and sobbed as he picked each stone out of the carpet and gripped them firmly in his palm.

Diamonds are forever, Jen, like our love.

"*Love?*" he screamed at the top of his voice. "Is this love?"

The tree wobbled and seemed to nod in agreement when Jon asked the same question over and over again. It was mocking him too. The tree would have to die. He yanked it out of its pot and threw it out of the back door.

He still felt rage – the same, he imagined, that his wife had felt when she threw some clothes into her car, then his babies, and ended their twenty-year marriage with three simple words.

It's over, Jon.

His babies hadn't understood. It was Chloe's fault, she had sobbed, because she had lost the label on that present and wished she could remember who had given her it.

Another three words.

It doesn't matter.

Then another three:

Mummy knows who.

Then three final words before the car's engine started and two tearful little girls begged their mummy to let Daddy come with them on their adventure.

I hate you.

He hated himself more than Jen loathed him. The silence of Chloe's and Becca's bedroom filled his mind as he walked into their peaceful haven and sat on the floor sobbing, thumping his fist on the carpet, wishing it was concrete, and that it would break every bone in his hand. His heart was broken; a few more breaks wouldn't hurt.

He crawled on all fours, then ran his index finger along their bedding, their little white wooden chairs, their toys.

Daddy, come here, come and see this.
I love you, Daddy.
Anything for you, Jon.
I love you, darling.
I can't love you back, Jon.
Thinking of you.

Beth. Jesus. *Beth.* He had to warn her before it was too late. Her mother had not changed; she was still the evil monster who had terrorised not just Beth but now his own family.

She must know.

He switched on his mobile phone; it sprang into life. He had one message.

I'm so scared, but I can do this! Thanks for giving me the courage to do it – and have a wonderful day.
Beth x

He rang her. She didn't answer.

He tried again. Her phone went to voicemail.

Jen didn't answer either, although she could be driving, and loathed using her phone hands-free.

He texted them both.

Call me urgently.
Jon x

* * *

The meal was delicious. Kirsty and her mum had produced a near-Michelin star quality feast, according to the majority of the guests, and even Robert, who lived on fast food most of the time, had scraped his plate clean after two massive portions of turkey and roast potatoes.

Beth knew that Kirsty had been completely responsible for the success of the dinner; she had meticulously planned the timings, having written down a timetable and ticked each time and task off when she had completed it.

Although Robert has laughed at his sister and claimed she had OCD like his mum, he was deeply proud of both women in his life. They were the best; always had been and, even back then, in the darkest of times, he'd constantly believed in his mum, as his sister always had. And there she was today, albeit with a massive deal of assistance from Kirsty, showing just how capable she was, and just how beautiful she could look; despite the scars, the origin of which he still did not fully understand and, quite honestly was terrified to find out whoever or whatever had caused them. Today though, his mum didn't care who saw the scars and to him, that was progress. She used to hide behind a mask of thick makeup and jump at the sight of her own shadow.

He poured Beth another glass of champagne before lifting the glass and standing up. "I would like to raise a toast to the two wonderful women who have made today possible. To Mum and Kirsty – cheers!"

Everybody agreed and raised their glasses to the women who were smiling proudly at each other; except one – Beth's mother. She wanted to throw the liquid over the bitch's head or into her ugly face. But that could wait. Andrew would not approve.

"Congratulations, Kirsty and Beth, dear. It was a lovely meal; most surprising."

Andrew and his father raised their eyebrows in shock and nodded approvingly at Brenda, who finished her meal and smiled falsely at them. How stupid they were. Did they really believe in their wildest dreams that she really could accept her daughter as a normal human being? Clearly they did, and, as they cleared the table and pecked Beth on the cheek, her bright eyes shone deep into her mother's, who could not look back into hers or reciprocate. Her eyes still scared her, but the champagne would hide it for a little while. Alcohol was good at shielding pain – and memories.

"Anybody for another drink?" she asked, opening yet another bottle of wine.

"It's time for the gifts, Mum," Beth replied before putting on the infamous Christmas CD and jiggling her bottom to the Slade number. "Dessert, and more drinks, can follow later."

The guests all agreed and Sara smiled excitedly at her husband, knowing that Beth would simply adore the present she had worked so hard on. She sipped her orange juice before jumping up and down.

"Me first, me first," she yelled, passing Beth the neatly wrapped parcel. Beth's hand shook as she carefully removed the paper, knowing how important this present was to Sara. Beth held the item tightly and smiled at her friend. And when Alfie's eyes emerged from the gift-wrap, they seemed to smile at his owner once again. Her tears smudged her makeup as they cascaded down her face.

But that didn't matter anymore. Beth was healing and, along with so much else, the sadness she had previously felt at the loss of her beloved pet, had, at long last, dissipated. It was her joyful memories of Alfie that had made her weep, along with the fact that Sara, her closest and dearest friend, had worked so hard to make this wonderful portrait for her.

Once again, she was crying tears of joy. She embraced Sara, who smiled warmly at Beth. "Thank you, Sara; I will never forget this moment in all of my life."

Sara met her friend's eyes and kissed her gently. "Me neither," she replied, before sitting down next to Jason and gripping his hand tightly. She too was healed; the love of the people in this room had made that happen.

"No more pain, Lizzie," she added, gazing at Mrs Pritchard, who was sniggering. *What a stupid girl,* she thought. *No more pain? We'll see about that.* She poured a glass of burgundy and, once again, slugged it back in a few mouthfuls.

The mountain of presents grew larger by the minute, but the piles of discarded paper, bows and sticky tape didn't worry Beth at all. It was a perfect day. Her father walked into the living room carrying a pile of parcels; Beth beamed at him.

There were two identical large boxes – one for Kirsty and one for Robert, a soft package for Dave and three gifts for Beth. The large one intrigued her. She knew that it could be fragile, and her mother had ordered her father to carry it very carefully and place it gently against the wall until Beth had opened everything else. The sack of coal from her childhood had been heavy and bumpy; this package was large, square and fragile. Perhaps, after all these years, she had finally redeemed herself. She smiled as she studied Beth's package. Her daughter's eyes were twinkling and her heart was fluttering with excitement and anticipation. She was so happy.

Beth's children sat quietly, cross-legged. It reminded her of earlier Christmases. Tommy had been there too but was now working abroad, teaching children in Africa. They missed him terribly, but knew that he was happy there and would never return. 'I belong there, Dad,' he had said to them. That had been three years ago and he had never looked back.

Kirsty and Robert's eyes remained fixed on their gifts. Their mum and dad had given them much-needed money, along with the usual smellies, underwear and clothes. But these gifts from Nan and Granddad intrigued them. It was their turn to be excited.

"Open them together," Brenda ordered, passing each grandchild their present. "This is an extra-special gift to make up for the years I wasn't allowed to see you." She fell heavily into the armchair and glared at her daughter.

Andrew left the room. This was going to be so difficult – he wanted to kill her still, but had to control his rage. He ran up the stairs to see his precious baby; little Lizzie always made him feel relaxed. She slept peacefully. He held her tiny body against his chest and closed his eyes, listening to her shallow breathing and feeling her delicate heart beat against his.

The children were flabbergasted when they opened the boxes and placed their gifts, in unison, on to the carpet. They had not expected this; an iPad each and an iPhone 5. Kirsty stuttered as she managed a shocked 'thank you' before running to kiss first her granddad, then, albeit very nervously, her nanny. Robert struggled to speak before thanking them, then bursting across the room to hug them both. He'd wanted a new phone for ages but couldn't afford one; he could now throw away his old Blackberry! Kirsty was already planning her photo library of her new-born baby five months on.

Dave smiled at his children. It brought him such pleasure to see how happy they were. Beth was smiling too. She spoke warmly as she addressed her parents. "Dad, Mum, thank you. I'm speechless; you have been so kind, considering…"

Richard brushed down his shirt in an attempt to eradicate the creases, which, despite ironing it earlier, had reappeared. He strode across the living room towards the other gifts the Pritchards had purchased and grabbed a large parcel from the pile of gifts.

They gave Natasha a DVD player and a video camera; he thought back to *his* Lizzie and hoped that Andrew's and Nat's baby would be able to *genuinely* smile into the camera and provide them with precious memories they would never forget. Natasha kissed him before thanking Mrs Pritchard, who was appalled at the extravagance of the gifts. Richard was stealing the limelight again – it was her turn now.

Dave stopped her before she could retrieve the last of her presents for Andrew and Beth. He wanted Beth to open her gifts from him next – in front of everybody. He'd planned this moment meticulously, as Kirsty had the meal.

He gathered three items from beneath the tree and crawled towards Beth before kneeling in front of her. He had an audience, including her mother, who was reeling with anger, and also Andrew, who wouldn't have missed this moment for the world.

Dave's eyes met Beth's. "My first gift to you, my darling, is a sign of my commitment and a request for you to be my wife – officially." Beth opened the small box and gasped. The diamond sparkled on the white gold band. Dave slipped it onto her engagement finger; the room filled with warmth and love.

"Elizabeth Pritchard, I love you, and I can't wait for you to be Mrs Lewis."

Beth's eyes remained fixed on Dave's, which flickered and shone brightly like the Pacific Ocean on a beautiful warm day. They needed no words. She loved him. She edged forward and placed her lips on his. The other guests clapped, cheered, and joined the couple in hugging, exchanging kisses and best wishes.

She'd left the room to meet her new granddaughter. She towered over the fragile baby as it wriggled, then cried from hunger. She was horrified at the resemblance – this brat also had the eyes of the devil. "Look at you, you pathetic creature. Scream all you like – they won't hear you." She closed the door behind her, knowing that nobody downstairs would hear its cries.

She smiled before re-entering the room. "Now, what have I missed?" she asked, joining in.

His second gift was simple, but special. Beth had been looking at the brushes for months now but hadn't treated herself to them due to money worries. Kirsty had bought her the palette, Robert the watercolours, and Dave had completed the kit. Everybody had come up trumps and Beth hugged him again before placing them in a neat pile, then staring at the gift from her mother. It all fit into place. She now knew what her mum had bought her – it was obvious! Her list had revolved entirely around her passion – painting. Three out of four of the items she had written down were positioned neatly here on the living room carpet. The easel was there too – she just hadn't opened it yet. Her eyes met her mother's, which for once looked warm and no longer hostile. Dave distracted Beth before passing her his final gift: a large envelope.

"Beth, this is my final present to you, my remarkable, perfect princess." Once again, everyone fell silent and Beth tentatively opened the envelope before bringing the sheet of paper close to her face to ensure that she wasn't imagining it. It was a signed and approved plan of an extension. He'd designed an art studio for Beth, and the building work was scheduled to commence on the fifth of January.

"Your dream, Beth," Dave whispered before Beth stopped him.

"Has just come true," she replied before jumping up and down and cracking open yet another bottle of champagne.

There was just one final perfect moment to come for Beth; the one when she forgave her mother for everything she had done in the past. Closure for Beth, and for her family.

Her eyes flicked towards the large object propped against the wall.

"May I, Mum?"

"Of course, dear, of course – I know that Dave will approve."

She gripped her glass firmly, watching her daughter tear off the paper. Beth folded it neatly beside the bubble wrap that covered the item. It was wooden, no doubt, expensive, possibly; hence the wrap protecting it.

Everyone watched silently. She peeled off the Sellotape and unwrapped the paper. Beth's heart was thumping as she lifted the heavy item and studied it closely, looking at each individual wooden slat. Her audience gasped and smiled, realising that it was the gift that Beth had yearned for.

Beth's heart sank when she finally tore off the remaining paper.

The slats were for clothes; her mother had done it again and had bought her a clotheshorse, not the artist's easel she had so desired. Yet again, she had won.

Beth's face flushed and a lump formed in her throat as she studied the item for a second time to ensure that she was not mistaken. Her stomach churned and her vision blurred. She turned towards her mother, who was laughing. "Dave gave me your list, but knowing how tight finances were for you all, I figured that this would save on the electricity – you know how much tumble driers cost to run these days."

Andrew started to walk towards his mother, anger written across his face. A tiny hand stopped him. A tiny word begged him to stop.

"No."

Dave stood by Beth, horrified at her mother's cruel trick. After all the years she had promised to love his angel and had wormed her way, yet again, into their lives, she hadn't changed. She was still torturing his princess. It would never stop; he was sure of that now.

He held Beth's hand, before a single tear escaped from his eye and ran down his cheek.

She turned to face her fiancé. Her enormous, sad eyes met his before she took five brave steps towards the woman who had, yet again, humiliated her in public and had, once again, hurt her. But this time she was prepared for it. She had not forgotten the years of torment and abuse; she had to confront her mother.

Now was the time.

She stood up straight before taking a deep breath.

"Why, Mother? Why do you hate me so much?"

Gloria could take no more. She had been a party to Beth's horrific nightmares too many times and, despite adoring Beth, she could not face this – not today. Not at Christmas; a holy time, a time to rejoice over the birth of Christ.

She went to rise, only to fall back into the comfortable and deep cushion. She laughed, probably due to nerves, and Sara joined in. It was too much for her as well, and she hoped that they could break the ice and interrupt Beth.

Mrs Pritchard stared coldly at the two women. *Is this the best you can do in terms of friends?* she thought. *A fat black woman, a dumb girl and a gormless husband?*

She then studied her daughter.

The laughter stopped. The tension grew. The silence was uncomfortable, almost unbearable. Gloria, Sara and Jason held hands. Dave moved next to Beth, supporting her. Andrew wrapped his arms around his dad and nephew. Kirsty moved closer to her parents, seeking comfort and reassurance that everything would be fine. She sucked her thumb as she had done as a child. She was frightened. So was Beth.

"I asked you a question, Mother, and I demand that you answer it. I need to understand why you despise me and why you still continue to hurt me, mentally and emotionally."

Beth examined the scar on her wrist before forcing herself away from Dave and kneeling to face her mother. Glaring into her grey eyes, she leaned against her, trying to intimidate her.

"*Why?*"

Elizabeth's eyes made her shudder. The evil little tyrant pushed her body against hers, forcing her weight onto her, as those other bodies had so many years ago…

They had laced her drinks first, but the euphoria of her drunkenness and light-headedness had simply added to the whole magical experience of the festival. They'd been friendly to her, as well as generous with the drugs, and one guy, the dark-eyed man, had shown an enormous interest in the Black Widow. He wanted her. She was flattered.

The Black Widow wasn't really a drug-crazed cult member, though. Sure, she had joined a group of hippies she'd met at university, but, other than taking the odd joint and maybe the occasional trip on LSD, they didn't do much wrong. Life to her group was all about having fun – nothing violent, sordid or dark.

Brenda, unlike the others, was a virgin and had hoped to save her virginity for the man she would eventually marry. She was proud of herself, proud of her integrity and her loyalty to her boyfriend back home. Her parents had approved of Richard straight away and, once she was ready to settle down, Brenda had agreed to marry him. She didn't love him, but he was rich and money could buy a great deal of happiness. She really was a good girl, despite her name.

That's what she tried to tell them endless times, before they pinned her down and raped her one by one on that horrific August evening on the Isle of Wight.

'Please stop,' she screamed as they forced her hands behind her back and tore away her blouse, then her bra, laughing like hyenas, pinning her down and watching her writhe in pain as they stubbed out their cigarettes on her stomach before tearing away her skirt.

I beg you, please, please don't hurt me. Please don't do that to me. I'm a virgin. I'm a good girl! Please, I beg you, stop. Let me go. Please.

They didn't listen. Their leader demanded that they remove the remainder of her clothes and let him go first. He pulled at her tights, then ripped off her panties before dropping them on her stomach.

My clothes, please, no, please let me go.

One of the gang members wanted to leave; he wasn't going to hurt this girl, no matter how high he was. He wanted to get the hell out of here.

Damien stopped him as he attempted to escape.

Your turn after me. Hold her down harder. Shut her up, man.

Nooooo. Stop, please. I can't do this. I really am a virgin. I'm Mummy's little angel.

Damien had heard it all now. He sneered. She sobbed and desperately tried to escape. He ordered his accomplices to pin her hands down and forced her panties into her mouth. She coughed; he laughed, then spoke to her in a controlling monotone. "You are a lying, deceitful, drug-crazed slut, belonging to a crazy cult. You promote the fact that you love the occult by naming yourself the Black Widow. You act like a slag all afternoon, flirting and kissing us all. Yet now you claim you're a fucking virgin – what a joke! I'll teach you a very hard lesson for lying to me."

"I am the leader, Satan's follower, and I will not be deceived. You will pay the price with my spawn. You will be reminded what a stupid, lying, filthy, dirty bitch you are every time you see the child. But, more importantly, you will see *me* every time you see my spawn. You will never forget today. Mummy's little angel will suffer. Nobody ever betrays Damien. You will pay the ultimate price."

He raped her one final time. His ebony eyes seemed to bore into her soul as he ejaculated deep inside her, creating a new life.

Now what will Mummy's little angel do?

She had no idea. Cowering in the mud, nursing her cuts and bruises, she rocked backwards and forwards which, somehow felt comforting.

The reluctant cult member who'd tried to escape before being forced to assault her threw up before removing the panties Damien had stuffed into her mouth to shut her up. "I am so sorry, please forgive me… I believed you when you said that you were your Mummy's little angel. He shouldn't have made us do that to you. I have to go..."

She gasped for breath as he ran off towards his friends. They laughed and pointed in her direction while she mopped the blood from her legs with her panties, shaking frantically.

"Mummy's little angel," she whispered, as Beth, Gloria and Dave watched her rock backwards and forwards in the large armchair, tears flowing down her cheeks. The remaining audience had dispersed into the kitchen and dining room. The tension was too much; the woman's memories too painful.

Richard coughing from the dining room brought Mrs Pritchard back to the present. She closed her eyes as she remembered the question her daughter had asked so many times, yet she had never, ever answered. *Why do you hate me so, Mummy?* Maybe it was time. Maybe then everybody who had judged her as being a bad, evil woman would sympathise with her and support her. She needed that now. She had to tell her. Andrew would then love her again – and so would everybody else. Once they knew the truth.

Beth remained leaning against her mother's knee. She finally responded.

"I want everybody here to know why," Brenda said coldly, shoving her daughter away from her and onto the carpet. Beth moved backwards until she reached the support of Dave and her daughter. Dave put his arms around Beth's waist. Brenda remained motionless.

Other than Natasha, everybody was back in the living room. The CD had stopped playing and the baby was quiet. The silence was eerie but now was her moment. At last they would understand.

She poured herself another drink and knocked it back. Her words slurred. She spoke loudly to the room. "You are the result of a gang rape, Elizabeth Pritchard. Your father, Damien, raped me over and over again, along with his gang members. Then I was forced to marry *him*." She pointed a fat, nicotine-stained finger at Richard, who was shaking with rage and shock and horror.

He had no idea what had happened to Brenda. He'd married her when she had returned home and declared that she would not be returning to university in the autumn. She had offered him no explanation, other than saying she felt she didn't fit in there. Yes, their wedding had been rushed, but he had loved her so much and had proposed to her countless times before she had left home to study French. When she'd suddenly quit her studies and agreed to marry him instead, he'd been the happiest man alive. The news of the baby so soon after their wedding had made Richard's every dream come true.

Now he felt shattered, destroyed even. He staggered towards his wife, his eyes filled with tears and pain. "Brenda, why couldn't you tell me? I loved you so much and I could have helped you. Why did you suffer in silence? Why did you make Lizzie pay for this horrendous crime instead of the monsters who raped you?"

The silence was deafening. Brenda forced herself out of the chair and pushed her husband away, looking hatefully at him. "You would never have understood. Come on, Richard, look at yourself. You are as weak and pathetic now as you were then. I hoped that the pain would disappear. I hoped that I would learn to love you, in time, and forget the past. But she – that hideous daughter of mine – was a constant reminder of the rape ... and you? You provided me with the money I needed for my *real* baby – Andrew. He was all I cared about. You counted for nothing, you idiot. I just wanted your money. Not you. And definitely not *her*... just my darling, my precious Andrew."

Richard left the room to throw up in the lavatory. She continued to scream – this time at Beth. "Your bloody grandparents were to blame as much as your real father. I had disgraced them, and I could never have had an abortion as they were fucking Catholics. I knew how much Richard adored me, so I was forced to marry him. Surprise, surprise – eight months later, you were born. We were a typical, suburban, middle-class happy family, Elizabeth – which was exactly what my parents had hoped for. But every time I saw you, I saw your evil father, the devil, raping me and mocking me and hurting me again – again and again. Your father was – *is* – evil, Elizabeth, and you are his double. Every time I look into your eyes, he's there, staring at me. Every time I touched your hair as a child, it was his hair. Your lips, the same lips that forced themselves onto mine as he raped me repetitively – everything I see in you is *him*. *Everything,*

Elizabeth. Now can you understand why I hate you so much? Can any of you understand?"

Sara was the first to cry. Her baby kicked hard. Jason comforted his wife; he too wept tears that he'd never known had existed. Until today, he had not understood what real pain was. His break-up with his ex-girlfriend had been easy compared to this. This was the real stuff, real pain. Agony, even.

Gloria was not easily shocked. In her profession, she had seen the most heart-breaking things imaginable. This was, however, close to her worst experience. Her daughter's suicide had torn her family and marriage apart and had ripped her heart into shreds. But this was right up there with the worst things she had seen and heard.

Poor Mrs Pritchard.

Poor little Lizzie.

Gloria moved closer to her friend, who had collapsed onto her knees and was curled into a ball, her fiancé holding her tight, stroking her hair, crying like a baby. Kirsty was curled over her mum's back, rocking back and forth, seeking comfort too, sucking her thumb and sobbing.

The sorrow flooded through the room. Robert held on to a cushion for comfort; Andrew held his father outside in the hallway. Natasha was still upstairs, oblivious to what had been said.

Brenda sat alone. She looked away from her daughter, got up from the chair and took the five steps required.

Bending towards Beth, she apologised.

Nobody heard.

It no longer mattered. Beth didn't care anymore. She found the strength to lift her body away from Dave and her daughter. She thanked everybody for coming and ran upstairs to the comfort of her own bedroom. Natasha was holding baby Lizzie. Beth ran past; Natasha came to see what the matter was. She saw Beth wiping her face, roughly removing her makeup with cotton wool.

"I don't want to look like my father," Beth sobbed.

"Are you okay, Beth?" she whispered, trying not to wake Lizzie again.

"I will be," Beth replied before entering her bathroom. "I just need a few minutes alone, if you don't mind."

The young woman understood that she wasn't needed; although she'd only been told snippets about Beth's former life, she knew from her husband's nightmares that it had been quite horrific. Beth must have been affected so badly and, judging by the scars, attacked many times as well. She tiptoed down the stairs to be met by numerous pairs of eyes.

"Is she okay?" Dave asked, desperate to comfort his fiancée.

"She just needs to be alone for a while," Natasha replied, going to her husband for comfort. His red eyes filled with tears and, once again, she held him, close to her chest, and comforted him instead of her baby.

"I need to see my mum," Kirsty sobbed, running up the stairs, waking Lizzie and running desperately towards her mum's bedroom. She burst through the door; Beth was sitting cross-legged, close to her chest of drawers. On her lap was a box: an old shoebox with a dog painted on the front. Kirsty joined Beth and held her hand as it followed a trail of thick paint, which formed the outline of a golden retriever. Beth's finger led her daughter's over the green collar before lifting the lid and placing it beside her.

"What's this, Mum?" she whispered, moving close to her for reassurance that things would be okay.

Without raising her head, Beth replied softly, "It was my life, sweetheart."

Beth lifted out the diary, which contained the dates of her mother's attacks on her. She removed each page. She tore each page into pieces then placed them back in the box.

She put the dog collar into Kirsty's hand.

"This was Alfie's," Beth said, remembering the kind pet-shop man who'd given her some free dog biscuits the day she had purchased Alfie's new collar.

A trinket fell from the pink tissue paper. It was a fairy or something similar.

"From Jason," she smiled, "when I was in St Thomas's."

Beth returned it to the box before lifting a fine, faded pink piece of fabric from it. She untied the ribbon at the top and carefully removed the watch. It still worked, Beth knew that. Every week she gently wound it up and it still kept precise time. Kirsty studied the delicate item in her mum's hand.

"My nan left me this; it's all I have to remember her by. Please look after it Kirsty, for me."

Her daughter could take no more. Why was her mum giving this stuff to her? Why now? She asked the question, terrified of the response she may hear.

"I need closure, Kirsty," Beth said, knowing that her daughter was questioning everything she was doing.

She was close to the bottom of the box now.

The letters from Dr Jonathan Davies formed a neat pile to one side. On the other side was a discoloured envelope; she removed some locks of hair from it. Beth recollected that night – the night where her mother had cut her hair, forcing her head against the worktop as she sheared the locks away from Beth's scalp.

"The night I met your dad," she whispered, returning the items to their envelope, not thinking of the fact that she had attempted to kill her mother for the first time that dreadful evening.

The scissors were still glistening; they still looked sharp. No comment was necessary; she knew exactly what these had done.

Her second failed attempt.

"Why the scissors, Mum?" Kirsty asked. She nervously watched Beth run her finger along the sharp blade, not flinching when the blood seeped from the fresh wound.

"Hold my hair as I cut it, Kirsty, I'm begging you."

Kirsty forced her hand against her mum's.

"Mum, why are you doing this?" she asked, horrified. The bedroom door opened. Dave entered the room and quietly joined them, taking the scissors from Beth.

Beth's eyes were distant as she explained why she needed them. "If I cut my hair short and dye it, say really blonde, I won't look like *him*."

She turned to face Dave, who was kneeling before her.

"I could also get some contact lenses," Beth added, "and change my eye colour too. Then I won't look like my real dad, and she might really love me then, and be kind to me, and say the words I desperately need to hear from her. She might say she loves me."

Kirsty's and Dave's hearts bled with pain for her; it felt like their hearts had been punctured by the blades of the scissors. Beth's was broken again.

They said very little. They replaced the items in the box and then held Beth tightly before responding.

"Don't change anything, please," Dave whispered. "We love you for who you are – *please* don't feel that you need to look different for her sake. You now know why she hated you. And you now know that it's nothing you did. You've done nothing wrong. We love you – surely that's enough. Please let that be enough."

"It's over, Beth," Dave added, lifting her tiny body and placing her on the bed. "Rest now, I'll take care of everything else."

She closed her eyes and tried to force sleep upon herself. At least she understood why her mother hated her. But that still didn't justify why she had tortured Beth all her life. *Beth* hadn't raped her mum; Beth was simply the result of a hideous attack on her mother; she too was a victim. They were both victims of that man, that cruel monster Damien. What would have happened if her mum had told her the truth earlier? They could have been friends. Her mum could have even loved her. But at least she knew the truth now.

Beth was very sorry, but she'd changed her mind.

There **would** be a third time lucky.

And soon.

She had so much to do, and so little time.

* * * * *

34. VODKA AND PIE

2014

The bottle of vodka had not helped. Nor had the remaining chipolatas from breakfast.

Jon's head thudded with pain; his heart thudded even harder. He'd heard people quote the word 'agony' numerous times in practice, and had nodded at them all in a knowing way as they poured out their hearts and shared their painful, *agonising* memories with him.

He now felt like a patronising, condescending moron – he hadn't had the faintest idea what his patients had meant. Not until now – Boxing Day.

Jen had not replied to his texts, or to his calls. Eventually, he telephoned her mother who, reluctantly, had admitted that Jen and their girls were staying there for a while. 'Before they find somewhere to live,' she had added rather sternly.

The girls were asleep, and Jen was exhausted. She didn't want to speak to Jon.

Game over.

No, it fucking wasn't.

Not for him, anyhow.

* * *

The smell of bacon awoke Beth. Her eyes felt puffy without her even touching them. She knew this feeling well, and her throat was sore – again; incessant crying had caused this, and she had cried enough tears last night to fill a reservoir.

The bedroom was warm; Dave had obviously turned up the radiator for her. She recalled shivering frantically, despite him tucking her in to bed and adding a blanket over the duvet in an attempt to warm her up. Her whole body had been in shock.

This, combined with the alcohol and additional medication, meant she'd been in a pretty bad way on Christmas night.

Beth lifted herself up and plumped up the pillows to support her back as she stretched and closed her eyes. Her head felt clear, despite yesterday's events and, surprisingly, she was hungry. Her tummy rumbled; she fancied bacon and eggs with toast. A large mug of strong coffee would be nice as well. With three sugars, of course.

She felt amazingly good, despite her sore throat and eyes. She would soon be free.

After wrapping her body in the fluffy new dressing gown Kirsty had given her for Christmas, she pulled on her enormous pink, floppy-eared rabbit slippers which Robert had bought her. Sure, they were daft, but it was the thought that counted and, heck, they were comfortable.

Beth carefully took one small step at a time, trying hard not to fall down the stairs in the oversized slippers. In the kitchen, she was welcomed by her father and Dave, who looked completely exhausted. They threw a weak smile at Beth, who sensed the tension in the room and realised that she wasn't the only one who had suffered at the hands of her mother. Her dad's sad eyes gazed across the kitchen, as he sat motionless.

Beth went over to him, and brushed his arm with her hand. It seemed so peculiar having to be the strong one, and even stranger that her father had also suffered at the hands of that evil woman, her mother.

"Dad, are you okay?"

He'd spent the night discussing his various options with Andrew and Dave. Natasha had left soon after Brenda's tragic confession, and Brenda had agreed to leave with her. She'd submissively entered the car and Natasha had said very little during the journey home. There was nothing left to say. Other than she was sorry about the rape – but even sorrier Brenda had made Beth pay the price for the crime when things could have been so very different. She vowed never to see the woman again.

Richard would start divorce proceedings. He would continue to rent the flat he was currently living in, and apart from collecting a few of his belongings, he need not see her again. It was over. Almost.

He thought of his former home, and the woman living in it, one last time. Despite knowing how much she hated him, and that she had only married him for his money, he could not bring himself to sell it and leave her homeless. He thought back to happier times, with her singing a lullaby to Andrew, and smiling as he took a photograph of them. He recalled seeing her alone, crying. He now knew why. If only she'd told him about the rape, he could have helped her. He could have supported her through the years and made her realise that none of it was her – or Beth's fault. He could have taught her how to love her daughter. *Her* Elizabeth. It was, however, too late now.

He lifted his head as Beth placed a large mug of coffee in front of his hand, and then proceeded to fry some more bacon.

"Drink the coffee, Dad, then, if you feel up to it, we'll talk."

She was amazing. His little princess was still being kind to him, despite now knowing that he wasn't her father – had *never* been her father. Brenda had been right. He was weak and pathetic – he couldn't have helped her or Beth. He had ignored his wife's tears, her addiction to drinking, and had never been brave enough to ask her why. He had failed to notice the abuse of his little girl for all the years she had been tortured. He had ignored the tell-tale signs of desperation from both women. He'd even taken photographs of his Lizzie who, in hindsight, was in a terrible state. He was pathetic. Who was he trying to kid when he'd said he could have helped?

He was to blame.

The tears flowed down his cheeks and his hands trembled as he spoke to his daughter.

"It's all my fault, Elizabeth. If only I'd have seen what was obvious, this would never have happened."

Beth shuddered at the memory of her mother's twisted features when she'd told them about the events that had led to Beth's conception.

The rape.

The eyes of the devil.

She resisted the desire to cry, and gripped the worktop for support before replying in a soft whisper. She must not weaken or her mother would still be controlling her. "Dad, it's not your fault. It's not mine. It's his – Damien's... my biological father. He's to blame, along with Mum – she should have told us all. We could have helped her but, instead, she tortured me for all of my life."

Richard shifted on the stool and swung around to face his daughter. Dave nervously watched Beth as she sipped her coffee then methodically spread some butter onto two slices of bread, neatly positioned the bacon and formed a perfectly symmetrical sandwich. She cut the sandwich into quarters and placed them on a plate, before offering her dad and Dave one.

"I'll make some more," she added, after the two men devoured the sandwiches in a matter of seconds.

She made more; exactly the same as before. Precise and square, cut into symmetrical quarters.

"What's this about, Beth?" they asked. "Why the sandwiches? Why such perfect quarters? What are you trying to tell us?"

She had no idea; she was just hungry and so were they. Beth had always made her sandwiches this way, ever since her nanny had taught her how to when she'd been a little girl.

"There is no hidden code. I'm hungry and so are you," she replied indignantly.

Her father studied Beth, concern spreading across his face. He feared that her *friends* had returned, as did Dave.

She glared at them and reassured them that she was okay. "Dad, Dave, you have to stop questioning why I do certain things and why I act in certain ways. Just like," she paused, "just like I've stopped asking why *she* tortured me since I was born." Beth chewed her sandwich before taking a mouthful of her coffee. "We now know why. Everything from today – from now on – is black and white. It's as simple as that. You're not guilty, Dad. I'm not guilty. She is! "And, she concluded, I am not mad nor am I insane. She is."

The crumbs from the sandwich stuck in Richard's throat; he coughed loudly. Beth passed her dad a glass of water before taking one for herself, with her medication.

She studied both men's facial expressions before adding her final statement. Beth tried to imagine the horror of the rape. She could almost picture it – she'd come close several times when she had been a prostitute, when she'd been bitten, tied up and repeatedly used for sex. Yes, she knew what her mother had suffered.

"Yes, *he* is to blame. The rapist – my biological father. But *she* is far worse – far, far worse. Torturing me for something that was out of my control. Making me suffer for my father's actions. Making *me* pay the price for the rape."

Beth slammed her fists on the worktop; her coffee spilled onto her hand. It didn't matter – she'd suffered endless burns during her childhood. She rubbed her leg unconsciously before continuing. The men were silent.

"She was drunk," Beth went on. "She was high. She wasn't Mummy's little angel, as she wanted to be thought of. But she tortured me."

Again, she cried, although she thought she had used up all her tears the night before. She spoke softly to her father and to Dave. "Mummy's little angel will be …"

Richard jumped off his stool and stopped Beth as she started to speak.

"No, Elizabeth, sweetheart. It's over. No more."

She stopped crying and nodded in agreement before finishing her sandwich and running upstairs to shower. Dad was right, of course. But this was not the game plan, and it wasn't quite over. Her mum had pushed it too far and Mummy's little angel would still become Mummy's little killer.

"Third time lucky," she hollered, while shampooing her hair and scrubbing her body clean. "Third time lucky!"

* * *

He didn't care that it was Boxing Day and that he had yet another shocking hangover. He had a few things to do first, and then he would drive to Kent, and *order* Jen to let him see his girls. If it took all day and night, then so be it. Jen, Chloe and Becca were his life and now it was time to prove it – once and for all.

Anything for you, Jen, absolutely anything.

Geoffrey had always been a tosser, Jon thought. As he stood in his pretentious porch of his pretentious bloody house, staring at his bedraggled and clearly distressed partner, Geoffrey didn't even have the decency to invite him in.

"What's up, old chap?" was all he could say, blowing cigar smoke into Jon's tired face.

Jon didn't care anymore. He loathed the other man – he was greedy and uncompassionate, who cared not for his patients, but only about money and status.

"Everything's a fucking statement for you, Geoffrey, isn't it? The car. The house. The trophy wife – who, by the way, is shagging your accountant." Jon threw his arms in the air before angrily pointing at the house, then at the Porsche on the driveway. "It's about this, isn't it – possessions. Don't you care about anything else, mate? Is this it? Is this all that matters in your fucking pathetic, narrow-minded world?"

Geoffrey, embarrassed by his partner's actions and allegations, pushed Jon into the hallway, hoping to God that the neighbours had not overheard him. He quietly closed the door, before speaking softly to Jonathan.

"Jon, my wife and kids are asleep. Keep the noise down, will you? What the hell has got into you?"

Jon glared at Geoffrey. "It's you. It's the practice and all your greed, Geoffrey. I'm offering you my third for £50,000. It's a bargain – my clients alone are worth that in future revenue, and I put almost that amount in a decade ago."

Jon thought of his marriage to Jen, and how excited they both were when they started their new life together, after St Thomas's. They had hoped that a small rural practice would be the dream they had yearned for. It had taken years to save the £40,000 but, right then, it had been worth all of the scrimping and saving.

Geoffrey's shocked face studied Jon as he fidgeted nervously in the hallway.

"Are you serious, Jonathan?"

"Absolutely. I need an answer now, Geoffrey, or I'll approach Mark next. Your choice."

Jon hated Mark even more than Geoffrey but, knowing how greedy he was too, he knew that he'd jump at the opportunity of owning two-thirds of the practice.

Geoffrey re-lit his cigar and adjusted the belt of his dressing gown before clearing his throat. "Okay, Jonathan. You have a deal. Where do I sign?"

Jon had already prepared a semi-legal document and presented it to his soon to be ex-colleague. "Here," he replied. "And I want payment tomorrow. Do you hear?"

Geoffrey inhaled a large mouthful of cigar smoke before nodding in agreement. "Done, old boy," he replied, believing that all of his Christmases had come at once. "Glass of champers, my friend – for old times' sake?" he asked, patting Jon on the back before rubbing his hands together in glee.

"No," Jon replied, letting himself out. "I'll clear my office instead, then once I've completed the last two items on my list, I will have some champagne."

Geoffrey had no idea what had got into his colleague. Ringing his partner Mark later, he rubbed his hands together again at the thought of the additional income the practice would bring in, knowing that he would have no more NHS patients to fuss over – not even the woman his old pal had shown such compassion over. Maybe that's what all this was about. Maybe it was something to do with her.

He disregarded the thought almost immediately. Although Jon was stupid at times, he was not mad. He would not jeopardise twenty years of practicing psychiatry for the sake of one patient.

Never.

Nobody would.

Not unless they were insane.

* * *

Beth needed some air; although the shower had helped her to re-focus on her life, she needed to be alone – just for a little while.

After clearing the remnants of breakfast and making yet another jug of coffee for her guests, she checked the time.

It was 9.50 a.m.

Perfect.

Grabbing her car keys, Beth skipped towards Dave before planting an enormous kiss on his lips. Richard gave a strained smile and, after gulping down his third cup of coffee, stood up and held Beth tightly.

"Drive carefully," they told her, before deciding they needed yet more bacon sandwiches to ease their hangovers.

Beth reminded herself of their kind words. It was difficult, though, as she always found it hard to concentrate when she was excited. She slipped on her boots and an old hoodie, and tucked her hair under the hood. The latex gloves were already in the pockets, along with the key – not that she'd need it. At least, she didn't expect things to have changed that much over the years.

Finally, adjusting her top, she waved to her men. "I won't be long," she chirped, before starting the car's engine and defrosting the windscreen. Heck, it was freezing today, she thought, but that was good. Perfect, in fact. Absolutely perfect.

* * *

He'd never liked being totally alone. Jon blamed his feelings of uncertainty and nervousness on the fact that he was one of five children, and during his childhood his house had never been completely empty. He'd therefore become conditioned to always having company – welcome or not – and subsequently, whenever he was in an empty room, he felt uneasy; nervous, even.

His home had felt so cold this morning. Despite opening his last present from Jen and forcing a sad smile on his face, the emptiness had consumed his every thought, his every breath, which, right now, as he stood in his once warm and friendly office, he wished would stop, along with his heart.

She'd bought him a plastic custard pie – similar to the ones you see in comedy series or belonging to a clown, except Jon's hadn't got a real filling – just bright yellow, custard-like plastic. It was supposed to have been a joke. Jen's gift tag had read: 'This is the only pie in your life from now on,' but again, like the broken heart pendant, Jon hadn't been totally convinced that she had been thoughtful when she'd purchased it for him. The only gift he really cared for was on his back – his babies were there with him too, next to his heart – which, despite him hoping would stop, still beat hard within his ribcage.

He'd bought a few boxes with him. Carefully emptying his drawers, Jon studied his certificates and removed them from the wall, placing them in the cardboard box and protecting them with bubble wrap. The photo of him and Jen with the girls was next.

Their smiles, however, haunted him. Jen's eyes haunted him. The whole, idyllic picture did – as, lying next to it, was the card that *she* had painted for him: the perfect family scene. Jon, Jen, Chloe and Becca with those eerie smiles. Still haunting him.

As she was.

After writing a few notes for his ex-colleagues, and clearing out his junk, Jon collapsed into the green leather chair that he – and Beth – had loved so much.

Thank you so much. I don't know what I'd have done without you, Doctor.

I can't love you back.

It would have to stay. The chair held too many painful memories too. He closed his office door for the final time and turned the key in the lock. Jon said goodbye.

This part of his life was over – well, almost.

He had one more thing to do – and so little time to do it in.

* * *

The roads were completely clear and, after precisely twenty-eight minutes, Beth had reached her destination. She pulled on her woollen gloves, a daft bobble hat that Kirsty had brought her back from Paris, and slipped on an old cagoule which she kept in the car for emergencies. She'd forgotten to put on a proper coat before leaving and so, Beth figured this would do just fine.

She wouldn't be long.

The frost had created a bright silver sheen across the playing fields of the park. A few straggling leaves from the summer clung desperately to the bare branches, hanging on for dear life, glistening and shimmering in their final moments of glory – before falling onto the ground, rotting and disappearing forever.

Beth rubbed her hands together, hoping that the friction would warm them. It was bitterly cold – below freezing, but she had to do this.

The gate was painted bright yellow. The enormous catch that she'd recollected as a child was, in fact, tiny. Funny how one's perceptive on things was so different when you are all grown. She shrugged her shoulders as she slammed the gate shut and studied the slide – the slide she had played on countless times; the slide where Alfie had waited at the bottom patiently, wagging his tail and panting. The slide that had made her laugh, made her happy, set her free for a short while.

Free from the pain.

It was cordoned off by red and white tape. Graffiti had been sprayed on the main slide section, which was broken into three jagged pieces, bent into sharp metal shards. Extreme vandalism.

She turned away, unable to look back, unable to console herself.

The chains of the swings had been twisted over and over again, forming a huge mass of rust with a seat hidden somewhere among the mangled metalwork. Beth remembered swinging high into the clouds, swooping like an eagle into the sky; flying away to freedom. Pushing the swing hard, it slammed back into her chest, making her stumble.

Nothing ever stayed the same.

She shivered again. She closed the gate for the last time, and walked along the once winding paths, which were now hidden from view and caked in mud and weeds.

Alfie, come here, come and fetch your ball

All just distant memories now. Everything had changed.

The Avenue, however, had not. As Beth crossed the tree-lined road, she studied the individually designed homes with their bespoke features and luxurious family cars parked on the driveways.

They were still stunning, despite being older and some of the roofs having moss on them now. It was reassuring to see the smoke billowing from their chimneys, and Beth stopped dead as she observed a little girl with cute little pigtails sitting close to the fire in one house. She was giggling. A woman, probably her mummy, was tickling her tummy; that was the kind of memory Beth had always yearned for. She had had dreams – that she had hoped would, someday come true.

They hadn't, though.

Her mum had never loved her.

Beth wished she had.

Beth's eyes remained fixed, staring at the vision through the magic window. The woman spotted her and stared back at her; a strange woman in a cagoule. Bowing her head, Beth ran towards the familiar back garden, away from the happy families, away from the beautiful homes, away from the dreams she had always hoped for.

Back to this.

Her prison.

The gate still had not been painted; scraps of paint clung to the wooden planks, like the leaves had to the branch in the park. Everything, it seemed was holding on to what was left of its short life.

The gate didn't need to be unlocked. The half-bent hinges had rusted, just like the chain on the swing. Beth forced the gate open. Its base dragged across the muddy lawn, forming a clump of mud at the end.

She had to be careful now. She needed the plastic bags.

Despite the lack of security, the back door, as always, remained unlocked. The light was off and Beth stood motionless, holding the handle tightly. This was to be her moment of glory, yet, as her hands shook, she ducked as a shadow darted across the hallway, then disappeared as quickly as a flash of light.

She studied her watch.

Eleven a.m.

She had plenty of time.

The shadow had been her imagination; her mother, in all the years she had known her, had never been awake at this time of day in her own home. And, now that she had started to drink again, Beth knew that she'd have enjoyed several drinks by now. She would be fast asleep.

No, there had been no shadow. She was nervous – terrified, even; it was simply nerves and her vivid imagination.

The latex gloves felt tight over the woollen gloves, but they stretched just far enough. Beth pushed the door handle down. She held her breath, expecting the door to creak as she pushed it open, but it remained silent; Dad must have oiled the hinges after all.

She could hear her own breathing. She removed her shoes, and placed two more plastic bags over her feet.

She must be careful.

She could not make any mistakes – not this time.

Never again.

The scissors had gone, yet her mother had kept the cheap stainless steel hanger on the wall, which now contained a collection of keys and ridiculous key rings with photographs in them. Beth was tempted to pause to study them, but resisted. The noise from the hallway made her stop. She could hear her heart thudding now, as well as her breathing. Her head filled with tension; she stood completely motionless, listening intently for her mother. Silence again; she should have taken the Abilify today as well. Her imagination was going crazy; all she needed now was that bloody dog and the girls to return, then, once again, her plan would fail.

"Stay calm, Beth," she told herself before entering the hallway in which she had suffered at her mother's hands so many times. Nothing had changed, although the parquet flooring was tatty and discoloured now. The walls were still stained where Alfie had rubbed his muddy coat along them after his long walks with Daddy or Beth and, as she bent down and squinted, she spotted the bloodstain. *That* was still there too, despite her mother doing a pretty decent job of clearing the evidence, after battering her daughter for lying.

Beth struggled to compose herself as she strode up the thirteen wooden steps. *Her* bedroom door was open; the bed was empty.

Where was she?

Beth's body heaved with terror. She *was* here. Beth had *not* imagined the noises or the shadow. Her mother was probably awake and, once again, was winning the game of terror.

Beth took a deep breath before making her final journey.

The first thing she noticed in the attic room was the window. It had a new pane of glass in a brightly painted frame, and a pretty lace curtain surrounded it. A single pink curtain had been hung and was tied back by a pink velvet sash. Beth ran her finger along the wooden sill, expecting to feel the indentations she had made over so many years, but they had disappeared. Somebody had rubbed down the wood, erasing the proof of her years of torment in an instant. She rubbed her arms as a blast of cold air shot through the room, sending shivers down her spine. This old house still gave her the creeps all these years on – it was probably her mother playing mind tricks on her, but Beth needed closure.

"Let me end this my way, Mother," she sobbed, slumping onto the new divan which had crisp white linen on it and goose down pillows. A minute feather lifted, then floated into the cold air as Beth plumped the pillow; it reminded her of a scene from *Forrest Gump*, where the feather followed the direction of the wind; an unknown path. Like her own life, really, she thought. Uncertainty surrounded her every move; even now, even at this point of her life … the end.

The tiny feather landed at her feet. She smiled and popped it into her pocket before taking a final look at the room she had been held prisoner in. It was almost over.

She descended the three staircases, expecting to hear the throaty, evil laugh of the gargantuan creature she loathed so much. Unexpectedly, there was a stillness in the house, and a silence that was unfamiliar.

Even the radiators were quiet. As she passed them, Beth realised that they were switched off. Strange – her mother had always felt the cold. The boiler must have broken, or she was so drunk that she hadn't noticed. Beth crossed her fingers, hoping for the latter option – perhaps, after all, it was not too late to end it all.

A lamp in the living room was on. Beth tiptoed into the room. She saw her. Her tormentor, her torturer, was in the armchair, a familiar empty glass next to her, wearing a hideous dress, unconscious again.

Beth's heart rate quadrupled. She edged towards the sleeping woman. She held her breath before reaching the armchair.

She must remain silent.

She could not mess up now.

Not this time.

The fire was still burning; a small log glowed bright orange. She lowered herself to the carpet and crawled towards the fireguard. Turning her head, she checked again. Her mother was still asleep. The coast remained clear.

Be quiet, Elizabeth; stay silent, child.

It was incredibly difficult, but she could do it. She would find the strength to move it, even at this awkward angle.

The fireguard was heavy. Beth strained against the weight, trying not to drop it or drag it across the hearth. She relaxed after positioning it close to the edge of the quarry tiling; just far enough away.

Perfect.

The logs were plentiful too. Beth scattered the tinder over the hearth, and added a few firelighters for good measure. She strategically positioned the logs so that, should something go terribly wrong, there would be a simple explanation for what happened.

Carelessness due to drunkenness.

The largest log was too big to fit in the grate – it would have to be sawn in half to get it into it; this would, however be perfect for Beth's assignment.

Hurry up, child.

Time was running out. She laid some smaller logs on the burning fire, joined them up to the larger one on the tiled hearth, added some tinder and some more firelighters. Checking behind her again for safety, Beth bent towards the flames and blew gently. A twig glowed, and when she blew again, a tiny flame danced away from the main fire and along the twig, towards the hearth.

She smiled; how she longed to stay. But she had very little time. She crossed her fingers one last time. No more to do, though. It was all done.

The woman remained motionless, and for a brief moment, Beth felt remorse. The woman she had loathed so much had herself been hideously abused; she could, perhaps, be saved after all. If only she had told Beth what had happened to her, it could have been so very different. They could have loved each other as a mother and daughter should.

It was too late.

411

The fire was spreading. A spark from the log shot into the air and fell beyond the hearth, the rug smouldered, ignited, then burst into flames.

Her mother did not wake.

Beth dashed out of the back door and ran out of the back garden, past the houses in The Avenue, through the park, then towards her car. She wished she'd hung around to watch the flames destroy her home, but it would have been far too dangerous. She could not be caught – not this time.

Her heart pounded, but she remained motionless, her eyes fixed on the cloud of black smoke in the distance. She envisioned the flames licking through the windows and escaping through the roof and into the sky, disappearing high above the clouds – as Beth had wished she could so many times as a little girl – only to be joined by more enormous flames, desperate to escape from that godforsaken place. She pictured her mother, gasping and fighting for breath, as Beth had when her mother had tried to drown her in the bath. She imagined her mother feeling the searing agony of burning flesh; the same pain she had subjected Beth to when she had stubbed cigarettes onto her little body.

The blaring and shrill of sirens brought Beth back to reality. She drove steadily away from The Avenue and took one final look at the perfect homes with their perfect families. She no longer felt envy, and knew that, very soon, she and her family would be as happy as those in her dreams. She stopped suddenly and gave way to a fire engine. Its blue lights were flashing and its anxious crew sat in the front cabin. They smiled at Beth as they drove past.

She had succeeded.

At least, she hoped she had. There was no need to cross her fingers any more. Twice, she'd failed to murder her mother, but this time – she was absolutely positive – this time she had struck gold and had finally succeeded.

"Third time lucky, Beth," she whispered as she started to drive slowly towards the comfort of her own wonderful home. She stopped for a final time to watch the fire engine turn into The Avenue. She thought of the charred remains of her old house, reduced to a pile of rubble. She thought of the charred remains of her mother's body. Then she cried.

Ashes to ashes. Dust to dust.

"You're at peace now, Mum. At last you will be Mummy's little angel."

With that, she wiped away her tears for the very last time.

It was over.

She was free.

* * *

How clever we humans are, he thought as he adjusted his seat belt and smiled at Becca, who was fiddling with the remote control for her very own TV set. The brain was an incredibly magnificent organ that stored mountains of data which, when required, could be accessed and used for a multitude of tasks. Memory was an amazing tool, he knew that for sure – it had saved his marriage, he was positive of that. The voices in his head agreed.

Jon noticed how much Jen had aged over the past few months. Two grey strands ran through her hair, shining against her auburn locks. It was quite frightening what stress could do to your body. Jon watched her rub her face; it seemed that the eczema she'd suffered from as a child had flared back up too, along with her IBS. Her tired eyes met his and she strained a smile at her husband as he whispered to her, "Thank you for forgiving me. I love you so much. I promise to do anything for you, Jen – absolutely anything."

She had heard that line a thousand times and, although he seemed to be full of remorse, her heart still felt empty and raw. She strained to read the menu on the small computer screen, and decided to watch a comedy later – after all, she had about ten hours to kill before they landed at Singapore. She also needed a distraction from the real world; a funny movie may help a little. She scratched her face; blood encrusted beneath her fingernails. She licked it and the blood disappeared in an instant. If only pain dissipated as quickly. Nevertheless, she felt much better than she had before. She felt a little happier now Jon had proved how much he loved her.

She thought of her friend who had lived in Australia for over a decade, and how on Boxing Day, Jen had called her, hoping for the offer of a holiday – a break from everything. The invitation had led to a job offer to teach at a private school and now, just three days on, they were heading for what could be a new beginning for them all. Jen thought of the impact of this decision; the effect it would have on Becca and Chloe. Jon would cope – he always did. Him and that bloody pie of his. But the girls? Only time would tell, she guessed. She continued to plan the three-week holiday; they would juggle relaxation with interviews and find out how they could qualify for a work permit. Jen crossed her fingers before meeting her husband's tired, empty eyes.

She studied Jon. Jen noticed that he had also aged. He'd gained a couple of wrinkles, and he looked sad, which made her feel uncomfortable and guilty. She moved her gaze away from her husband and held tightly to Chloe's hand as the safety video began and the air hostesses pointed out the closest emergency exits to the passengers.

Becca felt sad. She loved 'Engerland' and she adored her nanny and granddad too. Leaving them was not nice, but she knew that when Daddy had visited them all at Nanny's house and had told Mummy that everything bad had gone away, they had suddenly become friends again. She didn't know what exactly Daddy had said, but it had made Mummy smile, which she hadn't done for a long, long time. Daddy had also said that funny saying of theirs: *Anything for you, Jen, absolutely anything* which had made her Mummy cry. Becca gripped her daddy's hand tightly wishing that he would protect her for ever. Especially from the Big Bad Wolf, who she hoped would never find her in Australia.

Jon felt his daughter's tiny hand within his palm. His thoughts were elsewhere as he recollected the events of the past few days. He thought of Geoffrey, the greedy blood-sucking leech who paid him, as ordered within twenty-four hours of his visit to him. The fifty thousand pounds would enable him and Jen to pay a deposit, at least, on a new home in Perth – if they were accepted, that was. Jon had agreed to lie low for a little while, as Jen settled into what they hoped would be her new life of teaching in Australia. Maybe, someday soon, Jon could teach too. He'd like that, and he figured that with his great ability to listen and absorb information, he would be a pretty good teacher or lecturer of psychology. He was also intelligent; very clever, in fact. Nearly a genius. Finding a new job would be simple.

Jen sent a strained smile at her husband. It wasn't going to be easy, but he had given up everything, including *that* woman, once and for all and, for that, Jon deserved one final chance. It couldn't have been easy quitting the practice he'd loved so much. Or Beth. She was also relieved to hear that he'd taken care of her mother too, and she hoped that the evil woman would spend many years in prison to punish her for terrorising so many people.

The plane lifted into the sky. Jon closed his eyes. The John Legend CD was playing his favourite track, 'Asylum'. He tapped his fingers to the beat, delighted with the end result. *How ironic*, he thought, while listening carefully to the words. It had been written for him, and Beth too: the two of them…

It had been far easier than he had imagined it would be; in fact, it really had been amazingly simple.

She never locks the back door.

She hadn't.

She always passes out after her morning drinks – about half past ten.

She had, and it was just before then, when she was cleaning the upstairs bathroom, that he had sneaked into the kitchen and laced her vodka with sleeping pills.

How convenient it had been learning of her mother's routine from the moment she awoke to the moment she slept. Beth had supplied him with every single detail he needed in order to eliminate the problem once and for all. OCD clearly ran in the family; perfect timing had helped him sort everything out and win back his family.

He'd thought of a prescription too, along with the possibility of an autopsy, which he now knew, following the convenient house fire, would be highly unlikely. Nevertheless, the prescription had been in Mrs Pritchard's name, and he'd left a copy of it in the bathroom cabinet, along with some sleeping pills – just in case.

There had been a minor interruption when he'd hidden in the hallway and she finished off the bottle of booze, before passing out, never to wake again. Jon suspected that he had heard the arsonist – but he'd been smart, crawling on all fours and leaving by the study window at the rear of the house. It was often unlatched, due to Beth's father having smoked cigars for years and her mother hating the smell, which apparently still lingered even though he no longer lived there. He'd even listened to Beth when she'd explained how she'd got away with trying to murder her mother the second time; he had worn latex gloves and had placed plastic bags over his shoes to protect himself forensically.

He didn't need to worry; the fire would have destroyed any forensic evidence. He was free now, as were his family – and Beth. The song finished. He set it to play again, thinking of her huge brown eyes and long eyelashes, imagining her sitting in the old green chair with her feet tucked beneath her. He recollected her smile, her beauty and the amazing strength she had demonstrated throughout the twenty years he had treated her. He'd known her during her most desperate of times – the young and fragile Elise he'd met during his training, Lizzie … dear Lizzie, fighting bulimia and depression, and now Beth; the wonderful, beautiful Elizabeth Pritchard, who had finally faced her demons and started to heal. One woman in three different eras of her life, all shared with her doctor, who was flying thousands of miles away to save his marriage.

How he missed her – his Beth. He hoped that she would be happy and finally find the closure she had so desperately wanted. He fought the desire to cry, wiping his eyes and taking a deep breath in order to compose himself. The heart key ring in his back pocket dug into his flesh, reminding him of where he was and who he was married to.

Jen smiled at her husband as he reclined his seat and tapped his fingers to the rhythm of the song. Clutching his wife's hand as the music played, he smiled warmly at her.

"No more pie," Jen said softly, pecking her husband on the cheek. Jon gripped his wife's hand and closed his eyes, hoping for some rest during the flight. The houses below became minute dots in a minuscule landscape, and the voices that he'd recently become so used to agree with his wife.

Holding hands and giggling, Jon's friends skipped along the aisle, nodding at him as he tried to sleep.

"No more pie," they laughed before disappearing into thin air. "No more pie."

How wrong they were.

* * * * *

ABOUT THE AUTHOR

JW Lawson was born in the mid-sixties and unlike the characters in 'Third Time Lucky' and 'Mummy's Little Angel', was blessed with a happy childhood. She is happily married to Andrew and has two lovely sons, Christopher and Matthew, along with a wonderful family and some great friends.

Working full time as a Company Director, Jo writes purely for pleasure and relaxation. It's a hobby that has become highly addictive: Book Three is already in her head! In addition to writing, she enjoys travelling, spending time with her family and walking in the countryside.

For further information, see www.jw-lawson.com

If you enjoyed *Third Time Lucky*, you'll love JW Lawson's *Mummy's Little Angel* featuring Jonathan Davies and Beth.

MUMMY'S LITTLE ANGEL

Joanne didn't believe that her life could become worse than it already was. She had lost everybody and everything she had loved. She was alone. Surely she had suffered enough?

The press had called her identical twins *psychopaths*. Her Maggie. Her Annie. But she still loved them, even though one of them had killed her husband, Jeff. Joanne still believed that his murder had been an accident. How could one of her daughters be a murderer? She knew them better than anybody else. They were good girls really. Her babies...

The brutal murder of her god-daughter Laura had never been solved. Items had been missing when Laura's remains had been discovered – clues that could lead to the capture of her killer. One of them was Laura's doll ... the doll that Joanne later discovered in her home.

Joanne is facing the most horrific dilemma of her life. Has the wrong woman been imprisoned? Could her daughter really have used such brutality against a six-year old child? Or could both women be innocent after all?

She needs to find somebody for her daughter to confide in – somebody she will trust. She needs a miracle.

There is only one person who can help. He is compassionate and caring, with an amazing ability to gain the trust of the most difficult patients.

He is Joanne's only hope.

He is Jonathan Davies.

24036794R00238

Printed in Great Britain
by Amazon